IN THE FOOTSTEPS
OF THE BEHEMOTH

First Published in Great Britain 2013 by Netherworld Books an imprint of Belvedere Publishing

First edition: 2013

Any reference to real names and places are purely fictional and are constructs of the author. Any offence the references produce is unintentional and in no way reflects the reality of any locations or people involved.

A copy of this work is available through the British Library.

ISBN : 978-1-909224-40-7

Netherworld Books
Mirador
Wearne Lane
Langport
Somerset
TA10 9HB

In The Footsteps Of The Behemoth

By

Sam Leeves

Netherworld Books

Chapter One

The moon lit the path languidly, piercing through the darkness with apathetic impulse. The breeze whispered by, calling names nobody heard.

His heavy footsteps swept up clouds of dust around him; a metronome beat in the night. His thoughts hung burdensomely on his mind, intensifying the already vehement fear that he was too late. He tried to push such ideas away into some fathomless reach of his being, yet he had always been one to brood; a fault in himself he knew all too well.

He paused, finding a tree beside him. Yes, he was perhaps late, though he was only a man and one who had been walking for days at that – he needed rest. Yet, just as he moved to sit beneath the ancient, dying tree, something caused him to halt. In the corner of his eye he saw but a wisp of vermillion, though it was enough to garner his attention and distract him from even his most tempestuous thoughts.

He turned to where he had seen the curious effigy and looked further up the path. Of course, he was correct in what he thought he had seen; his were not the kind of eyes the light played tricks upon. Indeed, the light venerated him, spurned him, would cast him away at each opportunity it was given to do so; he had known this for some time.

He inspected the apparition, far away though it was. It stood like a man, with a shape that vaguely matched, though the colossal horns atop its head caused some confusion. Yet, upon noticing the substantial spear in the right hand, it all fit together. The horns were a feature of an arrogant helmet, worn by a man in vermillion lacquered armour. He stepped forwards, tearing himself from the shade into the light of the moon and revealing an iron mask, contorted into an expression of profound, anguished fury. The mouth; slung open into a violent roar. The eyes; bulging and wide, threatening disaster to all who believed themselves to hold the fortitude to gaze into them directly.

The man in the vermillion armour seemed to regard the weary traveller. He tilted his head slightly, the angle gifting the expression on the mask an even more potent ferocity. Upon completing his examination, he took a step back as if to steady himself.

"Who goes there?" he called, his gravelly voice echoing off the mask giving it a metallic tone. "Who goes there in such malevolent apparel?"

The traveller took a moment to consider himself. He supposed that his black clothing was somewhat mysterious and his tattered, faded, crimson cape even more so. Yet, neither could match the suspicions that the gargantuan sword strapped upon his back wrought.

The breeze swam by, catching his matted black hair, blinding him for a moment. When it ceased, his hair fell back into place, shrouding the left half of his pallid face and trailing over his shoulders.

"A mere traveller," he said. His voice was no more than an effortless whisper, yet it inexplicably reached the armoured man – distant though he was. He watched with his glowing amber irises as the armoured man regarded him with the same tilt of his head.

"Of course," he said in that metallic voice. "Pale skin, dark hair, amber eyes; you're a shadus!"

The shadus said nothing.

"No doubt you've heard of me, shadus," the man in the vermillion armour said. "I am none other than the infamous Vaiske Parlet."

The shadus ran his eyes over Vaiske Parlet.

"I do not know the name," he said.

"I assure you," Vaiske said in an angered tone that struggled past his mask, "it is a name that holds some weight."

The shadus said nothing.

"Tell me, shadus: what is *your* name?"

The shadus slowly raised his right arm and ran his hand through his thick hair, though his eyes never left Vaiske Parlet. He only answered once his arm had fallen back down to his side.

"My name is Lament Strife," he said.

"Lament Strife," Vaiske said, as if he was tasting the name. "Then tell me, Lament Strife, what brings a shadus to the Northern Continent?"

"Personal business," came the reply. "And business I must be getting back to at that. Excuse me."

He walked towards Vaiske with slow, dragging steps, his heavy black boots whipping up flocks of dust with each pace he made. His cape swam lazily behind him, beneath which the wooden hilt of his gargantuan sword poked out. As he passed Vaiske, the spear shot before him, blocking the path. Lament suspiciously rolled his eyes towards the warrior.

"I'm afraid that answer doesn't suffice," Vaiske said, leisurely slanting the horrific mask in the direction of the shadus.

"It is as much of an answer as I have," Lament replied.

He was now close enough to notice Vaiske's mouth curl into a sly smile, though the warrior's eyes still eluded him behind the iron mask. Lament peered into the apocalyptic face; what was disaster to him?

Vaiske perpetually met his look, causing Lament to frown slightly. Gradually, the warrior's smile faded.

"Well then," he said, "I'm afraid you go no further!"

With this roar, Vaiske drove his spear at Lament, the shadus only avoiding the strike as he turned his back on the warrior, causing the tip of the spear to meet the gargantuan blade on his back. Lament drew the sword, pushing Vaiske away, only for the warrior to drive the tip at the shadus once more. Lament parried the strike, wielding the sword as if it was a slight dagger.

The wooden hilt should not have supported the blade as easily as it did, thin as the cylinder of wood was. The guard was a mere rectangular slither of oak attached to the top of the hilt, more for some kind of angular decoration than any practical purpose. The blade was sharp on only one side like a katana, though it held not even a hint of a curve. All in all, the sword matched the height of the shadus comfortably (the hilt alone was the length of his forearm) and, when on his back, the blade was almost as wide as him. But, despite all of this; despite the size, the weight, the impracticality of the sword; he swung it in one arm with ease.

As the duel raged on and each strike was parried, blocked or dodged, the men became more desperate; the moon glinting off their weapons and singing death to the night. It was then, when his mortality seemed most upon him, that Vaiske drove his spear at Lament only to catch his cape, though the warrior struck with enough force to pin the shadus to the tree.

Vaiske leapt backwards as Lament tried a wild swipe with his sword only to find the trap too constricting for such an attack. Vaiske laughed mechanically and knelt, taunting the shadus.

Lament tore himself from the tree, ripping his cape in the process and found a haze in his eyes as Vaiske released dust from his hand. Blinded, Lament clawed frantically at his eyes, audaciously trying to regain his blurry sight.

He turned, his eyes correcting themselves, and saw Vaiske kneeling upon the shadus' moonlit shadow. The warrior drew a platinum dagger from his belt and plunged it into the ground on which his shadow was cast.

Lament fell, agony ravaging his entire body, trying to make sense of the sensation but finding nothing. Moments later, Vaiske was stood above him, the dagger in his hand; now obsidian black.

"Forgive me, shadus," Vaiske said. "No doubt, although a stranger in these lands, you are a good man. More important still, you were a worthy opponent; I only overcame you through the use of my less reputable tactics, but please know this was nothing less than necessary.

"I know you can feel the life draining from you, so I shall be as brief as I can. Know that your death was not in vain. Indeed, here today, you have been a part of history, for this is the moment that future generations shall look to as heralding the age of peace. Your death shall save many lives."

Lament watched, amber irises still glowing in the world of black, as Vaiske Parlet, silhouetted by the crying moon, thrust the dagger into his own chest.

Darkness.

*

He left Farras, the town of his birth and childhood, as his mission dictated; under cover of night. There were moments that he feared the moon would exonerate him and whisper to his kin of his leaving. But the moon, and all light with it, was soon hidden behind a thick blanket of cloud. On he walked, passing the outskirts of his beloved hometown and into unknown fields.

Spring was slow in coming. The late winter air froze his lungs and restricted his blood as each breath drew yet more sharpness into him. His black robe did little to warm him, though he was thankful for the camouflage in the night.

But, as easily distracted as he could have been by the cold, only one thing was on his mind: where was Master Snow? His teacher had promised to return by the first sign of winter and yet now, with winter waning, he gave no indication of re-appearing.

Thusly, Arvan Deit, young apprentice to the greatest swordsman in the world, ventured into the impenetrable darkness of that night on his first adventure.

*

Rain, so complete to fall almost as a sheet, crashed down upon him as he watched the immense frame wander gracelessly away. The Behemoth, malevolent monster to most, harbinger of death to others, ignored the rain as only something of its size could. It towered above all, only mountains competing to succeed it in height. Fitting, for its skin was as hard as rock, save for the few places that its tangled fur grew from.

He chased after it, though he never managed to convince himself that he had even a shade of a hope of not losing it. One stride for the creature was one hundred paces for him and the lumbering beast was deceptively fast. Even if he'd had a horse he could never have kept up with it. How many times had he lost it now only to mistakenly happen upon it a few days later? Enough for him to have lost count some time ago, yet that was all he knew. He often considered submitting, but told himself that it was not an option; his research was far from complete.

It was then that he witnessed the most peculiar behaviour the Behemoth had exhibited yet. It stopped and turned, as if aware of his minute presence, fixing its listless white eyes upon him. They seemed not to comprehend him, but to encase him.

He should have been excited – such behaviour was unknown to him, even after the time he had studied the beast and there was nothing in the millennium worth of research he had read that suggested similar conduct. No, this was a new discovery. Though all he could think of was the oblivion that surely awaited him. The oblivion that awaited all who garnered the attention of the Behemoth.

The creature ruptured its mouth open and screamed viscerally.

His hand wrapped uselessly around the hilt of his katana. His usually calm heart sped to a beat he had never known before. Remembering every duel he had ever fought, he tried to ease himself in some meaningless effort of control, and inhaled slowly.

The listless white eyes left him and the creature turned away.

His heart fluttered as he realised he was still alive and supposed that, after the way of life he had been engaged in so far, he should have grown used to the threat of death. He sighed in a thankful breath as the breeze whispered past. He would not be joining it that night.

He held his white robe closer to him against the cold and continued to track the Behemoth. Though he smiled subtly, knowing he would lose it once more, soon enough.

Chapter Two

He opened his eyes to the lacerating light of dawn, awakening with an idiosyncratic nausea. The sword upon his back lay weightily upon him, causing him to struggle for breath in the insipid morning air. His arms, wrapped in the bandage-like cloth of his sleeves, were before him; realising this he pushed himself onto his back and breath came more easily.

Lament sighed, looking at his pallid hands. It may have just been the juxtaposition of his white hands against his black clothes, but he appeared to be even more sallow than usual. His silken skin was so thin, so translucent, that he thought he could see the blue veins beneath. He told himself it was just his imagination, yet a certain vividness suggested reality.

Already exhausted by the day's activity, he let the back of his right hand fall down upon his forehead to find it hot and wet. He caressed his brow with his fingers and placed them before his eyes, seeing beads of sweat traverse the printed tips. He couldn't remember his last fever.

He was ailing, that much was certain. What had caused the malady, on the other hand, was shrouded in mystery.

It was then he remembered the duel from the night before.

Lament tilted his head back and rolled his eyes as far as they would go, expecting to see the body of Vaiske Parlet, but he saw nothing. No armoured man, no discarded spear, no platinum or obsidian black dagger piercing the bloodied chest of a suicidal warrior.

Did the dead walk? If so this was a strange land indeed. Unless, of course, Vaiske Parlet had survived. But what motive, other than suicide, could he have had for plunging the dagger into his chest?

"You've not the time for this," Lament whispered to himself. He tried to sit up but the slight increase in height caused his nausea to intensify and he retched violently. As he fell back to the ground an alto-pitched ringing began in his ears. His heart throbbed, blood threatening to burst through the threshold of his vascular system. He groaned and let the malaise wash over him.

It soon passed and quelled into the lesser symptoms of before, so intense had his suffering been in these few brief moments that he barely noticed this diminished plain of despair. Yet, he dared not try to raise himself again lest the anguish begin once more.

He lay there, helpless, in the shadow of the dead tree, trying to make sense of the affliction he found himself victim to; his eyes perpetually fixed on the tree. It was grey and shrunken, though not unimpressive in height. The bark was no more than an outer shell now; blighted by fissures and holes from decades of animals making a home of the skeletal life-form. Its limbs had long since been amputated by time, leaving only the withered and malformed branches that had come to birth mere weeks before the death of the great tree. That is, save for the one remaining vast arm that reached out to the sun, though now even this was wilting under its own weight. Yet, the tree held no answers as to Lament's suffering, nor did it bring further clarity to the events of the night before. Frustrated, he rolled his head away and looked upon the endless vista to the south where the immeasurable nothingness of the plains rolled on, eternally uninterrupted.

Lament closed his eyes, for in his impotent state the feeble morning light caused him pain. Besides, the darkness helped him think. Though, when the thoughts fell upon his mind, he soon found himself wishing them away.

He had long been aware of the truth that he may have been too late for the encounter he had set out to reach, not that it was known his presence would be at hand. Still, he would rather arrive unannounced; after all, his objective dictated it. Surprise would benefit him, for to give his opponents a chance to prepare would surely spring tragedy and death for him.

He forced those musings from his mind. In his current condition the event of reaching that place was ever more unlikely and thoughts of it brought him no solace.

Instead, he turned his thoughts to the events of the night before. His attacker, Vaiske Parlet, was motivated by more than simple xenophobia – he was sure of that. His time spent on the Northern Continent had revealed to him that these people were certainly fearful of strangers, shadus in particular, though he had never faced violence because of it before. It wasn't unreasonable to assume the warrior wanted only to test his skill, until Lament recalled the words Vaiske had spoken to him as the shadus lay defeated.

"Your sacrifice shall save many lives."

The words wandered around his mind, repeating themselves for some time, yet all he could make of them was that his adversary had thought Lament's death to be for what he would surely deem 'the greater good'. But the obvious fact of the situation was that Lament hadn't died – he'd had no reason to. Vaiske Parlet's spear never reached him, never pierced his skin. In fact, neither of them had drawn blood. But still, the shadus had fallen, feeling the life fade and flicker within him. It was a peculiar sensation and one he'd rather not have to remember, but he found himself thinking of it all the same.

His nausea flared and he groaned. He could make no sense of the situation, especially with his sickness pressing ever more fervently on him. What did it matter? Understanding would not release him from this grievance.

He cleared his mind and allowed himself to slip from the grip of consciousness.

The shadows were at their shortest by the time he managed to sit up, though he still required the tree for support. He had not fallen into unconsciousness as he had expected, instead he had drifted into same strange daze somewhere between sleep and wakefulness. Still, the rest, slight though it had been, seemed to have waned his symptoms; sitting had not been the challenge it was before, though it had taken considerable strength.

He could still piece together little reason for his current plight, but he found himself no longer caring. He imagined that was worrying enough.

He gazed at the horizon, isolated on the already lonely scene. He arched his head skywards seeing the sun at noon, but it threw no heat down on him. He shivered against the cold, thinking how small the sun looked; almost insignificant.

To allow himself to sit comfortably he'd had to remove the sword from the straps on his back. This had been an effort. In spite of the ease he usually wielded the sword with he had not found the strength to lift it and had resorted to shaking it free from him. It now lay listlessly beside him. He looked at it. The sensation may have been born from his current enfeeblement, but the sword too looked weak, merely a weight for him to support and one he was unable to at that.

He was distracted from his ponderings when his ears picked up the merest padding of feet, running quickly in his direction from the west. He turned his head and peered up the path as a wolf came into view. It was a mangy beast with thick grey fur, yet Lament could still see the wolf's ribs protruding through its taught skin.

The wolf stopped and looked at him.

He had heard of wolves eating wounded travellers before. In fact, he had heard many stories of such happenings since he's arrived on the Northern Continent, some involving prouder and less predatory animals than wolves.

His amber eyes never left the wolf, nor did the starving wolf's stone grey eyes leave the shadus.

It took a step towards him and Lament tried to lift his sword as a warning, but could not find strength. The wolf continued in its approach and the helpless shadus could do nothing but let it come, those predatory pupils always upon him.

He could feel the beast's cold, cloying breath on his face, but never did he look away, not when death, and release from his ailment, was so close. The wolf's eyes seemed to soften and it nuzzled Lament's neck affectionately, as if urging him to rise. It licked the sweat from his face, tricking the shadus into believing his fever was no more than his twisted imagination. Unfortunately, the wolf could not cure his nausea or dry his fever sodden clothes.

The wolf whimpered sympathetically as Lament stroked the scrawny creature's tufty mane.

"You would do well to eat me," the shadus said. "And I would do well to be eaten. But you are a noble animal, no doubt, and would rather catch your prey yourself."

The wolf laid its head in Lament's lap and looked mournfully up at him.

8

"I can offer you no food, save for myself, and you have declined that meal already."

The wolf yawned with a high-pitched sigh and closed its sorrowful and starving eyes; the grey lids closed with a heavy laboured sliding.

Lament took the time to consider his situation. He was inexplicably diseased on a road so close to the Central Desert that it was unlikely he would ever be found. He had few choices and one of those was death; no choice at all. His symptoms appeared to be lessening, or he was growing used to them. Either way he would have to fight against them and find a way to stand, only then could he seek help. Only then could he make it to his encounter.

But the shadus was weary and, if he was to continue on his journey, he would need his strength. He allowed his eyes to close and sleep washed over him.

His eyes shot open to the dark night, the bile rising in his gullet. Choking, he fell forward and vomited violently, the strain pulling on his stomach muscles and burning his throat. When all was gone he spat, trying to rid the putrid taste from his mouth, and collapsed back against the tree.

Although the sleep had not assuaged him of his symptoms, he at least now had some energy. Rejuvenated and rested, his body would surely be able to ward off the worst of this sickness if he would give it some time.

The wolf still lay motionlessly beside him. Lament laid a hand on the sleeping beast and was met by winter-cold skin. It osmosed through to him, until he could feel the freezing chill in his bones. He removed his hand and looked moodily into the distance: the noble beast had starved to death, rather dying itself than hurting another being. Still, it had some company in its last moments – that was something. Lament wondered if a shadus would have been company enough for a dying man on this continent and concluded not, though it did not pain him as he thought it would. He was still pondering the unjust ending of the wolf's beating heart.

He stood, easier than he had been expecting, and picked up his sword. It bore not the encumbering weight of before and he found no trouble in strapping it once more to his back. His nausea was still present but no longer threatened him with tumultuous expulsions.

Despite his slight recovery, as he moved to leave, he found his gaze falling upon the slumped body of the wolf. It lay there, innocent and inert, already attracting attention from nearby insects.

"Forgive me," Lament said, "for I have nothing with which to dig you a grave, though I think you deserving of more."

He took a step to the east only to fall to his knees as his bilious stomach rose and caught him. He clutched at his heart as if to rip it from his chest and end this madness.

It was then the delirium overcame him.

Chapter Three

The sun rose lazily and Arvan watched in wonder as the sky was painted a lustrous blue. It was still crisp, too cold for spring, and the grass wet his sandaled feet with dew. He breathed in the sharp air and continued west, putting the distraction of dawn behind him.

He tried to remove his hunger from his mind – he had neglected to bring provisions with him; a mistake so grievous he, for a second, doubted how well Master Snow had prepared him. He smiled, supposing hunger was just a part of the adventure.

They would discover his departure soon, that much was certain. He wondered how Darkla and Mirr would react. Mirr would be typically understanding. Darkla would be hurt, though hopefully not so much that she couldn't forgive him. He'd often spoken of leaving to find Master Snow, after all, he had been gone a suspiciously long time and had never been late returning to Farras before; a student couldn't help but be concerned. Then again, he'd find him soon enough now.

Day had fully dawned when he saw the figures on the horizon. He had hoped they wouldn't have been as early as that, or maybe he'd been walking too slowly.

He knelt, observing the mounted soldiers pacing and busying themselves with morning rituals. To the north of them, glowing through the early morning mist, stood Pale Castle; the terrible white stone piercing the low visibility to a meaningless sentiment. It glimmered as the eerie moon in the insipid light. Although some ten miles away out at sea, it was a mammoth visage, dwarfing even the hulking bridge that led to it.

"Careful lad," said a voice behind Arvan. He turned, whipping the air forcefully around him and gripping the hilt of his katana. Before him was a kind-faced, if clumsily built, man in a purple robe. He held a staff in one hand whilst supporting a bag of provisions over his shoulder with the other. The sun reflected lightly off of his bald head.

The bald traveller looked at the carven-faced youth disapprovingly but without any suggestion of malice. He supposed the boy was too scruffy looking to be a true warrior; his robe was slightly too large for him and his brown hair flopped over his eyes.

Arvan blew his fringe from his sight.

"I'm no 'lad'," he said, relaxing. "I'm a fully grown man."

"Is that so?" said the bald man, wearing a subtle smile. "My apologies. I wanted only to warn you against trying to pass Lord Riit's cavalry in the light of day."

"I had planned on passing Pale Castle last night," Arvan said, softening further. "Though it appears my journey from Farras was slower than I had anticipated."

"You left Farras last night and have made it this far already?" the man said, eyes widening. "It sounds to me as if you're making fantastic time."

"Thank you," Arvan said, smiling.

"If the question is not too intrusive, fellow traveller, might I enquire where you are headed?"

"The Final Resting Place of the Empire," Arvan replied before frowning, annoyed at himself for giving the information so readily. Though, there was something disarming and harmless about the man whom he spoke to. He felt as if he had known him for some time.

The bald man smiled. "I hoped as much. I too travel there. Mayhap we could travel together? I often get rather lonely on the road and would adore the company."

Arvan stroked his fringe from his eyes.

"I suppose it is safer to travel as two," he said. "I heard a whisper that the Behemoth is headed for the West Lands."

The bald man seemed to pale slightly and his eyes took on a grave look. Then he took on his usual good-humoured, if humble, smile once more.

"If that is true then I fear I won't be of much assistance," he said. "Though you speak wisely, there is *some* safety in numbers."

He looked past Arvan and his face became grave again. Arvan turned and saw the cavalry much as before.

"But come," the bald man said, "we have stood here long enough and should on with our journey, lest we attract some undesirable attention from Lord Riit's men."

They turned south and walked for some time, the bald man singing tunelessly, yet cheerfully. When they were out of view of the cavalry, (though Pale Castle still lurked ominously in the distance) the bald man stopped and turned, causing Arvan to almost walk into him.

"I've been terribly rude," he said. "My name is Kyagorusu Kagaron." He bowed slightly.

"My name is Arvan Deit."

"Well, Arvan," Kyagorusu said, smiling. "Would you care to eat with me?"

They sat on the foot-beaten path and ate a meal of bread and cured meat. Arvan thought it may have been the length of time he had gone without food, but he found the simple meal as delicious as any he had eaten back home. When they were finished and Arvan was suitably full, Kyagorusu forced a lemon scented cake upon him.

"Meal times don't come around as often as one would hope when travelling," Kyagorusu said. "You should eat while you have the chance."

Once Arvan had finished his cake, Kyagorusu suggested they rest a while, though Arvan soon grew restless. Still, the experienced traveller had been gracious enough to allow Arvan to travel with him, so the boy surmised he had no right to complain.

"Tell me, Arvan," Kyagorusu said. "How old are you?"

Arvan frowned slightly, though Kyagorusu seemed not to notice.

"Nineteen," he said warily.

"Ah," Kyagorusu said, smiling. "Neither one thing nor the other."

"I'm sorry?"

"You're spring, Arvan," Kyagorusu said. "You've awoken fully but haven't quite bloomed into summer. Neither boy nor man."

"I assure you," Arvan said, not masking his annoyance quite as well as he had intended. "I'm definitely a man."

Kyagorusu smiled. "If you say so, Arvan. Though, spring is pleasant enough, more comfortable than summer at any rate." He eyed Arvan and noticed the youth's stern expression. "Forgive me, Arvan; I fancy myself as something of a philosopher. I sometimes forget that my musings are not to everybody's taste."

Arvan softened, though his face retained its carven shape.

"That's quite alright, Kyagorusu," he said. "I fear I have had my mind turned to grave thoughts for long enough that I take all things too seriously."

"You're troubled?" Kyagorusu asked, sympathetically. He sat up and met Arvan's hazel eyes. Upon meeting the boy he had thought him to be older than nineteen; he was stern of face in a way more akin to someone twice his age, brought on by the worries and trials of life. Then again, he supposed the boy's hard features had something to do with that.

Arvan pursed his lips ponderously, then released them into a sigh.

"'Troubled' is perhaps the wrong word," he replied. "Though my thoughts are somewhat darker of late than I would like." He looked up and saw the sun almost at noon. "Might I suggest we continue? We have made little progress and I would feel more at ease were we further from Pale Castle."

Kyagorusu ran his hand over his bald head. "Of course. How foolish of me; I'd almost forgotten. At this rate we shall never reach the Final Resting Place of the Empire!"

They rose and Kyagorusu moved to venture further south.

"Would it not be pertinent to travel west now?" Arvan asked. "We are out of sight of the Riit clan."

"I find the warlords rarely travel into the Central Province, especially close to the Central Desert. Although it will take longer, we will be far safer."

Arvan said nothing and followed after the man with more experience.

*

She discovered his empty bed with the dawn. It didn't look as if it had been slept in, but the dream realm was known to often be elusive to Arvan so she didn't allow the worry to fully overcome her until she had searched the temple too.

It was no longer a place of worship; the people of Farras, along with the rest of the Northern Continent, had abandoned the gods as they thought the gods had abandoned them. A millennium of fear and war will distort one's faith, or so it seemed. They found themselves caught between the Behemoth and the warlords, finding no respite in religion. Hope wanes so easily.

With faithlessness came the disrepair of the temple. Centuries of neglect allowed the walls to crumble and fall, leaving only the stone framework standing. Yet, despite the disrepair and his own disbelief, this was Arvan's preferred domain of meditation or training and, as such, he could be found there more often than not.

Although, as Darkla stood there in the sterile dawn, the myriad of candles Arvan had lit for Master Snow in hope of his return dancing mournfully around her and glowing off of her white dress, he wasn't there. There they had found her; her blonde hair clinging to her catatonic face.

Now, sat across from Mirr in their dining room, she finally let a tear escape from her eyes and trail down her face. She couldn't look at Mirr, the maternal face holding sympathy, but no solace, for the disappearance of Darkla's lifelong friend.

"He'll return soon enough, Darkla," Mirr said softly. "And he'll return with Master Snow."

Darkla failed to speak. All of her concentration and will was focused on holding back the countless tears that gathered inside of her, plotting their torturous escape.

"If you're concerned about his safety," Mirr continued, trying to find some aspect of the situation that would soothe her, "you know as well as I that Master Snow has trained him exceptionally well."

Still Darkla said nothing. She refused to even meet Mirr's eyes, the effervescent allure of which had yet to fade in her fortieth year.

"I know he's impetuous, Darkla, but he's far from arrogant. He knows when to back down from a fight."

Mirr reached across the table and gently clasped Darkla's hand in hers. The girl yielded. She looked at Mirr and tears streamed from her eyes, bursting on and staining her white dress with small puddles and a thousand tinier ones all around. She allowed her thick hair to fall before her usually contented and exquisite face. Her body sighed so fervently that she fell forward slightly, shaking rhythm-lessly with each convulsive sob.

"I'm not worried, Mirr," she said through the wall of inconsolable tears. "I know Arvan will be fine and he'll return, much the same as he ever was."

She tried to compose herself, but the resistance caused the tears only to leap from her eyes more forcefully. She let them surmount her, finding she could do little else. She wanted to speak, but could only repeat what she had already said. "I'm not worried."

"Then why do the tears ravage you so?" Mirr asked.

For the briefest of moments, Darkla managed to strengthen herself with a hard, sharp inhalation of breath. But with her words returned her sobs.

"Why didn't he ask me to go with him?"

*

The afternoon proved to be just as cold as the morning. A glacial breeze seemed to wrap itself around them. Did the dead take an interest in their journey? If so, Arvan wasn't sure whether to feel comforted or haunted.

"The dead are restless today," Kyagorusu said, smiling lightly. "I wonder what has them so excited."

"Does it not unease you?" Arvan asked, crossing his arms in an attempt to hide his shivering.

"Not particularly," Kyagorusu replied. "I'll join them one day; I'd rather my companions get to know me now."

Arvan looked at Kyagorusu sceptically but said nothing.

"My apologies," Kyagorusu said. "Philosophy again. Unfortunately it has a bothersome habit of creeping up on me and invading my speech."

Arvan forced a smile, though he was uncertain of how convincing it was.

"Tell me, Arvan," the bald philosopher said. "What draws you towards the Final Resting Place of the Empire?"

"I'm a student of Lawliet Snow," Arvan replied.

"*The* Lawliet Snow?" Kyagorusu gasped, stopping and turning. His eyes were wide and fixed expectantly on the face of Arvan.

The boy smiled and blew his fringe from his eyes. "You know of him?"

Kyagorusu smiled knowingly and they began walking again.

"I've heard many fantastic tales," he said. "I'd rather not ponder on how exaggerated they are, though, if he is even an iota as brave as they suggest, he is a phenomenal specimen of a human being indeed. Yet..." He glanced at Arvan and paused.

"Yet?" Arvan prompted, amiably.

"Perhaps it is best left unsaid."

"Please, Kyagorusu. I am not easily offended."

Kyagorusu gave him a sidelong look and sighed. "Yet, the way of the sword troubles me. I find it distasteful... no, disgusting and vile, that a human being could find it him or herself to kill another."

Arvan nodded solemnly.

"You'd be surprised," he said. "Master Snow feels the same way."

"So the stories are true," Kyagorusu mused, his smile returning.

"I'm sorry?"

"The stories say he is troubled by each death he causes. Even those of the men some would say were deserving of their fate." He paused, pensive, for a moment and Arvan saw a serene peace fall over the bald man the likes of

14

which he was rarely witness to. "And what of you, Arvan? How does the killing make you feel?"

"It is an experience that has, so far, let me be."

"Ah," Kyagorusu said. "Let us hope that it stays that way. However, none of this explains why you are going to the Final Resting Place of the Empire."

"Master Snow visits my town when he has an opportunity. He was called away in the spring of last year on urgent business from Lord Thean."

"Of course," Kyagorusu said, as if to remind himself. "Lawliet Snow is one of Lord Thean's most trusted retainers."

Arvan nodded. "Master Snow promised he'd return by the first snow of winter. But winter has now almost faded into spring and he has yet to return."

"But why go to the Final Resting Place of the Empire?"

"Master Snow has some associates who have been stationed there for some time. I hope that he may be staying with them or, at the very least, they may have some idea of where he is."

Kyagorusu smiled. "Ah, the adventures of youth." Then he went back to singing his tuneless, blissful song. Arvan couldn't help but join him in his smile.

The sun was setting as they passed into the Central Province. Had the sun been larger, as it would inevitably be in summer, Arvan imagined the canvas-like sky would have been coloured even more lustfully than it currently was. Instead, the azure heavens were dappled with powdered cloud. They dragged their lengthy shadows along beside them, contemplating when to stop and rest.

Arvan hadn't expected the journey south to take them as long as it had. He had his suspicions that he would have been closer to his destination by now without the companionship of Kyagorusu. Then again, he doubted he would have been in such a good humour.

"I never asked you, Kyagorusu," he said. "Why are you going to the Final Resting Place of the Empire? A matter of philosophy, no doubt," he added with a sly smile.

Kyagorusu laughed heartily. "Very droll! Though your scathing sarcasm isn't completely wrong. I'm a scholar. Well, a dilettante of a scholar really; I've had little formal schooling, but I have a mild interest in all things. I'm sure that there is much to learn in the great city of the west."

"I thought you were rather too well informed about certain things to just be a traveller," Arvan said.

"Oh, I don't know about that. You'd be amazed by what you can learn on the road. Life's a knowledgeable teacher." Kyagorusu smiled and ran his hand over his head. "But that's philosophy again. Come, let's eat! The more food I have in my mouth the less likely I am to spout nonsense! We have walked far today and we will go further yet tomorrow. Rest is needed."

Kyagorusu struggled for a long while to light a fire, though he smiled and

15

sang to himself for the entire length of time he monotonously rubbed the sticks together. Even when it grew too dark to see and he lost part of his tinder, he never ceased his joyful song. In fact, when the fire was finally lit and the flickering flames lit Kyagorusu's face once more, Arvan saw that the large bald man was smiling wider than ever.

He cooked a meal of boiled rice and handed a bowl to Arvan. The portion was rather too large for the boy, rather too large for any one person really, but he ate it anyway, wishing not to offend Kyagorusu. They spoke little as Arvan realised he was far wearier than he'd originally thought.

Chapter Four

The darkness clung to him as it always had, the breeze swirling around. No wonder he had always thought himself something to do with death.

The fever gripped him more firmly and he tried to claw himself free of its oppressive clutches. But in his delirium he knew not what was happening. Each time he broke the grip he slipped and then had the fear of breaking himself to contend with, only to be gripped again, tighter than before, threatening to wring the air from his lungs. His response; to break the grip and face his doom, finding breath shortly, then being caught in that tyrannical grasp once more. This repetition would surely be the end of him.

Eventually, freedom found him. He fell from the clasp but didn't shatter as he had been expecting. No, true liberation met him.

He swam in an ocean of nothingness so absolute that he could never know light as he once had. Even with his evolution-enhanced shadus eyes, the darkness was insurmountable, but still he journeyed through the sea of nothing, the black welcoming him encouragingly into it.

"Come," it said, wordlessly. "Why fear? Rest. Haven't you had toil enough?"

"Yes," he seemed to reply in his usual whisper of a voice. "May I lie beside you once more?"

"Not yet, my love. Not yet. It seems you have more to venture through."

"Must you smile so when you speak such ill-fated news to me?"

"Would you have it any other way?"

He had the sensation of being lifted, but ostensibly remained for even now he failed to pierce the darkness. He moved to speak, to plead to stay, but found no words to say and so his removal from the world of black went unchallenged, but the voice spoke again.

"Haven't you something you still must do?"

He woke in the shadow of the tree as he had the day before, the lustre of the morning sun burdening his unconditioned eyes. His sword strained his breathing and he forced himself to stand, then waited for the inevitable side-effects. But none came. He didn't collapse as he had so many times the previous day, nor did the malady strengthen and move to strike him down. He put his fingers to his brow and found his temperature slightly raised, though his fever had almost dissipated entirely. His nausea still haunted him, but after having perpetuated itself so vehemently the day before, he could now almost ignore it.

He breathed pleasantly in, the air cold but fresh, and he allowed his eyes to fall upon the body of the wolf, but it was gone. A subtle trail of crimson blood ran eastwards along the path. It seemed a larger predator than the insects that had been ravaging the corpse had come and taken the wolf for itself.

"That's twice you've saved my life," Lament said, though his words were only known by the light breeze that crept past. "If not for you I would surely have been the prey. You have my thanks, paltry though the payment is."

He moved to venture east and continue his journey to his encounter when he found upon him the grudging, tauntingly subtle suggestion of his illness and stalled. It was far from potent enough to strike him down, but it was nevertheless present. With time whispering on, he pondered what to do. There was a part of him that doubted if he was in much of a condition to journey east. If the sickness came upon him again, could he survive it?

As if to aid his thought, he stepped from the shadow of the tree and into the full light of the day when something attracted his attention. There was something strange about the ground on which he stood. It took him some time to place the sensation because he struggled to believe his eyes, but they were never wrong. His sight was so evolved, so perfect, he could never doubt what he saw. Then the fear came upon him.

Despite the slanted light of the early morning when the shadows were at their longest, he cast no shadow.

He moved, telling himself it was a trick of the light. Yet, wherever his body went, no shadow followed him.

The image of the platinum dagger plunging into his moonlit shadow and slowly turning black shot through his mind. Of course, it made sense now. He recalled the shadus elders telling him a tale of how one could steal shadows with a certain mythological dagger, though they had also said that a man who had his shadow stolen would die almost instantly. But Lament suffered only an illness, severe though it was.

He sat, stunned, on the path once more, trying to make some sense of the situation. But as hard as he thought, forcing his mind to wrap itself tightly around the facts, no answers came.

It was then he remembered the most disturbing part of the tale.

A man with two shadows can be killed by neither time nor weapon.

By stabbing himself with the black dagger, Vaiske Parlet must have taken Lament's shadow for himself. The final words he had spoken to Lament wandered around the mind of the shadus, tormenting his already loose grip on sanity.

"Your sacrifice shall save many lives."

So, the man in the vermillion armour plotted something, supposedly for the good of many. However, Lament had learned that what these men-of-the-north *thought* was right and what was *actually* right were often two different things. He would have to find Vaiske Parlet and reason with the shadow thief, hoping that he didn't find him too late. Yet, what of his other duty?

He looked north, to where his journey should have taken him if he had just managed to reach the easternmost point of the path.

"Forgive me," he said. "I wish not to condemn you to your doom, yet is this not more pressing?"

He stood and looked around him. Where could Vaiske Parlet have gone?

It was then, as the sun was approaching noon, that the breeze swept west, unleashing a cloud of dust along the entirety of the path, and Lament Strife saw two silhouetted figures approaching from the east.

*

The tickling, bright light of dawn permeated through his eyelids and made a nuisance of itself, slowly dragging him from his sleep. He became aware of a shuffling around him and the unmistakable clatter of cooking pans. The smell of frying bacon aroused him further.

He smiled and opened his eyes, expecting to see Darkla's excited face telling him of the plans she had for the two of them on that say. But, instead, he saw Kyagorusu sitting by a fire with a frying pan, leisurely cooking breakfast.

"You look disappointed," Kyagorusu said, smiling in his typical fashion. "Do you not like bacon?"

"It's not that," Arvan answered. "I was just expecting something different."

Kyagorusu gave the boy a curious look.

"I have eggs," he ventured.

Arvan laughed. "I'm sure whatever you cook will by splendid, Kyagorusu."

"I'm glad to hear it," the bald man said, poking the bacon inquisitively. "It's almost done. Did you sleep well?"

"I think so," Arvan said, rubbing his eyes to expel the last notion of his drowsiness.

"You don't sound *sure*," Kyagorusu said, looking up from the almost-cooked meat.

"I'm not entirely. I don't remember waking in the night, but I certainly don't feel well rested."

"Those are the words of a man used to sleeping in a bed," Kyagorusu laughed. "You'll soon be used to it. I often find the first few nights of a journey an ordeal too. Here." He passed Arvan a plate of bacon and fried bread. "You'll soon feel better after you've eaten."

Arvan ate uncomplainingly. The hot food warmed him against the bitter morning air and distracted him from his thoughts of home. He kept to himself that the bacon was more brittle than a butcher would ever have intended; he was just grateful for the food.

Once they had finished, Kyagorusu re-packed the equipment and they continued on their journey, the bald man singing his cheerful song as they went. The walking was easy work and they turned west against the Central Desert earlier in the day than Arvan was expecting.

Kyagorusu stopped singing and sighed pleasantly.

"Spring will be here soon," he said, smiling. "I imagine it's already sprung back home."

"Where are you from, Kyagorusu?"

"Port Fair; a small town on the Southern Continent. I go back when I have a chance, or a reason. I haven't had either of late."

"I suppose you don't have to worry about the warlords so much there."

"Not recently," Kyagorusu said.

"Or the Behemoth," Arvan mused.

"Oh, we see the Behemoth regularly," Kyagorusu said, rousing slightly. "Still, it's never done Port Fair any harm."

Arvan thought about this for some time. He often heard the Behemoth roar when it was out on the plains near Farras, but he had never actually seen it. The high pitched shrieks kept him awake as a child, but he was now so used to them that he could now sleep through the night. That wasn't to say he didn't respect its power; upon its birth, or so the legend said, it had levelled the great city in the east, now known as the City of the Dead. Anything with such destructive potential was the subject of fear.

Eventually, Kyagorusu spoke again.

"What did your parents say when you told them you were leaving for your first adventure?"

Arvan looked away, up the road. "I… don't have any parents to tell."

Kyagorusu ran the palm of his hand over his head.

"Forgive me," he said. "My inquisitiveness got the better of me."

"That's okay, Kyagorusu," Arvan said. "You didn't know." He forced a smile. "Besides, I'm nineteen. I can do what I want."

Kyagorusu smiled. "You can at that. I think I was wrong about you, Arvan. You might very well be summer, after all. Early summer, at least."

Arvan's smile widened. "And how about you, Kyagorusu; how old are you?"

"Let's just say I'm autumn, or approaching it and faster than I'd like. Then, once again, I'll be neither one thing nor the other."

It was then, as the sun was approaching noon, that the breeze swept west past them, unleashing a cloud of dust along the entirety of the path, and the two travellers saw a silhouetted figure standing in the middle of the road.

It was an abstract figure, with a hauntingly obscure shape. For a time, they stood, observing. Arvan struggled to make it out until he realised it was human, or vaguely human, at least. The waves he had seen at the top of the apparition were part of the thick, matted hair. The flowing entity attached to the person; a cape. There was nothing distinctly masculine about the effigy, but he believed it to be a man by the simple fact that there was nothing particularly feminine about it either.

As if to aid his sight, Arvan blew his fringe from his eyes.

"Careful, Arvan," Kyagorusu said, quietly, almost as quiet as the breeze that whispered around them. "There are some less than reputable characters on the road."

Kyagorusu watched as Arvan's hand wrapped around the hilt of his katana.

"Yet," he said, "there is also no need to be impetuous."

Arvan gave Kyagorusu an embarrassed glance and let go of his sword. Slowly, they began their approach.

Lament considered the visages, his hand grasping the hilt of the gargantuan sword on his back; his last encounter on the road hanging heavily on his mind. He could feel the breeze dancing mournfully around him.

They were a strange pairing, no doubt. One effigy was a large but neat man; the other was slender and messy. He could tell by their way of walking they were males, though, other than that, they remained a mystery to him.

They stopped as the breeze died and the dust began to settle.

Kyagorusu's hand met Arvan's chest and the boy stopped walking. The man ahead was still an abstract figure, though Arvan could now see he was a collage of monochrome, save for the tattered crimson cape that swam lifelessly behind him and those glowing amber irises. The man released the hilt of the enormous sword on his back.

"What a strange looking person," Arvan whispered.

"Of course," Kyagorusu said. "He's a shadus."

Arvan's head turned involuntarily to the bald man. "Shadus?"

"You might know them better as 'shadow people'."

Arvan gave Kyagorusu a blank look.

"Perhaps not," Kyagorusu said, smiling. "They're humans, not so different from us, but they come from the Shadow Isles – a land where it is night for nine months of the year. As such they took some rather different evolutionary steps."

Arvan looked upon the vague man in the distance but could make little of him, except that he had never seen such a mysterious person in his life.

"Then what's one doing here?" Arvan asked.

"That I don't know," Kyagorusu said. "Still, I doubt he's any more dangerous than you or I, despite the size of his sword."

Arvan had been attempting to ignore the sword on the back of the shadus. It matched him in height and was almost the width of his broad shoulders. Yet, it didn't seem out of proportion, slender though the man was. It was almost as if there was more to the shadus than where the dimensions of his body ended.

"We mean no harm," Kyagorusu called to him.

"Nor do I," the shadus said in a whisper that somehow reached the pair.

"May we come closer?"

The shadus seemed to shrug, then turned and gazed into the distance.

"Do as you wish," he said.

Although Arvan was sure he would normally have suspected such a situation of being a trap, he found himself in a mood of unconventional trust. There was a sorrowful calm that swept over him at the shadus' words and, with that wave of sedation, the suspicion was washed from him. Still, he found himself a few paces behind Kyagorusu.

The bald traveller stopped and turned. "Are you coming?"

Arvan nodded resolutely and followed.

As they neared the shadus, Arvan marvelled at his features. In truth, there was nothing particularly extraordinary about the features themselves, but the ghostly pale, almost translucent, skin gave them a quality that Arvan couldn't quite comprehend. Anything especially different about the man's features, Arvan supposed, could be put down to him being of a separate race. Yet there was something more than that. He had a small, but sharp, nose, centred on a face that was bordering on gaunt, accentuating his cheekbones. The shape of his eyebrows made it seem as if he had a faint, though perpetual, scowl and, combining this with his slightly pouting lips, made him look reminiscent of a sullen child. Arvan surmised the shadus couldn't have been much older than him, but he wasn't sure what he was basing that on. There was merely something about the way he held himself that suggested youth. Even had he not been a shadus, he would have been striking to the boy.

"Hello stranger," Kyagorusu said.

The shadus glanced at them both in turn, then back to Kyagorusu. He nodded abruptly.

"Are you a fellow traveller?" Kyagorusu asked.

The shadus looked moodily into the distance.

"I was," he said in the same haunting voice as before.

"I'm afraid that I don't understand."

The shadus didn't respond.

"Well... farewell, stranger. Mayhap our paths will cross again one day."

Kyagorusu moved his head sharply as if to tell Arvan to follow him and the pair began on their way.

"Wait," the shadus said, behind them. They turned and he spoke again. "Forgive me, please; I was attacked on the road and have spent the last two days in the throes of some malevolent fever. I fear my wits are still not completely about me."

"My dear man!" Kyagorusu said in a gasp and strode towards the shadus. He gripped the ailing man by the shoulder. "Where were you headed?"

The shadus looked away. "To the north. Though my plans have since changed." He paused and his eyes rolled towards Kyagorusu. "Tell me, if you would be so kind, where on this continent would a man go if he wished to make an impact in the world?"

The bald man thought for a few moments before answering.

"The Final Resting Place of the Empire, I suppose," he said. "It's the only city still standing."

"How can I get there?"

"It is as far west as the continent allows," Kyagorusu replied. He smiled in his warm way. "But never mind that! You may travel with us; we too are headed there."

"You have my thanks," the shadus said, his voice and expression unchanged. "Though, I do not wish to be a burden."

"Burden?" Kyagorusu asked. "I know of no such man. You will come with us, but first we must eat."

At the mention of food, the shadus retched.

"No," he said. "Please, let us walk some way, at least; I have been in the same surroundings for days and wish to find something other around me, As for food…" he retched again, "I fear I couldn't digest it."

"Very well," Kyagorusu said, sympathetically. "My name is Kyagorusu Kagaron. This is my newest friend, Arvan Deit."

"My name is Lament Strife."

"Well, Lament Strife, we shall continue to the Final Resting Place of the Empire as a three." Kyagorusu paused and turned to the boy. "That is, if Arvan doesn't mind."

Lament's eyes followed Kyagorusu's to Arvan. The youth blew the fringe from his eyes and looked Lament in those amber irises. The shadus gazed upon the features of the stern faced youth. He had a strange demeanour for one so young; his features hard and strong as if the bones beneath were carved from rock by a master sculptor. Eventually, however, his look softened and he smiled placidly.

"It's fine with me," he said. "With the Behemoth possibly in the West Lands, I'd rather have more people travelling with us than fewer. Besides," he smiled, slyly, "perhaps you could philosophise to Lament rather than me?"

Kyagorusu laughed. "So it's settled. Come Lament; the road ahead is long, but together, we shall reach our destination soon enough."

Kyagorusu left Lament's shoulder and began walking west along the path, Arvan at his side.

Lament turned and looked north to where he would travelled. He told himself that he was probably too late to have done any good anyway. The breeze seemed to sigh around him.

"Forgive me," he said to the far-flung north. Then he followed the other travellers.

They walked on in the afternoon under the fractured light of the alabaster sun. Kyagorusu and Arvan talked pleasantly when the bald man wasn't singing his tuneless song. Lament politely feigned interest. Twilight was soon upon them.

23

"So, Lament," Arvan said, "what draws you to the Final Resting Place of the Empire?"

"You heard him earlier, Arvan," Kyagorusu replied. "He seeks to make a different in the world."

"Actually, no," Lament said in his usual whisper of a voice. His companions turned to him, slightly shocked that he had spoken.

"Well, dear fellow, what do you mean?" Kyagorusu asked.

"I..." Lament stopped himself and looked away. Kyagorusu and Arvan paused a few steps ahead of him and turned to look at the shadus. Arvan tried to follow Lament's gaze but found nothing for the shadus to be looking at.

"I believe a man may have gone there," he finally said. "A man of no particular malevolence, but extreme arrogance. What his actual plans are, I do not know, however I do not trust him and he must be stopped."

Arvan considered Lament, the shadus' glowing amber eyes now almost outshining the light of the day. He couldn't quite make out the face that Lament wore, though he thought it ostensibly no different that when he first looked upon it. Yet, those slightly frowning eyes seemed to hold something Arvan hadn't noticed before and, just as he thought he was about to understand it, it faded into nothingness, shrouded in mystery forevermore.

"Should we be concerned?" Kyagorusu asked, his voice, uncharacteristically grave.

"I'm not entirely sure," Lament replied, turning and meeting the bald man's eyes. "Though the realisation enough was potent enough to make me change my plans."

"Important plans?"

Lament paused. The breeze appeared to spiral around him as day dissipated into night and the darkness clung to him. He moved uncomfortably, as if to shake it away.

"They could have saved a man's life; and one dear to me at that."

Arvan glanced between the two, but could make nothing of them or their conversation. Kyagorusu's face was so different to his usual calm smile it seemed it belonged to a separate man. He hoped never to see the bald man's face so severe again, but, as time seeped on and night darkened further, the calm smile showed no signs of returning.

Lament stared into the distance once more, submitting and allowing the darkness to cling to him. "I fear I have condemned him to death."

"You have your reasons," Kyagorusu said.

Lament looked at the bald man. "I would make haste, lest I am still not too late."

Kyagorusu nodded. "Of course, but it is dangerous to travel at night, for us north-men at least, and it has been a day of hardship. Let us sleep and eat."

Lament retched again.

"Please," he said. "You two eat but cook nothing for me. No good will come of me eating."

Kyagorusu nodded and sent Arvan to look for some firewood.

As Arvan stumbled in the black night he struggled to remove Kyagorusu's reaction to Lament's words from his mind, but he failed, despite the fact he was focused more fervently on that than his task of finding firewood. He could make little of what the shadus had said, it seemed he merely lacked the resolve to save the life of his friend and had taken a path that could forgive his distraction.

The thought left his mind and he found himself holding a few dead branches in his arms. As soon as he had left the path he had begun finding them, though he couldn't see many trees nearby. He supposed they had been scattered by the breeze. Then again, the lack of a sighting of a tree could have just been because it was godlessly dark.

Kyagorusu's face shot through his mind again, so pale as to rival Lament. Gone was the quiet, constant optimism. Yet, Arvan could still find nothing terribly ominous in what Lament had said. Then again, living a life spent in fear of warlords and the Behemoth had made him numb to many other springs of fear.

He turned and began to walk back to the camp.

Lament sat wearily, his arms resting on his knees, his head resting on his arms, and tried to ignore his nausea. Kyagorusu readied a pot of rice for when Arvan returned with the firewood.

"I happened to look at the ground around you at sunset today," Kyagorusu said, glancing at Lament. "When the shadows were at their longest."

Lament said nothing, though his eye rolled from its pitiable position to fix on the bald man.

"At first it didn't concern me. I've never met a shadus before and I thought controlling one's shadow might have been one of the evolutionary steps that you've taken." He paused, eyes widening. "But the man you're after... he stole it, didn't he?"

Lament nodded abruptly.

"I read a book on the subject," Kyagorusu said. "Well, shadows were covered, at least. There's a school of thought that believes shadows are more than just an obstruction of light – your experience proves that to be true – that shadows are part of the soul. It claimed that if a man lost his shadow..."

"He would cease to live," Lament interrupted.

"Indeed," Kyagorusu sighed. "The man who stole your shadow took it for himself, didn't he?"

Lament nodded in the same manner as before.

"So," Kyagorusu said, staring into the dark night. "There is a man out there with two shadows, by all accounts an immortal." He turned to Lament. "And you journey to the Final Resting Place of the Empire to take your shadow back."

Lament nodded, glancing at the gargantuan sword lying beside him. "Think of what an immortal could do if he had the ambition."

"Of course, you realise if he wishes to keep your shadow there is little you can do."

"That's inconsequential," Lament said. "It is my duty. I cannot save my dear friend without a shadow."

"Ah, that again," Kyagorusu said, natural curiosity gaining the advantage over his fear. "Where, exactly, were you going? Who were you going to save?"

"That is a story for another time," Lament said. "But one I shall undoubtedly tell, as you have made me tell many things I would like to have kept to myself. And I am still going there, I have merely suffered a setback – though I am most probably too late to be of much help now."

Kyagorusu pried no further as the quiet footsteps of Arvan came drifting in from the black. The boy placed the firewood down wordlessly and helped Kyagorusu light a fire. They ate a meagre meal of boiled rice (Kyagorusu had managed to make it taste of nothing but salt, in spite of the fact he had no salt on him) and then they slept; the toil and worries of the day paling against the forever incoming ebb of tiredness.

Chapter Five

The star speckled sky dripped light onto the Wastes as he strode tirelessly on. In the distance he could see the city of stone with the backdrop of the colossal mountains. He had not expected to reach the Final Resting Place of the Empire so soon, then again he hadn't rested – he needn't ever again. He was immortal now.

Vaiske Parlet smiled behind his horrific mask and gazed upon his new shadow. It was cast by the moon as when he had first seen it, though it had then been attached to another man. Somehow it retained the shape of the shadus. That was the only thing that irked him, however he imagined that it was only just that an aspect of the shadus remained in the world now that the man himself ceased to.

His thoughts were interrupted as he spotted a group of figures on horseback approaching him. He took the time to count them and found nine, riding fast. His spear, though tall (reaching the tips of the horns of his helmet), was light in his grasp and he found himself struggling to stay his hand – wishing to try out his new power and his already known skill.

The riders stopped just before him and Vaiske observed the lead-rider. He was a young man, whose blonde hair fell down to his chin. He was clean shaven and wore a pure white cavalry jacket, left open, with immaculately shined silver buttons on each breast. The rest of his uniform, a grey t-shirt under the jacket, black trousers and black boots that climbed half way to his knees, were equally well kept and the expression that the man had on his face suggested to Vaiske he was well aware of this. Strapped to his belt was a small scabbard that held a dagger with a golden hilt. He was a slender man, but his physique suggested power despite the fact he wasn't particularly muscular. His eyes, grey as the mountain rock of the city of his birth, glimmered in the moonlight and, without even a hint of fear, he looked Vaiske Parlet in his hideous metal-shrouded eyes.

The lead-rider stroked his dull-grey horse's mane and cooed soothingly. The noise calmed even Vaiske, though he didn't allow himself to admit it. The horse sighed pleasantly to the man's touch.

"State your business, stranger," the lead-rider said. His voice was deep but gentle and, though his words were imperative, his tone was nothing less than pleasant.

"I journey to the Final Resting Place of the Empire," Vaiske replied, finding himself slightly disappointed that the lead-rider shivered upon hearing the ghostly-metallic tone.

"Is that so?" the lead-rider asked. "I am Captain Lind Starling of the Great

King's Cavalry. These are some of my men." He gestured to the men behind him. They were a group of men who had obviously tried to match their Captain's standards of self-grooming, though had yet to master the art as he had. Their jackets were a dull-grey, save for the man next to the Captain whose jacket was black.

"This," he continued, gesturing towards the man in black, "is Lieutenant Damske Fernarl."

Vaiske tore his eyes from the Captain and looked at Fernarl. He was as slender as Starling, though slightly shorter and his features were darker; his eyes a deep hazel, his hair a well-kept sculpture of chocolate brown. He too was clean shaven, giving his face a look of the grave.

"Tell me, stranger," Captain Starling said. "Who are you?"

"I am the infamous Vaiske Parlet," he replied and watched, satisfied, as Starling's men failed to supress their surprise. They stifled their gasps, instead settling for concerned glances.

"Infamous?" Captain Starling said. "I seem to be slightly out of touch. The name is new to me." He looked at his men, then back to Vaiske, smiling. "Though my men seem familiar with it. Do you know the name," he turned to Fernarl, "Lieutenant?"

"Yes, sir," the man in black replied. "He is a warrior of some repute."

"Would I know any of his exploits?"

"He once survived battle with the Behemoth."

"That could be said of us."

"He once defeated an entire division of the Riit Clan in battle."

Starling smiled. "That, too, could be said of us. Then again," he ran his eyes over Vaiske Parlet. "I suppose we are not of such extraordinary appearance."

"Please don't feel bad, Captain Starling," Vaiske said. "I fear I haven't heard of you, either."

"And all the better for it," Starling laughed.

Vaiske sneered behind his mask, though all the Captain could see was the horrifically anguished face of metal. Vaiske wondered who this undisciplined man thought he was and why his men held him in respect. If he was under this man's command he would surely mutiny. Vaiske could never follow such a man. Then again, he wasn't one for following anyone any more.

"Tell me, Vaiske Parlet," Captain Starling said. "Why do you journey to the Final Resting Place of the Empire?"

"I seek an audience with Great King Eremmerus," the immortal replied.

"Is that so? Well, I suppose that can be arranged. Though, I'd imagine I should ask whether or not you're dangerous." He smiled. "So, *are* you dangerous, Vaiske Parlet?"

Vaiske gripped his spear tighter.

"Perhaps you would care to find out?" he asked in as pleasant a voice as he could muster.

Captain Starling raised his head and looked down at Vaiske, his golden hair falling before his left eye. For a moment he was an effigy of wrath, yet his face held no anger. Just as Vaiske felt he was about to decipher the look, the Captain softened.

"Very well," he said. His hand trailed down to the side of his horse and he seemed to grasp for something that wasn't there. He frowned and looked to Lieutenant Fernarl. "Who dressed Titus today?"

"That would be you, sir."

"Ah…"

"Is there a problem, sir?"

Captain Starling smiled a convincingly efface smile. "I seem to have forgotten my spear."

"I did remind you to fetch it whilst we were in the stable, sir. I even offered to get it myself."

Starling's smile widened.

"Well, the result's all the same," he said, turning to Vaiske. "I'm afraid I've forgotten my spear. Though, I suppose I could use my dagger, if you would prefer?"

"Choose a champion," Vaiske growled.

"Well, I'm afraid I can't do that," Starling said, smiling again. "The men and I have a rule; don't we, men?"

"Yes, sir!" came the reply.

"Do you wish to say it?"

"Yes, sir!"

"Well…"

"No man is to draw his weapon before Captain Starling," the men recited. "He will be the first into battle and the last out. He will lead every charge and feel every death as if it were his own."

"So you see," Starling said to Vaiske, "I can't oblige you in your generous offer. I'll just have to let you see the Great King and disarm you before your meeting with him."

Vaiske sneered behind his mask.

"Perhaps you'd like to ride with us to the city?" the Captain continued. "Titus is a strong horse and can carry two riders rather easily. It's faster than walking."

"No thank you," Vaiske grunted, unable to disguise his incandescence.

Captain Starling smiled and rode wordlessly away with his men. The sound of galloping hooves gradually faded and the cavalry faded from sight. Vaiske Parlet walked after them – he didn't need the assistance of cowards like Starling. He strode across the cracked Wastes towards the Final Resting Place of the Empire, the moon and stars lighting the arid land eerily. Soon, despite his two shadows, Vaiske Parlet was completely alone.

The gate was sickly pale, somewhat juxtaposed with its immense dimension; strength itself. He touched it to find it cold with the late winter air, so glacial as to permeate through his gauntlets and whisper solemnly to his skin.

He tapped on the stone structure with the tip of his spear and a quiet chime reverberated through the night. He waited as a monolith to be let in but there was no movement from the gate, nor sound from within the city walls. His spear met the stone again; harder this time, louder. He waited, but still nothing replied, save for the creeping breeze. As the deathly cold touch of the breeze reached him, Vaiske Parlet regarded the sensation with intrigue. It caressed his armour gently before shooting away. What could the dead know of an immortal?

Eventually, the gate edged open with the churning of cogs and the clinking of chains. As the gate opened and the darkness of the city seeped out of the laceration, Vaiske could make out the figure of a man astride a horse. He sneered behind his mask as the moon caught the blonde hair and white jacket of Captain Starling.

"Ah, Mister Parlet," the Captain said, Titus walking slowly from the city. "I thought I heard something. We weren't expecting you to arrive quite so soon. Still, better to make sure wouldn't you agree?"

"Quite," Vaiske said through gritted teeth. However, they parted, into a smile, when he had the pleasure of seeing Starling writhe once more in the throes of the metallic voice.

"I believe you wished to see Great King Eremmerus," Starling said. "Please, follow me."

The Captain led Vaiske through the labyrinthine city, riding Titus at a slow walk. Quite how the Captain knew his way through the maze of stone buildings, Vaiske couldn't fathom. Each building was uniform in shape and size, the only thing that seemed to differ was the amount of moss crawling up the stone walls.

Even in the faint light of the midnight the city was grey. Vaiske wondered for a time how so monochrome a city could breed a man as effervescent as Captain Starling. He then decided the Captain of the Great King's Cavalry was too insufferable a man to both think of and be in one's company.

He watched the Captain move rhythmically in the saddle of his horse as if the man and beast shared a heart, or that their hearts beat in time with one another. Whether such synchronicity was possible, Vaiske had no idea, but it seemed to him to be the only explanation as to how the man could find such ease in his affinity with the animal.

"He doesn't sleep anymore," Captain Starling said, quietly.

The speech took Vaiske by surprise, though he said nothing.

"The Great King, I mean," the Captain continued. "He merely sits in his throne looking bored, his head tilted at an angle, as if he's playing some game; seeing how far he can move his head before his crown falls off. Of course, he'd never let anybody see him like that, except me. He tells me things; things that I'd rather not know. Most of the time they're mere ramblings, but every now and then…" He shuddered.

"The Blood Lust is on him, I fear. Not even a year ago he had to fend off the attacks from the warlords; that's what caused that monstrosity out there." He gestured behind them, through the winding city, and Vaiske knew he meant the Wastes. "He misses the blood. He misses the death. You didn't seem to notice it, but the breeze is thick out there; so thick one can hardly breathe. I sometimes catch him out there, struggling for breath and relishing in the asphyxiation. He says it cures his insomnia, knocks him out, you know? But only I've seen him like that and he'll keep it that way.

"Of course, he blames me. He says our victories were 'too absolute' and I, as Captain of the Great King's Cavalry, have scared off all competition. I'd rather the city was safe, but Eremmerus demands to have his place in history. Please, don't misunderstand, I believe he truly does want peace, only he wishes to be the founder of it. He's no monster; merely a man who wants to leave his mark. And to think we were once such good friends…"

Starling stopped talking and sighed. He ran his hand through Titus' mane and slumped, ever so slightly, in the saddle; such a subtle increment that Vaiske doubted he would have noticed it, had he not been searching for some weakness in the Captain.

"Why are you telling me this?" Vaiske asked as they came to a set of colossal steps that led some way up one of the mountains.

"Who said I was talking to you?" Starling said, wearily. He stroked Titus' mane before dismounting and turning to Vaiske. "Still, you'd have been wise to listen. It helps to know about the Great King when you speak to him."

The immortal looked upon the young face of Captain Starling. "How old are you, Captain?"

"Too young for anyone to call me 'Captain'," he replied, smiling. Then, the smile faded and he frowned, so slightly and so briefly that Vaiske almost missed it; in fact, he debated with himself whether or not it was a trick of the light.

"Wait here," Starling said, and he began up the steps; his heeled boots clicking with erroneous pleasure in the night.

Vaiske tried to think of something other than the Captain while he waited. He attempted to come to some conclusion about whether or not such a young man being in charge of an entire cavalry was either just or wise, but merely stumbled over the youth of the Captain. He could have been no older than twenty-one, but he seemed to have a wealth of battle experience already. Indeed, he claimed to have fought the Behemoth.

Vaiske knew that Great King Eremmerus was young also; thrust into the throne at nineteen after the death of his father. As he recalled, that was two years ago, however men can age quickly under poor circumstances and Vaiske could think of none poorer.

The Captain soon re-emerged at the zenith of the stairs and gestured for Vaiske to approach. He did so, his footsteps heavy on the carved rock, but, immortal as he now was, he made short work of the climb and was soon stood before Starling.

"He says you can see him," the Captain said. "I'll have to take your spear though."

Starling held out his right hand and raised his eyebrows playfully. Vaiske grunted and thrust the wooden handle into the Captain's grasp.

"Thank you," Starling said, taking the spear and holding it loosely at his side.

"Are you not going to search me?" Vaiske growled. "I could have more weapons on me. What if I aimed to assassinate the Great King?"

Starling laughed lightly.

"So *assassinate* him," he said. "Save *me* the bother."

Vaiske moved to walk past the Captain, only to find his own spear pushed in his path.

"Of course," Starling began, "not a word of anything I've said to you should leave your lips. Not for my sake; he's a private man, no doubt, but, to his mind, I've committed worse treacheries than speaking ill of him. No, don't repeat anything I've said to you, even if you qualify it with 'Captain Starling said…' or the like. He *will* think it's your own mind and he's not a man you would enjoy being an adversary of." He looked away, down the stairs, into the darkness of the city. "I know I don't."

Starling turned to Vaiske and moved the spear, allowing Vaiske to continue into the palace. There was no door; the palace had been carved into the mountain – leading straight into the throne room. 'Beautiful' could never describe it, though it had never been intended to, nor was the room intended to be it. It was a feat of stone masonry, holding up the rest of the mountain with the bare minimum of pillars. Vaiske wondered as he approached the centre of the room, how the engineers had managed it.

"That's far enough," a tired voice said.

Vaiske stopped and looked around for who had spoken, but found nothing.

"If you're wondering about the architecture," the voice continued, ignoring the confusion of the masked warrior, "my ancestors, as well as I, enjoyed viewing the city from the throne." The voice sighed. "Lind! You're in the way of my view."

Vaiske turned and looked out of the entrance. The silhouette of Captain Starling shrugged and disappeared behind a pillar, leaving an unobstructed view of the city and the Wastes beyond.

"Stunning, isn't it?" the voice said. "Of course, it's better when one doesn't have the nudging thought that the worm, Lind Starling, is out there blighting the landscape. Still, I suppose he has his uses. Bringing me the great Vaiske Parlet - his most recent achievement."

Vaiske smiled behind his mask and turned to where he believed the voice to be coming from. His eyes fixed upon a faint glimmer of metal where the moon, or one of the brighter stars, caught a part of the Great King's crown. He could just make out the frame of the mammoth, stone throne, large enough for two men at least. The Great King, dressed in a white suit, complete with a white cape, was lounged on it, his crown at such an angle as to be perpetually on the verge of plunging to its doom.

"Taciturn, aren't we?" Great King Eremmerus said, his features obscured completely by the darkness.

"Only when in the presence of greatness, your majesty," Vaiske said, unsure how sincere his words would sound once they were filtered through the iron mask.

"Oh, you're one of *those* are you? Good. I could do with more of *those*."

"'Those', your majesty?"

"People who know their place." Although the voice of the Great King was weary he enunciated each syllable. Every word was formed in his mouth with the deliberateness of a sculptor's chisel. "Then again, I know of your exploits and you seem not far from greatness yourself. I need men like you. Unfortunately, I tend to get men like Lind Starling."

"Insufferable fellow, isn't he?"

The glint of metal rose slightly as the Great King lifted his head.

"Address me correctly, Parlet," he said, slowly.

Vaiske took a step back and tilted his head at the Great King.

"Insufferable fellow isn't he, your majesty?" he said through gritted teeth. Who was this man who thought himself above Vaiske Parlet?

"I quite agree," Eremmerus said as if Vaiske had made no misdemeanour at all. "Needless to say, I do have my reasons for keeping him close. He will win a battle with a cavalry charge, even if it does take the challenge out of it. He's a rather good bodyguard also. Don't let the dagger fool you; he's deadlier with that than most are with a sword. Why he disarmed you, I'll never know.

"Unfortunately, he's become rather less fond of me of late. Not that it bothers me - I've held a distinct loathing of him for some time now. I have considered executing him (it would assuage me, at any rate) but who would lead the cavalry? The men adore him, not that I'm sure why."

The Great King paused and the glint of metal rose once more, only to fall gently back into place; out of place. There was silence in the throne room for a few uncomfortable moments and Eremmerus sighed.

"But you've come to talk of matters other than Lind Starling," he said and the glint rose again.

"Yes, your majesty," Vaiske replied. "I heard a whisper that you were planning on ridding the continent of the warlords."

"Whisper?" Eremmerus spat. "There is no *whisper* about it, Parlet. I am amassing an army. Every man and every boy in the Final Resting Place of the

Empire shall lift spear and sword until we are rid of those damnable warlords once and for all!

"It started as an empty promise; something to tell the populace to keep them hopeful whilst we were under attack. Then it dawned on me – it was a fantastic idea! Of course, it requires considerable manpower, but it shall be done. And there I shall stand; at the forefront of the battle, blood stained and magnificent – the harbinger of the age of peace!"

The Great King's voice grew tender and Vaiske smiled behind his horrific mask. He had expected Eremmerus to be open with his plans but the weary voice of before belied his now animated tone. It was now he could reveal the secret of his own.

"A masterful machination indeed, your majesty," Vaiske said. "And how much easier would it be to achieve if you had but one immortal in your army?"

The glint of the crown tottered from side to side.

"Immortal?" the Great King said.

"Yes, your majesty."

"It sounds as if the enjoyment, the danger, would be removed from the battle."

"It seems to me, your majesty, that now is not the time for waging war for the mere joy of battle – now we must wage war to win. We can rid this land of the scourge that is the warlords if we but lift a hand in defiance. With an immortal your victory is assured. That is not to say that the pleasure need be removed from battle, far from it! With an immortal at your side you need fear no sword or arrow of your opponent reaching you. They will concentrate their efforts on stopping the unstoppable foe; you need only concern yourself with spilling the blood of your enemies until there are none left."

The glint of the crown moved slightly forwards, as if pondering some great problem. It then rose and shuffled from side to side.

"An excellent point," the Great King said. "But it is only hypothesis. I have no immortals and so my glorious war must be ever in danger of failure."

"But, your majesty," Vaiske said, grinning wildly behind his mask. "An immortal stands in this very room."

The Great King lifted his crowned head interestedly.

"I am no longer merely Vaiske Parlet! I am the man-with-two-shadows!"

Chapter Six

Lament spent the night feeling the grip of the breeze on him, the dark of the night clinging to him and the fever coming once more upon him. He didn't sleep. Other than the sickness-enforced unconsciousness of the recent days he hadn't slept in some time. There was something about the light in this land that unsettled him; such perfect lustre rising and falling each day, only a short spell of darkness interrupting to accentuate the light. Not only this, but the moon was small here, the stars dim. There was something about the atmosphere in the Shadow Isles that magnified the night, the loss of which he had yet to grow used to in the land of the north-men. Though, he knew the truth was that he had not slept long before he noticed any of this; long before he came to the Northern Continent even.

He lay just off the foot-beaten path staring up at the stars. He needn't rest at night, it would serve only to slow his progress, yet Kyagorusu and Arvan had shown him kindness – he couldn't just leave them, even if that meant death for a man.

He turned his head and gazed upon the shadow-less ground. Had he retained his would the sight have been any different? It was too dark to tell and he had no need for conjecture. The fire still flickered limply, throwing light his way. He was far from it and grew cold, though Arvan and Kyagorusu slept soundly enough. Lament stood and wandered over to the dying flames, placing more wood on them. The fire gorged itself and grew, rising to the height of Lament's hip. He turned and looked to the ground once more; no shadow.

"Why do you look?" he asked himself in his usual whisper. "It will not return by its own volition."

He heard a gentle groan and his eyes fell on Arvan, stirring. The youth opened his eyes and looked at Lament.

"My apologies," the shadus said. "I was cold. I didn't mean to wake you."

Arvan sat up and smiled weakly. "It's not you, Lament; I'd have woken anyway. I'm still unused to sleeping without a bed."

"You don't travel much?" Lament asked, absent-mindedly.

"This is the first time I've left my town."

Lament rolled his eyes towards the boy. "And why do you go to the Final Resting Place of the Empire?"

"I think my master may be there, Lawliet Snow. Do you know of him?"

"I don't follow the tales of the north-men."

Arvan lay back down.

"He's the greatest swordsman in the world," he yawned. "And a great

35

adventurer…" He trailed off and when Lament peered on the youth's face he saw he was asleep.

Lament lay back down, closer to the fire this time. The stars gazed down on the earth, disinterested but attentive.

"These plans of men," Lament said. "What are they? Still, I'd rather this than have naught to do."

He closed his eyes but, as he expected, no sleep came.

Lament watched the sun rise without wonder. The first time he had witnessed it, he thought it magical; the light slowly washing over all below it, expelling darkness only to where the orb could not reach. It was different than in his homeland, when the day didn't arrive so much as the night seemed to fade; the short Day Months, a mere rest for the night. But here, to be blessed with a rising sun every day, and he had become indifferent to it.

He rose and strapped his sword once more to his back. It had been a long night and he was unsure of how many similar ones he could experience before he could take no more. Not so many more, perhaps not even one. Lying awake, alone, in the darkness left him vulnerable to his thoughts and those musings were laden with more darkness at best.

"Did you sleep at all, Lament?" Arvan asked, rising.

Lament was taken quite by surprise, thinking himself the only one awake. He looked to the youth but took some time to reply. "I…"

"Of course he didn't, Arvan," Kyagorusu said, sitting up in his blanket. "He has a lot on his mind. Well, don't worry, Lament; we shan't keep you waiting much longer."

Kyagorusu and Arvan breakfasted on the last of the bread and a slice of the cured meat each.

"We're almost out of food," Kyagorusu said. "I suggest we make the remainder of the journey as short as possible. I did only pack enough food for one person, after all."

"It's a good thing you're not hungry, Lament," Arvan said, wrapping up his blanket. "We'd have run out of food yesterday."

Lament looked at Arvan and the boy dropped the blanket, realising just what he'd said.

"That's not to say it's fortunate that you're ill!" he hastily added.

Kyagorusu laughed. "Perhaps it would be best if we just went along? The less chance Arvan has to trip over his words the better. Still, I suppose we should be careful he doesn't trip over his feet instead, eh?"

Lament set a quick pace for the day, which did not allow for conversation. The mood of the shadus seemed to have infected the rest of the group. Arvan was surprised that he managed to keep up, but supposed that his teaching with Master Snow had included quite a lot of endurance training. Even

Kyagorusu didn't struggle, the clumsily built man using his staff as if it was an extra limb.

By noon, the ground on which they stood had become harder, before turning completely to rock. It was then they knew they had reached the West Lands.

"The Rock Flats!" Kyagorusu said. "I hadn't expected to get here so soon. This is quite a pace you've set, Lament."

Lament stopped and turned as if to reply, only for his legs to enfeeble and he fell to his knees. Kyagorusu caught him and lowered him gently. The shadus' brow was littered with sweat and he had grown paler than usual.

"My dear man!" Kyagorusu said. "Perhaps you should rest a while. We've come further in half a day than I would usually expect to in a whole one as it is."

"We don't have time," Lament said, lifting himself only to fall back down. His breathing was laboured, more from frustration than exhaustion.

"Then we'll make time," Arvan said, gently. "You can't go far like this, Lament."

Lament said nothing. His eyes were fixed on something far in the distance, something his companions couldn't yet see; his superior shadus eyesight stretching a fathomless length past that of the others.

He forced himself to stand and tore his sword from his back. He held it heavily in his right hand, the blade tipped down towards the rock ground.

"It's not a case of my objectives," Lament said, his whisper sharper than usual. "We have to leave because…"

The ground shook violently as a deafening crash sounded. Arvan and Kyagorusu fought to stand, though Lament had steadied himself upon the sight of whatever held his attention.

Just as Arvan and Kyagorusu regained their balance the same thing happened again and Arvan fell.

"It's coming," Lament said. He hauled Arvan to his feet and took the boy in his free hand. Kyagorusu, knowing what was coming next, broke into a run, effortlessly keeping pace with the ailing Lament.

The ground continued to shake, perpetually intensifying and making each swift stride a challenge. Arvan stumbled, stretched by Lament's grasp, and only managed to continue for the shadus dragging him along. He allowed himself to look back – the figure was far away, but still he could tell it was immense in frame. It was then he realised that the footsteps were timed perfectly with the quakes of the ground; reverberating outwards. It was the Behemoth! Growing ever larger in his sight.

"We won't make it!" he cried. "We can't escape it!"

Lament stopped running and released Arvan. The boy stumbled backwards and fumbled for his katana, but he could not draw it; his eyes fixed upon the forever nearing effigy of death. A hand fell on his shoulder and he saw Kyagorusu.

"Calm down," he said, smile inexplicably intact. "There are tales of men who have survived encounters with the Behemoth."

Arvan said nothing for the boy had death so firmly planted in his mind that the bald man's words held no meaning. He looked at Lament, a few paces between them and the approaching Behemoth.

The shadus held the gargantuan sword in both hands, his feet stubbornly placed on the rock beneath them. The pale man in black clothing stood atop the grey, his crimson cape fluttering listlessly in the breeze. How he was so calm, Arvan couldn't comprehend.

"Go," Lament said, his whisper inexplicably audible over the booming footsteps.

"We can't leave you!" Kyagorusu called.

"If nothing else, I can give you time to escape."

"We're not leaving!"

"I've condemned one man to death through poor conviction and maybe many more through carelessness. At least let me save you. At least let me die with honour."

Lament's eyes never left the Behemoth. Nothing else existed to him. Kyagorusu realised that there was no use arguing – the shadus wouldn't change his mind.

The bald man grabbed Arvan's arm and ran.

They ran until they could no longer feel the quaking ground, but still they did not feel safe. They ran until they had left the Rock Flats, yet comfort still eluded them. Their lungs burned, their legs ached and their hearts screamed disaster. They fell to the grass of the plain and drew air into themselves, trying to assuage the pain in their bodies. But even as that was relieved the sorrow took hold of them. Lament was surely dead. Although it was true that men had survived encounters with the Behemoth before, but theirs were tales of war when the Behemoth was outnumbered by legions of warriors and even then few escaped.

They lay on the soft grass until their breath returned and their hearts no longer screamed. Arvan felt a great serenity come over him, but he tried to wish it away; his peace was out of place. He turned morosely to Kyagorusu.

The bald man was sat, slumped, his face red with effort, his eyes large and unceasing. Eventually his breath slowed and he looked more like himself, but gone was the ever-present smile. He simply stared into the Rock Flats from which they had just escaped.

The land of stone was motionless, the glass sky hanging loosely above; ready to crack in an instant.

The shriek of the Behemoth cut through the breeze as if to shatter the false jewel overhead.

"What now?" Arvan asked.

"We have to keep moving," Kyagorusu panted, forcing himself to stand.

"I won't feel safe until we're in the city."

He pulled Arvan up and the boy met his eye.

"I ran away," Arvan said, weakly. "I couldn't even draw my sword."

Kyagorusu laid a hand on his shoulder. "It's happened to more experienced men than you, Arvan. Sometimes running away is the wisest thing to do."

The shriek rang out again, louder and more ferocious than before.

"Like now!"

They began running west again, less urgent than before though still as fast as their exhausted bodies would allow. The thought lay heavily on Arvan's mind, so heavily that he found himself speaking it before he had committed his mouth to the task.

"Master Snow wouldn't have run away."

Kyagorusu said nothing.

Lament turned and watched his companions disappear from his sight. Oblivious to the shaking ground, his attention was still and absolute. Once the figures were finally gone, he turned back to the Behemoth, still growing in his sight. The man shaped beast shrieked with such volume that he thought he would never hear again. Yet, once the roar was over, the din of the footsteps returned.

The fever overcame him and his sword felt heavy in his grasp as it never had before. He was glad for the bandage-like cloth on his hands and forearms without which the hindrance of the sweat would have been too much. He calmed himself with a deep breath and tried to push the malady away.

The Behemoth was now close enough for him to make out specific features: feet like hooves, the dark fur covering its thighs and biceps, the stone-esque skin, the listless white eyes. It clenched its fingered hands into fists and looked upon Lament, pausing.

Lament gripped the sword tighter and braced himself.

The breeze swirled around him, catching his cape and dancing with it.

"May I lie beside you once more?" he asked.

The breeze ceased and his cape fell to wrap around him comfortably.

Lament Strife, the gaze of the Behemoth still hard upon him, lifted his sword with his right hand above his head, the sun glinting off the tip of the blade, sending a path of the light up to the head of the Behemoth. The beast moved its arm as if to break the lustrous trail but succeeded only in shielding its eyes.

Lament dropped the sword slightly, destroying the path and readied himself for his defence.

"You need wait no longer, my love," he said as the Behemoth raised a colossal fist. "I have come to join you on the breeze."

Day was beginning to darken as the last of their energy finally left them.

The sunset bruised the sky into a collage of purple and navy, giving golden light to the abstract edges of the grey clouds.

Kyagorusu and Arvan collapsed, exhausted, on the bank of a river, the gentle flowing of which almost soothed them into a complete sleep. It took Kyagorusu shaking him to lift Arvan's weary eyelids. Panting, they drank from the river and Kyagorusu split the last of the food between them. Once their breath and energy had returned, they sat by the river for a while.

"How far did we run?" Arvan asked.

"Quite a way," Kyagorusu replied. "And no distance at all."

Arvan tried to smile but the philosophical comment didn't tickle him in the way Kyagorusu's musings usually did. Instead, he merely blew his fringe from his eyes.

"I mean it," Kyagorusu said, solemnly. "It was a long way for us, but for the Behemoth it's a fraction of the distance."

"Do you think it will come after us?"

"I doubt it."

The image of Lament standing resiliently as the Behemoth approached entered Arvan's mind. He spoke as if his death meant nothing, less than nothing in fact, as if it was no death at all.

"It's okay to feel sad," Kyagorusu said. "But you mustn't blame yourself."

Arvan looked at Kyagorusu and instantly knew that the bald man was right. He felt as if he had known the philosopher for far longer than the few days he had. Still, he supposed they had been eventful.

"We only met him yesterday," Arvan said. "And he gave his life for us."

"He was a brave man."

"Is there any chance that he survived?"

Kyagorusu didn't answer.

For a moment, Arvan's thoughts left Lament and he felt sorry for himself. He was cold, tired and starving with still some way to go to the Final Resting Place of the Empire. Then the scathing pit of his stomach began to burn.

"I ran away," he said. "What will Master Snow say when I tell him?"

"He will say you were wise to do so," Kyagorusu replied, sympathetically. "There is no glory in a foolish death. Lament's death was heroic, sacrificing himself for us. Were either of us to stay as well we would have been fools."

"If I never have a day as shameful as this one I will die happily."

Kyagorusu sighed.

"It's not over yet," he said, looking downriver.

Arvan peered around the large man and saw a small group of figures on horseback headed towards them. He groaned, just wishing for sleep.

"Should we run?" he asked.

"I don't think I can run any further? Can you?"

Arvan shook his head and together they waited for the figures to come closer. Arvan found his hand wrapping around the hilt of his sword, but he doubted he could do much with it if the riders were a threat; he couldn't even draw it when confronted with the Behemoth. His hand moved away and clutched at the grass on which he sat.

"Not many travellers in these parts nowadays," said the lead-rider. He was a scrawny man, dressed in tattered rags; then again, so were the men who rode with him. "What business have you in the West Lands?"

"We mean no harm," Kyagorusu said, his voice sounding tired. "We just want to go to the Final Resting Place to the Empire."

"Do you?" the lead-rider said with a sly smile. "Scarsk!"

"Yes, sir?"

"Tell his Lordship what we've found. I think he'll be rather interested."

The messenger rode away but Kyagorusu and Arvan were too tired to watch him. They exchanged a grave look and let another man bind their hands. Would this day never end?

Night had fallen fully when the torches appeared. Two men with flaming branches rode alongside an underfed man. Behind them a column of men of similar stature walked, each armed with makeshift spears or rusted swords.

"Bow to his Lordship!" the man who bound them barked.

Arvan and Kyagorusu, too exhausted to disobey or question, lowered their heads. When they looked back up the column of poorly armed soldiers had halted and the man on horseback, lit by torches, towered above them. He was gaunt, his eyes sunken and hollow. His tattered rags could have easily fit another man inside.

He looked to the lead scout.

"Who are these men?" he asked, wearily.

"Travellers, my Lord. I thought we could use them to bargain with Eremmerus."

The warlord shrugged.

"I'm not sure how much Eremmerus has to give," he sighed. "I'm not sure he's in a condition to give anything, mentally at least. Still," he glanced over the prisoners, "if nothing else we can embarrass him in front of his people."

"Yes, my Lord."

"They will walk beside me. I would have new company tonight." He looked upon them. "You are alone?"

"We once had a third," Kyagorusu answered. "Though, he was taken by the road."

"A familiar story," the warlord said. "Come, I have heard the Behemoth is in the West Lands. If that is so then I would rather keep moving."

The scouts hauled the prisoners to their feet and they joined the column beside the warlord. Arvan's hunger deserted him, as did his weariness and he was left forsaken by all feeling save for the visceral nothingness that exuded itself upon him. This warlord was not how they were supposed to be. The stories suggested that he would be a vile man who would kill any helpless peon who stood in his way. Yet, although he was far from charming, or even pleasant, he wasn't the monster Arvan had always thought the warlords were.

"What are you going to do with us?" Kyagorusu asked.

The warlord sighed. "Trade you for food. If Eremmerus saves you from us, you're two more supporters to his mind, and he needs all the supporters he can get. Of course, we'll have to make it look like we'll kill you if he doesn't give us what we want." He glanced at Arvan. "Don't misunderstand, if he doesn't give us the food we need, I *will* kill you – you're still another two mouths to feed, and I don't just have my men to worry about."

"Family?" Kyagorusu asked.

"A wife and three children in the South Lands. They get what food they can, but they're starving. The men aren't doing much better."

Arvan looked back at the men that marched behind them; a collage of morose looks, stumbling on, using their weapons to keep them upright.

"They don't look like they want to follow you," Arvan muttered.

"They don't," replied the warlord. "But they had to choose; live under the tyranny of the Great King or live under the tyranny of me. They've made their choice." He paused and added quietly, "And I've made mine."

"But you could all go back and live regular lives again!" Arvan cried, his voice cracking with sincerity.

"And leave ourselves open to the injustices of another clan, maybe even Eremmerus? They say he's amassing and army larger than ever seen..."

"You could all lay down your weapons!"

"Who would agree to that? My enemies have weapons, so I have weapons. And what of you, young man? My scouts say you were armed with a katana before they disarmed you."

Arvan said nothing.

"War breeds war," Kyagorusu said, solemnly. "And we've all been touched, pulled into the cycle. But we'll never have peace if we don't make a conscious effort."

"Yes," the warlord said. "And I fight for peace."

Kyagorusu smiled sadly; the light of the torches just bright enough for Arvan to make it out and he warmed.

"I met another warlord who said exactly the same thing," Kyagorusu said.

The warlord didn't reply. They went on under the sickly moon in silence, except for the coughing of some of the men behind. An imperfect sky reigned, they grey clouds rolling in from the west, until, eventually, the moon was obscured.

After some time the warlord looked to one of his scouts.

"Gag the prisoners," he said. "I'll not have such treason spoken in my company."

Filthy rags were thrust into their mouths and tied so tightly around their necks that Arvan could barely breathe. He retched many times and felt the convulsion of oncoming vomit but nothing came. Kyagorusu nudged him as if to pass on some strength.

"My wisdom is absolute," the warlord said in his tired voice. "My power is absolute. I will win, for my men are on my side. I will win, for the right is on my side."

The river flowed on as they walked beside it, seemingly forever and unceasing, until they came to a small lake that was its source. They had walked north for many hours with little on Arvan's mind except death and war. When the company stopped there, despite his dire situation, Arvan collapsed to the soft grass and slept a dreamless sleep.

The lake shimmered, reflecting the depressed clouds overhead as the breeze weaved its way through the company of men. They lit fires, tearing branches from the trees that circled around the area, creating a clearing between the lake and the trees. The soldiers drank but the good cheer that alcohol usually brought remained elusive.

Kyagorusu knelt next to the sleeping Arvan, his bonds so tight that his hands had gone numb. He rubbed his fingers together, attempting to bring the appendages back to some semblance of life. He succeeded to an extent, but as soon as he stopped the numbness returned.

He stared out to the lake, beautiful but for the company he was in. He knew where they were; the Lake of the Fallen Hero, named after a man long dead. Kyagorusu knew all of the tales; the man was honoured in some, demonised in others. Kyagorusu couldn't quite decide which the truth was, to his mind each man had a reason for his actions and, though they may not always be in the right, he could be sure they always *believed* themselves to be in the right. It was no different for the Fallen Hero. He began recounting the most famous tale in his mind before he remembered his current situation and his thoughts returned to the present.

Many of the soldiers were starting to go to sleep, the alcohol combining with their empty stomachs, bringing a weary haze over them. A few armed guards were positioned around the poor excuse for a camp, though they were some way from Kyagorusu and Arvan.

Kyagorusu lay down, as if to go to sleep, or so it was intended to appear to the guards. He looked out to the lake once more, a lone cherry blossom tree catching his eye on the west bank. It was practically bare, but, on the tip of a small branch growing from a sturdy limb, was the merest whisper of a white bud trying to bloom. Despite his danger and his gag, Kyagorusu smiled.

'Spring is finally almost here,' he thought.

He cautiously glanced around, taking careful note of the positions and distances of the guards. They were far enough away for him to try what he had been planning, though not far enough to do it with full vigour.

Waiting for a more perfect opportunity, he settled for biting and chewing his gag. The taste was rank and he attempted to remove his mind from the task if only to relieve his taste-buds, but the vileness leapt around his mouth. Still, he bit, every time with more force, his jaw aching from the effort.

He heard the faint sound of stitches tearing and he knew it was working. Eventually, the rag tore entirely and he spat it from his mouth, leaving nothing but the vulgar aftertaste of the grime-ridden cloth.

Kyagorusu looked around again. The guards had abandoned their posts once they were certain the warlord was asleep and were now huddled around one of the further fires, drinking and speaking mutiny.

Now was his chance!

Kyagorusu noted a sleeping soldier nearby with a sword resting at his side. He crawled over, slowly, his eyes perpetually fixed upon the undisciplined guards, but they never even thought to check. Soon he reached the sword and sat with his back to it, grasping the hilt clumsily in his bound hands. He watched with terror as the blade tapped the sleeping soldier while Kyagorusu fumbled with the sword, but the soldier never stirred.

The blade was blunt but, with more time than he wished to invest on the endeavour and repeated, exhausting effort, it cut through the final chord of the rope around his wrists. He placed the sword gently beside the sleeping soldier and crawled back to Arvan.

Arvan woke with a start, his breath returned and his hands freed, to the sight of Kyagorusu kneeling over him.

"Not a sound," the bald man whispered. "Or at least, not a loud one. Most of the soldiers are asleep, but I'd rather not risk waking them."

Arvan nodded. "Where are our weapons?"

"It's too dark to find them and I don't want to spare the time. Besides, with these numbers, I doubt they'd do much good anyway."

"I suppose," Arvan whispered. "Though, Master Snow gave me that sword."

"He'll understand," Kyagorusu said, looking at the guards by the fire. "He'd rather you were alive, I'm sure. Now, come on; crawl over to those trees." He pointed to some trees to the west of the lake and they made their slow way over to them. Arvan was so tired he could barely move, before they were even half way to the trees he was out of breath, but Kyagorusu slowed to the pace of the youth and encouraged him along.

Once in the line of the trees, they sat for a while, regaining their energy. When Arvan had some breath to spare, he spoke.

"Do you really think we can escape?"

"They'll come after us when they realise we're gone," Kyagorusu said. "I'm not sure how long that will be though. We're not in much of a condition to travel quickly; but neither are they. It's not far to the Final Resting Place of the Empire; at the very least we can make it difficult for them to recapture us."

Arvan nodded defiantly and, together, they slipped from the trees into the darkness of the night.

The breeze swirled around, so thick as to stifle his breathing. For a time, it did and he thought he was choking, but never did the air leave him endlessly and relief was always soon upon him. It suffocated his skin with heat, so close to him he thought himself in some hell long forgotten. If his torment was never to end he would not have known.

The sky above was faulted, black and grey warring with one another until each was too weak to claim victory. The moon was spurned, the stars torpid, and he knew, other than the breeze, he was completely alone.

But that was fine; he knew they would soon come.

They were both too tired to run, but they walked as swiftly as they could. The sun was beginning to dawn as they stepped onto the Wastes. Arvan, struggling to breathe as it was, found the thickness of the breeze insurmountable but suffered on, inhaling sharply, each breath further lacerating his already maltreated lungs.

He peered back and saw the figures of the scouts on horseback approaching from the distance. He stopped walking.

"Well, Kyagorusu," he said, "we almost made it." He looked west again, gazing at the tauntingly close city of grey stone. "We almost made it."

Kyagorusu grabbed Arvan's robe by the collar and pulled him up to his face.

"You're not giving up!" he roared. "Your Master's in that city and he's waiting for you! Now come on!"

He took the youth's arm and dragged him along behind him as he broke into a laboured run. Where Kyagorusu had found this new energy even he didn't know but he wouldn't question it. He tripped and stumbled, the slight weight of Arvan behind him still enough to unbalance him at intervals, but on they ran, unprepared for death.

The riders drew forever nearer, their pace quickening while the energy left Kyagorusu and he slowed.

But something ahead had caught Arvan's eye. An abstract figure, both slender and large, a mass of waves with no hard edges. He couldn't make out where the effigy ended and the rest of the world began, all he knew was that, somewhere, it did.

The visage moved subtly and tore itself from obscurity into Lament, effortlessly holding the gargantuan sword, his cape fluttering in the breeze.

"Step aside," he said in his usual whisper.

Arvan and Kyagorusu ran either side of him and turned back, the riders now uncomfortably close.

"Don't kill them," Kyagorusu pleaded. "They've made bad choices, but they're not bad men."

Lament glanced at him. "I'll do what I can."

They watched, both inert and amazed, as he lifted the sword over his head, taking a small step back, and, using all the strength he could muster, struck the ground with the colossal blade. He sent a rift tearing through the arid ground of the Wastes towards the riders with an almighty growl of the earth. The riders tried to avoid the lengthening fissure but were thrown from their horses nevertheless, landing unconscious on the ground. The wise animals rose and ran back east.

"How did you escape the Behemoth?" Arvan asked, gradually overcoming the spectacle he had just witnessed.

"There will be time enough for that later," Lament replied. His eyes were perpetually gazing at the horizon.

"I haven't known you very long," Kyagorusu said, "but I know that whenever you do that it is unfortuitous news."

Just as he finished speaking, a great multitude of silhouettes appeared on the horizon. It could only be the warlord force.

"I don't suppose you could fight all of those?" Kyagorusu looked at Lament's face and saw the exertion of the one strike; it had brought on his fever once more. Sweat condensed on the shadus' brow and he wiped it away with his sleeve.

"It's not far now," Arvan said. "If we run we might just make it."

Kyagorusu smiled. "That's the Arvan I know!"

Lament placed his sword on his back and turned from the charging soldiers. He pointed to another force approaching from the city on horseback.

"If they don't get us first," he said.

Still, they ran west, running towards the figures on horseback. Lament, somehow fresher than his companion, remained a few paces ahead; his right hand perpetually wrapped around the hilt of his sword.

Arvan looked back. The rested warlord army was moving faster than they could ever hope to. When he looked forwards again, the mounted force had stopped just before them. Once they reached the lead-rider they stopped running.

"Well," said a man in a white cavalry jacket, holding an ivory-white spear in his hand, "you brought an entire warlord army with you, I won't thank you for that. But I'll not deny you the help. Lieutenant?"

"Yes, sir?" replied a man in black.

"Take Flint and Strahl and get these men to the city. Give them food and set them up in my quarters. I'll take them to see the Great King once they've rested."

"Yes, sir!"

Before Arvan knew what was happening, he was hauled onto a horse behind its rider and found himself hurtling towards the city, Lament and Kyagorusu in much the same condition. Behind them the crashing of steel on steel, muffled only by a cacophony of hooves, raged. The sound was so fervent that it hadn't even died by the time they reached the immense gate of the Final Resting Place of the Empire. Yet, Arvan knew nothing of this. The heavy but soothing rocking of the horse had lulled him into sleep.

Chapter Seven

For days she woke and expected to find her disappeared with the night, gone in some arbitrary direction in search of company. Yet Darkla was almost always in sight of Mirr, or easily found. Often, she was sat in the temple as Arvan used to in some state of severe meditation. Each morning she lit a candle for Master Snow, the temple now full of miniscule stars, the flames of which never died out.

And so it was that morning as Mirr ascended the eroding stone steps to the temple, no longer even a shell; merely four stone pillars, holding up the sky where a roof used to be, and a stone floor. Darkla sat in the centre of the room, surrounded by the flickering candles that shimmered off of her white dress and gave new sun-kissed lustre to her blonde hair.

Mirr stood at the entrance, wishing no disturbance to the entranced girl, and gazed up at the cyan sky. Great waves of surf-white clouds ebbed into view, cascading into each other and becoming one before drifting on, driven by the endless tides of breeze. The sun was lost behind the flow at times, only for its light to burst around the clouds and renew itself, washing the world in unending luminescence.

"You can come in, Mirr," Darkla said, ending Mirr's reverie.

"I don't want to disturb you."

Darkla turned to her with a faint smile. "It's no disturbance. I'm not meditating, I don't know how. Why Arvan and Master Snow do it I'll never understand. Please," she moved and gestured towards the ground beside her, "I'd enjoy the company."

Mirr entered and sat beside Darkla, bending her body in such a way that only a child could be used to. When she looked on Darkla's face the girl showed no signs of having cried recently, yet, despite the faint smile, Mirr could see sadness exuding itself from somewhere within her.

"You're using their names flippantly today," Mirr said.

"They're just names," Darkla said, still smiling. "Anyway, they'll be back soon enough."

Mirr wondered for a time how Darkla had become so philosophical about what only three days ago she was distraught. She considered that perhaps it was an act, but dismissed it on her previous knowledge of her. She was an honest girl, one who didn't deny her emotions. Still, that didn't explain this sudden change.

"Do you know what day it is today?" Darkla asked, interrupting Mirr's thoughts.

The dark haired woman shook her head.

"It's nine years today since Lord Riit's men murdered my parents," she continued, every bit as calm as before. "Do you remember it?"

"Of course I do," Mirr said gently. "And so do you."

"No I don't," Darkla said, looking away as her smile faded. "That's the worst of it. I remember my mother smiling at me and stroking a tear from my cheek with the last of her strength. I remember my father telling me that everything would be okay. I remember them both slipping away. I don't have any memory of the Riit Clan riding into town; I suppose I must have blocked it out."

Mirr touched Darkla's arm softly but said nothing. The breeze whispered past, dancing with the flames of the candles and Darkla smiled, only for the curl of her lips to escape in an instant.

"I don't usually think about it," she said. "Even on the anniversary. Arvan distracts me; he plans a big adventure for the day. He's so good at it that last year I didn't even realise what day it was until the day after and it was too late to be sad about it then."

Her voice was quiet and she spoke pensively. She looked at Mirr with a fragile smile.

"Is that why you were so angry at Arvan for leaving?" Mirr asked.

Darkla sighed. "I suppose that's part of it, as much as I don't want it to be. He's my friend, usually a very good one, but he was so worried about Master Snow that he felt the need to leave. I didn't comfort him or distract him well enough. I let him down."

"I'm sure Arvan doesn't feel that way."

Darkla shrugged.

"Well," she said, "I do."

Chapter Eight

Arvan woke to weak darkness that could only belong to the very early morning. Lethargy swept over him at once and he pulled his covers over him, smiling as he realised he was in a real bed.

The events of the day before returned to his mind. The eternal running from the warlord clan, the cavalry charge. Then darkness. Still, he seemed safe enough now.

"I'd suggest getting up soon," a familiar voice said. "Captain Starling said he'd like to get some sleep eventually."

Arvan peered out of the sheets and saw Kyagorusu sat at a small table, eating a slice of cake and drinking a glass of red wine. He looked rested and as happy as ever, his smile marred only by the glutinous crumbs of the cake.

"Kyagorusu," Arvan said. "How long have I been asleep?"

"Almost an entire day," Kyagorusu laughed. "Don't worry. I've only been awake an hour myself, though I managed to stave off sleep until we entered the city."

Arvan blushed.

"Come now," the bald man said. "There's food, and good food at that. Besides, as I've said, Captain Starling needs his rest too."

"Who's Captain Starling?"

"I am," said a figure appearing in the doorway near Kyagorusu. It was the man in the white jacket from the cavalry charge. He was leaning, hands gripping his belt buckle, in the doorframe. "And you're in my bed."

Arvan scrambled from the bed, embarrassed at himself for keeping a high ranking man waiting, only to find that he wasn't dressed. Blushing further, he grabbed the blanket and wrapped it around him.

Captain Starling sighed and rolled his eyes towards Kyagorusu.

"We found those on the battlefield," he said, nodding towards the staff and katana in the corner of the room. "They didn't match the equipment of the warlord army."

Kyagorusu nodded. "Thank you, Captain."

"Please, Kyagorusu, call me Lind. I'm too young for anyone to call me 'Captain'."

"Thank you, Captain," Arvan said, now dressed. "That katana holds a very special place in my heart. I am eternally grateful."

Starling smiled, watching as Arvan placed the sword back in his sash.

"You too, Arvan," he said. "My name's Lind. Now, before I get any sleep, I'm required by city law to take you to see Great King Eremmerus. I've already broken regulations by waiting this long. He's not particularly fond of me as it is, so I'd like to take you as soon as you're ready."

"Of course," Kyagorusu said, standing and collecting his staff. "We can leave immediately."

"Not quite yet," Starling said. "Arvan hasn't eaten. I wouldn't wish anyone to see Eremmerus while having an empty stomach; suffering two such pains would be torture. Anyway," he smiled, "the young man has yet to make my bed."

Arvan blushed, eliciting light laughter from Kyagorusu. He picked the blanket from the ground and set to work.

"I do have one question," Arvan asked as he struggled to tuck the far side of the blanket beneath the mattress. "Where's Lament?"

"Why," Captain Starling said, "he's waiting at the palace, of course."

The sun pulled itself apathetically over the horizon, eventually blossoming into a glorious pink dawn. The light passed gracefully between the stonework of the city until it reached the mountains, casting giant teeth-like shadows out onto the ocean.

Lament leant, arms folded, against a pillar that led into the Throne Room of the Palace, watching the sunrise as the four halberd-wielding guards eyed him nervously. He'd been waiting for some time, sleep eluding him as it so often did, but he could do nothing until Kyagorusu and Arvan had rested. He'd been told that it was city law for groups who entered the city together to see the Great King together. At least this would be a convenient opportunity to thank them for their kindness and bid them goodbye.

He peered around the pillar into the Throne Room. The figure dressed in immaculate white was lounged in the stone throne on the far side of the room, seemingly content to ignore the patient shadus.

"Careful, shadus!" one guard snapped. "One more look at the Great King and I'll cleave your head in two."

Lament snorted in an amused fashion and returned to leaning against the pillar, gazing out upon the city. It wasn't long before he heard footsteps on the great stone staircase and his companions, accompanied by Captain Starling, came into view.

"Sorry to keep you waiting, Lament," Starling said, his right hand scratching at his chin before returning to his belt buckle. "I had to make sure my guests were well rested. You're sure you won't sleep?"

Lament shook his head. "I have lost too much time in my journey already. Thank you, but I would continue."

"Very well," Starling said. "Of course, regrettably, I will have to disarm you all."

Kyagorusu handed the Captain his staff and Starling passing it to one of the guards, then he did the same with Arvan's katana. Lament pushed himself from the pillar, tearing the gargantuan sword from his back and passed it to Captain Starling. The Captain looked at it and smiled humbly.

"Private Cassus?" he said.

"Yes, sir?" replied the man who had threatened Lament.

"I'll let you handle that."

Private Cassus gave the soldier next to him a grave look, then handed him his halberd. He anxiously walked over to Lament. The shadus gestured the sword towards him and the Private grasped the hilt just beneath where Lament held it.

"I've got it," he said when Lament didn't let go.

The shadus' faint scowl became more pronounced than usual and his hand left the hilt. He took a step back, narrowly avoiding being struck by the blade as it went clattering towards the ground, Private Cassus still attached. Eventually he let go and looked at Lament.

"How can you lift that?"

Lament said nothing.

"Well," Starling said, smiling broadly, "I suppose that's as good a place for it as any; you're effectively disarmed. Unless you've an objection, Lament?"

Lament shook his head. "No objection."

He shot Private Cassus a glance that breathed death, then turned and entered the Throne Room, his footsteps a metronome beat, his cape fluttering behind him. Starling entered and gestured for Kyagorusu and Arvan to follow.

The light of the dawn poured through the narrow entrance into the Throne Room, the stone pillars obstructing the lustre, casting giant shadows the length of the room. The men who entered too cast large shadows, save for Lament who swiftly moved into the shade of a pillar; he did this so quickly that the motion was complete before the rest of the group had entered.

Great King Eremmerus lounged in the Throne, immersed in the morning light. Beneath the perfectly tailored white suit was a painfully thin figure, as frail as an old man despite his mere twenty-one years. On his face sat a juvenile beard, thin and patchy, only visible because of the way the light caught it. His lank, light hair crawled out from beneath the angled crown, the gold jewelled and shining. Still, he did not look at the group. He sat counting the steps idly and only spoke once they were halfway across the room.

"That's far enough," he said.

The group stopped.

The Great King sighed.

"Lind," he said , wearily. "I believe these men arrived a day ago. Why have they only just been brought to me?"

"I had urgent news to see to, your majesty."

"Such as?"

"There was a warlord army that looked to assault the city, your majesty."

"Ah, yes," Eremmerus seethed, "your cavalry charge. I don't recall ordering that."

Starling frowned. "You ordered me to protect the city while patrolling the Wastes, Eremmerus. I followed your orders."

The Great King sat up, gripping the arms of the throne as forcefully as his frail body would allow.

"Address me correctly, Lind!" he roared.

"I did," Captain Starling sneered. "You're no king. You're certainly not a Great King. You're a war mongering coward. Now, if you'll excuse me, I've sleep to catch up on."

He turned and made for the light, his boots singing with that sensual click of the heel.

"No, Lind," Eremmerus said, calm once more. "I want you and a detachment of men in the Wastes. I hear the Behemoth is in the West Lands. I don't want any nasty surprises."

Starling stopped and turned.

"Eremmerus," he said, softly, "I haven't slept in two days."

"Two days?" Eremmerus laughed mockingly. "I haven't slept in almost a year. Go, Lind; I tire of you."

Captain Starling clenched his fists and stormed out of the palace, disappearing behind one of the pillars. Eremmerus returned to lounging on the throne.

"You'll find me a fair ruler, so long as you do as I say," he said, flicking a ringed finger into the air. "Captain Lind Starling fights me for popularity among the soldiers. Why, I don't know; the army's always been loyal to me. Still, the less said about him the better. You'd do well to stay away from him. You might not have to make much of an effort – hopefully he'll be crushed by the Behemoth."

A vulgar grin crept across the Great King's face and he closed his eyes as if viewing the scene. Arvan and Kyagorusu exchanged concerned looks, though Lament remained typically distant.

"Of course," the Great King continued, "the only reason the Final Resting Place of the Empire still stands is because of my lineage. I'm sure Starling would have you believe it was his doing, but my family has defended this city from the Behemoth for a millennium now. Queen Rasset was the first, though she wasn't strategic enough to stop the rest of the empire falling."

He smiled that vulgar smile once more. "It won't be long now, though. We'll have it all back and we can end this foolish bickering between warlords. And there I will stand; executing Riit and his like."

He opened his eyes and passed them between each member of the group. Arvan knew little of the Great King, often finding a story about him available but, disinterested, he poured enthusiastically into one of Master Snow instead. He could see that the Great King was only slightly older than him and, though he would usually hold some respect for such a figure, he doubted the Great King was particularly sagacious.

The gaze of Eremmerus seemed to linger on Arvan for an eternity, studying the young man who shuffled uncomfortably in his sight. Arvan frowned, annoyed at his lack of discipline; unable to meet the Great King's look. Eventually, the dead eyes moved on and Arvan felt a great relief come upon him.

"It's a long history," Eremmerus said. "I can go into it if you wish."

"I've not the time," Lament said, his whisper even more ghostly than usual as it reverberated around the stone frame of the room.

"Then you'll make time!" Eremmerus roared, pounding on the arms of the throne.

Lament didn't react. He stood, as unemotional as ever, and met the eyes of Eremmerus; the gaze of the amber irises never failing.

Arvan felt his hands becoming clammy, freezing his palms on the already cold day. He looked to Kyagorusu who gave him a comforting smile, then to Lament; the shadus' angular features, only obscured by the thick black hair that fell before the left half of his face, never turned from the Great King.

Eremmerus sat, panting, in his throne for a long while. He was dwarfed by the structure, made to look even feebler by the sheer scale of his city's stonework. The plateau of the sun caused pale light to fall on his face, making him rival Lament in a war of the sallow. Heavy dark bags pulled on his eyelids, open perpetually and unblinking.

"Upon the news of the Behemoth's creation," the Great King began, slowly and deliberately, "Queen Rasset ordered every soldier of the empire back to this city, then called Mandra. But, as her soldiers were leaving New Mandra, once called Genko, the Behemoth attacked. Their foe was new and unprecedented; New Mandra unprepared and weary from battle. General Tegus ordered his entire force to attack, but they could not even injure the Behemoth. When he knew defeat was upon him, he ordered a retreat to the docks, boarding the naval fleet with the remaining troops; leaving the citizens to their doom. The Behemoth levelled New Mandra to rubble, thusly we have the City of the Dead; no city at all.

"But that was not the end for Tegus. Once the city was destroyed the Behemoth went after the naval fleet, the cannons only slowing the beast. None survived, save for an army scout, left on the docks, spared the Behemoth's wrath for hiding amongst the rubble. He made for Mandra, riding his most trusted horse. He rode hard and fast, never allowing the creature to rest. The horse finally died somewhere in the Rock Flats, the Behemoth forever gaining on the scout. He left the horse and ran.

"His energy eventually left him and the Behemoth passed him. But no warning from the scout was needed.

"A few days before the birth of the Behemoth, Mandra was assaulted by two men! They killed the soldiers that obstructed them, but, as most of the army was returning from the Central Desert at the time, they did little damage to the Mandran numbers. They made off with something of little importance."

"A tale of the Fallen Hero," Kyagorusu said, smiling.

"You call *that* a hero?" Eremmerus snarled. "A murderer, traitor and a thief?"

Kyagorusu fought the urge to retort. He ran the palm of his hand over his bald head and smiled pleasantly.

"Still," Eremmerus said, "I suppose this wasn't the worst thing he'd done. Indeed, the shock was enough for Queen Rasset to put the returning troops on the defence of Mandra, fearful the ghost of the world's past would return. Imagine their surprise when the Behemoth appeared! By all accounts even more fearsome than the Fallen Hero.

"It took nigh on ten thousand men, but they turned the Behemoth back. The scout arrived the next day and told the events in the City of the Dead. The empire was lost, the age of glory had ended swiftly and the Heroless Millennium began. Queen Rasset changed the name of Mandra to the Final Resting Place of the Empire until such a time that our nation was great again. I doubt she expected it to take as long as it has, but it won't be long now."

He smiled slyly, the crown tottering down his brow and stopping just above his eyes. The angle, combined with the skeletal appearance, gave him the look of a king long dead, awaiting rebirth. Such a haunting effigy and still he continued to speak.

"Of course, the Behemoth wasn't done with the city. It attacked again, always thwarted by superior planning; Queen Rasset and my ancestors that followed her, heroes in a heroless age! Only the Final Resting Place of the Empire stands against the might of the Behemoth's malevolence!

"As much as I abhor them, the Riit Clan should be commended for protecting Pale Castle for as long as they have. Though, they have failed to defend the rest of the North Lands…"

His eyes widened as if awakening or returning from a trance. He looked on the group for the first time in a long while, his eyes wandering continually through his tale of history. He stroked at his childish beard and smiled, his crown still halfway down his head.

"But you've not come to hear of history," he looked at Kyagorusu. "Especially not history that you already know. So, tell me, why *are* you here?"

Kyagorusu smiled his usual humble smile. "I'm a scholar, here to learn all that I can."

"How tiresome," Eremmerus groaned, lounging on the throne once more. "I knew you were a scholar as soon as I saw you. You've all same look." He looked at Arvan. "You're not a scholar, though, unless you're a particularly dishevelled one. So, why are *you* here?"

"I'm looking for my Master, Lawliet Snow," Arvan said, quietly, scratching at his arm as he spoke.

"It's a vast city," Eremmerus yawned. "I don't know everyone in it. Indeed, I've started to forget you two already." He looked to Lament, smiling that sly smile again. "Now, you're no scholar. A less scholarly looking man I've never looked upon. Though, you know more than you'd have me know."

"I too seek a man," Lament said.

"How boring," Eremmerus said, closing his eyes. "As I've said, I don't know every…"

"You'd know this man," Lament said, interrupting.

Eremmerus peeled one eye open and rolled it towards the shadus. "I would?"

Lament nodded firmly.

"Well," Eremmerus said, "I suppose that's slightly more interesting. I'll humour you, shadus; who is this man you seek?"

"He's a warrior of some repute, or so he claims."

Eremmerus smiled. "We've a few of those."

"Upon his face lies a mask of anguish."

"Oh?" Eremmerus said in a tone of mock interest.

"He wears vermillion armour, with a horned helmet."

"He does?" The Great King sat up in his throne.

"His name is Vaiske Parlet."

Eremmerus moved his mouth as if tasting a delicious, if novel, meal. He raised his eyebrows before frowning severely, tilting his head just enough of an increment for Lament to notice.

"And is there anything else extraordinary about this man, this warrior, this Vaiske Parlet?"

Lament paused, then said, begrudgingly, "He has two shadows."

Eremmerus smiled.

"Could it be?" he said as if to himself. "Humour me, shadus. Would you step into the light?"

Lament looked to Kyagorusu and the bald man shrugged.

"You'd have to show someone else at some point, old boy," Kyagorusu said. "It may as well be now as at any other time."

Lament glanced at Eremmerus, the Great King's smiled forever widening; his teeth clenched together, mountainous and saw-edged. His cheeks rose, the muscles taught and overworked, returning colour to his grey face. He seemed to wake as the excitement pulled on his ever unclosing eyelids, until they were torn an unfathomable distance apart. In those moments he seemed to live as no man ever had, blood pouring through his emaciated veins: a skeleton, given once more the gift of flesh and life, returned to this world to exact the worst of his shrouded and forgotten beliefs.

The shadus moved uncomfortably on his feet, eyeing the lustre emitted on the ground beside him, the he looked as the boy stood next to him, eyeing him suspiciously. Lament sighed and stepped out from the shadow, supposing his hesitance was answer enough for the Great King, but not for Arvan.

As Lament cut in front of the path of luminescence, he caused not even a flicker of darkness to fall upon the ground. Not even half a week ago, the slender man whose scale was complex would have borne a shadow that blanketed the Great King in darkness, but Eremmerus sat, smiling, bathed in glorious light. Had the sky been just slightly less perfect, the effect would have been fractured to the point of absolution.

Arvan gazed at the floor washed with unobstructed light, blinking; his eyes unbelieving. His mouth drew itself open and remained there, slightly agape. He turned to Kyagorusu as if to speak, but no words came and the boy contented with blowing his fringe from his eyes, then looking back to the shadow-less ground at Lament's feet.

"I'd heard a whisper that stealing a shadow was possible," the Great King said, lecherously. "No – more than a whisper. It was said plainly to me. But it does raise a question: How are you still alive?"

"Do you know the man of which I speak?" Lament said, sharply.

Eremmerus's smile widened. "I couldn't possibly know where you'd find a man like that."

"Where is he?"

Lament leapt forwards only to be stopped by the sound of longbow string being pulled back. He glanced over his shoulder and saw two archers at the palace entrance.

"I tire of you," the Great King said, reclining further. "No doubt, you'll be of some amusement to me once again in time, but for now…" He waved a weary, if theatrical, hand.

Reluctantly, Lament turned away and left, Kyagorusu and Arvan following. As they approached, the archers stepped aside and stayed their bows, allowing the trio to pass. They stepped out of the Throne Room and found Captain Starling standing there, obscured from the Great King's sight by one of the pillars.

"I hadn't noticed the shadow," he said, his voice more serious than usual. "Or lack thereof."

Lament said nothing, his attention seemingly drawn towards the city.

"I would speak with you further, all of you," Starling continued. "Please, return to my quarters. I'll be with you once more, just as soon as I can be."

Lieutenant Fernarl, who had arrived sometime during the group's meeting with the Great King, stepped forward. "I shall run the patrol, Captain. You need your sleep."

Captain Starling smiled warmly and placed a hand on the Lieutenant's shoulder. "No, Lieutenant. Eremmerus would court-martial us both if he found out. Besides, you've been awake almost as long as I have."

He bid them a wordless goodbye with a subtle hand gesture and made his way down the stairs.

Lament gazed over the vast and unceasing city. Even to his eyes it seemed never to end, though he knew the Wastes and the rest of the world was out there, somewhere in the beyond.

"I must search for him," he said, turning to his companions. "I fear this is where we part."

"Not just yet, Lament," Kyagorusu replied, sternly. "Captain Starling has things to tell you more than he does Arvan or me, I'm sure. Anyway, you've yet to tell us how you escaped the Behemoth."

Lament looked away. "I suppose I owe you that much." He paused. "No, I owe you far more."

Kyagorusu smiled. "Your company for a short time longer is payment enough, Lament. You forget that you saved our lives."

Lament's mouth curled into the closest expression Arvan had seen the shadus to smiling. Still, his face seemed not to have changed with that perpetual scowl across his eyes.

"Very well," the shadus said. "I will tell you." He turned and looked down the great staircase at the disappearing effigy of Captain Starling. "Though, I feel I should tell that man too."

"I'll come too, if nobody minds," Arvan said. "Captain Starling may know something of Master Snow."

"Of course he does," replied Kyagorusu.

"And what of you, Kyagorusu?" Arvan asked. "Why do you need to see him?"

The bald man smiled.

"My dear boy," he said. "I go where the information is."

Effortlessly, Lament lifted his sword and strapped it on his back, ignoring the concerned looks of the guards and glancing back into the Throne Room at the vague figure of the Great King. Fernarl suggested they leave, and the group followed the Lieutenant down the stairs and away from the palace.

The Lieutenant had led them through the labyrinthine city as if it were no more than a short, straight street. There were no signs, as far as Arvan could see, to aid his direction.

They now sat in Captain Starling's quarters, just left by Lieutenant Fernarl. Arvan sat on the bed, staring at the well-lit ground around Lament, the shadus standing on the threshold that led to the balcony. How he hadn't noticed it before his attention was forced upon it, he didn't know; it seemed so obvious a thing to be missing. Still, he said nothing of it, supposing Lament an idiosyncratic figure and fearing how he might react.

Kyagorusu, sat at the same table as before, folded one leg over the other and leaned back in his chair.

"Well, Lament," he said. "I suppose now is as good a time as any. You can tell us how you miraculously escaped the Behemoth."

"Very well," he said. "But I should warn you; my tale shall contradict everything you have heard of the creature, or anything I have heard at that."

"Whatever do you mean?" Kyagorusu asked. "You didn't slay it, did you?"

"Far from it," Lament said.

"Then what?" Arvan asked, shuffling uncomfortably on the bed.

The shadus' eyes rolled towards the young man and then closed. When he opened them again he was looking at nothing in particular; his pupils diluted, shrouded by his amber irises.

"Very well," he said. "You had just left me…"

*

"You need wait no longer, my love," he said, as the Behemoth raised a colossal fist. "I have come to join you on the breeze."

Knowing even a sword as gargantuan as the one he held would do little against a creature of the Behemoth's size, he placed it once more upon his back. The fist came hurtling down towards him, the shadus already feeling the rushing air despite the hand's apparent distance. Ready to acknowledge his mortality, though ever unprepared to stare it in its face, Lament closed his eyes.

The breeze swirled around him, tickling his skin and, just for a moment, he thought he was holding someone's hand. He smiled inside himself, only for the sensation to dissipate as soon as he had perceived it. The breeze seemed to whisper his name lovingly. What good was hallucination and delirium to a man who would soon be dead? Nothing, except comfort, which, although welcome, he dismissed as his malady.

The rushing air colliding with his body ceased abruptly and he knew then that it would be mere seconds before the fist met him, blinded by his own eyelids. He opened his eyes, wishing no more obstruction to his doom; no dream dead to hold his hand or call his name, no darkness to soothe his all-seeing eyes. He would know his end.

'So, death,' his mind called to the ether, 'you have come for me? Then show yourself. Take my hand and drag me from this abyss; I've had toil enough. Your grip, the breeze, has been on me often enough of late. Do you care to clasp me further and crush me? Here I am; ready for you. Do what you brought me here for and be done with it.'

But as his eyes focused on the Behemoth, harbinger of death, destroyer of life, he realised he would not die that day. The creature had stayed its fist.

The hand, still some distance away, shook as if in horror at what the Behemoth had sought to do. The listless white eyes of the creature gazed at its own fist, unable to look away.

"Do it," Lament whispered. "Take me."

As if to force the creature, his hand wrapped around the hilt of his sword.

The Behemoth shrieked, the piercing tone cutting through the seething air, but it did no more. Its eyes moved to Lament, encasing him as they did before and the shadus' hand left his sword.

He took a step forward and the Behemoth took a step back, like a timid creature a fraction of the creature's size. Then, the Behemoth turned and stalked away, the ground shuddering with each thunderous stride.

Lament stood, thinking of what he had seen for some time, somewhat shocked that he was still alive. Then, just as he concluded that there was no conclusion to come to, he followed after Kyagorusu and Arvan.

*

They listened, attentive and silent as Lament spoke; the laconic shadus lost his taciturnity, yet he spoke in that same ethereal whisper. He removed from his story his words to the breeze, his taunting speech and his more melancholy thoughts; it would do no good to tell his companions of those. However, he told them of everything else in as vivid detail as he was able. Once he finished speaking, the room was silent for a time, until Arvan spoke.

"Lament," he said, "what exactly are you saying?"

"The Behemoth isn't evil," Lament said, amber eyes fixed on the boy. "It's just like any other animal. It fights when it's cornered."

Kyagorusu nodded, certainly. "It seems a reasonable assumption," he said, his voice serious. "Now that I think of it, in every story I've heard of it, mankind has attacked first; not that I think that's strange. It's only natural to fear something of that size. Yes, it was that way in every story, save for its birth. Though that was so long ago now that I suppose the truth could have been distorted somewhat."

"Perhaps it's drawn to violence," Arvan said. "They say it was born in a time of great war."

"It's possible," Kyagorusu mused. "There are many tales of the planet creating such things to end war, though this would be the first I've heard of that was alive. One thing is still a mystery, though; what drew it towards us?"

Lament turned towards the bald man, a mass of waves and a symphony of shuffling clothes. He gestured with a thumb to the sword on his back.

"Do I not look as an apparition of war to you, Kyagorusu?" he asked.

"Then we should warn people!" Arvan said. "Then we won't have to live in fear of the Behemoth anymore!"

"I'll do nothing with the information," Lament said, looking away from Arvan. "I have too much for one man to accomplish as it is."

"So you would doom all who oppose it?"

"It's only hypothesis, Arvan," Kyagorusu said. "We're basing the destruction of a one-thousand year old opinion on one short experience with the creature and my own interpretation of a few stories. At best you could stop people attacking it, but could you stop mankind warring with itself?"

Arvan said nothing and looked down at his hands.

"I understand how you feel," Kyagorusu continued. "But we have very little evidence."

"I will tell Captain Starling," Lament said to Arvan. "Even if we are

59

wrong, which I'd imagine we are, the information could still be of some use to him, even if only to dismiss it."

"You won't need to tell him," a familiar voice said from the doorway. The group turned to see Captain Starling, his usual immaculate appearance in tact. "He's already heard."

"How long have you been there?" Kyagorusu laughed.

"Long enough to hear the theory, if not the story," Starling replied. "As so often happens, I forgot a weapon save for my dagger. Since I had to return to the barracks as it was, I thought I may as well see how you were settling in." He looked at Arvan, still sitting on the bed. "A little too well, perhaps," he said, smiling.

"What do you think?" Kyagorusu asked.

Captain Starling shrugged. "It's an interesting idea, if nothing else. I'll experiment with it if I can, but if it's drawn to violence then the Great King's Cavalry is a target and I'll not risk the lives of my men. We've lost too many men to it as it is." He paused and looked at the floor for a time. "But I didn't come here to talk of the Behemoth. I've some time before Eremmerus realises I'm disobeying his orders. Is there anything I can help you with?"

Arvan looked up at the Captain enthusiastically, forgetting about the Behemoth.

"Do you know where I can find my Master?" he asked. "He's the infamous Lawliet Snow."

Starling smiled. "I've had little time to hear tales of heroics recently. Indeed, I've been living my own. How would I know him?"

"He's a retainer of Lord Thean."

"Thean…" Starling mused. "They wear white robes with a fuchsia sash and emblem, yes?"

Arvan nodded. "And he has dark hair, much the same as mine."

"Ah," Starling said, "messy fellow is he?"

Arvan frowned and blew the fringe from his eyes.

"There's a man who matches that description," Starling said. "He's staying with another Thean man not far from here. I'll take you to him when I've the chance."

Arvan leapt from the bed and bowed before Starling.

"Thank you, Captain!" he said. "You've no idea how long I have waited for this!"

Starling grimaced.

"Call me Lind," he moaned, then his voice returned to its usual pleasantness. "Now, I've something more pressing to share with you."

"Oh?" Kyagorusu asked.

"Yes," Starling said. "A concerning subject, really. One I'd rather know nothing of."

He met Lament's eyes.

"I know the man you seek," he said. "I know Vaiske Parlet."

Chapter Nine

"He arrived two days ago," Starling said, severely. "One of the first things he did was to challenge me to a duel. Naturally, I declined, though Eremmerus seemed rather more impressed by him."

"What do you mean by that?" Lament asked.

Starling rested the index finger of his right hand on the handle of his dagger. He wore a troubled expression that seemed to lurk just beneath his contented face.

"The Great King has made Vaiske Parlet his champion," he said. "Who better than an immortal? Already the man-with-two-shadows has taken over many of my duties; Eremmerus instead settling on sending me out to the Wastes, waiting for me to die. That *I* took you to see the Great King was sheer stubbornness on my part and we can count ourselves blessedly lucky that it was a rare occasion that Parlet wasn't there."

"Where can I find him?" Lament asked.

Starling met his look once more.

"You can't," he replied. "Or at least, not yet. He disappears for long periods of time inside the palace; he's Eremmerus' most welcome guest. What Eremmerus doesn't realise is that Parlet's using him."

Starling paused as if waiting for an interruption of some kind, but none came. Silence coagulated itself in the room, causing a stagnant reverie among the group. Starling moved his weight from one leg to the other as he thought it might end the miasmic mood that had come upon them. Of course, it did no such thing.

Arvan had sat back on the bed, never removing his attention from the Captain, but finding little to say of the situation. He yearned to leave and find Master Snow, but was insufferably intrigued by Starling's tale.

"What Parlet plans or how Eremmerus fits into it, I can't even guess," Captain Starling continued. "Every time I get close to him, Eremmerus sends for me and gives me new orders. Needless to say, Eremmerus trusts Parlet more than he trusts himself. I'll never find out what he's planning as long as Eremmerus is so fond of him, especially with the Great King loathing me so."

"You're sure his intentions are malevolent?" Kyagorusu said, ripping himself from his trance.

"If not malevolent then it's a type of goodness I can't say I care for."

Lament moved uncomfortably, his scowl tautening.

"When he stole my shadow, he seemed to think that my death was for the greater good," the shadus said. "He said my sacrifice would save many lives and herald the age of peace."

"That doesn't sound so terrible does it?" Arvan said. "Surely everyone wants peace."

Starling looked at Arvan sceptically. "Peace by death? I certainly don't like the sound of that." He looked to Lament. "Eremmerus has called for a ceremony tomorrow in the Coliseum. The entire city will be there, including the army. I hear he plans to introduce Vaiske Parlet to the troops."

"Well, at the very least, that should assuage your concern, shouldn't it?" Kyagorusu said. "You should find out his plans then."

"Unfortunately not, Kyagorusu. The whole event has an air of finality about it. It's not so much the plan that concerns me, but the way he's gone about it."

"What do you mean?" Kyagorusu asked.

Starling sighed, his elegant posture slouched with tiredness. "Think about it; Vaiske Parlet sought an alliance with Eremmerus, but Parlet is an immortal, by all accounts he could wipe out the entire army of the city and not concern himself with even pulling a muscle. Of course, it would be an effort, but he's not a lazy man. Eremmerus is far weaker than Parlet, but Parlet has latched onto him as if he's the one who needs help. It's just peculiar."

"I see your point," Kyagorusu said. "Is there nothing you can do to stop him?"

Starling smiled, grimly. "How do you stop an immortal? I had rather hoped that Lament would have a plan."

All attention turned to the shadus, still stood by the balcony. His brow glistened with fever-induced sweat, but he showed no other signs of his illness, save for his perpetually livid skin. As usual, he didn't move his head to face them, he merely rolled his eyes over of them in turn; the amber orbs surrounding the sun of black in the centre.

He'd been contemplating what to do when confronted with Vaiske Parlet for some time now but had come to no decision. Currently, as he was pressured into coming to some conclusive action, he could think only of his nausea and the night that had brought it to fruition.

"He's a driven man, but not a monster," Lament said. "I once planned to reason with him."

Starling frowned. "Perhaps you're right. But I don't think he's a reasonable man. Besides, Eremmerus wouldn't stand for it."

"You mean the Great King won't let Lament get close enough to Parlet to reason with him?" Kyagorusu suggested.

"Quite the opposite," Starling said through the curl of a smile. "There's only one thing I'm sure of about this whole situation; Eremmerus wants Lament and Parlet to meet."

"What for?" Arvan asked.

"His own entertainment. The Blood Lust is upon him, surely you noticed. He speaks sensually of war and death. If Vaiske Parlet is using Eremmerus then Eremmerus is using Parlet, no matter how much he trusts the man. Imagine it; a grudge fight between an immortal and the man whose shadow he stole – it would be the duel of the century." He looked once more to Lament. "The Great King will gift you the opportunity to end this tomorrow. For the sake of us all, I hope you take your chance."

"And tell me, Captain Starling," Lament said. "How do you propose I kill an immortal?"

Starling looked away at the carven wall of the room.

"I don't know," he sighed, then he looked back to Lament. "But I shall be there to help you any way that I can. Though, you must remember; my hands are bound far tighter than any of yours whilst under the gaze of the Great King."

Lament sighed, turning away from all in the room and walking out onto the balcony. The barracks were placed halfway up one of the smaller mountains in the city, but it still towered some way above all else in sight. He looked morosely over the city, leaning over the railing. Somewhere out in the view was Vaiske Parlet and tomorrow they would meet again.

"Such is my place in the world," he said in the whisper that somehow reached the three men inside. "I must prepare. Farewell."

He grasped the stone rail of the balcony with one hand and launched himself off the side of the building, disappearing in a cacophony of material fluttering against the resistance of the breeze. Arvan ran out to stop him but, as he peered over the side, the shadus was gone.

"We'll see him again," Kyagorusu said. "Though we'll probably wish we hadn't."

Arvan entered, his stony face an apparition of insurmountable angst. He sat on the bed and stared at the floor. He had hardly known the shadus three days, but he had already lost count how many times he had disappeared. After the fourth day, Lament Strife would most likely cease to live.

"Come now, Arvan," Starling said. "I'm about to take you to your Master. Would he wish to see you in such a manner?"

Arvan peered up, smiling. "You would really take me to him?"

"It's on my way," Starling said. "I must return to the Wastes as it is. Will you accompany us, Kyagorusu?"

"I wish that I could," the bald man replied. "Yet, I must find more permanent lodgings. I cannot deprive you of your room for eternity. Arvan, should your Master require you to stay elsewhere, you are more than welcome to lodge with me. I should imagine I'll be easy enough for you to find."

"Thank you, Kyagorusu," Arvan said. "For everything you've done."

"I'm sure we'll see each other again soon enough, Arvan," the bald man said, his humble smile returning to its rightful place.

"I'm sure you're right, Kyagorusu. And thank you, Captain Starling. I've known you so short a time and you've already done so much for me."

Starling sighed, then smiled softly at Arvan.

"For the last time, Arvan," he said. "Call me Lind."

The slow, clipping footsteps of Titus that rang out through the streets were enough of a call for the citizens of the Final Resting Place of the Empire to move from their path. Arvan, riding on the grey horse, holding Captain Starling from behind, thought the spectacle rather strange. Starling was too modest a man to expect them to move, yet that modesty seemed to be the very reason the citizens moved for him. He held the perfectly crafted, white spear limply in his right hand, his body moving rhythmically with Titus. Man and animal shared an affinity that Arvan hadn't witnessed before; it almost appeared as if they could communicate, if only simply.

The citizens were dressed in torn, tattered rags, their expressions ones of frustration and desperation, only brightening upon the sight of Captain Starling. He smiled at them, as if it would help and by the time he rode past, it seemed the citizens were in a better humour. However, as Arvan turned back he saw them return to their lives of quite despair, some looking longingly at the disappearing effigy of hope; the white clad Captain Lind Starling.

"It's a sorry sight, I know," he said, as Arvan began to shudder at the anguish he was surrounded by. "But there are those who are trying to help. Eremmerus once was one of them, but, since the War of the Wastes, he's forgotten about the people; his mind fixed only upon the satiation of his Blood Lust. But I've said more than I care to of Eremmerus today, and his name is unwelcome in this part of the city. I'd advise you not to speak it, but, if you must, say it quietly and only to those you trust."

Arvan said nothing, his attention drawn to a small boy holding a baby, both in the near-uniform rags, no adult so close as to be their parent. Arvan sighed and thought of his own childhood. Was it really so different?

They went on in silence save for the clicking of Titus' hooves and the subdued murmur of the citizens. Eventually, they turned and found themselves in a secluded street in an altogether quieter part of the city. Starling led Titus some way down the road until he stopped at a building that was much the same as the others, except the moss covered the windows as well as the grey walls.

"Here you are," Starling said. "The residence of the Thean men."

"Here?" Arvan asked, sceptically.

"Of course," Starling said. "Lord Thean and Eremmerus are enemies. Thean couldn't very well place his men in the centre of the city, could he?"

"Enemies? Then why haven't you stopped them? Why are you helping me?"

Starling shifted in the saddle, turning to face Arvan so the boy could see at least part of his face. The Captain was smiling.

"I'm not sure if you've noticed," he said. "But I'm not the most obedient soldier in the Final Resting Place of the Empire. Now go, you've waited long enough to see your Master."

Arvan dismounted and made for the decaying wooden door of the house before turning to Captain Starling. "Thank you, Lind."

Starling smiled. "Anytime, Arvan. Well," his hand grasped his belt buckle, "I'm sure I'll see you again, soon enough."

He nodded goodbye, then stroked Titus softly, causing the grey horse to saunter lazily down the street. Arvan watched as the Captain faded from his vision. When the captain was gone from sight, Arvan knocked on the door.

He waited some time but no answer came and he knocked again. Still there was no answer. Frustrated, he blew his fringe from his eyes. After knocking a third time, he spied the handle and let himself in.

The door opened into a room cloying with dust, though he could see this only due to the light pouring in through the open door behind him. He left the door as it was – the only source of light in this land of accursed darkness. The shadows deceived his eyes, creating effigies of evil and violence in the stone walls, grabbing at him. Dust swam in the air before him and caught his throat as he inhaled it. The smell was vile, something akin to mould, though not altogether the same.

He had to fight to calm his breath as he tripped over a mound of precariously stacked books. Could Master Snow really be living in such squalor? Back in Farras he was clean, meticulously so, being around this filth for any length of time would have driven him to insanity.

Arvan heard the breeze whisper solemnly outside and the door creaked closed, condemning him to an apparent eternal black. He paused in the room and allowed his eyes to adjust to the new profound darkness. His pounding heart threatened to leap from the cage of his chest, the possibility ever more likely with each explosive beat. He clenched his fists and tried to focus his mind on the tightening pressure around his fingers, anything but what lurked inside the darkness.

Gradually, his sight returned and he could make out the shapes in the room, if not the colours. Ahead of him, only a few feet or so, a figure sat, slumped, in a chair.

"Master?" Arvan asked.

The figure didn't stir. For the briefest of moments, Arvan thought he saw another man in the corner of the room, but, as he moved to look at him, the form disappeared and his attention returned to the figure in the chair.

Arvan approached, careful not to stand on any of the piles of books, which he could now see were vast in both number and size. As he got close he saw the figure was slumped further than he had originally imagined. The head hung limply, resting on the right shoulder. The body had slid halfway down the chair, dominated by the ancient furniture.

The apparition was certainly male, although the hair had grown long and unchecked. Beneath the robe the slouching man wore were toned muscles, clinging tightly to his strong bones. Yet, there was a weakness to the man that could not be waved away by the mere fact that he was unconscious.

Arvan was now so close for the smell of the man to overpower the stench of the room. Cherry blossoms; a soap familiar to that which Master Snow always used. Arvan frowned. How had his Master grown so feeble?

The boy reached out a hand and prodded the man gently in the chest. He was cold to the touch, hauntingly so, the merest suggestion of a connection to the man's skin invading Arvan's fingers and chilling him to the bones of his nimble fingers.

The figure didn't stir.

"Master?"

He moved to touch his Master on his head and inevitably wake him, but, as his hand was just an inch away, the man slumped further and his robe drooped flaccidly away from his chest, revealing a dark mark.

Arvan leaned over the man to get a better look, met by a subtle smell that reminded him briefly of sword training with Master Snow. Cautiously, Arvan caressed the stain on the man's chest. It was a miasmic fluid, viscous and vaguely adhesive to the touch. He brought the fingers up to his eyes but could see the liquid no more clearly. He sniffed at it, the smell from before stronger but still mysterious.

He licked it with the tip of his tongue; savoury sensation, suggestion of salt, the faint taste of iron.

Blood.

Blood from where he had been stabbed in the chest.

Arvan's will left him and he took a step back, gasping. Then, bravery returning, he leant forwards and shook the man.

"Master…"

The dead man fell further forwards and Arvan leapt back. He scratched at his hands, his weight shifting from one leg to the other.

He felt the grasp of a powerful hand on his shoulder. Fear tore his eyes open as wide as the lids would allow. Remembering the hand-to-hand combat techniques Master Snow had taught him, he grabbed the wrist of the hand on his shoulder, twisted it and ripped the clasp from him.

Arvan turned to face the assailant and drew his katana.

The symphony of his percussive wind-struck clothes was deafening. As he hurtled towards the ground, Captain Starling's quarters drifting ever further above him, he wondered how much longer he could test luck in such a way before it would claim him. Already he could feel death was close and his nausea flared.

As he neared the ground, the breeze wrapped itself around him, as if he was held by some giant hand, and he slowed, allowing him to land gracefully and unharmed.

Lament brought himself back around to the present, his sword cutting effortlessly through even the thick breeze of the Wastes.

'You must avoid these distractions,' he thought. 'If it were to happen tomorrow, what then?'

Yet his malady hung onto him, a dragging weight in the already cumbersome atmosphere. He swung his sword as if to wave the feeling away, but his sickness showed no sign of leaving.

He was some time out on the Wastes when he saw a familiar figure approaching on horseback. Captain Starling, his pure white jacket shining in the day's sunlight, his blonde hair thrown back as the wind whipped passed. He stopped not far from Lament.

"You gave Arvan quite a scare," he said. "Of course, Kyagorusu and I knew you would be alright."

Lament glanced at the brilliant spear in Captain Starling's hand. "Vaiske Parlet too fights with a spear."

Starling frowned. "Yes, and far better than I do, I'd wager. I know what you're suggesting, but when I fight I do so out of necessity. Besides, I've a tendency of playing for keeps."

Lament said nothing.

"Well, Lament, I'll wish you luck. I'm sure I'll see you at the ceremony tomorrow."

He rode away, wordlessly, and Lament was left only with the company of the breeze. He sighed and swung his sword.

Arvan stabbed at the man with his katana, only for the blade to go past. When he tried to withdraw his arm for a second strike, the man clasped Arvan's sword-arm to his side, and then held the boy's head to his chest. Arvan writhed, trying to break the man's grip, but he was too strong.

"In about two minutes' time," the man said, "a sizeable force of the Final Resting Place of the Empire's army will burst through that door. As it is they will find a sword wielding boy, two men from the Southern Continent and a dead army general, killed by said men from the Southern Continent.

"You've a choice; you can come with my associate and me, escape and live, or you can stay here and be felled by the local army without having a chance to explain the situation. Now, which will it be?"

He released Arvan and the boy looked up at the man, but could make nothing out in the darkness.

The door burst open, sending splintering wood flying into the room. There, silhouetted by the light, were a dozen soldiers in the employ of Eremmerus.

"Well," the man said, "it seems your decision has been made for you."

He grabbed Arvan's arm and hauled the boy into another room, just as a slew of arrows impaled the wall by which they'd been stood. Arvan had no time to protest as the man dragged him through the near pitch-black house, the boy constantly tripping over discarded piles of books, the sound of the soldiers' rushing footsteps never far behind them.

Just when Arvan was giving up hope of ever seeing daylight again, he saw an open door at the end of the narrow hall the man was leading him down. Another man stood in the doorframe.

"Running away are we?" the second man said as they stopped just before him.

"Yes, and so should you be," answered the first.

"My apologies," the second man said in a voice that sounded as if it had been filtered through a smile. "I'd move if I were you."

The first man, Arvan still in tow, dove past the second and into a deserted street. Arvan turned and watched in amazement as the man in the doorway cut down two arrows headed towards him with one stroke of his katana which he sheathed directly after using.

He turned to them. "Shall we?"

The first man pulled Arvan to his feet and the three fugitives ran, soon coming to the busy street that Arvan had ridden down with Captain Starling. Just as Arvan realised his relief, thinking they would be harder to find in such an area, he noticed the white robes of the men. The *idiosyncratic* white robes of the Thean House. Perhaps they would be rather easier to find after all…

As they careered down the street, pushing past the citizens who weren't quite fast enough to move from their path, Arvan took the time to study the men he was with. The first man was somewhat older than the second, though Arvan (still being led by him) could only see the back of his head, yet the hair was grey and closely cropped to his head, revealing the shape of the skull beneath.

The second man was somewhere around the age of thirty to Arvan's eyes, falling somewhere within a few years either side of the age. His hair was darker than Arvan's, closer to black than brown, with eyes to match. His hair was neat, but far from short; styled into a fringe that swept to the left in one great wave. He was tall, standing a few inches above Arvan with a toned, if not particularly muscular physique.

Arvan looked past the younger man to see the soldiers, encumbered by their heavy armour, had lost them some time ago. Yet still they ran through the streets of the city, the mountains getting further from sight with each step.

"Where are we going?" Arvan asked.

"Somewhere they'd never look for us," the older man replied.

It wasn't long before the immense gate leading out of the city loomed ahead of them, but they didn't enter the Wastes. The older man led Arvan up a set of steps and stood atop the perimeter wall of the Final Resting Place of the Empire. The older man released Arvan and the boy fell to his knees.

He gazed upon the grey city, a haunting kind of beautiful he supposed. The mountains pierced the cyan sky far in the distance, the myriad of a city all that stood between him and them.

"Alluring, isn't it?" the old man said. "I'm not sure I hold with it, though. They destroyed a lot of the mountains to build the houses. Still, everyone has to live somewhere."

Arvan turned his head to look at the man. He had a grizzled face with eyes that were beginning to lose their colour. His skin was tanned and leather-like from years of living almost entirely outside. He was the same height as Arvan, though his extra muscle contrasted with the boy's somewhat awkward frame.

He helped Arvan to his feet.

"Alright, boy," he said, sternly. "What were you doing in our headquarters?"

"I was looking for Lawliet Snow," Arvan said, snatching back his arm from the man.

The older man frowned. "What business have you with Lawliet Snow?"

"He's my Master."

The younger man smiled.

"Ah," he said. "Lawliet's famous student; it's Arvan."

"*You're* Arvan?" the older man said, suspiciously.

Arvan nodded.

"Well, I suppose Lawliet never did say much for your common sense," the younger man said. Arvan thought to protest, though everything had fit together so well in his mind he had to speak of other things.

"I know who you are too," Arvan said. He looked at the older man. "You're Grimoire Groan." Then to the younger man. "And you're Distance Valentine. Master Snow's told me many tales of your adventures."

"I see Lawliet's just as informal when we're not around," Grimoire said, a slight smile on his lips. "My correct title would be General Groan, and that's General Valentine. Then again, I suppose we can make an exception for a student of Lawliet, eh, Distance?"

"If not a student of Lawliet then who else?" Distance replied.

Arvan smiled. "Is Master Snow here?"

Grimoire's face became severe once more.

"Arvan," he said. "How much do you know of what Lawliet was ordered to do last time Lord Thean spoke to him?"

"Nothing at all."

"I can see this might be rather more complicated than I had hoped. Distance, how about you tell Arvan of *our* orders first?"

"Gladly," Distance said. "In its simplest form, Lord Thean ordered us to observe Great King Eremmerus. Lord Thean fears a full scale war is about to erupt on the Northern Continent and, if it does, that Eremmerus will be the one to start it. Of course, he's right. Over our time here the army of the Final Resting Place of the Empire has trebled. Unfortunately, recently, things have gotten rather more complicated.

"A few days ago, a warrior by the name of Vaiske Parlet arrived in the city, though that isn't particularly salient right now. However, his presence has led to added tensions within the army. One of our informants, the army general you found slumped in the chair, wanted to side with Parlet and came to kill us. Luckily, we saw this coming and Grimoire here dealt with him accordingly. In fact we'd been setting up today for some time, those books you tripped over were all misinformation on why we're here. Your presence complicated things for us slightly, but no harm done.

"After the ceremony for Parlet tomorrow (I'm sure you've heard of it) we're leaving to report back to Lord Thean. War's coming, Arvan; unless we can think of something soon."

Arvan paused for some time, thinking of what Distance had told him. Everything in his life recently seemed to connect to Vaiske Parlet in some way. After a few minutes, he spoke.

"What's that got to do with Master Snow?" he asked.

Grimoire sighed and looked hopelessly at Distance with a tilt of his head.

The breeze whispered past, out to the Wastes, and Arvan's gaze followed the invisible, unknowable force. What awaited it? Who had joined it? Who would join when this unpleasantness was over?

When he looked back, Grimoire was looking at him with a sympathetic expression.

"Did you come all this way looking for Lawliet?" he asked.

Arvan nodded stiffly.

"Well," Grimoire said, "perhaps it would be best if I left it at this; he's not here, he's not in the city. I suggest you go home when you have the chance."

"I'm not averse to adventure," Arvan said, clenching his fists.

"Adventure's got nothing to do with it," Grimoire said. "Lawliet's orders were separate from ours, but connected in a way most could never understand."

"I suggest you tell me," Arvan said, his eyes unmoving, his hand wrapping around the hilt of his katana.

Distance folded his arms and eyed Arvan suspiciously. There was something unnatural about the expression; not that Arvan could see it. The boy bowed his head, his eyes obstructed by his fringe.

"You'd attempt to cut down two Thean generals for a scrap of information about Lawliet?" Distance asked.

"I'd do anything for Master Snow," Arvan whispered.

"As would we, Arvan" Grimoire said. "But…"

Arvan stopped listening. Grimoire's words could never reach the boy on the plain of sorrow he had been taken to. He had been so sure that he would find Master Snow in the Final Resting Place of the Empire, or at least information of his whereabouts. That information was stood before him, yet intangibly unreachable.

A familiar itching feeling made itself known behind Arvan's eyes, a sensation he had known so well as a child, yet familiarity and solace were very different things. He shuddered as the sensation gained intensity and he forced his eyes closed. Still, the tears seeped in convulsive sobs.

"I came so far," he said, interrupting Grimoire. "I thought that I'd die, more than once. I met people who I had no choice but to trust. I saw the best and worst of mankind. Along the way my hope strengthened and waned in turns, but I never submitted because once I got to this city, if I got to this city, I would find Master Snow. I would have died for that cause, but it was a waste."

"You had quite an adventure," Grimoire said, quietly.

"Could it really hurt, Grim?" Distance asked. "How much worse could he feel if you told him?"

"And hurt the boy?"

"I'm no mere boy!" Arvan shouted, his head jolting upright, an unblinking gaze fixing on Grimoire. Arvan's face was tear-stained and flustered, but his eyes were hard and as stern as ever, despite his stony features showing an aspect of malleability. "I'm a man!" he roared, wildly flinging a fist out beside him. "A man who travelled far and went to too much effort to leave here with nothing."

Grimoire sighed; a thousand thoughts passing behind his eyes in each merest moment.

"Very well, Arvan," he said. "As we've said, Lawliet's task was separate from ours, but, at the same time, one couldn't completely remove it from what Distance and I have been doing. Lord Thean is trying to bring about an age of peace where we'll have no war and no fear, but we've got more to worry about than the Warlords and Eremmerus."

"The Behemoth," Arvan said within a breath.

"Yes," Grimoire said. "Arvan, Lawliet was studying the Behemoth. He was following it, making a note of its behaviour over a long period of time – so far man has only known of it in short moments. Lord Thean wanted Lawliet to discover every aspect of it, hoping that understanding the creature would help him create some plan for peace in the future. Only, Lord Thean, nor myself or Distance, have seen any research."

"What?" Arvan said, weakly.

Grimoire sighed. "Lawliet's been missing for many months now. We don't know exactly what's happened but it's not unreasonable to assume, considering the little we do know, that he was killed by the Behemoth."

The breeze seemed to wash over Arvan and he lost the power of speech. The temperature of his blood dropped to that of the late winter air. His breathing became heavy and laboured and the world seemed that much emptier.

Master Snow was dead. He had travelled all that way only to discover that fact. The man who had been the closest thing he had to a father, or any parent in his later years. More than this he was killed by the Behemoth. Lament and Kyagorusu had been correct; it was just a theory after all.

He could feel his head becoming light as the blood rushed from it and he struggled to stand. Distance rushed to him and grabbed him by the shoulders.

"Come on, Grim," Distance said. "Let's get Arvan somewhere a little more comfortable."

Rushing footsteps, like a cacophonic waterfall rushed in their direction.

Distance lifted Arvan and Grimoire led them from the wall.

When the soldiers got there they found only the breeze and the endless vista of the Wastes.

Chapter Ten

Turbulent dreams and words of war dispersed and re-condensed; lost souls, people he once knew, painted on the black canvas of his mind. He was called to by the dead man in white in words he couldn't understand.

The boy felt old, as old as death itself – the morbid tradition both unceremonious and final. He let the darkness sweep over him; fighting it held no reason.

Arvan woke in an unfamiliar room, the pink light of dawn washing in through a large window. He hugged the covers closer but it brought him no comfort; solace could not exist in a world without Master Snow. Already it felt so empty as for Arvan to be completely and perpetually alone.

'Why exactly did you leave Farras?' a quiet melancholy voice inside his head spoke. 'Are you a man now? Does his death promote you to his rank?'

He had no answers to these questions, save for the nothing that existed in his mind.

He turned in the bed and saw Kyagorusu sitting patiently by the door. The bald man looked at Arvan sympathetically.

"So you *are* awake," he said, gently. "You were verging on catatonic when you came here yesterday. I suppose you don't remember."

Arvan stared at him, but said nothing.

"We're in my current residence, near the palace. I happened upon you with the Thean Generals, running from the army. Someone had to hide you all; lucky I found you really."

Arvan sat up, wrapped in the blanket. It was coarse and made his skin itch but he didn't care. When the unpleasant sensation came he scratched at it, yet, when it didn't abate, he merely let it express itself. Were he to banish it, it would only reappear later, soon enough.

"Distance and Grimoire told me what happened. I'm sorry."

Arvan looked at the window of the stone room. There was no glass, merely a hole cut in the wall; the masonry as perfect as anywhere else in the city. The light poured in, illuminating the room and the world outside, too early for the full events of the day to begin to transpire, yet there was movement nonetheless.

He turned to Kyagorusu. The large bald man with the clumsy features sat with a concerned expression. Arvan thought to speak, if only to give himself freedom from Kyagorusu's gaze.

"I never thought he'd die," Arvan said, his voice raw with emotion.

"We seldom expect it," Kyagorusu cooed. "Not of those we love. Were we to do so we would lose our hope."

"I keep asking myself why I left Farras. Yes, it was to find Master Snow, not that there was much point. I have friends there; Darkla and Mirr. With Master Snow that was closest I ever had to a family. But I left and I didn't even tell them."

"If you wish to return I'd gladly travel with you," Kyagorusu said. "This city holds less wonder than I had hoped for."

Arvan shook his head and stared at the stone wall. He wore no expression, he didn't know how to convey such a profound sorrow and so he merely didn't. It was, after all, the simplest act.

"How can I go back?" he said. "I always told myself I'd return a man and I thought finding Master Snow is what would make me one. Yes, I always call myself one but..." He trailed off. "Besides, it doesn't feel like home anymore."

"'Man' is just a title, Arvan. It holds little meaning. There are boys as young as thirteen who could be called men and men as old as fifty who are mere boys. I wouldn't think too much of it. If you wish to return they would accept you."

"No," Arvan said, still blank. "I would stay with you, as your student."

Kyagorusu looked at him, clearly surprised, and said nothing.

"You've done so much for me!" Arvan said, kneeling in the bed, pulling the sheets to his chest. "I'd like to repay you, though I can't even think how I could begin. I think that I could learn much from you."

Kyagorusu smiled faintly as Arvan gazed at him.

"I am still learning, myself," the bald man said, running the palm of his hand over his head. "If that is your wish I will not deny you. However, know this, I cannot teach you the way of the sword; if that is your desire you must pursue it yourself. And you shall not be my student, we will live as equals. Is that understood?"

Arvan nodded.

"Do not replace Master Snow with me," Kyagorusu continued. "That will not end well for either of us."

Arvan nodded. Then his eyes glazed over and he was silent for some time, clearly deep in thought. In those moments he didn't move, he hardly seemed to breathe. A statue in a city of stone. Eventually, he spoke.

"We were wrong about the Behemoth," he whispered. "But I was so sure."

"It was just a theory, Arvan. We all considered it."

There was a faint knock at the wooden door Kyagorusu was sat by, then it opened revealing Distance and Grimoire. They entered looking much the same as the day before.

"I suggest we leave soon," Grimoire said. "The crowds are beginning to move through the streets. If we wait much longer we'll be alone and too easy to spot."

Kyagorusu nodded and stood, then looked to the wordless Arvan. The bald man opened his mouth to speak but found nothing other than silence residing inside.

"Arvan," Distance said. "I know how you feel. When I first suspected the news of Lawliet, well I... I didn't think the world was what it once was."

"But," Grimoire added, "if what Kyagorusu tells us of Vaiske Parlet is true, then we'll need every sword-arm we can acquire. I can think of none better than a student of Lawliet."

Arvan looked at them listlessly, a huddled mess in his blanket.

"Very well," he said, solemnly. "I suppose it's all part of the adventure."

*

Eremmerus gazed with a lustful smile strewn across his face as the Coliseum filled, each inch of stone in his sight being replaced by flesh. The frozen blue sky above showed no sign of turning to anything but further flawlessness and he shivered with pleasure. Once his sensual satiation was at its pinnacle he sat in the throne of the Royal Box, just as colossal and impressive as the one in the palace.

The Great King turned to the man-with-two-shadows, stood dutifully next to him.

"Tell me, Parlet," he said. "What do you think of my Coliseum?"

"It is magnificent, Eremmerus," Vaiske replied in his metallic voice. "Building it atop the mountain was a stroke of genius."

"Built atop the mountain?" the Great King laughed. "How quaint! The mountain was removed from around the Coliseum. It's quite a story – I shall recount it to you sometime."

Captain Starling eyed Eremmerus. As he was always appointed to at such events, he was stood on guard on the left of the Great King. With his left hand he held the silver buckle of his belt and rested his right hand on the hilt of his dagger. He allowed his eyes to drift from the sly smile of Eremmerus to the agonised mask of Vaiske Parlet.

His second shadow, the shadow of Lament Strife, was cast upon the Great King. Over the last few day Eremmerus had always had Vaiske Parlet stood in such a fashion, as if it was a good omen for the Great King.

Vaiske glanced at Starling, but the Captain refused to remove his gaze. Even if he wasn't an immortal Vaiske Parlet would have been a formidable opponent. His entire body was shielded by the vermillion armour he so proudly wore. His mask, that ghastly apparition of death that had met so many just before their doom, was wrought metal thick enough to withstand even the most potent blow from a weapon. Yet, it was what lurked behind the mask that Starling feared most. He still hadn't discovered Vaiske's plot and, with each second he was bathed in ignorance, it came closer to fruition.

'Can you achieve this?' Starling asked himself. 'Can you kill an immortal? Even with the help of Lament your cause is hopeless…'

He removed the thoughts from his mind and looked out over the sand-swept ground of the Coliseum. Already the army was in place, the Great King's Cavalry in formation too, Lieutenant Fernarl at its head, just visible for his black jacket amidst the torturously still ocean of men.

The seats were now full as well. He passed his eyes over the stone for a glimpse of the shadus, but failed to make him out.

"You look nervous, Lind," Eremmerus said. "Scheming are we?"

"Not with your champion so close," Starling replied. "I just don't like being so far from my men."

Eremmerus waved him away and looked out over the vast vista of flesh.

Starling and Vaiske met one another's looks.

'Do you know what he plans, Vaiske?' Starling thought. 'Do you know he has brought you here only for his entertainment? But you would gladly do battle; you would gladly kill Lament, or any other for that matter.'

Starling tried to look away from the mask of anguish, the bull horns, the vermillion armour and the tall spear, but he could feel Vaiske's shrouded eyes on him. He could never be in comfort with them pointed in his direction.

*

Vaiske sneered behind his mask. Could it be possible that Captain Starling would obstruct his divine machinations? Vaiske Parlet, harbinger of peace, ceased in his perfection by the self-indulgent boy of a man; he who claimed to know all of sacrifice, only to risk his life for meaningless causes. It was laughable. The utopia that the man-with-two-shadows would create held no place for a man such as Captain Starling. Still, Vaiske knew better than to wish him death.

Eventually, Starling looked away and Vaiske laughed to himself, only to be stopped by a twinge of pain in his side.

His second shadow was squirming.

This was unprecedented. Of course, the shadow could not reject him fully, nor deny him his immortality. He needed not concern himself with such trivial matters as insubordinate shadows. Still, he couldn't look away from it; the crawling darkness writhing across the unknowing Great King.

He mused on it for some time, only for the shadow to calm and be still once more. He reassured himself; he was dealing with the supernatural, of course peculiar happenings would occur.

His mind followed his eyes, gazing on Eremmerus; the white clad Great King, his crown angled precariously on his head. He too was plotting, nothing as malevolent as Starling, but a man who had the Blood Lust on him as fervently as Eremmerus did could not be trusted; all he cared for was death and he would not be denied.

The Great King turned and smiled that sly smile, his mouth as a gash cut by a sword. "What say you, Parlet?" he said. "Shall we begin?"

*

The breeze gathered around him, his clothes making fluttering noises in the resistance, but none more so than his cape, swimming in the endless tide of life. He peered down at the amassed army in the Coliseum, approaching fifteen thousand or so, still with room to move in the immeasurable arena. And there, in the Royal Box, noticeable for his extraordinary appearance, the-man-with-two-shadows; Vaiske Parlet.

Lament stood atop the wall of the Coliseum, some way above even the highest spectators, closer to the eternal sky than the ground.

He drew his sword and rested the gargantuan blade on his shoulder. The breeze gripped him more tightly, waving away the hint of nausea. He hoped that fondness brought good luck.

*

They had taken their seats under the cover of the crowd, which shielded them from detection. Though now, seated only four rows from the front, even Distance and Grimoire showed signs of nerves at their proximity to the armed forces of the Final Resting Place of the Empire.

"Lament," Distance said to Kyagorusu. "He's a good swordsman, is he?"

"I certainly hope so," Kyagorusu said. "If not, the sword he carries is an arrogant statement."

"What do you mean by that?" Grimoire asked.

"You'll see," Kyagorusu said with a thin smile, his staff resting in his hands. "Besides, even if Lament is no match for Parlet, we've friends in high places." He looked up to the speck of white in the Royal Box.

"Ah, yes; Captain Starling," Grimoire said. "He's aided us on many an occasion. I assume you're ready should the worst happen, Distance?"

"You worry about yourself, old man," Distance replied. "There's nothing wrong with *my* sword skills."

Grimoire glanced at him but decided not to retort.

"And you, Arvan," he said. "Are you ready?"

Arvan shuddered. He had never killed a man before, though he always imagined he could do it if the need arose. But, with Master Snow on his mind and an immortal to face, he wasn't his usual assured self. Yet, he still nodded stiffly in reply to Grimoire.

"I don't mean to put you in a position in which you must kill, Arvan. Though, I find myself with little choice."

Arvan said nothing.

*

Eremmerus stood, holding the hip height wall before him with both hands.

"My people!" he called, ceasing the speaking of the audience immediately into a contemplative silence. "I am humbled that you would heed my words so respectfully as to attend with the numbers you have. I am honoured to be in such a position that I can call you my subjects and myself your Great King.

"My people! You have faced hardship during my time on the throne; I realise this. I have made it my utmost duty to end your suffering: this is a task I have not delegated – I have taken it upon myself – and know this; the end of your anguish is nigh!

"We live in a world of war, in a time that has come to be known as the Heroless Age. We are caught between the Behemoth and the Warlords. Were we to lose our vigilance for but a brief moment we could be obliterated. The Warlords threaten you and end your travel; they poison your water-supplies and block food routes so you would die of thirst or starve. The Behemoth is ever present and keeps your children awake at night. It screams so loud as to silence even the breeze!"

Captain Starling watched Eremmerus with vague interest. The Great King was far more animated than he had seen him in a long while. His body jerked as he spoke, his arms waved and he articulated his words even more than usual. Starling had doubted that the Great King had the strength to project his voice to each audience member in the Coliseum, though he had managed this effortlessly; aided by the ingenious architecture that accentuated each sound made. But he knew one thing further. The Great King was not excited by his speech, far from it. He waited only for a time when Vaiske Parlet and Lament Strife could battle unhindered. A time when his Blood Lust could finally be assuaged.

"And who protects you from these dangers? The army that stands before you!"

The crowd cheered, a gentle rumble echoing throughout the Coliseum.

"My ancestors!"

Again, the crowd cheered, softly shaking the foundations of the Coliseum.

"The mountains themselves!"

The crowd cheered louder than before, their fervour rolling down to the very base of the mountain.

"Captain Lind Starling of the Great King's Cavalry!"

The crowd cheered matching the enthusiasm of their previous outburst, but holding it for longer. For a time it seemed it would never dissipate. Eremmerus snarled at the smiling Captain.

"What can I say?" Starling said, quietly, shrouded by the cheering. "I'm a man of the people."

Eremmerus grunted and turned back to the crowd. He held up a hand calling for silence, eventually the crowd obeyed.

"And," he began, "of course, your Great King!"

The cheer that followed was lacklustre, save for the seats directly by the Royal Box, reserved for the Final Resting Place of the Empire's wealthiest citizens.

Eremmerus glared at Starling but the Captain said nothing.

"You have all lost someone dear to either of these evils," the Great King continued, his voice tenderer than before, but maintaining the same volume. "Some of you have lost loved ones to both. I, myself, lost my father to the cowardly Riit Clan and all of my brothers to the Behemoth. Destroyed and distraught by the tragedy, my mother took her own life and that of my dear sister, leaving me to rule alone. We have all lost."

'Yes,' Starling thought. 'We all lost the true Eremmerus to the Blood Lust in the War of the Wastes.'

The Great King paused for some time, realising he had the audience back in his grasp. He sighed, pleasured, and smiled, thankful that even the nearest member of the audience was too distant to see the curl of his lips.

"You all know what kind of a king I am by now. I make promises, but never ones that I cannot keep. I promised you that we would win the War of the Wastes and we did. I promised you that I would make sure that you always have enough food and I have done. I promised you that I would make the Final Resting Place of the Empire a military might once more. Well, is the army stood before you not vast?"

The audience cheered, so fervently this time that it rivalled the one that erupted for Captain Starling. Rivalled, but not exceeded.

When the noise died down, Eremmerus continued.

"Well, I cannot promise you that we will lose no more to the Warlords or the Behemoth. In fact there is great loss still to come. This army may be a fraction of the size once I have brought peace to the land. But I can promise you this; there *will* be peace! And the Final Resting Place of the Empire shall bask in it and we shall reclaim the name of greatness: Mandra!"

The audience erupted with the greatest cheer of all.

*

"Why do they applaud?" Arvan asked, weakly.

"Because they must," Grimoire replied. "The Great King truly does want the best for his people but he doesn't know how to go about it. He realises there must be unity so if they do not cheer, they are punished. They can escape with little acts of insubordination like the cheer for Captain Starling, but a blatant refusal to cheer would mean death for acts of treason."

Arvan said nothing. He was too amazed by the sheer volume of the citizens' response; the raised, triumphant fists and the air-thrust weapons of the army. If this wasn't true support, it was an excellent imitation of it.

*

"You see, Lind?" Eremmerus said, smiling slyly at the Captain. "I will always be in their favour."

Starling said nothing and the Great King moved to silence the audience.

"My people! You may ask yourselves how I can make such a promise. How can I be so sure that such a time will come to fruition? Allow me to enlighten you.

"Upon my right stands the infamous warrior, Vaiske Parlet. But he is no longer as he once was; he is no longer a mere man. No. He is now the man-with-two-shadows. Vaiske Parlet is an immortal! And he had sided with our city to destroy the warlord clans and bring about the age of peace!"

Once more the audience erupted. Their cheers ravaged the eardrums of all in attendance and seemed to shake the entire city. Starling's soul sighed in frustration at their obedience.

Eremmerus smiled.

"Well, Vaiske," he said, quietly. "Would you care to show them what you can do?"

Captain Starling watched in horror as Vaiske threw back his helmeted head and laughed mechanically.

"Nothing would give me more pleasure!" the man-with-two-shadows roared. He grabbed the short wall with both hands and vaulted into the arena.

*

Arvan watched, stunned, as the horned effigy fell through the air and landed on his feet on the sand of the arena, as if the height from the Royal Box had been the mere bottom step of a staircase. The immortal called to the officers of the army and made the troops form a perimeter at the edge of the arena, creating a colossal circle for Vaiske Parlet to perform in.

He moved as if he and the spear understood one another, speaking a language only they knew; a language spoken by the smallest movements of the smallest muscles and heard by the attentive wood of the spear's shaft.

Each step swept up flocks of sand at his feet. His movements all so fluid that he could have been involved in some visceral dance of death.

For a moment Arvan felt ashamed, he wished to one day be as skilled as Vaiske Parlet. But was it so wrong to respect him as a professional? He was clearly a masterful warrior and Arvan suspected that even the peace loving Master Snow would have been intrigued by him. Then again, Master Snow wasn't in much of a position to hold an opinion anymore and certainly not to speak it to his protégé.

Arvan sighed. This world was still very new to him.

"Talented, isn't he?" Kyagorusu said.

"Terrifyingly so," Grimoire sighed. "Even if he wasn't an immortal I wouldn't want to face him."

"I hope your friend makes his move soon," Distance said. "The crowd's beginning to warm to him."

Arvan watched in awe as Vaiske struck the ground before him, sending up a wave of sand he cut directly in half. Something even Master Snow could not achieve.

*

"Where are you, shadus?" Eremmerus said to himself. "You'll never have a more perfect opportunity than this. You'd be unwise to fail me now; I'd kill you far slower than Parlet would."

Starling, still stood next to the Great King, tautened and his hand gripped around the golden hilt of his dagger. If Lament wouldn't strike then he would have to face Vaiske himself. He sighed but felt no relief.

Lament's words whispered through his mind in the melancholy voice of the shadus. 'How do you propose I kill an immortal?'

Starling sighed again. "Well," he said to himself, "I'll just have to find out, won't I?"

Then, just as he was drawing his dagger from the small scabbard in his belt, his hope was restored as he saw a speck of black and crimson atop the wall on the opposite side of the Coliseum.

Starling smiled.

And so it would begin.

*

Even to the superior eyes of the shadus, Vaiske Parlet was practically indistinguishable at that distance. He moved vaguely and minutely below.

The breeze, which for so long had danced around him, faded and Lament was left alone on the wall. His cape fell back around him.

"Now?" he asked. "Very well. Should I fail, my love, I shall meet you on the breeze."

He stepped to the edge of the wall and peered over into the arena once more. The faint vermillion effigy was almost in the very centre.

He clasped his eyes on it, and leapt.

*

Arvan tried to look away from Vaiske Parlet, but he was mesmerized by him. It was more than just his skill – it was everything about him. He moved so easily, despite his heavy armour and the length of the spear. His eyesight must have been obscured by the mask, yet his accuracy was perfect, as if he could pick out a single grain of sand in each cloud he threw up with his violent strikes. His appearance itself was enough to entice Arvan; a horned demon, materialised by the breeze, armour stained red by spilling the blood of his enemies. He fought for peace and would continue to do so until that peace was absolute.

Was it not distasteful? Arvan felt that a man who was so experienced and talented at killing should have disgusted him. But why couldn't he look away?

"What's that?" Grimoire asked, pointing to something hurtling through the air.

Arvan tore his gaze from Vaiske Parlet to what Grimoire was pointing at. It fell so quickly that it was a blur of black and crimson, a streak of silver leading the way. The effigy seemed to forever gain velocity and tumble through the air in some ferocious grace, but it still had far to go before it hit the ground. No, the ground wouldn't be good enough for this mirage – it had a target. It was shooting straight towards Vaiske Parlet.

"Yes," Distance said. "What *is* that?"

Resistance gathered around the falling force, as if the breeze itself wished to slow it, but succeeded only in creating a ball of pale blue energy around it. Arvan could liken the sight only to a shooting star.

Kyagorusu smiled beside him, garnering the attention of the Thean Generals.

"You what it is, don't you, Kyagorusu?" Grimoire said.

"Of course I do," the bald man replied. "That's Lament."

*

"Finally!" Eremmerus roared. "So the shadus makes an appearance and Parlet has no idea! This could be quite a spectacle, eh, Lind?"

Starling looked at the Great King. The man he was once so close with to call a 'friend' was salivating with the prospect of the duel. His body hunched with tension, waiting to be released at the first clash of their weapons.

Starling looked at the falling Lament. Would that be enough to kill an immortal? Indeed, the shadus would strike Parlet with considerable force, but that was nothing to a man who had an eternity to face. Besides, there was no guarantee that Lament would survive the impact.

"I asked you a question, Lind," Eremmerus said, glaring at the Captain.

"It will be more than a spectacle, Eremmerus," Starling replied, before his voice fell to a whisper. "This will be death itself."

Eremmerus laughed.

"Fantastic!" he growled.

Starling glanced at the Great King, then back to Lament, ignoring his usual revulsion at what Eremmerus had become.

Lament gained yet more velocity as Vaiske Parlet continued to perform obliviously. There was no way the shadus could survive the crash, but that didn't seem to bother him an awful lot.

Starling shuddered.

*

He held the gargantuan sword before him. If he moved it just slightly he would lose his balance and collide with the ground, not his target.

Vaiske Parlet, the horned vermillion warrior, grew in his sight, the shadow-thief's performance becoming ever fiercer. But he would soon be interrupted…

*

Arvan had expected Lament to face Vaiske in an honourable duel; appearing before the warrior and challenging him. Foolish? Perhaps, but it was noble. This sky-borne ambush was a thing of desperation, the act of an already defeated man. Of course, Arvan could not begrudge Lament a slight advantage, after all he did go into battle against an immortal. But there was something about Lament's plan that Arvan couldn't accept.

The pressure built up inside of him and he clenched his fists so tightly that they soon went numb.

What would Master Snow have said of such an attack? The greatest swordsman in the world would surely have condemned it; Arvan felt he knew Master Snow well enough to assume that much. Master Snow would gladly have fought an immortal himself, no matter how hopeless his position.

Yet, Master Snow was no longer there and it appeared that honour and nobility in battle had died with him.

Arvan tried to stifle it, but the cry left before he even knew what it was.

"Watch out!"

*

'Watch out?' Vaiske thought. 'Whatever for? Did you not hear Eremmerus? I am an immortal.'

He thrust his spear before him, eliciting a subdued cheer from the somewhat distracted audience.

Vaiske felt an intense pain in his side and his second shadow seemed to try to tear itself away from him, before receding into unpleasant convulsions.

The pain soon subsided and then Vaiske felt it, the approach of a sword behind him. He spun around, blocking the attack with his spear. He caught but a glimpse of the gargantuan blade.

The attack must have hit him with some force, for as he absorbed the strike with his legs, the ground shuddered and the Coliseum was engulfed in a tsunami of sand and dust.

Chapter Eleven

In the grained obscurity of the sand and dust there was no life. Everything was as it was not. To breathe was to choke. To move was to be lost in the land of sediment. There was not an eye in the Coliseum that could be said to hold sight. There were few that even dared open.

All was still, save for the shifting sand. Even the breeze ventured not to whisper past, lest it displace the last fragment of stability or sanity,

Yet in this land where life could not be said to roam and death feared to enter into, stood two men, locked in an embrace of war, whose senses were at their height.

Lament gazed into the mask of anguish he had first seen not even a week ago. He remembered it as vividly as if he had been looking at it the entire time he had been searching for Vaiske Parlet. The shadus was close enough to the man-with-two-shadows to see through the eye-holes his mask and into the immortal's spheres of sight. They were contorted into a fervent scowl. His mouth, visible only for the mouth of the mask being slung open in so vehement a howl, was thrown open, teeth clenched, in some expression of vengeful fury. Lament thought that if he removed the rest of the mask, the face beneath would look no different.

Vaiske glared at the shadus, his pale face holding no expression except that faint frown he always wore. His amber eyes glowed hauntingly through the sand, the left barely visibly as his matted hair fell before that half of his face. No different from that night so long ago, unless he counted the hangdog weariness in the shadus' eyes.

So he *did* have a weakness. But it did leave a question: how did he survive the extraction of his shadow?

Vaiske smiled behind his mask and threw the shadus back with an impossibly strong swipe of his spear, expelling the obscuring sand from the Coliseum.

Lament landed on his feet on the opposite side of the arena.

"Forgive me shadus," Vaiske roared. "But I've forgotten your name."

The crowd watch in silent awe, gradually adjusting to the return of the light, as Lament held the gargantuan sword effortlessly in one hand. The shadus looked around and, feeling the glares of the audience, rested the blade heavily on his shoulder.

"My name is Lament Strife," he replied in his usual whisper. He watched as his voice reached the audience and sent a shudder around the Coliseum.

"Ah, yes," Vaiske replied, laughing mechanically. "I knew it was something ludicrous."

Lament said nothing.

Vaiske spun his spear theatrically in his hand before taking up an attacking stance, the weapon lifted above the horns of his helmet. "So, you sought to kill me with that strike?"

"No," Lament replied, his sword still self-consciously resting on his shoulder. "I didn't come here to kill you."

"Then why try such an aggressive manoeuvre?"

"To attract your attention. You were in quite a reverie."

Vaiske took a step forward and let his spear fall to his side.

"You wouldn't kill me?" he growled. "Then what would you?"

"I came only to reason with you. I require my shadow."

"You do?" Vaiske asked, conveying mock-interest even through the filter of his mask. "Well, I fear I have yet to be done with it."

"That too is of concern to me," Lament said.

Vaiske moved his head so that his eyes were fixed on the shadow, tilting slightly, then, without the mockery of before, he spoke. "What do you know of what I plan?"

"Not a thing," Lament said. "Yet, that you would need to be an immortal to achieve it is disconcerting enough."

"You would seek to stop me?" Vaiske asked, his voice becoming quieter.

"No, I would seek to reason with you. But if that should fail, you would leave me no choice but to stop you."

Vaiske thrust his spear at the distant shadus.

"And how do you propose to kill an immortal, Lament?" he roared.

"I don't," Lament replied. "But if you would force my hand I'm sure I could find a way."

Vaiske sneered behind his mask. "I shall not return your shadow."

"What would you do, Vaiske?" Lament asked. "Slaughter the warlords and their armies until there are none left? Until the breeze is so thick with the dead that a man can hardly breathe, until he can reach out and grasp it?" Lament brought his free arm up and clasped his hand as if clutching an invisible entity. "Would you make the breeze so thick that we can almost see it? Is that your age of peace?"

"I would give mankind a hero!" Vaiske roared. "What would you give these people; the broken rhetoric of peace?"

Lament shook his head. "I would do worse. I would give them nothing, but a nothing they could trust."

Vaiske paused. His second shadow had calmed, replaced by a fury of his own. That the shadus would question his motives showed an insolence beyond comprehension. Who was he to question this immortal? A man who, by all rights, should be dead, dared to suggest he could rival the man-with-two-shadows and, yet, was that not the very basis of this rivalry; that he should be dead?

Vaiske tilted his head, contemplatively. "And, Lament," he said. "What would *you* do if I returned your shadow to you?"

"There is a man who needs my help," the shadus replied. "I am in no condition to rescue him as I am; shadow-less."

Vaiske threw back his head and laughed mechanically.

"You would condemn the world to war for the sake of one man?" he said. He fixed his gaze back on Lament. "Pathetic."

"I would save him and all others you would kill," Lament said.

Vaiske smiled behind his mask. "Why, Lament, you still have no idea of the peace I seek to bring. But enough talk; I grow weary of this. Come, we must fight!"

Vaiske lifted the spear above his head and watched as Lament stayed as he was. The shadus remained standing inertly, his gargantuan sword resting on his slender shoulder.

'How do you propose to kill an immortal?' a quiet, melancholy voice inside Lament's head asked.

He didn't reply; why justify a hopeless cause? It was what it was and nothing else.

As he grasped the sword, placing his left hand just below his right and holding the weapon before him, he was thankful he knew a loving presence on the breeze. It whispered around him, dancing with his cape as it so often did. It caressed him gently and he felt the comfort the breeze always brought him. But this sensation of the breeze wasn't merely 'it' but 'her', or so it was in his thoughts.

The breeze subsided and Lament looked to Vaiske. The warrior was stood as he had been; for what did he wait? Why did he stall the shadus' inevitable death?

Lament sighed. He would wait no longer and, with that decision, he charged at Vaiske Parlet.

The sword trailed behind him, as his cape, his heavy footsteps a percussive war-cry that his silent mouth would not reciprocate. But no, for the sand muted the sound of his feet so that even the most inescapable aspect of his fury was a non-entity. Still he charged on, wondering just how long it would take the man-with-two-shadows to end his life when their weapons met once more.

Vaiske stood, motionless as a monolith, Lament's gaze upon him, persistent and unwavering. So, even the opponent of the shadus considered him no threat; so be it.

Lament threw his arms above him, the sword cutting through the air, then let them fall, ready to cleave Vaiske Parlet's helmeted head in two. Still the immortal didn't move.

The sword met its target, hitting the very centre of the top of Vaiske's helmet, equidistant from each horn. Yet, despite the force of Lament's strike, despite the accuracy and the weight of the gargantuan sword, the strike did not so much as dent the armour.

Vaiske stood as if nothing more than a light breeze had hit him. His eyes, one either side of the blade, were fixed upon the shadus. He didn't speak. He didn't move. He merely watched and blinked.

*

For a time, all was still. Lament wouldn't move his sword from its defeated position and the audience dared hardly to breathe. Arvan looked to Kyagorusu and the Thean Generals. Not one of them moved, petrified as the rest of the Final Resting Place of the Empire. He looked back to the paused duel in the arena. At least nobody would say anything of his warning Vaiske.

*

The silence broke with the metallic voice of Vaiske Parlet. "An excellent strike, Lament," he said, his roaring voice filling the Coliseum. "Though, certainly to my mind, you found your mark rather too easily. So," he paused and his expression contorted once more into a scowl, "allow me to retort."

The spear jolted upwards, towards the left eye of Lament. The shadus stepped to the right, narrowly avoiding the tip and replied with a swipe at Vaiske's chest. The spear countered, once more aimed at the eye of Lament, the shadus only avoiding being blinded by striking the long handle. He succeeded in knocking the spear off target, but brought himself little relief as Vaiske struck with his spear in a downwards motion. Lament leapt backwards, just dodging the tip.

The barrage of attacks they unleashed upon one another continued. A seemingly endless slew of attacks, counters and parries. Always graceful. The intent to kill never waning. But Vaiske forever had the advantage. What did an immortal need to worry about defence?

*

Arvan watched in a mesmeric wonderment at the skill of each combatant. If Vaiske fought as though he and the spear understood one another, then Lament fought as if he and his sword were one, a shared consciousness and much more. Lament's actions with the sword had always seemed effortless, yet, since his training the day before, it seemed he was pained when not attacking with it. But still he wore that remorseful expression.

Surprisingly, Arvan found himself thinking of Lament as the more skilled warrior. To have his own mortality hinted at with each strike from Vaiske and still have such accuracy was nothing less than a spectacle of talent. Indeed, had he not been fighting an immortal, Arvan was sure that Lament would already have won.

Though, there was still such mystery around the shadus, and it was a mystery that Arvan could not help but distrust.

*

Vaiske stabbed at Lament's chest only for the shadus to parry the attack and leap backwards, far enough to be out of Vaiske's reach and far enough to move if the man-with-two-shadows was to charge at him. Each held their weapon ready for the next stage of the duel.

Lament drew in air, stinging his lungs with every breath. The nausea was burdensomely upon him, so vehement that he had to fight against his desire to retch.

"Had enough, Lament?" Vaiske roared. "For how much longer do you think you can do battle with that sickness?"

Lament didn't answer. For a brief moment he had the fear that his heart had ceased to beat and he fell to his knees, his sword resting beside him. When the sensation of life returned to him, he sighed though he wasn't sure if that was from relief or despair.

He forced himself to his feet and took up his sword, resting the giant blade on his shoulder.

"When the sword becomes too cumbersome to swing, it is time to give up the fight," Vaiske said. "Yes, I would still take your life, but only to ensure you wouldn't meddle in my affairs again. You fought bravely, shadus, even more so than when last we met, but it is useless to fight an immortal. I shall allow you to die with your sword in your hand like the warrior you are."

Vaiske spun his spear in his hand before grasping it, ready to attack. He took a slow step forward.

"Tell me, Vaiske," Lament said in his usual whisper. Vaiske fought the urge to shiver; the way the breeze seemingly wrapped itself around the words of the shadus was truly haunting. Still, he continued his approach. "What do you know of the shadus?"

"As much as I care to," the immortal replied as he walked towards his static prey. "Now; come, shadus. Take this time to choose your final words."

Sand sighed under the feet of Vaiske as he neared Lament. The audience remained in its silent reverie.

Lament's amber eyes never moved from Vaiske. The apparition of imminent death continued to make its approach, but the shadus showed no allusion to concern. Vaiske thought that, perhaps, the shadus had accepted his mortality. Good, that would make this easier.

Then as Vaiske's shadow crawled onto Lament's feet and surged onto the ground around him, creeping further up his body, the shadus did something that Vaiske had never expected him to. Lament smiled. Yes, it was thin and vague, only one side of his mouth curled and his remained emotionless and uncaring, still maintaining the faint scowl, but it was a smile nonetheless.

88

Vaiske stabbed at Lament once more but his spear only met air. Lament had disappeared.

*

The audience erupted into a cacophony of gasps and angry shouting. What they had witnessed was being debated and interpreted.

Arvan looked to Kyagorusu, but the bald man merely shook his head.

"No, Arvan," he said. "I don't understand either. Though there's still much we don't know about the shadus people; Lament especially."

"If you had to guess?" Grimoire asked.

Kyagorusu sighed. "They say the shadus have mystical abilities. I'd venture this, whatever *this* is exactly, was one of them."

"Well, at least it's confused our immortal," Distance said before looking at Arvan. "We should be thankful for that; he doesn't need any more help."

Arvan said nothing and looked back into the arena.

*

Eremmerus pounded his fists onto the short wall.

"Just as we were about to see blood!" he growled. "What do you know of this, Lind?"

"Only that you shouldn't be as upset as you are," Starling replied. "This means that the duel will continue longer."

"It's hardly a duel if you can't see one of the combatants," the Great King mumbled.

"I wouldn't worry, Eremmerus. I'm sure we'll see Lament soon enough."

The Great King snarled. "We'd better. He'd be wise not to fail me."

*

Vaiske paced the arena, his spear perpetually readied. The soldiers positioned around the perimeter watched him warily, his demeanour unknowable behind his mask.

The breeze whispered past, waltzing with clusters of sand as it went. Vaiske eyed it cautiously but nothing more came. The world around him was one of noise and impatience, both of which were un-disciplines he could not afford.

He spun around, thrusting his spear into air where he thought Lament was. He grunted.

"Where are you, shadus?" he said to himself.

He stepped forward, the displaced sand cooing to him. It had no choice but to move for his immortal foot.

Before him leapt a figure of black and red, the gargantuan sword swiping

89

and his hip. Vaiske blocked it, only for Lament to sink away again.

"What is this trickery?" he asked himself. "Where do you go, shadus? Besides, even if you struck me, what could you hope to do?"

Vaiske paused in his pacing and looked to the ground. Nothing lay there, save for his two shadows. He smiled behind his mask.

"Of course," he said.

He stabbed at Lament's shadow only for the tip of his spear to meet sand. He paused, taking his spear from the ground, then he tried the same with his own shadow, achieving much the same result.

The sword shot from his own shadow and met his abdomen; again, it did nothing but touch his armour. Then, slowly, it sank back into the shadow.

"Lament, you conniving runt!" Vaiske roared. "Face me like a warrior!"

The audience fell silent at the illustration of the immortal's fury, yet still a faint noise remained. Rushing air, coming from above.

Vaiske looked up and Lament hurtling towards him once more, sword first, already prepared to land. In that moment, Vaiske felt a niggling terror – he fought an adversary of which he knew very little. The apparition of crimson and black landed before him and struck at him three times, Vaiske sidestepping each attempt, then Lament sank back into the immortal's shadow.

The shadus treated shadows as if they were a miasmic fluid, yet to Vaiske they remained a mere obstruction of light. Even as Lament sank into them, Vaiske's spear could only meet the ground. Yet, one question remained; how had Lament gotten above him?

Vaiske looked around for an answer and saw that his second shadow was delving into that of the Coliseum, connecting them. He concluded that Lament could travel from shadow to shadow if they were connected. He managed to leap from above as, technically speaking, the shadow was also cast upon the highest seats of the Coliseum.

"Very clever, Lament!" Vaiske roared. "Can all shadus utilise this trick?"

Lament rose from Vaiske's shadow, his sword held in his right hand, resting at his side.

"Yes," he said. "Though you have made it rather easier for me by having more than the standard issue of shadows."

"Hence the term 'Shadow People' I suppose," Vaiske said. "But, tell me," he smiled behind his mask, "how do you propose to use this to kill me; an immortal?"

Lament said nothing.

Vaiske laughed mechanically.

"So you still have no plan! And when noon comes there shall be no shadows for you to hide in. Then how will you escape my attacks?"

*

Kyagorusu smiled solemnly. "Unfortunately, Parlet is correct. As long as he has two shadows there's nothing Lament can do. He can use every trick he knows but Vaiske is still an immortal. It's a fascinating skill, though. One I should love to ask Lament about. Though, I suppose I won't have the chance now."

"He's not dead yet, Kyagorusu," Grimoire replied. "He can always use the shadows to try and escape."

"I wish he would," Distance said. "He'd be an excellent addition to Lord Thean's force."

But, inside, they all knew that Lament would not leave. Even if his pride would have let him, Vaiske would not.

*

The duel waged on. Each strike was so powerful that, as the weapons met, they screamed war into the very back of the Coliseum. Lament leapt from shadows only for Vaiske to predict where he would emerge and counter his attack.

"What do you propose we do, shadus?" Vaiske asked between strikes. "We're an even match. I have yet to land a blow and your strikes cannot harm me. All there is to separate us is time. I have an eternity to live for, how long do you have? Must we fight until you are unable to continue?"

"You mean to suggest that you would let me leave?" Lament asked.

"Of course not!" Vaiske roared. "I would kill you now and spare us both the effort."

Their weapons met, but neither went for another strike. Instead, they pushed against one another, straining with all their might. Then, with an explosion of his immortal strength, Vaiske pushed Lament away, the shadus once more on the other side of the arena.

Lament landed, kneeling, then got to his feet. He was weary, struggling to stand, and knew that Vaiske would soon take his life. The sickness ravaged him, but still he readied himself to charge the man-with-two-shadows.

"Well, my love," he said as the breeze clung to him. "It seems we are about to meet once more."

He grasped his sword with both hands and readied it for an attack.

The mountain began to shake. At first it was a gentle rumble, but it grew into a fervent tremor, the Coliseum swaying in its grasp like a ship in the midst of a storm.

It was a haunting rhythm that Lament feared he recognised.

Vaiske laughed mechanically.

"So it's finally here!" he roared above the ever growing din.

Lament turned.

The fist of the Behemoth punched through the wall of the Coliseum.

Chapter Twelve

It matched the height of the Coliseum wall with ease, towering above all around it. The audience ran from their seats as the Behemoth continued to tear through the stone as if it was no more than a silk sheet. Some of the less disciplined soldiers began to run from the arena, though the officers managed to keep the majority of them in position.

Lament peered up at the Behemoth. It had not changed at all from their previous encounter, other than its ceaseless frenzy. It shrieked, the listless eyes flitting around.

Splinters of rock flew past, further into the Coliseum, as the Behemoth continued on through the wall. The gigas of oppression moved as a man whose limbs were new to him. Each movement seemed to trail, offhand and unplanned.

The shadus looked to Vaiske who was stood next to him.

"I expect you're rather more glad to have an immortal with you now," Vaiske said.

"You plan to kill it?"

Vaiske nodded.

"How?"

"With ease, shadus," Vaiske said, striding towards the Behemoth. "With ease."

Lament's scowl tautened as he watched the immortal walk arrogantly away. Even for the man-with-two-shadows the Behemoth was a daunting, impossible foe, yet Vaiske strode to it as if it were a mere man. The shadus held his sword lifelessly in his right hand and sighed.

"Fear not, Lament," Captain Starling said, appearing beside the shadus. He looked typically immaculate, his hand resting on the hilt of his dagger. "We've driven the Behemoth away before, though it's never gotten this far into the city."

The Captain looked to the silent shadus and smiled at him, then to the Behemoth. "Lieutenant Fernarl!" he called into the assembling chaos.

The Lieutenant, mounted atop a horse that looked vaguely similar to Titus, was soon with them.

"Yes, Captain?"

"Take the men and place the horses in the stables; we'll need all the room we can get. Place the men with the archers – they'll need protecting if the Behemoth gets too close."

"Yes, Captain!" Fernarl saluted and began to ride away.

"Oh, and Damske," Starling said, causing Fernarl to turn. "Feed Titus whilst you're in the stable, would you? I've yet to do it today."

Fernarl saluted and rode away, the cavalry following in an arrow formation.

"Well, that should give us a little more room," Starling said, walking towards the Behemoth. "I'll see you in the chaos, Lament."

The Behemoth stepped into the arena, causing another tremor to assail the mountain. Soldiers stood in its path only to be trampled or swiped away, thrown into the walls, crushed with the force. Lament could see Vaiske, climbing up the seats of the Coliseum, some plan working its way through the immortal's mind, though the shadus couldn't fathom what it was.

*

The audience around them had almost completely evacuated, giving them a clear pathway to the arena. Without knowing it, Arvan had already stood and drawn his katana.

"Well," Grimoire said, "there's not much use sitting here talking about it. We'll have to fight it."

"I'll help as much as I can," Kyagorusu said, gesturing with his staff. "I'm far from masterful, though I've had to defend myself more times than I wish to recount."

"How do you plan to kill it?" Arvan asked absent-mindedly. He hadn't thought to ask the question, far from it. His mind was on revenge. The killer of Master Snow stood before him, by all accounts an invulnerable creature, but impossibility meant little to him in those moments. He was there to avenge his fallen master.

"When I was your age," Distance said, "my sword teacher spoke to me some very true words."

All looked to him, save for Arvan whose eyes were fixed upon the Behemoth.

Distance drew his katana and smiled. "Very little survives a beheading."

"That's reassuring," Grimoire said gravely. "Now all we have to do is get to the head."

"That could be a challenge," Kyagorusu said.

"Not for a man who can leap through shadows," Distance said.

Kyagorusu and Grimoire nodded at him. Then they made for Lament.

*

Soldiers tried, without success, to stall the Behemoth. They thrust spears at its feet but were soon trampled under the weight of a millennium of war. The beast continued to shriek and roar, swiping at those who sought to kill it.

Lament watched, inert, as a volley of arrows flew over-head, only to be thrust away by the mighty hand of the creature. What did these men hope to do? Kill something that had survived a millennium of assassination attempts?

He was torn from his pensiveness as Kyagorusu approached with two men Lament didn't recognise.

"Not to be blunt, Lament," the bald man said. "But we need you to use the shadows to get to the head."

Lament pointed to the sun, approaching noon. "The shadows are waning."

Kyagorusu looked to the Behemoth. The shadow it cast was still expansive, but directly under it; of little use to Lament.

"Besides," the shadus continued. "I came here only for my shadow."

"You'd think of that at a time like this?" Grimoire asked, shocked.

"I do not presume to battle with entities whose evil I doubt. I've a man's life to save."

"You still think the Behemoth may be benevolent?" Kyagorusu asked.

Lament nodded. "Even the best of men find themselves amidst acts of violence these days."

"Benevolent or not," Distance said, "it looks as if it will wipe us all out if we don't do something soon."

Lament strapped his sword to his back and sighed. "Why must I fight these immortals?" he muttered, prowling towards the Behemoth.

"What can we do to help?" Kyagorusu called after him.

"Cast a shadow for me," Lament replied, never stopping, never turning.

Kyagorusu turned to the Thean Generals.

"We'll need a fire," he said.

"A large one," Distance agreed.

Kyagorusu watched as Lament walked calmly towards the perpetual destruction of the battle, his cape dancing elegantly with the breeze as he went. How many times had he seen the shadus approach near certain death now? Still, this time his hope was greater than that of the others.

He smiled. "Arvan, gather everything flammable you can find."

But when he looked, Arvan wasn't there.

*

Arvan darted along the seats of the Coliseum, katana held at his side. The breeze rushed past him, singing fatally as he neared the Behemoth. He dived at the leg, jumping over the failing soldiers and plunged his sword into the beast. The tip met the stony skin but failed to penetrate and the boy fell amongst the fray.

Before he had a chance to become aware of it he was back on his feet, joining the slew of attacks at the legs of the Behemoth. The served only to stall it, gifting the beast penance to its movements. If they could just keep it still they could save the city.

Arvan had no time to be afraid. He found himself unwittingly following the orders of the officers; when to attack, when to retreat, when to charge; yet always vengeance for Master Snow was on his mind.

The Behemoth swiped at the soldiers, the young reflexes of the boy saving him as he ducked, though the soldiers around him were less lucky. The action tore Arvan from his murderous delirium. He watched as the Behemoth lifted a giant fist. Arvan heard the call for the retreat, though it meant nothing to him, merely two syllables; unconnected and abstract.

The fist surged through the cloying air of the Coliseum towards the ground where Arvan stood alone. In that moment Master Snow left his thoughts and all that the boy could think of was the eternal, unknowable abyss that awaited him. The fist continued, a complete blackness against the noonday sun, azure sky obscured behind it. The stone of the skin was cracked from a millennium of weathering. How much had the beast seen? What wisdom did it hold?

A blur of white and a mane of golden hair lunged past, pulling Arvan from certain death and into the lustre of the day. He sat on the sand, shocked that he was alive. He laid his sword beside and hugged his legs to his chest.

"The idea is not to get killed," a familiar voice said beside him. "That's much easier to accomplish if you're not crushed."

Arvan looked up and saw Captain Starling stood majestically, gazing at the battle before them.

"They're pulling the majority of the soldiers out," he continued. "This is a job for a large force that can move quickly or a few warriors. The cavalry can't manoeuvre well in here so we're trying the few warriors approach."

"It killed Master Snow," Arvan said weakly, his words muffled by his knees.

"Yes and it will kill you too if you stay," Starling said, his hands fondling the hilt of his sheathed dagger. "If that happens I'll have nightmares, and I don't sleep well as it is."

Arvan said nothing. Did his training count for nothing now that Master Snow was dead? He had always imagined his first battle would be fought beside his master, the pair a formidable unit that could defeat any and all that would oppose them. Yet, without the support of Master Snow it seemed Arvan could do nothing. He didn't notice Kyagorusu lumbering over to them.

"Get him out of here," the ever amiable Starling said to the bald man. "We've no need for the corpses of boys."

Arvan rose to his feet, fists clenched. "I'm no mere boy!" he roared. Then he burst into tears. "I'm a man!" His legs enfeebled and he fell to the sandy ground in a huddle. "I can fight!" he wailed. "I can fight."

In the darkness of his closed eyes he felt a pair of arms embrace him and he let them do so. His tears fell into the coarse robe, the rough fibres scratching his skin giving him some solace, if only for their familiarity.

"Yes, you can fight," Kyagorusu said. "But that doesn't mean that you should. Come, Arvan; there are those here better suited to this than us:

Lament, Captain Starling, Grimoire, Distance, even Vaiske Parlet. All are capable. There is nothing more we can do."

He let Kyagorusu pull him to his feet and lead him away. He had a morbid thought that he did not vocalise; though he did acknowledge it with a fervent sob.

'If the Behemoth could kill Master Snow, it can kill them without effort.'

*

Vaiske launched himself with his immortal legs from the seats of the Coliseum and onto the forearm of the Behemoth. He held the matted fur that grew from it and drove his spear into the skin for extra grip. The tip pierced through the stone and the Behemoth shrieked. It waved its arm wildly, the force of the creature nothing to his immortal strength.

"You'll not shake me free!" Vaiske roared. "You'll not break my grip!"

The herculean creature brought its arm before it and went to swat the man-with-two-shadows. He took his spear in his hand and leapt from the arm, goring the tip into the centre of the beast's chest, holding the handle of the weapon with one hand.

The Behemoth shrieked as the faintest trickle of deep-crimson blood seeped from the tiny wound. It brought its hands up in shock but made no effort to remove the spear or Vaiske. The sound of the pained scream reverberated throughout the Coliseum as an army of mourning ghouls, the soprano ringing burning the eardrums of all around.

Vaiske gazed to the sky overhead as a vast volley of flaming arrows arched over the head of the Behemoth casting a giant shadow across the arena for a brief few seconds.

Lament emerged from the shadows and appeared on the Behemoth's shoulder. He took the sword from his back and rested the blade on his shoulder. The breeze swept violently past, throwing back his hair and tattered cape, though he ignored it. His amber eyes rolled down to Vaiske.

"Lament, you contemptible cur!" Vaiske roared. "You seek to kill the Behemoth and take the glory for yourself?"

Lament shook his head. "I came only for my shadow. The sooner we are rid of this creature the sooner we can end our duel."

Vaiske laughed mechanically, gazing at the easily balanced shadus.

"Well then," said the man-with-two-shadows, "help me up onto the shoulder and we shall tackle the head together."

Lament plunged the blade of the gargantuan sword into the more flesh-like skin between the collar-bone and neck. Viscous blood dripped from it and he struggled to hold onto the hilt; once more he found great help in the bandage-like cloth of on his palms.

He hung with his left arm from the sword and reached for Vaiske.

They were so entrenched in their concentration that neither noticed the

Behemoth swing a wild fist in frustration at the wall of the Coliseum, sending a colossal boulder hurtling over the Royal Box.

*

Grimoire saw it first. He pulled on the robe of Distance and they fell to the stone surface, narrowly avoiding the boulder. The archers around them were not so lucky and many were dragged over the wall with it. The Thean Generals looked at each other grimly as they realised it was headed for the retreating soldiers.

*

Arvan leant on Kyagorusu, oblivious to the dejected looking soldiers around them. That they could do nothing in a battle so significant was a source of great shame. Arvan felt it too, though he wasn't aware he was far from alone in the sentiment.

He walked with laboured steps in time with those around him. The metronome. The rhythm of defeat.

Kyagorusu was strangely silent. The boy had ceased to hear his words some time ago, and so he didn't speak. All there was on the winding road leading down the mountain was the chiming of the soldiers' armour and the intermittent shrieks of the Behemoth.

It was the ending of this that caused Kyagorusu to look back.

There was what sounded to him like an explosion, though muffled and stunted, yet for a time he saw nothing but the extensive stone of the Coliseum.

Then the boulder arched over the wall.

He pushed Arvan away.

Darkness.

*

Their hands met and Lament threw Vaiske onto the shoulder that the shadus once stood on. The immortal then pulled Lament up with him, the man in the crimson cape tearing his sword from the Behemoth as he left. The pressurized blood spurted, though the beast seemed not to notice.

The men looked to one another, emotionlessly, though Vaiske's face was hidden by the anguished mask. The thought came to both of them at the same time; here, on the shoulder of the Behemoth, in the diminished space, neither held an advantage. It was the perfect place to end their duel.

Lament swung his sword over his head, though Vaiske moved first; the tip of the spear catching the shadus in his left eye.

Lament lost his balance and tumbled from the Behemoth.

97

The black and crimson caught Captain Starling's eye against the grey of the mountain stone and the blue of the perfect sky. He immediately knew that it was Lament; the sword fell, end over end, beside him.

He gestured to Grimoire and Distance to launch another volley of fire arrows, though soon realised their unit was greatly depleted and even if a shadow was cast Lament may be unconscious. If he was, it was unlikely he could disappear into shadows.

Starling ran towards the falling shadus as swiftly as he could, his eyes never leaving Lament.

There was a muted sigh of the sand as the gargantuan sword landed blade first in the ground beside him, just missing the Captain. Though he didn't think of his fortune, only of Lament's imminent death. Still he ran on, wishing he was galloping towards the shadus on Titus.

Fire flew overhead once more, lessened but still large enough to cast a shadow of the Behemoth across the arena.

Lament vanished, then emerged lying down next to Starling.

The Captain knelt beside him. The shadus' left cheek was bloodied from the mangled wound to his left eye, though he was conscious. He rolled his good right eye towards the Captain, silhouetted against the sun.

"Thank you," Lament said. Then he allowed the pale eyelid to close and condemned himself to the world of darkness.

Vaiske took no time to bask in his victory over the shadus. Indeed, he thought him dead once already – that it should take two attempts brought a fury upon him the likes of which he had never known.

Instead, he readied himself to finish off the beast. If one stabbed it hard enough the skin could be pierced, that much had become clear. He decided that if he threw the spear through the temple of the creature he could destroy the brain, assuming the beast had a brain.

He fixed the temple in his sight and lined up the spear for the shot.

Flames of lustre swooped overhead and a trailing arrow caught Vaiske's arm. He kept hold of the spear, but was struck with enough force to be knocked off balance.

Once he had steadied himself he knew his chance had been ruined. The listless white eyes of the Behemoth were turning towards him and the far arm came up to swat him from the shoulder.

The impact winded him and he plummeted from his perch, crashing into the stone seats of the Coliseum. A cloud of dust from the destroyed architecture rose around him. He pulled himself to his feet, unharmed, though he lacked the resolve for a second attempt to kill the beast.

He watched, his will dissipating, as the Behemoth slunk away through the hole in the wall, the ground rumbling with each step.

*

Arvan was dragged from his self-pity by the trail of blood on the path where Kyagorusu had once stood. After crushing the harmless scholar the boulder had continued down the mountain, claiming the lives of the more inattentive soldiers.

He knelt by the blood, no body to mourn, and wept at the death of his new, though close, friend. He didn't look up, even when the Behemoth exited the Coliseum and skulked away, down the side of the mountain and into the ocean.

Chapter Thirteen

The next day they gathered in the Throne Room. The Great King seemed far healthier than his ailing appearance of days past. His skin held colour where before it was pale, his frail physique growing into that of a slender young man. He sat powerfully in his throne, a thin smile strewn across his face, his eyes bright as the sky of the spring morning.

The rest of the congregation stood sullenly, the defeat of the day before still playing heavily in their minds, save for Vaiske. Arvan looked to him. He stood strongly, his spear upright in his hand, refusing to wilt into the posture of a beaten man. What unknowable expression did he wear behind that horrific mask? Arvan didn't want to know and shivered as the image of Kyagorusu's blood, swept across the mountain path, entered his mind. He held the bald man's staff in his hands, lovingly.

Distance and Grimoire stood together, the older man wearing a stoical expression. However, the younger looked mournfully at Kyagorusu's staff, only to look away when Arvan looked to him for comfort in their shared sorrow. Distance glanced back and then bowed his head to look at the floor. Grimoire refused to look anywhere but at Eremmerus.

Starling stood alone to the far right of the room, taking a position between the Great King and the rest of the group. Eremmerus' rejuvenation seemed to have come at Captain's expense. His current appearance, despite still being perfectly dressed, reminded Arvan of Lament at his sickest. The heavy, dark rings beneath Starling's eyes suggested he was the only person in the room to have not slept that night. Arvan knew the reason for this.

After the battle they had found the body of Lieutenant Fernarl on the mountain path. He had been returning from placing the horses in the stable, so eager to help Captain Starling against the Behemoth that he left Flint to organise the troops and follow in a few minutes time, when the same boulder that had killed Kyagorusu came tumbling towards him. It had not crushed him, but the glancing blow had done irreparable damage to his skull and he bled to death in moments.

Starling looked to no man. Indeed, he seemed to look nowhere in the room. Arvan saw the gaze of a man forever discovering the death of his best-friend.

Laboured footsteps in a metronome beat sounded, climbing the steps towards the palace. They all turned to see Lament enter. The army doctors had worked over him for some time, but they couldn't save his eye. When he woke he removed the bandage they had placed over the empty socket and replaced the it with a rag torn from his already tattered cape. The doctors then proceeded to muse over his sickness but came to no conclusion; and so he was condemned to live in a half-blind mystery.

He stood beside Arvan, his gargantuan sword strapped to his back despite the protests of the guards outside. He folded his arms, his fingers wrapped around his biceps, and rolled his amber eye to Vaiske. In spite of the loss of his left eye, his scowl was not diminished. He didn't look away until the man-with-two-shadows shuddered.

Arvan looked to Kyagorusu's staff. Surrounded by people, yet the shaft of wood was the only company he had.

"Well, now that the shadus is here, or most of him at least, I'll begin," Eremmerus said. "Captain Starling; you knew that the Thean Generals were in the city; is that correct?"

"Yes, your majesty," Starling replied.

"'Your majesty'?" the Great King mused with a smile.

"I've not the mood or the energy for insubordination today."

"I'm glad to hear it." Eremmerus turned to Distance and Grimoire. "And I suppose you were here to kill me?"

"No, Great King," Grimoire said calmly. "We were here only to ascertain whether you had an army to go to war with. You did, however after the heavy losses you suffered yesterday, it could be some time before you have a force strong enough to trouble the continent."

"How true," Eremmerus said bitterly. He passed his eyes over all in the room. "I could execute all of you for treason. Indeed, I had planned to gather you here for that very reason. But, having looked upon you and seeing what a sorry company I've brought here before me, I've changed my mind. You look as if you'd enjoy death. No, I've decided to be cruel. I sentence you to live. You may all leave here with nothing to help you forget the events of yesterday. There is just one aspect of this that I demand be explained." He turned to Vaiske. "Why are you here?"

The man-with-two-shadows made no effort to avoid the question and denied himself the grandeur with which he usually spoke. He didn't move.

"I required an army large enough to attract the Behemoth."

All heads snapped towards him, though he said no more.

"Expand," the Great King said with a sly smile.

"I've tracked the Behemoth for many years. It started as a mere childish dream; Vaiske Parlet, the man who killed the Behemoth. Then I realised it wasn't childish at all. A more adult feat has never been accomplished, but that is unimportant.

"I soon learned its behavioural patterns. It roamed as any other beast, until it sensed something; then it would make for heavily populated areas where there was a large force of armed men. The beast abhors violence!

"This was my most significant discovery in many years of following it. Unfortunately, once I had made this conclusion, I lost the creature. I set about making a name for myself as a warrior, taking on vast numbers of warlord soldiers. But, every time I came across the beast I was severely injured, only just escaping with my life.

"I realised I required more research. It was at this point I discovered the secret of shadows." He turned to Lament. "I'm sure you'll all understand if I don't go into too much detail. I've got rather a lot to lose if the information got into the wrong hands."

"Of course," Eremmerus laughed. "We don't want to take all the sport out of it."

"Quite," Vaiske said in his metallic voice. "Needless to say, I stole the shadow of our friend Lament to ensure my immortality and set out to kill the Behemoth. The research of shadows had taken me many years and the warlord clans' numbers were depleted in the War of the Wastes." He turned to Eremmerus. "But yours were far greater. So I set out here, gained your trust and gathered the troops in the Coliseum as bait for the Behemoth. The Coliseum seemed a perfect place to fight the beast – an enclosed arena where it could not escape."

"Ingenious," Eremmerus said.

"Perhaps," Vaiske said. "If our friend Lament hadn't arrived I might have killed it. Or, it may have been the same outcome with greater damage to the city."

Eremmerus lost his smile. For a fleeting moment Arvan thought he saw the Great King recede into his former ailing self, only to regain his strength.

"I commend you for your efforts," he said to Vaiske. "However, your means have wrought upon me damage that may never be undone. The Coliseum and army both need rebuilding. I could execute you; yet how can I do so to an immortal? Besides, your actions have satiated my Blood Lust, for now at least. I suppose I should thank you, but you have, at best, redeemed yourself only to the point of no action."

Vaiske said nothing.

Eremmerus turned toward Distance and Grimoire. "Back to your lord, I assume?"

"Yes, Great King," Distance said. "As soon as we've the chance."

"All in good time, General." He looked at Lament, his sly smile returning. "And what about you shadus? Where do you go now?"

"I've yet to reclaim my shadow," Lament said. He turned to Vaiske and held out his right hand. "You have lost the Behemoth. There is no longer an army large enough to use as bait. Even if there was, you cannot defeat it. You've no use for my shadow anymore."

Vaiske laughed mechanically.

Lament took a step back, his hand falling to his side. He frowned with no less fervour than ever and snorted sharply.

"The Behemoth was here but yesterday, shadus," Vaiske said. "The trail is still fresh. I can find it and I still require your shadow."

Lament wrapped his right hand around the hilt of his sword.

"Wait," Vaiske said. "I've a proposition."

Lament did not remove his hand from the sword but he drew it no further. His eye never moved from Vaiske.

"The events of yesterday have taught me one thing; even I, the man-with-two-shadows, cannot defeat the Behemoth alone." Despite the mask obscuring his face, the foul air in the room suggested to them that Vaiske Parlet was smiling. "But if I had an accomplice; a pale, one eyed accomplice; I could do it. I could rid the land of the Behemoth."

Lament's hand left his sword and he crossed his arms. "I see no gain for me."

"Once the Behemoth is dead I shall return your shadow."

The face of the shadus remained as emotionless as ever, yet there seemed to Arvan to be a new pensiveness to him. For a time he didn't speak and even Eremmerus dared not displace the silence. Lament's eye closed and he only answered when it opened and fell upon Vaiske.

"I would add one more clause," he said.

"Let me hear it," Vaiske said warily.

"You must first help me rescue the man I set out to."

"Out of the question!"

"Then we have no deal and I shall reclaim my shadow now."

Lament went for his sword and Vaiske levelled his spear, though neither moved for an attack. Captain Starling stepped forward.

"What's wrong with you both?" he growled. "Have not enough died? Will you not stop until this entire city is painted and bathed in blood?"

Lament sighed and took a more passive stance, though Vaiske remained ready to attack for some time longer. It seemed to Arvan as if the anguished mask was grinning homicidally.

The boy looked to Lament. The brow of the shadus was littered with sweat and he was clearly suffering from the malady. Arvan couldn't accustom himself to the sight of the one eye. Since he met Lament he was amazed by that two amber irises that danced like flames around the eclipsed pupils.

"Lament," he said. "When Kyagorusu and I found you were you on your way to meet this man?"

Lament looked to Arvan and softened. He nodded in reply.

"You were in the Central Province then. Where is he? *Who* is he?"

Lament frowned and paused. He folded his arms and closed his eye.

"He's a prisoner in Pale Castle," he said. "A pirate of some repute."

"It couldn't be!" Eremmerus exclaimed.

Lament opened his eye and looked at the Great King.

"His name," the shadus said, "is Captain Lavette Swift."

Each member of the room tried to conceal their shock that Lament's friend in need would be someone so infamous, but Arvan noticed the few tell-tale signs that each exhibited. He felt somewhat ignorant he had to ask.

"Who's Captain Lavette Swift?"

"He's a thief, murderer… well, pick a crime and he's guilty of it," Distance said.

"He's the latest in the line of the Swifts," Grimoire said. "A pirate family who have plagued the world for more than a millennium. Surely you've heard of the notorious ship the Valhalla."

Arvan nodded. He'd heard some of the stories, all horrific. Some of which he wished Master Snow hadn't recounted.

"Who he is is irrelevant," Vaiske said. "We'd lose the trail if we were to save him."

"So you *don't* know," Eremmerus said. "My intelligence suggests that the Behemoth is headed towards the Southern Continent. Couldn't a pirate grant you passage on his ship?"

"You've a navy," Vaiske growled. "Couldn't you help us get there?"

Eremmerus smiled his usual sly smile. "I've only the one ship I'm willing to spare in the pursuit of the Behemoth." He turned to Captain Starling. "And I've already got plans for that."

Starling bowed his head but said nothing.

Vaiske tilted his head towards Lament. He clenched his fist until it shook, then released it.

"Very well, shadus," he said. "We shall rescue Swift, travel to the Southern Continent, kill the Behemoth and then I shall return your shadow to you."

The shadus nodded stiffly.

"I'll come too," Arvan said, looking at Kyagorusu's staff. "I've more than one person to avenge now."

Lament rolled his eye towards the boy. "You'd be wise to return home."

"Nonsense!" Vaiske roared. "The boy's more than welcome. You know as well as I do, shadus; we'll need someone to stop us slitting each other's throat in their sleep."

Lament looked mournfully at Arvan, but the stony faced youth met his gaze forcefully. The shadus shrugged as if to agree.

"So it's settled," Eremmerus said. "Now, leave me with Captain Starling. We've a mission to discuss."

"Don't go too far," Starling said. "I would grant you all a fitting goodbye that my current situation wouldn't allow."

With that, they wordlessly left the Throne Room. A federation of different motives, forced together for the near future, at least. Grimoire and Distance walked beside them, glad in the knowledge that the Behemoth was not *their* quarry.

They waited for Captain Starling at the bottom of the palace steps. Arvan sat with Kyagorusu's staff resting on his shoulder as the bald man so often had. That the wooden stick was all in the world that was left of him was unjust and had led Arvan to the decision of returning it to Kyagorusu's hometown on the Southern Continent. Whether he would do this before or after felling the Behemoth he supposed would be determined by Vaiske or Lament.

Lament leaned coldly on a nearby wall, his eye pointed skywards as if he was studying the forever arching sun or conversing with the endless blue. Neither would have surprised Arvan after the revelation of the shadows. The boy's eyes fell to the ground around the shadus, the light still unhindered by his frame.

Vaiske stood typically sternly. His head never moved from facing the shadus as if he still didn't trust him. Arvan sighed. What threat could Lament possibly pose to an immortal?

Distance and Grimoire sat a few steps up from Arvan whispering to one another. They spoke too quietly for the boy to hear what was being said but their voices held ominous tones.

Arvan thought back to a simpler time when he knew of none of this. Master Snow's death, Kyagorusu's death, the plotting of Eremmerus, the battles of immortals and stolen shadows; all of this was still very new to him. It wasn't so many days ago that he lived a normal life with Darkla and Mirr in Farras. He found himself thinking of them more with Kyagorusu's staff in his hand. Perhaps Lament was right; Arvan should go home, but he had a duty to the fallen and it was one he could not shirk, nor would he wish to.

Eventually, the distinct clicking of Captain Starling's boots sounded and he could be seen descending the myriad of steps with another man. The second man had neat brown hair and was slightly shorter than the Captain. He wore the same black uniform that Lieutenant Fernarl once wore, though on him it lacked the stern ambiance of Fernarl.

"Sorry to keep you waiting," Starling said as they neared the group. Arvan was shocked to see him smiling. "This is my new Lieutenant, Airn Arnamous." He grasped the new Lieutenant lovingly on the shoulder. "He's a worthy successor to Lieutenant Fernarl, or as worthy as any man could be, and he's already grown use to calling me 'Lind'."

"It's a very exciting moment for me," Airn said, revealing his deep, though friendly, voice. "The exploits of Lind are notorious. To know that I shall be an accomplice in future ones is a source of great pride for me."

Starling's smile took on a sullen curl.

"Unfortunately, that exploit looks to be rather more perilous than we had hoped," he said. "Airn, ready the troops to board the Mjölnir. I've some small business to attend to."

"Gladly, Lind," the Lieutenant said. He saluted and left.

"A good man," Grimoire said.

"Rather too dutiful," Distance said. "He'll mature into a fine Lieutenant."

"He's mature enough," Starling said. "He's older than me at least, though he's still too young for what Eremmerus wants of us."

"What do you mean?" Arvan asked.

Starling sighed. "The Great King has put us in direct competition with you. He's sent the Great King's Cavalry to claim the Behemoth in the name of the Final Resting Place of the Empire. We're to leave immediately."

Vaiske laughed in his usual mechanical fashion.

"You can have as much of a head-start as you wish," he said. "You'll not kill the Behemoth with that force."

"Perhaps not," Starling said, shuddering. "Yet, orders are orders. It's just another mission Eremmerus doesn't expect me to live through, but I shall. I always do."

His voice took on a melancholic tone with this last claim that made Arvan shiver. He tightened his grip on the staff for comfort but the wood was cold in his hands.

"Anyway," Starling said, in a tone more like his usual amiable self. "I've come to wish you all luck and bid you a fond goodbye. I don't know most of you as well as I'd like and I know some of you better than I'd wish." He looked at Vaiske. "But, as we now depart, I've a present for each of you that will aid you in your quest to come. Follow me, please."

He led them through the labyrinthine city with his usual ease. It occurred to Arvan that the Captain walked as impressively as he rode a horse. The pace was singularly undemanding, yet they were far from the palace faster than they had any right to be. His boots clicked a rhythm that Arvan found himself walking in, absent-mindedly. The Captain swung his left arm as listlessly as any other man, though his right hand never left his belt buckle.

Arvan looked around him to find that only Lament was walking in a different time to the Captain. It was only now he realised that the shadus didn't so much walk as prowl, like a feral beast perpetually stalking a distant and invisible prey. They boy imagined that there was so much idiosyncratic about Lament that it was only fitting he should walk in his own beat. How Arvan hadn't been aware of the movement before he couldn't be sure, though he supposed he hadn't travelled particularly far with Lament. After all, he and the shadus were often split up.

It wasn't long before Arvan recognised his surroundings. They were near the mountain upon which Starling had his quarters. They entered a building of the same stone as the rest of the city, though it was a little larger than the others. It was a stable, though it didn't smell like one. The hay bales were neatly stacked and the floor had been mopped recently. Arvan didn't think he'd ever seen a place where animals were kept in that was so clean.

"I don't hold with keeping horses in filth," Starling said, noticing Arvan's expression. "Especially not one I'll have to ride."

He walked over and stroked Titus, the grey horse moaning with pleasure at his touch. The Captain turned and leaned on the door of the paddock.

"There are your presents," Starling said, gesturing to the other side of the stable. The group turned and saw five horses gazing obediently out. Starling walked to the horses and stroked a grey mare.

"This is Vanel," he said. "Titus' sister. Take extremely good care of her." He stroked her mane lovingly. "She was Lieutenant Fernarl's." He seemed to become trapped in this final sentence and Arvan saw he wore the same haggard expression he did in the throne room. He let go of Vanel and turned to the group once more. "You're welcome to all five; we keep them in reserve, though they're all near the end of their service now, save for Vanel and this beauty." He rested his hand on the head of a magnificent golden appaloosa. "Her name's Seln; too young to ride with us, to do what we must do."

Arvan noticed the other three were every bit as elegant and wonderful as Vanel and Seln. One was a great beast with hair of the purest black, the other two a deep brown.

"These are the brothers," Starling said. "Wander and Far. We never named the other. The men took, somewhat ironically, to calling him 'Nameless'. You're welcome to them for as long as you need them. Once you're finished with them they'll have no trouble finding their own way back home."

With that last word Starling seemed not to be in the stable with them at all as he gazed longingly outside. His eyes glazed over and titillated between his lids. Eventually he came around and sighed, taking to leading Titus out of the paddock and dressing him.

"I wish I could do more," he said. "But I'm not in much of a position to."

Once he had strapped the black leather saddle on Titus, he mounted.

"Well farewell," he said to the group. "The best of luck to you all. If I should happen upon any of you again, I'll wish it once more."

"Thank you, Lind," Arvan said. "You've done more than you know."

Lament nodded. "By all rights I wish you were to come with us. If it was not for you I would not have escaped from the battle with the Behemoth so lightly." He pointed to the rag over his left eye.

"It was an honour to battle in your presence," Grimoire said, bowing.

"We thank you for everything," Distance said, matching the older General's bow.

Starling smiled and looked to Vaiske, but the immortal said nothing. The Captain rode wordlessly from the stable, smile forever widening.

Grimoire turned to Lament. "We'll ride with you some of the way, if it is to your liking."

Lament nodded.

"Since when are you the leader, shadus?" Vaiske growled.

"Is your decision different, Vaiske?" Lament replied.

Yet, Arvan heard none of this. He merely watched the disappearing visage of the Captain astride Titus.

*

He sighed as he left the dark of the mountain tunnel and Titus' hooves met the wood of the dock. The sun fell on him gloriously, finally exuding the heat that had eluded his recognition for what seemed an eternity. The sky was a lighter blue than Starling could ever remember seeing, not even a hint of a cloud transpiring to ruin the perfection. The sea whispered either side of him, only obscured by the clicking of Titus' hooves and the readying of the warship Mjölnir.

So spring had finally begun.

When he saw Lieutenant Arnamous waiting for him on foot, a small mass of black in the otherwise bright day, he forced a smile.

"The men are all aboard, Lind," Arnamous said. "We were just waiting for the Navy captain, an able man named Ere, to give us the all clear. And you, of course."

"Excellent work, Airn," Starling said, looking to the ship. It was a perfect specimen of woodwork, with a multitude of cannons and cannon-holds. "Now, come. With each moment the Behemoth gets further from us."

*

They rode into the Wastes that night, after a day of needed rest. The city lay grimly still behind them and the breeze was thick. Lament led them on the nameless black horse, his crimson cape fluttering as he galloped into the night. Vaiske rode just behind, trying to overtake on Vanel, though the horse seemed to find the idea distasteful. Grimoire and Distance followed on the brown brothers, their white robes shining with the light of the moon.

Arvan followed. He hadn't ridden a horse alone before but the appaloosa, Seln, seemed not to need an awful lot of direction. The boy was grateful for it, though what was to come still lay heavily on his mind. Though not as heavily as what had already happened.

Chapter Fourteen

The miasmic breeze did nothing to assuage Lament's nausea. The coagulated air slipped viscously down his throat and clung to the sides of his lungs. It sat cumbersomely inside of him and he struggled to find relief. As they rode on he found the breeze getting thicker and shuffled uneasily in the saddle. Looking around he saw the Thean Generals and Arvan felt it too. Their breathing was as laboured as his, their faces a similar image of discomfort. If the immortal Vaiske shared in their worry he made no sign of it, or the sign never managed to crawl past his mask.

Eventually they came to the source of their unease. The nameless horse shied a little and Lament let it stop. The rest of the group gathered around him.

"What is it?" Grimoire asked.

It was only then Lament realised, even with the loss of his eye, his sight was still superior to that of his companions. The other horses were rather less nervous than his and he knew Nameless had not seen what he had, but sensed his rider's tension. He calmed himself and Nameless calmed with him.

"The breeze is uncomfortably thick here," Distance said.

"You see something," Arvan said. "Don't you, Lament?"

Lament nodded.

"What?" Vaiske asked suspiciously.

"I don't have the words for it," the shadus replied. "But you'll see soon enough. Then you'll wish you hadn't."

He rode on, far slower this time, in no rush to see the horror before him with any greater clarity. The breeze wrapped around him and, even with that oh-so familiar presence on it, he had to fight the urge to shudder. He heard the hooves of the others behind him, matching his sluggish speed.

Soon, they too saw it.

A vista of corpses, strewn across the arid land of the Wastes. An arm here, another limb, indistinguishable and deformed in death, there. Few of the bodies were complete, and those that were had begun to decompose; their wounds moving and alive with maggots and other more invisible beings who insisted to feed upon the flesh. The grey ground was discoloured with blood, dried and cracked; as an artist's abstract canvas, morbid and unending.

Nameless wished to go no further and tried to turn himself, but Lament righted him and rode him slowly on. He stroked the night black horse to calm him.

The horses trod carefully, their hooves meeting the crimson land and not the bodies of the men. But so complete was the littering of the bodies on the ground that Seln met a lone arm. She reared up, screaming into the night and the company halted but, before anyone could move to help the boy, Arvan rested her with a gentle stroke.

"It's okay," he whispered as he hugged her neck. "I'm terrified too."

Once Arvan looked up, Lament saw the boy had tears in his eyes. The shadus thought he was probably thinking of Kyagorusu and sighed.

"Captain Starling did this," Arvan said weakly. "Didn't he?"

Nobody replied but Lament knew the corpses belonged to the warlord clan that had chased Arvan and Kyagorusu into the Wastes. It was hard to believe the peaceful, mild-mannered, Captain Starling, along with the men under his command, created a scene of such repugnance. Yet, here it was.

"We should ride faster," Vaiske said, the mask giving his voice its usual metallic resonance.

"Pace will do us no good here," Distance said. "We've been lucky to have so few wrongly placed feet as it is."

Grimoire nodded and Lament rode on.

It was the warmest night of the year so far, though Lament felt cold in his bones; yet to expel the chill of the long winter. Or perhaps it was just his illness. He looked to Vaiske, the faint outline of the shadow that was once his was cast by the moon. Lament had noticed that it was unimportant which angle the light source was at; the shadow was always there, even at noon. He imagined it was even cast in total darkness, it was just unseen.

His thoughts returned to his horrific surroundings as he remembered the shadow was travelling over the bodies of dead men. He sighed and, with no other choice, rode on.

The moon caught the blood and lifeless faces as if in some haunting ethereal dream. Unbeknownst to him, Lament increased his horse's pace.

*

The sky was paling to violet by the time they passed the corpses and the end of the Wastes was on the horizon. Lament had thought to break into a gallop when the ground before them was clear but, now the situation had arisen, he found he could not bring himself to do so. The macabre landscape had destroyed his resolve and a distinct weariness had come upon him. Though, they all breathed easier, except Vaiske who needed not be encumbered with thoughts of mortality.

"Soon we shall see no more sights as that," the immortal said, his voice tender despite his mask.

"You believe killing the Behemoth will end all war?" Grimoire asked.

"No. But it will give Eremmerus, or someone else, the freedom to rebuild his army and unite the land."

"And should Eremmerus be unable to defeat all of the warlords?" Distance suggested.

Vaiske laughed listlessly and turned in his saddle so that the hideous mask, eyes bulging, mouth slung open in some gasp of horrific pain, faced the Thean Generals.

"Then I shall have to do it myself," he said.

"That is your age of peace?" Lament asked. "An all-out war?"

"A war with an outcome!" Vaiske roared. "Surely that is preferable to this endless conflict in which no progress is made."

"And should you be opposed?" Lament asked. "What would you do – kill everyone until there is only you left?"

Vaiske said nothing.

"Well," Lament said. "I suppose you would have your peace then."

Despite the heated nature of the argument, Arvan was aware that Lament's voice never rose above that plaguing whisper. How the shadus was calm, emotionless, at all times was a source of unending wonder to the boy. There was something, an aspect of Lament's being, that Arvan loathed to recognise but could never draw his attention from, that, in spite of all his morality and his sense of duty, was distinctly inhuman. He showed no love for any man or being and threw his body into danger as if death was nothing more than a new horizon awaiting exploration. Yet, there was a look in which his expression didn't change, nor did any other aspect of his demeanour, as if he was being embraced by the breeze. And it was so this loveless, inhuman entity maintained some fragment of humanity.

As if to distract himself from these unthinkable thoughts, Arvan moved to turn in the saddle and get one last look at the Wastes before they passed into the plains of the West Lands. He was stopped by Grimoire grabbing his robe.

"You don't want to see that again, Arvan," he said.

But Arvan acknowledged there was a part of him that did want to see it again, only from a different perspective. Still, he did not look back. He instead nodded, the near-colourless eyes of Grimoire meeting his. The General didn't look away until the desire to look back had entirely dissipated from the boy.

Arvan felt it leave him, like some malevolent sigh forcing itself from his chest as if only to let him know it dwelt within him. He slumped in his saddle and looked at Grimoire who glanced at him.

"How did you know?" Arvan asked.

"I was once a young man, too," Grimoire replied. "I thought to accustom myself to horrors I would once again see, when I was stopped."

"By who?"

"One I would get to know far better," Grimoire said with a smile. "A mere child at the time, and I do mean child. It wasn't wisdom that made him stop me though. He *had* looked back. It was the wish that nobody would see what he had seen if he could prevent it."

"What was his name?"

Grimoire's smile changed slightly, though Arvan couldn't quite comprehend what was different about it.

"Lawliet Snow."

Arvan said nothing and moved his gaze to the blonde mane of Seln.

"Of course," Grimoire continued, "together we saw many more sights such as that, worse even; until our fear of looking back was so great that we left battlefields with our eyes closed. And now I am an old man and he was no longer young when he was taken. Still, if I had to see those sights, indeed, *cause* those sights, then there are few I would have rather had at my side."

"It seems strange to think he's gone," Distance said mournfully.

"And with so many battles lying before us," Grimoire added. "It's somewhat of a mystery to me, but I have few memories of Lawliet that were not of battles and still every memory I have of him is a fond one."

Distance nodded in agreement but said nothing.

"I sometimes feel as if I'm in a different world," Arvan said, still staring at Seln's mane, his voice filled with sorrow. "I never considered that he would die. I still struggle with the thought that he has." He looked at Kyagorusu's staff in the saddle-scabbard and sighed. "Though that seems common to me of late."

If either of the Generals said anything to comfort him, he didn't hear them as his mind was loud with thoughts, and he had no desire to hear words of meaningless solace.

Lament led on wordlessly, Vaiske followed not far behind. They passed into the plains of the West Lands under a dawn that came earlier than any of them had expected.

With the light of the day came the dew of the grass beneath, a whisper that although spring had finally arrived, winter was still somewhat averse to fully relinquish its hold on the Northern Continent. As if to assert this, Arvan noticed just how weak the light of the sun was; no light at all, more like a different kind of darkness. Still, the sun brought some warmth with it.

They rode on slowly, the horses growing ever wearier. Soon however, before the day broke fully into true morning, they reached a place all too familiar to Arvan; though it was slightly different in the light of the day.

The trees still circled around, creating a small clearing between themselves and the lake. The water reflected the pure white orb, now gracefully risen into the powdered blue sky, still dappled with thin clouds lazily strewn across the heavens. Arvan gazed, still astride Seln, watching the water flow from the lake and cascade into the river. The last time he was there he hadn't had the time to wonder at the sheer size of the lake.

"Arvan," Distance said, tearing the boy from his reverie. Arvan saw everyone else had dismounted and Distance was holding the reigns of the horses, including Seln. "I'm take the horses to drink. You should rest."

Arvan nodded and dismounted, taking Kyagorusu's staff with him. He held it, lovingly as ever, and looked to the west bank where he and Kyagorusu had engineered their escape. A lone cherry blossom tree stood, surrounded by trees of green, the blossoms now reaching full bloom. The boy sighed; how unjust it was that his friend should not live to see the spring they had all waited so long for.

The clearing held no sign that the warlord clan had ever camped there, had it not been so ingrained in Arvan's memory he wouldn't have known himself. And so that was all that was left of the men who had tried to kill him; memories, corpses and the souls that clogged the already too-thick breeze.

Arvan's legs enfeebled and he allowed himself to sit on the soft grass, Kyagorusu's staff still gripped firmly. He wished the men no ill and knew that the bald traveller certainly hadn't. Times were difficult and men resorted to whatever means they had to in order to survive and feed their families. He thought of it often, it was no different in Farras. How many men had left to join Lord Riit? He couldn't count all of them, but they certainly outnumbered the few who stayed to starve. But this age of fruitless war would never end if something wasn't done.

It was only then he realised how hungry he was. His stomach growled but, looking around, he saw that nobody seemed to have brought any provisions with them. He had never gone hungry with Kyagorusu, or at least not for long. He lay down, clutching at his empty stomach, and fell into an unintended, dreamless sleep.

Lament looked to the sleeping boy, the staff of the dead man cradled in his young arms. The shadus tried to move the gaze of his eye to a less moribund view, the radiant lake only a tilt of his head away, but he couldn't. He felt as if it was his duty to acknowledge the sorrow of the boy, though interaction and comfort were two aspects of his being that he knew were somewhat lacking.

Vaiske stepped before him and Lament's gaze fell to his stolen shadow.

"Why have we stopped?" the immortal growled.

Lament met his look. "The horses are tired."

"Then what's the use of them? I could travel faster without them; *I* need no rest."

"You forget you travel with mortals. We cannot all share your perfection."

Vaiske snarled behind his mask and Lament took the time of silence to look at Arvan.

"We shouldn't have taken the boy," he said.

"Nonsense," Vaiske replied. "He's another sword. Besides, you mean to tell me you had no dreams of adventure when you were his age?"

Lament studied the face of the boy. How old was he? Young, though on the verge of manhood. Not so much longer than the shadus, though exuberant with a wealth more of youth.

Lament glanced impotently at Vaiske, then walked to the line of the trees, his cape trailing wearily behind. "None so grave as this."

The horses knelt, lapping up the water that ebbed towards their feet. Distance stroked the mane of Wander and looked out to the meandering river. He heard footsteps and Grimoire appeared beside him.

"Once we've rested we should head for the port alone," he said. "I don't want to get too close to Pale Castle; Lord Riit may see it as an act of war."

Distance nodded. "It's a distasteful place anyway."

Silence overcame them and they listened to the gentle tide of the lake – a reluctant movement as if all the water had ever desired was to be still.

"Grim?" Distance said after some time.

"Yes, Distance?"

"Do you think they can kill the Behemoth?"

The younger general turned to Grimoire and the older man was forced to look into Distance's dark eyes, a slight frown framing them.

"Do you fear that they will or won't?" Grimoire asked, his rough voice taking on a gentler tone.

"Neither," Distance sighed. "Whatever happens we have too many battles to come."

"Then what?"

Distance turned and looked to Arvan. Grimoire followed his gaze as Distance gestured with a nod.

"It doesn't seem right that the boy should have to die in a fruitless pursuit," Distance said.

"I'm more concerned about the company he's in." Grimoire said. "A bloodthirsty shadow-thief and a shadus I can't quite decipher. Not to mention a pirate soon to join."

"If they were men of valour they would leave him here while he slept."

"That would do no good," Grimoire said, smiling weakly. "He's Lawliet's student and adventure cannot be denied."

Distance turned back to the older general. "You know, you still haven't answered my question."

"I haven't?" Grimoire said, imitating a contemplative frown. "Forgive me, I'm an old man now, Distance. What was it you asked?"

Grimoire could keep up his pretence no longer and smiled. The sight of the older general's smile pulled on Distance's own mouth and the infectious smile appeared on him too.

"It doesn't matter," he said. "You wouldn't answer it anyway."

Arvan was woken by his hunger, almost nauseating in its intensity. The horses were now grazing freely in the clearing, though his companions, save for Vaiske, didn't seem ready to leave. Distance and Grimoire were talking by the lake, and Lament was nowhere to be seen. Arvan tried to return to sleep but, so ravaging was his hunger, he rose and walked to the lake, taking up water in cups made by his hands and sipping at the refreshing clear liquid.

Distance and Grimoire stopped talking and looked at him.

"How long was I asleep?" he asked, turning to them.

"Not long enough," Grimoire said.

Arvan didn't reply. He had caught a glimpse of himself in the lake, his rippled reflection not nearly distorted enough. He looked haggard, gaunt, his skin hanging poorly from his stony features. Dark rings lined his eyes. He touched at the meagre stubble that had grown the past week and he found he was slightly disappointed that his beard was not more impressive. He smiled.

"Maybe I am still spring," he whispered.

"Finally," Distance said. "A smile."

"It isn't an adventure without a few along the way," Grimoire said.

Arvan looked at them, his smile widening. "I wouldn't be so surprised. I'm not Lament, you know."

Grimoire chuckled in a way the boy hadn't expected from a man with the surname 'Groan'. Distance, conversely, merely let his smile grow.

"We've not the time for laughter," a metallic voice said behind them. They turned and saw Vaiske, mounted, spear in his hand. "Each second we rest, the Behemoth gets further away. We've already lost time with this damnable detour to save a pirate."

"You're welcome to leave whenever you wish," Grimoire said. "We've no wish to go to Pale Castle."

"You're not joining us?" Arvan asked, standing.

"I wouldn't go to Pale Castle to save anyone," Distance said. "Least of all a pirate. Perhaps if Grimoire was a prisoner, I'd attempt it, but even then I'd take a few thousand men with me."

"Even that would be brave of you," Grimoire said. "Besides Swift's been a prisoner there for two years now, or so I hear, awaiting execution. There's nothing to say he hasn't already been executed or gone insane from his impending mortality. No, we return to Lord Thean as soon as we've rested."

"I suppose that's for the best," Vaiske said. "I don't need all of you slowing me down. Now, where's that accursed shadus?"

It rushed from him, compressing all inside of him and wrenching the muscles of his stomach. Lament knelt, hunched over by a tree, grasping the trunk for support, and continued to vomit. It burned his gullet and throat, expelling itself violently, threatening never to stop, but, eventually, it had all left him. He spat the remnants in his mouth away but was left with the taste; bitter, acidic, a scent of burning flesh.

He pushed himself away and sat for a while, clutching at his screaming abdomen. He tried not to look at the liquid expulsions, though his eye soon fell upon it. He hadn't eaten in some many days and the puddle was perfectly smooth, a colour he couldn't describe. He supposed it was akin to grey, though somewhat more insipid, too filthy to be white.

He retched once more and turned away, his throat still burning, his gag reflex straining the tendons in his neck.

It had been a long while since the affliction had manifested itself with such vehemence, as if to remind the shadus of its power over him, warning him not to become blasé. Had he learned? His worsening fever was lesson enough, his clothes already drenched with sweat, clinging to him like the coagulated breeze of the Wastes. He shivered in opposition to the warmth of the day, the cold emanating from somewhere within him.

He decided to sit there until it passed. After all, it was the entire reason he had halted the company there.

His sword lay inertly beside him to his left, though he couldn't see it. He scratched at the cloth as if it was obstructing his sight, though removal would not improve his vision in the least. And to think he had once been so proud of his eyesight.

It was almost noon as Lament prowled from the trees and joined the rest of the group.

"Lament, you inconsiderate wretch!" Vaiske roared. "We've been waiting!"

Lament gave the immortal a one-eye glare. He was still astride Vanel, his spear perpetually ready for battle in his hand.

"We should spend the remainder of the day here," Lament said.

"Your laziness has already allowed the Behemoth to distance itself from us!" Vaiske said, gesturing wildly with his spear. "By the time we rescue that blasted pirate the scent may have gone completely cold."

"If you're still worried about me," Arvan said from atop Seln, "you needn't. I've rested now and I'm ready to continue."

Distance handed Lament the reigns of Nameless and the Thean Generals mounted. Wordlessly, Lament did the same. Vaiske led them east out of the clearing and the Thean Generals began to turn away.

"This is where we part," Grimoire said.

"Farewell," Arvan said.

Lament nodded in a silent goodbye, though Vaiske continued to ride on.

"I wish you all luck," Grimoire continued. "But yours is not our path." He turned to Arvan. "Remember, you've done Lawliet proud just to have come this far; don't feel as though you need to do more."

"Yes," Distance said. "If you were my student the you would already have surpassed my expectations of you."

Arvan smiled in polite agreement, though he said nothing more. The Thean Generals shared a grave look, then turned and began to follow the river south at a leisurely pace.

Before they were even out of sight, Vaiske was uncomfortably far ahead, but Arvan continued to watch the disappearing generals.

"Come," Lament said, causing Arvan to turn to the one-eyed shadus. "Vaiske will get too far ahead. I'm sure you'll see them again."

They turned and went after the immortal, once more into the Rock Flats.

Chapter Fifteen

The clouds, once a light dappling across the endless blue, grew bloated and grey, billowing into deformed visages, ominous and tormenting. At first the rain that fell was light, a mere sprinkling of water as if the clouds wished only for the return of the morning dew. But, gradually, it fell harder and more fervently, so complete as to fall almost as a sheet. It fell passively onto the clogging ground beneath the horses, each drop exploding upon impact and creating a thousand more infinitesimal beads of water.

Soon the thunder came, voracious, only knowable for its forcing itself above the din of the plummeting rain. Sheet lightning flashed, outlining the individual clouds an apocalyptic silver. If the storm would ever stop, it showed no sign of it.

The hooves of the horses crashed into the wet ground, sending up splashes of water the dirt could no longer hold. The force of each pummelling step climbed the beasts' legs and assaulted their riders, shaking them in the saddles, pounding their internal organs with unwanted and uncomfortable movement.

Arvan's hair was lank with dampness, falling before his eyes. He had to blow it from view every few seconds to ensure Seln was not straying from the route Vaiske, a vermillion figure obscured by the storm, was setting. His robe clung to him irritatingly. Every so often he would remove a hand from the reigns and tug at the garment to end its determined grip on his skin, only for it to fall into its cloying place once more a few seconds later.

The rain drummed on Vaiske's helmet, now so hard that he could hear nothing else save for the ravenous thunder roaring incessantly. Even he, an immortal, was plagued by the pulverizing force of the rain on his lacquered armour, the very resistance a detriment.

"Spring, eh?" he said, only able to hear his own words for them echoing behind his mask and around his helmet. This was his world, all in the parameters of the wrought metal, and even nature could not steal that away from him.

The vista lying before Vaiske was as abhorrent as what he led Lament and Arvan through currently. The clouds showed ignorance of any such event as an ending and spiralled into a fathomless distance, rain plunging violently towards the earth all the way. The grass, drowning in filthy water, continued on forevermore to his sight. Lament, however, could see further.

The one amber eye of the shadus pierced through the barriers of range, and further than the plain they traversed, into a land he would rather have not seen. The Rock Flats lay forebodingly, spanning on for an eternity as soon as they had begun.

Lament sighed and shifted in the moist saddle, no comfort to be found in any position. After all, the visceral movements of Nameless beneath him would only cause him to slip. He encouraged the horse on, trying to draw even with Vaiske. Rain fell against him, washing his fever induced sweat away, though the sickness remained and, with this unending dampness, would likely worsen. He often wondered if he would reach Pale Castle.

Eventually Vaiske stopped and turned to the shadus and Arvan. The boy thought the rain made him look like some murderous horned demon, crawled from the depths of a long forgotten underworld.

"You seem apprehensive, shadus," Vaiske said in his usual metallic voice.

"The Rock Flats lie ahead," Lament replied. "I've no fond memories of that place."

"Were it not for your damnable pirate I wouldn't venture into that place either, but needs must."

Arvan took on a distasteful frown and tried to hide it from Vaiske, but still the immortal caught it. "Something wrong, boy?"

"Nothing much," Arvan said, still frowning. "Only, you almost had an air of humility about you then."

Vaiske grunted and sneered behind his mask and then turned Vanel into the Rock Flats.

Lament glanced at Arvan. "I'd advise you against antagonising Vaiske."

"But he's with us," Arvan said. "Isn't he?"

"For now. Yet I see *it* in him."

"'It'?"

Lament looked after Vaiske, galloping away, then rolled his eye back towards Arvan. "The Blood Lust."

Lament gestured with his head and they rode after Vaiske.

Until a few days ago, Arvan had never heard of the Blood Lust, now it seemed a regular topic of conversation. Truth be told, he still wasn't entirely sure what it was.

"Lament," he said. "What *is* the Blood Lust?"

The shadus rolled the amber eye towards him, the sight of the red cloth over the left socket still new to Arvan.

"I fear I'm not the best person to explain it," he said. "General Groan or General Valentine probably have a better knowledge of it, though I suppose you can't ask them now.

"As I understand it, when someone is forced to kill, they can go one of two ways. The first is to grow a distinct hatred of battle and all that goes with it. The second; to fall in love with the killing and death, to the point that one becomes completely dependent on it. That is the Blood Lust. The craving of battle, the joy of the kill. If one suffering from it should go too long without satiating the Blood Lust they would grow weak and ill."

"Like Eremmerus," Arvan said.

Lament nodded firmly.

Arvan thought for a time how many people Master Snow must have killed and how he had hated all conflict. Never could a man be said to have had less of the Blood Lust. If his path was to be the same he hoped to grow weary of battle too, yet it still held some allure. General Groan and General Valentine seemed similarly inclined to avoid bloodshed. Then he looked to Kyagorusu's staff, the peace-loving scholar entering his mind. He sighed. Unfortunately, it seemed those lacking the Blood Lust didn't survive the battles.

"Lament," Arvan said quietly, barely audible over the rain. "Why don't you have the Blood Lust?"

"That's a story I'd rather not recount," the shadus replied quickly. "Come, Vaiske's getting too far ahead."

Lament urged Nameless on and Arvan followed. Soon, they drew level with Vaiske.

If the noise of the rain falling on the plains was deafening, the din of the rain bursting on the hard surface of the Rock Flats threatened to break their bones. Still, Vaiske rode hard, forcing Lament and Arvan to do the same.

On the land of grey stretched before them, only punctuated by the unknowably black storm-clouds overhead. From the dirge-ridden heavens stabbed a colossal trident of golden lightning meeting the stone ground some small distance ahead of the group, the assault dispersing the lightning into pathetic sparks, though the air took on a moist, burnt scent.

The travellers passed the point of contact wordlessly. The storm's wrath had burned an obsidian black, uneven, six-pointed star into the Rock Flats, the land's injury spreading in a perimeter greater than the span of ten outstretched men. Arvan looked in wonder but did not stop to survey it in it in any more detail.

The day seeped forth into the late afternoon and still the storm was unrelenting. Soon, evening came upon them, though they only had evidence of this due to the day becoming darker yet – there was no sun to be seen. What perdition was this?

Eventually it became so dark that Lament led his companions, blinded save for when the lighting lurched from the shadows. He slowed the pace of the company to that of an idle walk, out of the fear that galloping would merely lose them in the eternal black. He'd turn in saddle every-so-often to ensure that Vaiske and Arvan were still there; they were, though Arvan trailed behind. Lament sighed. The boy was slowing them down.

Arvan slumped in his saddle, exhausted. His stomach cried with unending hunger and wondered how long he would have to suffer. He could feel Seln withering beneath him, but knew that any suggestion to stop would be ignored or unheard. The only time he had felt so helpless with Kyagorusu was when they were being chased by the warlord clan, and that seemed an eternity ago.

He looked to the staff in the saddle scabbard. Already Kyagorusu's face was beginning to fade from his memory. The bald man's features were lineless, taking vague shapes in his mind. He remembered his way more than anything, all else was something of an ambiguity.

Even Master Snow was passing from his memory; his face nearly featureless now. All of his appearance the boy recalled was the white robe and the dishevelled brown hair.

He sobbed silently, masked by the rain and the thunder. Two men who had sought to teach him the ways of life were dead and he could barely picture their faces.

Arvan forced himself to sit upright and rallied himself; he'd had his time to mourn and could do so no longer. He blew his lank, wet hair from his eyes and caught sight of Vaiske, or at least the demonic outline of the immortal. The horned effigy sat majestically in the saddle, his right arm hanging strongly by his side, spear in hand. He was always ready for battle, and what glorious battle he did. Arvan thought back to Vaiske's duel with Lament in the Coliseum. The immortal had shown unparalleled skill. He loathed admitting it, but he imagined the man-with-two-shadows even surpassed Master Snow. And what use he aimed to put that ability to.

The rain ceased.

Lament halted the company and turned. Arvan and Vaiske grouped together, the man-with-two-shadows gazing up at the sky, the boy looking to the immortal. The clouds began to part, revealing the full moon. The benevolent figure oozed an insipid light, catching Vaiske's masking, making his ghostly appearance even more haunting than usual.

"Rather unceremonious," Vaiske said, levelling his head and looking at Lament.

"Is it not just the eye of the storm?" Arvan said.

Vaiske turned Vanel to face the boy.

"No," he replied in that same metallic voice. "It's over. You can rest assured in that."

"Come," Lament said, shuffling uneasily atop Nameless. "We've been here longer than any sane man could ever care to."

"Easy, shadus," Vaiske said, turning to him. "We're in no danger. Perhaps we should allow the horses to gather their breath."

The breeze rolled by and Lament shivered. It held him lovingly, swirling gently around, though the presence felt all too close to be comforting. Vaiske observed as the shadus seemed to squirm at the touch of it; his brow sodden with sweat, his skin so pale to rival the eerie light of the moon. He held the reigns of Nameless limply but warily, close to his abdomen as if in fear of his hands straying too far from his ever-empty stomach. He was slouched as Vaiske had never seen him. It occurred to the immortal that Lament looked long dead already.

"Does your mortality feel close, shadus?" Vaiske said, so quietly he could have been talking to himself. "Does the breeze call you?"

Lament's eye fell upon him.

Vaiske's second shadow flickered.

"No!" he roared. "Not now!"

The shadow lurched away and pulled the immortal from his horse. He fell to the hard ground with a heavy thud, barely holding onto his spear with the shock.

Lament tore his sword from his back and leapt from Nameless at Vaiske, the immortal blocking a torturously strong strike and pushing the shadus away. Vaiske stood and pointed his spear at Lament, his shadow still pulling on him. The shadus attacked again, Vaiske matching each blow with one of his own.

The intense pain shot through Vaiske's side.

He dropped his spear and fell to the floor, watching, inert, as Lament lifted the gargantuan sword above his head.

Lament's sword fell to the hard ground with a deafening clatter as something dove into his side and brought him down. He rolled his eye to the figure on top of him, pinning him to the rock. It was Arvan, eyes dark with fury, half covered by his hair.

"Do you think only of your own gain?" the boy growled. "What life would you condemn the world to just so you could have your damnable shadow?"

Lament said nothing and looked at Arvan with his usual emotionless stare.

The horned head of Vaiske appeared above him, his second shadow calmed and complete once more.

"I can't say I blame you, shadus," he said. "But try that again and I'll take your other eye."

He rested the tip of the spear on Lament's bottom eyelid. The shadus merely blinked.

They rode on saying nothing more of the skirmish. Lament rode some way ahead of Vaiske and Arvan, the boy riding with the immortal.

"That was a brave thing you did, boy," Vaiske said. "He could have killed you, and I wouldn't put it past him either."

"He has some skill," Arvan said. "Though, from what I have seen, he relies on underhand tactics."

Vaiske laughed. "Leaping through shadows? Yes, I suppose he is a contemptible fellow. Though, you speak of skill; you have some talent yourself. You took him down easily enough."

"I still have much to learn," Arvan said. "I am still inexperienced. Would you…" He paused.

"Would I…?" Vaiske prompted.

Arvan shuffled in his saddle. "I feel as though I could learn much from you. Would you care to teach me?"

Vaiske turned the horrific mask to face the boy.

"Arvan," he said, "I was hoping you'd ask me that! Of course I shall, but you will learn in battle. When we reach Pale Castle there will be much fighting to do. Stay close to me and watch carefully."

They left the Rock Flats and emerged in the North Lands, not so far from the Central Province. It was a hilly area, but Arvan knew it would flatten out a few miles on, creating the plains before Pale Castle.

"We'll rest here!" Vaiske called.

Lament turned, his glowing amber iris shining out into the night. "If we keep going we can reach Pale Castle and rescue Swift under cover of night."

Vaiske shook his head. "You mortals will need your rest if we are to assault Pale Castle. We're a comfortable distance away here."

Vaiske dismounted and Arvan did the same. Lament watched impotently.

"Arvan," Vaiske said. "See if you can find some firewood in the area. You must be hungry; I'm sure there's something to eat around here if you're clever about it."

Arvan nodded and left the camp.

Lament stayed a time, looking at Vaiske, his perpetual scowl subtle but unwavering. When the immortal went about setting up camp, the shadus dismounted and prowled into the night.

Arvan had collected some of the drier twigs he had found and fed himself on some foraged fruit, he had gathered some more for the horses. He was about to venture back to the camp when Lament appeared from the darkness.

"I'd advise you against getting too close to Vaiske," he said in his usual whisper. "Don't forget he has the Blood Lust."

"That's just your theory," Arvan hissed. "To me, he seems less bloodthirsty than you."

"He's a good man, I believe," Lament went on, as if Arvan had said nothing. "Though he doesn't know quite how to go about it."

"Unlike you. He hunts the Behemoth because it will benefit mankind. You only do so to reclaim your shadow."

Lament said nothing. He turned and prowled once more into the night.

When Arvan returned to camp Vaiske lit a fire effortlessly and told Arvan tales of his heroics. The immortal fed Vanel some of the fruit Arvan had gathered and stroked her mane lovingly.

Arvan fought off sleep, eager to hear more tales, but, eventually, his weariness became too much and he drifted off in the light of the flickering fire.

Chapter Sixteen

Arvan woke at dawn to find Lament had returned to the camp, his melancholic figure cut by the glass sky. How clear the day was compared to the one previous. The boy peered past the shadus, hills rolling into the distance like the heads of gods trying to break through a sheet of grass. Lament, surrounded by the vibrant vista, merely looked at the boy, the one amber iris forced to the side of his eye as Arvan tried to avoid his gaze. He showed his usual symptoms of a sleepless night, though they were so similar to those of his illness that it was becoming increasingly difficult to believe the two were not intertwined.

Vaiske too hadn't slept. He had spent the night on watch, for what Arvan wasn't sure though he had a suspicion the immortal's distrust of Lament was a factor. The man with-two-shadows rose and mounted Vanel.

On they rode through the hill-lands, often going between the hills but, when there was no other route, they led the horses carefully to the zenith. The time passed slowly, though the journey was mercifully short. Soon they crested the peak of the final hill and looked down upon the sight before them.

Pale Castle, connected to the mainland by the near-endless bridge built of the same white stone, stood menacingly in the distance, shimmering in the substance-less light of the morning. It seemed to watch them, each window, the large gaping door, a feature in a face every bit as horrific as the mask Vaiske wore. Indeed, even the immortal shuffled uneasily in his saddle.

Save for the castle itself, the view was empty. Despite the time of day, the early morning, in which the Riit Clan normally trained on the plain the bridge was connected to, not a soul could be seen. The breeze whispered around, waltzing with the amiable grass.

"This isn't right," Arvan said softly. "Almost the entire Riit Clan would be out here normally."

"It's a strange situation, no doubt," Vaiske said. "Still, it works in our favour. Out on the plain their superior numbers would have thwarted us without even having to try. On the bridge, or even inside the actual castle, the enclosed space makes their numbers count for little."

"You're right," Arvan said, though the enthusiasm in his voice was dubious.

The immortal gestured towards Pale Castle with the horns of his helmet. He and the boy urged their horses slowly towards it, but stopped when Lament didn't move. They turned and looked at him.

"What's the matter, shadus?" Vaiske said. "Having second thoughts?"

Lament's eye was fixed on Pale Castle, the haunting apparition sat uncomfortably between the differing blues of the sea and sky. Not a cloud ventured into the view. The sea crooned softly with the breeze, the warmth of spring finally finding the shadus.

Lament rolled his eye towards Vaiske and shook his head. He spurred Nameless on.

Upon reaching the plain at the foot of the hill, Lament's hand grasped the hilt of his sword, but it gave him little comfort. He became aware of Arvan and Vaiske eyeing him suspiciously but kept his hand where it was.

"That bridge must be near ten miles in length," Vaiske said as they approached the white stone structure.

"'Near' has nothing to do with it," Lament replied. "It is ten miles."

"But the castle's so large even now!" Arvan gasped.

"Accustom yourself to it," Lament said. "It shall grow larger yet."

They reached the threshold of the bridge and stopped. The horses would go no further, Arvan tried to spur Seln on further but she would not obey.

"Don't force it, Arvan," Vaiske said, dismounting. "The horses won't do us much good from now on, anyway." He stroked the mane of the grey horse lovingly. "Goodbye, Vanel. May you serve all of your owners as well as you have served me." He released the horse and it went galloping to the west. Nameless followed, Lament barely glancing after him.

Arvan dismounted and took Kyagorusu's staff from Seln's saddle-scabbard. "Farewell, Seln." The appaloosa whinnied graciously and chased after her companions.

Almost in unison, Vaiske and Arvan turned to Pale Castle. Lament's gaze had never left it.

"Do you think they expect us?" Arvan asked.

"We shall soon discover," Lament replied, walking towards the building of haunting white, his cape flowing gently behind.

Arvan turned and looked up to Vaiske.

"Stay close to me," the immortal said. "He knows something, or senses something at least."

"You think he's plotting against us?"

Vaiske shrugged. "I merely struggle to trust a dead man who roams with the ease that he does."

Vaiske gestured towards the castle with his spear and walked after Lament.

Arvan peered up at the ominous building. It dwarfed even the Coliseum in the Final Resting Place of Empire. Pale as death and just as ancient. He sighed and followed, grasping Kyagorusu's staff ever tighter.

The salt air was deceptively refreshing, betraying the danger Arvan knew the group to be in. The castle showed no signs of erosion from its thousands of years by the sea, perfectly maintained as it was, nor did it signify any life within. Who was this Captain Swift who could survive three years in so deathly a place? Arvan glanced at Lament. Only an acquaintance of that man could suffer three years of such anguish.

The cape of the shadus fluttered gently behind him, pulled by the breeze, almost in unison with the ebb of the tide. The one amber iris was looking at something far away, too far for Arvan to see what it was, though Lament's expression wasn't one caused by good fortune. Then again, everything about the shadus was morose.

Their footsteps were soft, muffled further by the ever present muttering of the ocean and the laughing of seagulls. The heat fell upon them, so heavily they may as well have been wrapped in untouchable blankets.

Vaiske flung a wild arm in the path of the boy and the trio came to a halt.

Two figures approached from Pale Castle, obscured by the wavering air.

Slowly, Vaiske readied his spear for attack. Lament bent his knees slightly and wrapped his hand around the hilt of the immense sword on his back. Unconsciously, Arvan's hand went to his sword too.

Still the figures approached, gradually gaining shape and becoming men. One wore a long leather coat that trailed with less life than Lament's cape. He wore a hat with a wide brim, walking with a gait that landed somewhere between a stroll and a strut. The second man was pulled by a chain, like some unruly pet, his hands and legs bound, making it impossible for him to walk with any speed and retain his balance.

As they neared, the companions didn't relax. If anything their tension grew, Arvan pulling an inch or two of his blade from the scabbard.

They were soon close enough to see they were both old men. The one in the hat had grey hair, trailing behind his ears all the way down to his shoulders, and a grey moustache flowing from his top lip in two great waves. The clicking of his boots, the leather of which climbed to his knees, silenced the ocean, the birds and the breeze. The colour of his hat was a deep brown, matching that of his boots and coat, his trousers an insipid tan colour, contrasted by the black shirt he wore. Across his chest shone strange ball-bearings Arvan had never seen, collected on two diagonal bandoliers. On the side of his leg was a scabbard, the length of which would have been long enough to fit a large dagger or small sword in, though it was wider than necessary for either of these and had the head of a strange weapon poking from the top of it.

The prisoner was more wrinkled than the first man, his eyes sunken and lifeless. He had long grey hair and an unruly beard that Arvan sensed he desired to cut away. He was so thin that his ribs could be seen in the gaps of the black rags that barely covered him at all.

The man in the hat stopped some way from the group and pulled on the prisoner's chain, choking him briefly. He eyed the trio one by one.

"You're going to Pale Castle?" he said in a gruff voice, every bit as old as his face. "Well, I won't stop you," he said when nobody answered.

"Who are you?" Vaiske asked.

The man in the hat smiled, hollowing the wrinkles in his face further.

"Sparrus Riona," he said.

Arvan gasped. He had heard the name before, many times; always spoken in the most hushed of tones, even by Master Snow. He was a man so fierce and so determined that few survived an encounter with him and those who did wished that they hadn't.

"The bounty hunter?" Arvan asked.

"It's not a very common name," Sparrus said, his brown eyes falling on the boy.

"What business have you here?" Vaiske growled.

"Aren't we an inquisitive lot?" Sparrus mused. "I came to find a buyer for my prisoner." He tugged on the chain, choking the prisoner again. "But they're not interested."

"Why?" Vaiske asked.

"They think he's just an old man," Sparrus said. Then he smiled and looked into the eyes of Vaiske's mask. "Which he is."

Lament looked to the Old Man in chains. He didn't seem to be paying attention to the conversation; his eyes flickered between the two shadows on the ground around Vaiske and the empty ground Lament stood on.

"Well," Sparrus said, "you've asked me enough questions, now it's my turn. Why are *you* here?"

Vaiske tilted his head menacingly.

"That's our business," he said in his usual metallic voice.

Lament glanced at Vaiske mournfully, then at Sparrus.

"We've come to save Captain Lavette Swift," he said. "Is he still alive?"

Sparrus turned his head back to Pale Castle and looked at a spire on the east side, then to Lament. He shrugged.

"He was when last I saw him, only a few hours ago," Sparrus said. "They said they'd keep him alive at least a little longer."

"What do you mean?" Vaiske growled.

"No doubt you've seen where the sun is?" Sparrus said, gesturing stiffly to the sky. Arvan looked up. Their time traversing the bridge had passed quickly and, though they were not even halfway across, it was almost noon. "They'll execute him at dusk. You've a few hours. But..." Sparrus paused.

"But?" Arvan prompted.

"But it's traditional for the Swifts to escape alone. Then again, Lavette isn't the man his ancestors were. I sometimes wonder if he's a man at all."

"You seem to know him well," Vaiske said.

Sparrus smiled.

"I should," he said. "I tracked him for over a year before I caught him."

In a flash of rage Lament tore his sword from his back and moved to fell Sparrus, only for the bounty hunter to draw the mysterious weapon he had. On the sight of it pointed at him, Lament stopped. He gazed at the weapon; a hollow shaft of metal curving into a wooden handle. Near where the two pieces met, a short string fuse poked.

"Easy, shadus!" Sparrus said. "I suppose you don't know what this is."

Lament said nothing.

"It's a weapon of my own creation. I call it the 'hand-cannon'. It works on the same principles of a cannon you might find on a ship: the powder goes in, the shot goes in, you light the fuse. It fires just as far as a good arrow, only twice as fast. Ingenious really. You've seen what a cannon-ball does to a wooden ship? Imagine this, tearing through a human body. It's not the sort of thing you get up from."

Lament's scowl deepened. He replaced his sword, falling back in line with Vaiske and Arvan.

"That's better," Sparrus said, re-holstering the hand-cannon. "I won't stop you saving Swift. You'd be doing me a favour, really. If he escapes then his bounty increases; I can catch him again and make more money from his capture. Just don't expect the soldiers to be so understanding."

"Where are the soldiers?" Arvan asked

"In the castle; guarding Lord Riit. They're on high alert."

"Why?"

The Old Man stirred and looked up at them.

"They fear the Behemoth is coming," he said in an ancient voice. "It was in the Final Resting Place of the Empire only a few days ago. But you know all about that."

"Silence!" Sparrus growled, slapping the Old Man with the back of his hand.

Lament turned away, flinching. Then he looked back at the Old Man. "How did you know we were there?"

"The Planet told me," the Old Man said as if he'd forgotten the retribution for his last utterance. "It often speaks to me of the Behemoth."

Arvan shuddered. Unwittingly, upon releasing his katana, he had grasped Kyagorusu's staff with both hands and held it lovingly to his cheek.

"What is it?" he asked. "Why does it torment us so?"

The Old Man smiled solemnly.

"It is what it is," he said. "The Defence."

"It killed my master and my friend!" Arvan erupted. "You call that a defence?"

The Old Man looked at him, unaffected. "I was only answering your question." He passed his eyes between Lament and Vaiske. "But my answers are rarely considered satisfactory." His eyes fell to the floor.

Sparrus sighed and leaned against the side of the bridge, supporting his aged body with his arms.

"He always does this," he said. "I'm not sure he knows what he's talking about. I found him in the Central Desert a few months ago; I think he went mad with the heat."

"You're sure there's a bounty on him?" Vaiske asked.

Sparrus nodded determinedly. "You hear some of the things he says, then you'll know; someone, somewhere, wants him."

Lament took a step forward, his permanent frown becoming one of curiosity. "What is the Behemoth a defence for?"

The Old Man met his look.

"Isn't it obvious?" he said. "The Planet. It was born from the Planet so that our world could protect itself from us. It was supposed to end our wars, but the Planet miscalculated what a juvenile race we are and, instead, we went to war with the Behemoth. It didn't solve anything.

"The Planet's older than us, that's for sure, but it certainly isn't old. We think it is because our lives seem miniscule compared to the life of the Planet. What is a lifetime in the context of a billion years? Well, what is a billion years in the context of an eternity, where there is no time and only movement? We lose ourselves in our own abstract concepts. The Planet is still a child in a sea of eternity. The Planet is still learning but, equally, it is older and wiser than us, trying to teach us but there are things it cannot yet teach because it doesn't know them itself."

"Then what does?" Lament asked in his usual whisper.

"The ether?" the Old Man asked, as if to himself. "I don't know and neither does the Planet. But that's okay because we can learn together."

"See?" Sparrus said. "Nonsensical ramblings. But they're ramblings that someone wants to hear."

"If the Behemoth is a defence mechanism then why does it kill?" Arvan asked, holding back tears his companions either didn't notice or care about.

The Old Man looked at him caringly.

"I don't know," he said. "The Planet never willed it that way. I think we tainted the Behemoth, making it like us. It still tries to stop war, just not in the way the Planet intended. War breeds war. But we've learned that now, or at least the Planet has."

"How are we supposed to live if even the Planet doesn't know everything?"

The Old Man smiled. "Tell me, young man. What do you think the meaning of life is?"

"Here we go," Sparrus sighed. "His favourite topic. He seems to believe he's something of an expert on 'purpose'."

"I…" Arvan paused. "I've never given it any thought."

The Old Man nodded understandingly.

"That's probably wise," he said. "Purpose can destroy a man. He can waste his entire life looking for it and still be ignorant of it as he dies."

He turned to Vaiske. "But you; you've thought about it. You're too old to not have."

"Thought about it?" Vaiske laughed. "I had no need to think about it. It

129

was decided for me. It's a man's purpose to secure his place in history. That way he can live forever."

"Is immortality so important?" the Old Man asked, smiling to himself. "Then again, I'm hardly one to talk."

Lament was about to ask the Old Man what he meant by that but was silenced by his ancient gaze.

"And you," the Old Man said. "You're no older than the boy, or not a great amount, but you've seen too much not to have asked yourself, or more than him at least. So, what is *your* purpose?"

Lament looked solemnly into the distance, though he knew the eyes of the entire group were on him. "Whatever the breeze wishes."

The Old Man smiled again.

"So you do know," he said. "I had wondered."

"Know what?" Vaiske asked.

The Old Man didn't answer, he merely waited for Lament to meet his look. Once the shadus had, he continued. "I'm not sure if the presence is a good thing or not, but the breeze is certainly fond of you."

Lament shuffled uneasily as the breeze spiralled around.

"What aren't you telling us, shadus?" Vaiske growled, turning to Lament.

"Nothing you need to worry about," the Old Man said. He moved his gaze to Vaiske's second shadow. "I see you've read my book."

Vaiske's head snapped back towards the Old Man. "Book?"

"You've two shadows. I assume you did it with that." The Old Man pointed at the platinum dagger in Vaiske's belt.

Lament's eye rolled towards the dagger. He hadn't noticed that Vaiske still wore it, indeed, he hadn't seen it since the night his shadow was stolen. Vaiske looked at Lament, feeling the eye of the shadus on him. He took the dagger from his belt and placed it on the side closest to Arvan. Slowly, he turned back to the Old Man.

"So you're the man who knows all about immortality," he said.

The Old Man smiled. "I wouldn't say 'all about'. I know more than most." He peered again at Lament. "The illness you're suffering; it's Shadowblight. The shadow serves an important function in the body's more spiritual aspects. It is a gateway and a barrier; a walkway for, and a defence against, the breeze. Tell me, you've been hearing or feeling her on the breeze more recently, haven't you? The breeze affects you in ways that it didn't before."

Lament said nothing.

"Denial won't save you," the Old Man said. "Without a shadow the body suffers Shadowblight where it simply begins to shut down, eroded by the breeze until it is your time to join."

"Eroded by the breeze?" Arvan said.

"It's the Planet's life-force," the Old Man explained. "But it's a life-force born from death. In a place where the breeze is thick you feel ill or uneasy, don't you? The shadow prevents the breeze from harmful contact. Without a shadow the concentration of the life-force is too great, too pure, too powerful for the body to withstand and so it is eroded by the breeze. Imagine the energy of the breeze; an eternity of death flowing through a living body. It's not so difficult to picture the effects is it?"

He turned to Lament again.

"I don't know why you're still alive; during our research the subject died of Shadowblight within a few hours. Then again, you're a shadus and your people are more connected with the shadows than others, though we never experimented on one.

"I don't know how long you have, but I can promise you this; it *will* claim you if you don't have your shadow back."

"He'll get it back, Vaiske growled. "When we kill the Behemoth."

The Old Man's eyes widened as he gazed into the grotesque mask of Vaiske.

"So that's where you're going," the Old Man gasped. "Is that how you plan to assure your place in history?"

"One of many," Vaiske said firmly.

"The Planet doesn't want us to kill the Behemoth, does it?" Lament asked. "Or you don't think that we should."

The Old Man smiled knowingly.

"No," he said. "The Behemoth has done as much as it can, though the Planet will mourn its passing. If you must kill it, grant the Planet, and the creature itself, one justice."

They all looked at him, expectantly.

"Kill it as swiftly and harmlessly as you can. It has suffered for a millennium and needs no more pain."

Sparrus pushed himself from the low wall of the bridge and tugged the chain, choking the Old Man.

"I think that's enough for this encounter," the bounty hunter said.

"Where will you take him?" Vaiske asked.

"The Final Resting Place of the Empire. The Great King Eremmerus pays bounties well and has interest in the singularly peculiar ones. Besides," he smiled, "his tales say he has some history there."

"Wait!" the Old Man pleaded, lifting his shackled hands. "I have one last question!"

Sparrus gestured impatiently for him to continue.

The Old Man passed his gaze between the trio. "You've gone far on your travels between you, yes?"

"We've been around," Vaiske replied.

"On your journeys have you come across black ash floating on the breeze?"

Lament shook his head, knowing he spoke for all three.

"Well, if you should come across such an occurrence, wish him well for me."

"Him?" Arvan asked.

"Oh," the Old Man said. "Nothing. Just days gone by." He smiled weakly.

Sparrus pulled on the chain again and they walked closer to the group. Arvan stepped behind Vaiske, clearing a path for them.

"I'd hurry if you want to save Swift," Sparrus said, passing. "There's still some way of the bridge left to go."

He walked past, the Old Man trailing carefully behind him and they faded into the distance together.

"Damn old fool," Vaiske grunted. "He doesn't know how to use immortality properly. That's why he'll never grasp it."

Vaiske walked towards Pale Castle once more, Arvan following dutifully behind. Lament sighed and joined them.

'Who are you, Old Man?' Lament thought. 'Are you sagacious or insane? How long have you lived and how much longer have you got left? What has the Planet taught you and what has it kept hidden? The same as has been from me, no doubt. Yet, you seem to wander less blindly through this miasmic darkness than I, sane or not.

'You speak of her, but how much do you really see? Do you see her arms draped over my shoulders and meeting across my chest, her head resting on my back, listening to by uneven and irregular heartbeat? Or do I betray myself; creating more of the breeze than there is? Yes, you spoke of presence, but do we speak of the same one? Still, I feel her whether she is actually there or not. If this delusion serves me ill then so be it. I would rather live this lie than the horrific truth the rest of the world seems intent on encumbering me with. Here there is comfort, mendacious though it may be.

'You talk of my mortality, Old Man, as if it affected you. What tragedy is it? That you should give me advice I suppose deserves my thanks. But my death is not the tragedy to me that it is to you. Then again, you have not your own death to mourn.'

On they walked towards Pale Castle, the structure surging in their sight. It seemed to live, in its own deathly way, as if their approach created some form of morbid excitement. How many troops moved behind those walls, ready and prepared to plunge their weapons into the group? How many cells and prisoners awaited them and which one was Swift?

The noon sun beat down upon them, the blows of heat softened slightly by the breeze. It drifted away from Pale Castle, pulling on Lament's cape. He shifted his shoulders as if to shrug it off but still it whispered by, catching the sword of the shadus.

Behind his mask, Vaiske eyed Lament. He was growing more curious all the time; what was it he sensed? The Old Man seemed to connect the shadus with the breeze in much the same way Vaiske had come to, though the immortal couldn't be sure whether the validation of his suspicions was fortuitous or not. He had spoken of a presence, of 'her', though Lament had maintained his emotionless disposition. Did the Old Man know of what he spoke, or were they as Sparrus suggested; nonsensical ramblings?

The boy wandered mournfully beside him, holding the staff of the dead man. His carven face had contorted into a scowl that rivalled Lament's and Vaiske concluded he was thinking of something the Old Man had said.

"Damn philosophers," he grunted, heard only in the sanctuary of his mask. The breeze ceased.

"Wait," Lament whispered, stopping; the sheer severity of his voice enough to halt the two with him. They still had some way of the bridge to traverse and Vaiske didn't take kindly to unnecessary stalling. However, he knew that Lament was in an even greater rush than he.

The shadus crossed Vaiske and Arvan, prowling over to the right side of the bridge. He peered over into the waters beneath.

"What is it?" Arvan asked.

Lament looked into the water for some time further still. Eventually he replied, his gaze never moving. "I thought I saw a ripple in the water."

"And now you see nothing," Vaiske laughed.

Lament didn't reply.

"Come, shadus," Vaiske growled, taking a step forward. "Clearly the Shadowblight is making you hallucinate and we've wasted enough time as it is."

Still Lament didn't reply. His eye stayed fixed on the impossibly calm water beneath the bridge, so steady there may as well have been no tide. The breeze did not blow. The gulls did not laugh. The company's breath was silent and Pale Castle showed no signs of holding a moving soul between its walls. There was nothing, save for the gentle cooing of the sea beneath.

The sea appeared to stare back at the shadus, unmoving. His amber eye was transfixed on the tiny waves, making their way to the shore.

He caught it. The merest ripple; a single pulse of a herculean heart beneath.

He lunged at Vaiske and Arvan, the untrusting pair readying their weapons, only missing him by a mere matter of millimetres. He brought them to the ground just as a giant fist pounded through the white walkway, but a hundred metres from them.

Stone was launched into the sky and came tumbling down, plunging into the ocean with the force of deities. Some smaller boulders landed by the group creating a faint clattering sound.

Vaiske recognised the arm immediately as that of the Behemoth. The skin of stone, the tangled fur, the immense presence that it wrought; so colossal that it blocked even Pale Castle from their sight.

It pulled itself further from the ocean, its shoulders destroying yet more of the bridge. Vaiske and Arvan, in their surprise, were pulled further away by Lament. Eventually, Vaiske threw the shadus off of him and stood.

"Fool!" Vaiske roared. "This is our chance!"

Lament shook his head calmly and pointed to the sun, now just past noon.

"The shadows are too few."

"Then just distract it for me!"

With these words a bombast rumble howled from the castle and the Behemoth seemed to consider this, only to skulk around the bridge and approach the castle. With obstruction of the Behemoth gone, Arvan could place the sound. From each available window, from the battlements, from the gate to the castle, were hundreds of cannons all following the path of the Behemoth, armed by hundreds more terrified, but organised, warlord soldiers. They fired again, causing the bridge to tremble. Despite the massive gap the Behemoth had created, the part of the bridge the group was on shook just as violently as the rest.

The cannon-balls collided with the Behemoth, though they only made the beast pause in its approach. It took a slight step back to steady itself and shrieked. The terrible sound, both creation and doom, rang listlessly into the bright day, so hollow yet so complete. It continued wading towards the castle.

Arvan had wondered just how it was possible for something so large to hide in the water so well, but, now that the bridge was no longer obscured by the bridge, he could see that the water crept up to its waist. If it lay, or even crouched, in the water the surface would cover it completely. But why wait? Why hide? It was then he realised it hadn't waited at all, it had just arrived, swimming under cover of the surface of the water, using its legs as some gigantic tail-fin, like an immortal shark bursting from the water to finally take its prey.

"The cannons aren't doing much," the boy said weakly.

"They're not supposed to," Vaiske said. "They merely want to hold it off. It's a good thing too. If they took my glory from me they'd have me to deal with."

Lament gave Vaiske a look of contempt but said nothing. The immortal didn't notice. His eyes were fixed on the scene before him. The cannons sounded again and again, the Behemoth taking the blows as a man is bitten by a bothersome gnat and on it went; now so close to reach out and touch the castle. It pulled back an immense fist and tore into one of the western spires. It crumbled and fell, the sultry air filled with the screams of those inside as the structure plunged into the waters beneath. Already the breeze seemed thicker.

Ignoring the continued barrage of the cannons, the Behemoth plunged another fist into the walls of Pale Castle, sending more of the haunting white stone into the ocean. Yet, it was the Behemoth's very ignorance of the cannons that allowed them to be re-placed. All now faced west, pointing directly at the Behemoth. Still it paid them no heed.

The trio saw the flash of the cannons first, then the smoke. The nauseating sound of the blast was followed by a great wave of reverberations. The force hit the Behemoth in the chest and it stumbled backwards like a winded man.

It shrieked painfully, but showed no signs of a fatal injury. Before the Riit men could reload and fire again it sank back into the ocean and skulked away.

They stayed there for some time in silence, watching the rippling in the water fade with distance. The tide sighed in relaxation and, save for the water, all was still.

Eventually, Lament spoke.

"Come," he said. "We must still save Swift."

"We'll never pass that gap," Vaiske said. "It's too large. Besides, the castle could fall down at any minute with the damage it took." His calm demeanour disappeared and he turned to the shadus, brandishing his spear. "Lament, you deplorable cad! Why didn't you tell us of the Behemoth before?"

Lament pointed to the rag where his left eye once was.

"I couldn't see it," he said calmly. "You took more than my peripheral vision from me, Vaiske. It's as if half the world has fallen away and, when I move to inspect the abyss, it returns, only for the rest of the world to fall away. Had I both my eyes we might have ended this today."

"The old fool could have said something," Vaiske muttered.

Arvan looked to Lament, the cape of the shadus as still as he had ever seen it. Though, the shadus stood as if they should all have been on continued alert.

"You saved us," Arvan said. "Thank you."

Lament said nothing.

"Well, we've lost the Behemoth," Vaiske said.

"I thought Eremmerus said it was headed for the Southern Continent," Arvan said.

"It probably was. But, when Lord Riit heard of the attack on the Final Resting Place of the Empire, he pulled his troops inside the castle and placed them on high alert. The Behemoth couldn't resist such a force."

"What now?" Lament asked.

"The same as before," Vaiske replied. "The Behemoth will go to the Southern Continent, though now we need a new plan to get there."

"My hometown isn't so far from here," Arvan said. "Maybe we could plan there."

Vaiske nodded. "It's as good a place as any. You two could rest for some time. Lead the way, Arvan."

Vaiske and the boy began back to the mainland, though Lament remained and looked to the eastern spire.

"Forgive me, Swift," he said. "Once more I have failed you."

They arrived in Farras that night, though they never made it to the town alone. A figure ran from the town-fence and towards them. Arvan didn't realise it was Darkla until she spoke.

"Arvan!" she gasped, grabbing his hand. "Come quickly!"

She ran, dragging him along, ignoring his pleas of protest and his questions. She led him up the steps to the temple.

The lights of the candles were almost blinding and Arvan immediately knew that Darkla had continued lighting them for him. He sighed inside himself when he remembered he would have to break Master Snow's death to her.

They stood, holding hands at the entrance and Arvan spotted a figure sat, meditating, within. He was dressed in a white robe with the same messy hair as Arvan, though slightly darker. He stood and turned.

He had a humble face with a short beard from months without adequate shelter. He looked lovingly at the boy. Arvan didn't recognise him until he saw the cherry blossom symbol of the Thean House on the man's robe.

Arvan gasped.

"Master Snow!"

Chapter Seventeen

Master Snow looked around at the myriad of candles around him.

"This shows a great deal of dedication," he said. "Was I really gone so long?"

Arvan nodded firmly. "It felt like longer."

He felt Darkla take his hand. He pulled her gently closer but didn't look at her.

Master Snow frowned contemplatively. "I was gone longer than I intended."

Arvan looked at him for a long while. Except the beard, he looked no different than ever. His hair was the same dishevelled mess. He had the same slender but toned frame. Even his eyes were the deep hazel they always had been. That was what bothered Arvan most; this lack of change.

He flinched, looking away.

"You're supposed to be dead," Arvan said.

"Arvan!" Darkla gasped, pulling herself from his grasp and giving him a look of contempt he usually would have associated with Lament.

"It's okay, Darkla," Snow said. "Of course, Arvan's right; I should be dead. It appears he knows where I've been all this time."

Darkla gave Master Snow a curious look, her thick blonde hair falling over her right shoulder and down her chest.

"Where have you been?" she asked.

Snow smiled gently. "Perhaps you should ask Arvan."

She looked to Arvan and he said nothing. He gazed at the stone floor of the temple, all that was left of it, and avoided the gaze of his friend and the gaze of his teacher.

"Arvan?" Darkla prompted.

Arvan sighed, realising he couldn't hide in his non-communication, and looked to her. "Master Snow has been researching the Behemoth."

Her sea-green eyes widened and she snapped her head to Master Snow, her hair flowing like a tail behind.

"That's incredible!" she said.

"I learned a lot," Snow said with a smile. "But I still have to report to Lord Thean. Though, from what Arvan says, it doesn't sound as if they're expecting me back."

"Why were you gone so long?" Arvan asked, his hard eyes meeting Snow's.

Master Snow looked at him sympathetically.

"I lost track of time," he replied. "It was difficult, being in the presence of the Behemoth, the majesty, the destruction; for so long it was a challenge to think of anything else. The leaves turned brown and fell. The snow came and melted away, but still I didn't feel that my research was done. It was only when the first signs of spring came that I felt I had something to report, but I still have much more to discover."

"That's all you can say?" Arvan sneered. "You're gone for so long that we don't know what to think and that's all you can say? I went looking for you, to the end of the continent. Distance and Grimoire thought you were dead. People died while I was looking for you!" He calmed, looking at Kyagorusu's staff in his hands. "I almost died looking for you; more than once."

Darkla took his hand again and he met her eyes. She smiled in her usual warm way.

"It's okay," she said. "You're back now, and so is Master Snow."

"I'm sorry, Arvan," Master Snow said softly. "But you've had a long journey. Perhaps we should discuss this in the morning?"

Arvan felt a wave of tiredness sweep over him and he could do nothing in reply but nod.

Mirr had been waiting for them and stood expectantly in the doorframe. She embraced Arvan but they exchanged no words, then Darkla led him to the room they had shared so often as children. It was small, but big enough for two with a single bed on either side of the aged wooden floor. The moon shone in through a tiny window and, as they sat on their respective beds, Arvan could just make out the outline of Darkla; the listless moon catching her golden hair.

"Arvan," she said.

"Yes?"

"Why didn't you tell me you were going?"

"I knew you'd want to come," he said. "I thought it might be dangerous. I was right."

"But it was an *adventure*!"

Arvan lay down. "I'll tell you about it tomorrow."

For a while there was silence, then Darkla spoke.

"I was really worried about you."

Arvan turned over in bed. "I didn't think I'd be gone that long."

Darkla laughed gently. "You sound like Master Snow."

Arvan smiled but said nothing.

Silence.

"Arvan?"

"Yes?"

"I'm glad you're back."

Snow sat at the small table opposite Mirr. She poured them both a small glass of red wine and Snow knew it wasn't good wine from the first sip, but, on his travels, he'd had none at all. He thanked her and observed the changes in her during his time away. Her face had grown gaunt, her eyes slightly sunken. Her once voluptuous frame had shrunk and her blue summer dress was ill-fitting.

"The town has enough to eat," he said. "Doesn't it?"

Mirr shrugged. "When Lord Riit doesn't take all of the food for his soldiers, we have a plentiful bounty."

"And when did that last happen?"

"Since you were last here," she said nonchalantly. "You know he wouldn't dare enter town with the great Lawliet Snow around." She smiled and sipped at her wine. "I was beginning to wonder if you were ever coming back."

He gazed into her all-knowing eyes. They still held the effervescence of their youth, green and lustful. He smiled and scratched at his beard.

"I'd have been back sooner if it was my decision," he said.

"If it was up to me you'd have never left."

Snow said nothing and sipped his wine, watching Mirr's eyes change. They sharpened, then softened and she looked away.

"But you're not staying, are you?" she said knowingly.

"There's a war coming," Snow said. "Great King Eremmerus is building an army and the weaker warlords are being whittled down. Soon there will be the battle for the continent."

"But why do you have to be the one to end it?" she asked, turning to him. "You've been fighting your whole life, isn't it time that someone else picked up your sword?"

"What do you want me to do, Mirr? Leave the fighting to the younger generation, so that Arvan and his like would have to fight and die? I'm forty this year, it's better that I go."

She looked at him, her mouth open slightly. Her eyes were wide. Then she blinked and they were barely open at all.

"So that's it?" she asked weakly. "You're going to give up and die, just so others don't have to. Do we have nothing?"

Snow met her look, the green of her eyes endless and ever-present. What was it they exuded; love, or just as close as a man such as he could ever come to it? He looked away.

"How much longer do you think I'll live, Mirr?" he said almost absently. "It's only luck and superior skill that have saved me this far. The breeze certainly doesn't favour me. How much longer can I try my luck before it fails me? How much longer before I come against a group so large that my skill is of no consequence? And yet you expect me to yield to my feelings for you."

"Haven't you been listening?" She grasped his hands in her own. "You don't have to fight."

He let her hands wrap over his; the warmth, the comfort. Her fingers curled over his in a touch he had long yearned for and remembered fondly.

"But you'd rather it was you," she said in his silence. "You'd rather have the prospect of us as something unobtainable." Her words cut despite her gentle tone. "Are you even capable of feeling how I do?"

"I was," he replied. "I think I've killed a few too many men to hold you as I once did. Though I yearn for nothing more fervently."

"You could have me, if you let yourself, and end this torment for us both," she said, standing. "If you had any decency you'd tell me how you really felt or you'd stop returning and let me get on with my life."

She began to walk away from the table but she stopped at the sound of her name and the loving caress of his hand on hers. She turned to him and sighed inside herself at the sight of his ever-contented face. They both yielded and fell into a long-awaited kiss.

They sat on the steps to the temple, Lament's gargantuan sword resting between them. Behind them, the flickering candles matched the light of the moon but more vibrantly, as if the flames lived and died as humans.

The night was cool and Lament felt a comfort that had eluded him for some time. Though, the night still reminded him of the one little more than a week ago in which he lost his shadow. The Shadowblight did not creep within him as it usually did and, for a time, he knew peace.

Before them was the house into which Arvan had disappeared. A single light was still lit within.

"That man in the white robe," Vaiske said. "He was the dead man, yes?"

Lament nodded. "Master Snow."

"Strange days indeed. Can nobody stay dead?"

Lament looked at the immortal.

"Some don't die at all," he said in his usual whisper.

Vaiske met the shadus' look. "Some of us need to ensure the dead cease to walk." He looked to the house once more. "Do you think we're welcome?"

"I hadn't given it much thought," Lament replied. "Though it would be a first."

Vaiske grunted. "Oh well. What is a bed to a man who doesn't sleep?"

"Naught more than a cage," Lament said. "And a taunting one at that."

Vaiske rested his spear on his shoulder and shuffled on the step. The candles cast his second shadow before him and he caught Lament gazing at it.

"You haven't tried to kill me tonight," the immortal said.

"Nor you I."

Vaiske laughed. "Don't speak like that, Lament. You're useful to me. You know as well as I do that I can't kill the Behemoth alone."

Lament looked moodily into the night and said nothing.

"Ah," Vaiske said, noting the shadus' look. "You don't think it's the right thing to do. Thinking of what the old fool said on the bridge?"

"Just so long as my shadow is returned when it is dead."

"Do you think me so dishonourable that I would betray our bargain?"

Lament rolled his eye towards Vaiske and gave the immortal a look he couldn't quite decipher. He had to turn his head more than he was used to owing to the loss of his left eye. He grasped the sword lying between them, rose and strapped the weapon to his back. He glanced once more at Vaiske, then prowled into the darkness, his cape trailing behind him in its usual melancholic way.

"That man carries death with him wherever he goes," Vaiske muttered to himself. He leaned on the step behind him and waited for the sun to rise.

He roamed the town with heavy footsteps in his usual slow rhythm. How many nights had he spent as this; endlessly awake? He supposed the throes of sleep had always kept their entrances subtly hidden from him, even in the land he had once called home, yet never so well that he had struggled to find them entirely.

These hours, where the darkness was at its most complete and the astral plain above lit the world most sparingly, he had come to think of as his. That another soul, save for the breeze itself, shared the night with him, seemed unnatural and there was no solace to be found in a world where he could not walk alone. How far would he have to wander before the night could take on the effect he had such a familiarity with?

In truth, he had never grown accustomed to the encumbering weight of the sword on his back, nor the act of carrying a weapon at all. Forever it pulled on him, threatening to drag him with its own murderous will and he didn't know how much longer he could resist it. Perhaps not for so much longer if the Shadowblight was to continue.

Eventually, he came to a secluded part of the town between two groups of houses. A place where the darkness was fittingly empty and the moonlight sufficient hollow. He let the night wash over him; these hours were his once more.

The night passed slowly, though Arvan had no recollection of it. He slept the night through and was the last to wake in the morning. He didn't remember his dreams, though he knew they were not the haunting images that had plagued him of late as for once he felt refreshed. He rose eagerly and ventured downstairs, into the kitchen.

Mirr, Darkla and Master Snow sat around the table eating a hearty breakfast. He couldn't remember the last time he had seen Mirr so happy nor the house so full. Lament and Vaiske sat on two chairs away from the table; Lament unable to eat and Vaiske not needing to.

Master Snow pulled out a chair beside him and gestured for the boy to sit in it. Arvan couldn't recall when he had last eaten a full meal. The shock of seeing Master Snow the night before had made him forget all about his hunger, but now, confronted by Mirr's near infamous cooking, his empty stomach ravaged him once more and he ate until he could eat no more.

When he was done, Mirr spoke.

"I think there's a lot of explaining to be done," she said, looking at Arvan and Master Snow. "Two people need to explain exactly where they've been." She turned to Vaiske and Lament. "And some of us need to confirm our identities and our presence."

Arvan spoke excitedly of his adventure. He told them everything; of Lament's stolen shadow, his encounters with the Behemoth, the warlord clan, Captain Starling, Eremmerus, the Thean Generals, even of the Old Man. He was an animated, if somewhat childlike, storyteller and his audience was captivated, none more so than Darkla who was forever urging him to go into yet greater detail. He only struggled to recount two parts of the tale. The first was the news of Master Snow's supposed death. He had carried the tragedy with him for so long, ever with it on his mind, only for the calamity to be shattered, though joy had yet to reclaim its rightful place. The second was Kyagorusu's death. His voice grew tender and he slowed, sometimes pausing for great lengths, though nobody rushed him. Even Darkla grew silent, staring at the staff Arvan had rested by the table. Eventually he finished the chapter and the rest of the journey became far easier.

Master Snow listened intently, though he didn't so much as glance at Arvan. His gaze was fixed firmly on Lament and Vaiske, unmoving and unwavering. The masked warrior met his stare, never looking away; yet the shadus seemed content to let Snow look and paid him no attention.

"Master Snow?" Arvan said when he was finally finished, tearing Snow's gaze from the pair and to him. "I'm sorry for I how I spoke to you yesterday. It was unacceptable."

"That's quite alright, Arvan," Snow said, smiling. "It must have been quite a shock; the dead aren't supposed to walk."

Arvan shook his head.

"No," he said. "I shouldn't have assumed you were dead. I should have known better of you."

"I'll die one day, Arvan. It was good that you were prepared for it. Already I feel…" He caught a sorrowful look from Mirr and stopped. "Well, let's just say that I'm not as young as I once was. Besides," he turned to Vaiske, "there's only one immortal in this room."

"So, you're leaving again?" Darkla asked Arvan.

"I still have to visit Kyagorusu's hometown," he replied. "I have to tell his family of his death; assuming he has a family. And I must avenge him."

Snow sighed.

"So you still want to go after the Behemoth?" he said. "Well, you're an adult now. I can't forbid you to go, but at least go prepared. I suppose I should tell you my research."

"Not just your research," Mirr said. "Everything."

Snow smiled. "I'm afraid there's not much else to tell. Upon leaving here last I reported to Lord Thean. He seeks to bring peace to the land, as well you know, but he knows two things must be accomplished; first the warlords must be quelled, hence Distance and Grimoire's mission in the Final Resting Place of the Empire. But man has an enemy greater than himself; the Behemoth. Even were we rid of every warlord and every soldier, we would still fight the Behemoth. So, Lord Thean gave me the task of researching it, so that we could understand it better.

"I stumbled upon it swiftly, not far from the Thean complex itself in fact, but it was moving decisively, on its way to some deathly engagement. Or so I thought. I was much the same as anyone at that point, thinking the Behemoth some malevolent entity. It had plagued and disturbed my sleep as a child as it had so many others'. I often wondered why its tragic hand had not befallen me, but I did not wish it to.

"Even looking upon it I, at first, found it distasteful. Whether the skin is actual rock or merely akin to it I am still not entirely sure. But its fur, from a millennium of war, has grown matted and patch-ridden, like some mangy beast roaming the land searching for its last meal. But even that is a visage of beauty compared with those spectral eyes. They gaze upon the world as if there was nothing there, like the creature lives in some violent blindness.

"I attempted to follow it, but it led me to the northern coast and into the ocean where it disappeared. I acquired passage aboard a vessel, but still the trail was lost. I spent a few days roaming the South Lands for some news of it, but heard nothing. Until one night, I was alone in the wilderness when I saw those white eyes coming towards me. I was certain I was the prey it sought and drew my sword, hoping to defend myself, at least to some extent. But it passed me, as if it hadn't seen me at all.

"I thought it was luck at first, but, over the following months, I had many such encounters. Strangely, I never saw it kill, though there was often news of it killing in some morbid battle where only it survived. But it never attacked me; I was no threat to it."

He sighed. "It was then I realised it's just like any other animal; trying to survive. Of course, I do believe what you say the Old Man told you. It really was born from the Planet to end war, but it walks life as aimlessly as a pack of wolves. It has places it prefers and places it will only go when it must. We *have* tainted it. It learned from us, waging war as we do, and grew ever more corrupt."

"You don't think we should kill it?" Lament asked in his usual whisper.

Snow looked at him. "They kill mad dogs. They kill lame horses. I suppose this is no different from that. Yet, there is something within me that mourns the very idea of killing the Behemoth. A part of me feels as though we would be killing the Planet itself."

"That doesn't really answer the question," Vaiske snorted.

"It's not evil, if that's what you mean. That became clear almost immediately."

"Malevolence has nothing to do with it," Lament said. "I find the idea of hunting and killing the creature vulgar. Yet, I cannot have my shadow returned until the Behemoth is dead, and so I must aid Vaiske in his quest., abhorrent though it is."

"The world will be a better place when it's dead," Vaiske said, his posture straight and tight. "You'll see. Then we can end this war between the warlords."

"Perhaps you're right," Snow said, leaning back in his chair. "The creature's grown melancholic, maybe it would be best to end its misery."

"But we've lost the trail," Arvan said.

"You spoke of places it preferred," Vaiske said to Snow. "Like where?"

"There's a meadow," Snow said. "It's in the centre of the Southern Continent. It's easy enough to find if you're willing to look."

"And how do you suggest we get there?" Vaiske said. "Swift is surely dead by now. Even if he is alive, the bridge is destroyed and we can't get into the castle. Besides, I'd not return to that odious place to save anyone."

Lament shot Vaiske a contemptuous look, then leant his elbows on his legs and slumped, gazing at the floor. Yes, Swift was surely dead. Sparrus had said they would execute him yesterday; that thought had ravaged him all night. It was possible he had even died in the Behemoth's attack.

"I too must return to the Southern Continent," Snow said. "Lord Thean keeps a small ship harboured at a port in the South Lands. You may accompany me."

Snow looked at Mirr, expecting some argument from her. She merely smiled and nodded, her gentle features all the more radiant in her submission.

"Fine. Go," she said. "But at least wait until tomorrow."

Snow nodded. "We've preparations to make as it is."

"Well," she said. "That's something."

Lament sat peacefully in the temple, where even the breeze didn't bother him. The candles had been extinguished and removed, the soft afternoon light washing gently over him.

He had never seen a place of worship before, even one that had eroded with the faith of the people like this one. The shadus people had no religion to speak of, rather trusting in the will of the Planet than unknown and unknowable entities. Yet, still he ventured to kill the Behemoth. Did the Planet will that?

He sighed, this was not what he had come here to muse on.

He had left Swift to die. Had he not been so reluctant or indecisive the pirate captain might still live. It was now clear that he would have been in a fit state to rescue him once his shadow had been stolen after all. He had survived battle with an immortal and the Behemoth; what were a few warlord

144

soldiers? Even on the bridge he'd had time to run towards the castle before the Behemoth emerged. Had he not been so inert, Swift would live. He had dishonoured himself.

Yet, despite this; despite his heavy thoughts, despite his faithlessness and his decidedly unholy surroundings; he was at peace in a way he hadn't known in an age. It emanated from within him, cascading through his veins from the tributary of his heart.

But this, like all the peace he knew, was shattered as he heard footsteps behind him. He didn't turn, but hey continued and Snow sat beside him.

"I don't wish to disturb you," Snow said.

"We rarely know tranquillity for as long as we would wish," Lament replied, closing his eye.

"Thank you for looking after Arvan for as long as you have."

Lament shook his head.

"I did little," he said. "Kyagorusu made sure he had all he needed. Since Kyagorusu's death Arvan has mostly kept care of himself." Lament opened his eyes and looked at Snow. "I have no delusions of what I am; a selfish man, consumed by my own motives. Even if I wished to tend to the boy I would not know how to show it."

"He says you risked your life more than once. That wasn't for the benefit of those you were travelling with?"

"Our motives are rarely so simple," Lament replied, looking away.

Snow took on a pensive expression. "Arvan seems fond of Vaiske. I don't think he's sure what to make of you."

Lament shrugged. "An immortal holds wonder and allure. I am a mere shadow-less man."

"I'd like Arvan not to get too much closer to Vaiske."

Lament rolled his eye towards Snow. "You don't trust him?"

"His objectives are noble enough," Snows aid. "Though I can't say I approve of his methods."

Lament nodded. "His intentions are honourable, but men of violence seldom end up doing the right thing."

Snow smiled. "I thought I was the one who didn't trust him."

"It's a challenge to hold a man who has tried to kill you in any faith, though I give him what credit I can."

"Well," Snow said, "let us hope that credit is well placed."

The grass danced gently around him as the breeze whispered past. He ignored it, only suggesting he was aware of it by holding his robe closer.

Before him stood a small grave-stone. The inscription on it read:

Ciadre Deit,
Forever missed.

So simple was the inscription demanded by his young self that Arvan pondered on the profundity of childhood. However, too much time had passed for him to hold onto that wisdom of youth.

He sat there, remembering his meagre family and held Kyagorusu's staff closer to him.

Darkla watched mournfully from a distance, considering whether or not to join him. He was a strange friend in many ways and, as well as she knew him, shared an affinity with him, she could never quite decipher when he needed comfort and when he needed to be left alone.

She was disturbed by heavy footsteps and the haunting effigy of Lament appeared beside her. He gave her a look that was no different to his usual expression, yet she read it as one of intrigue.

"His mother," she said.

Lament nodded. "My apologies."

They stood in a contemplative silence for some time.

"His father?" Lament asked.

"Much the same."

He rolled his eye towards her. "Yet there is only one grave?"

Darkla nodded. "I don't understand, myself."

The silence only death can create washed over them and they yielded to it. It seemed to bother Lament more than Darkla and he shuffled uneasily in his heavy boots.

"He doesn't speak of it?" the shadus asked, as if only to stop the silence grasping them too fervently.

She turned to him, her expression one of understanding. "If you lost one so dear to you, would you know how to speak of it?"

His amber eye endlessly met hers, but he said nothing.

The breeze whispered by and day began to darken. When Arvan rose they returned to Mirr's.

Chapter Eighteen

They left that night whilst Mirr was asleep, creeping from the house like expert burglars. There was a chill to the night that Arvan hadn't been expecting and he scolded himself for not taking more clothes from his bedroom, yet he smiled sadly when he remembered how Darkla hadn't even stirred as he left the room. Still, he couldn't return now and once more risk waking her. He would just have to hope that there weren't too many nights such as that one. He was becoming quite the professional at leaving without a word; it filled him with a strangely shameful pride.

Snow had left Mirr a note. They had known one another for twenty years, had supposedly been in love for most of that, and, upon his leaving her for perhaps the final time, he had left her a note. He shook his head thinking of his cowardice. Would waking her to say goodbye have been so difficult? Could he really not have waited until dawn? But he knew all of that was irrelevant. She would forgive him, reluctantly, undeservedly, and mournfully celebrate his return. Yet, this exit from Farras had a sense of finality to it that Snow couldn't quite shake off.

He thought back to the night before when they had drunk from one another; him, trying to find a reason to cease his swimming in her, yet the bewitchment of her touch growing, never receding, to the point that when they were both finished she stole from him again. He thought for a time of how her body had changed since last he was there, her seemingly fragile frame dictating that he control his lust, even as she urged him further on. She was insatiable, not knowing her own limits and that he had to be the one to enforce them brought him no end of sorrow.

He sighed as they walked through the town. Were they in decline now? He would be forty that year, not old but certainly older than he had ever expected, or cared, to be. For how much longer could he live that life? Grimoire was almost twenty years his senior and showed no signs of retiring soon. Was that what he wanted; a life filled with war?

He looked back at her house, barely visible through the dark of the night. Yet it was there, and always would he be welcome, no matter how long he was away for.

They were approaching the town fence when they saw an effigy moving on the outskirts. It shuffled as if to keep warm, growing in femininity as they approached.

"Darkla!" Arvan hissed as they got closer. "What are you doing?"

"I'm going with you," she said sternly. "I knew you'd sneak off and I wasn't going to be left behind again."

"But you didn't even stir as I left."

"Well that wasn't much of a feat considering I wasn't in the room."

Vaiske stifled a laugh but some of the sound escaped his helmet. Arvan looked up and saw Master Snow smiling broadly. Even Lament's lips had a humorously macabre curl to them. He frowned and turned back to Darkla.

"It's going to be dangerous," he said.

"Good!" she laughed. "It's so boring in Farras. I could do with some excitement."

Arvan looked around for some support from his companions but they remained silent.

Darkla held a bulging cotton bag. "I got some provisions from Old Yadlan. He said he'd rather we had them. I see you all over-looked the fact we'll need food along the way."

Master Snow scratched at his beard and looked away.

"She can't come, can she, Master Snow?" Arvan pleaded.

Snow looked between Arvan and Darkla.

"Well she's more prepared than we are," he said.

"But it's dangerous!"

"It's not the woman's place to stay at home, Arvan. Darkla's as ready for danger and adventure as the rest of us; more so, by the look of it. As far as I'm concerned she's welcome, but I'm not going all of the way."

Vaiske fixed his mask on Darkla.

"Just don't get in the way," he growled.

All eyes turned to Lament and the shadus shrugged.

"As long as I get my shadow back," he said.

"So it's settled," Darkla said. "I'm coming."

She threw the bag of provisions over her shoulder and they left town.

"But it's dangerous," Arvan muttered before following.

*

Mirr wasn't surprised when she woke alone. She had expected that to be their last night together; truth be told, she was somewhat amazed Snow had stayed as long as he had. Always was that soul roaming, even when the body was still. And his mind; was that ever with her?

She stroked the pillow next to her, long devoid of warmth. He must have left as soon as she fell asleep. Was it really so hard for him to stay?

The warm light of the spring morning seeped in through the gap in the curtains and she knew already he would be far away. If he was determined he may not even be in the North Lands anymore, but he'd always been distant.

She went to Darkla's room, only to find it empty, and she felt nothing. There was no understanding, no sadness, no joy, no fear for the girl's wellbeing. She had long since ceased to be pained by the leaving of those she loved. There was only what was; Darkla had gone with them, and now Mirr was completely alone. The realisation didn't wash over, or gently emerge, nor did it strike her swiftly and suddenly. It was merely there, as if waking from a restless slumber.

Thoughtlessly, she ventured downstairs and into the kitchen. There was a note to her on the table. She threw it away; he needed not explain himself. There had been many notes such as that one in their relationship. She wondered how many more there would be.

*

They watched, silent and still, as the column snaked on. Man after man marched south, driven by the will of Lord Riit and the knowledge that Pale Castle was not structurally unsound. The line seemed to go on forever, as did the direction in which they were moving. The very idea that they would ever find somewhere to stop, or would ever eventually march from sight, was laughable.

They peered from the wheat field, the crops just tall enough to shield themselves from sight if the crouched. The group had barely moved since night lifted, Snow cautious of any unwanted attention from the Riit Clan.

"How many men does he have?" Vaiske growled. "Will they never pass?"

Lament observed as Arvan shuffled uncomfortably. It wasn't so strange, they had been cramped in the same position for many hours now, yet the continuous fidgeting of the boy heightened his own anxiety. After all, they didn't camouflage well into the wheat field; they were still a collage of black and red, with the ever present hues of white from Snow and Darkla. Each movement shook the wheat around them and, on a day with so little breeze, gave clues to their position.

"Calm down," Lament whispered to Arvan. "We are safe so long as we control our fear."

Arvan nodded.

"I know," he said. "I just hate them so much."

"They steal food from Farras," Darkla said. "I can't count how many nights we went to bed hungry as children."

"They're moving away from Farras," Snow said.

"And still we cower here," Vaiske grunted. "We've an immortal among us, in case you've forgotten. I can slaughter that entire force with barely an effort."

"That's exactly what I'm trying to avoid," Snow said. "There's too much bloodletting to come to start spilling it now."

Vaiske turned to Snow but said nothing. Who was this roaming warrior to give orders to the man-with-two-shadows? He moved to leave the sanctuary of the crops only for Lament to pull him back.

"You'll give us all away," the shadus said. "We're not all immortal, and even you might miss a few." He pointed to a group of soldiers that were closer to them than the rest of the column, clearly watching the field.

"Do you think they suspect us?" Vaiske asked.

"Suspect?" a voice behind them mused. "I think it's gone a little further than 'suspect'."

They turned, finding some Riit soldiers in the grey uniform of their master pointing their spears at them. The man at the head of the soldiers was older than the others with the stripes Snow knew indicated he was a Major in the Riit army. He had a face that looked to have been carved by stone and neat brown hair.

Vaiske gripped his spear tighter.

"I wouldn't if I were you," the Major said. "We might not be able to kill you, Parlet (yes, we have heard the whisper of you and your immortality), but we can still kill your companions."

"Why would that concern me?" the immortal growled.

"Because no man wants the death of children on his conscience."

Lament rolled his eye towards Vaiske and watched as the immortal lowered his spear in an uncharacteristically fragile fashion. The shadus frowned further.

The Major smiled, then looked to Arvan.

"Hello, Arvan," he said.

The group turned to the carven faced youth; he was pale, sweating and an intense frown had burrowed into his brow. He held the hilt of his katana tightly, ready to tear it from his scabbard and cleave the Major's head in two. His wide eyes expression whispered death; yes, he could do it. Then he weakened, shuddering, and released the sword. He closed his eyes, hung his head, and looked away.

"Hello," Arvan said, then he paused. "… Dad."

They bound them, then disarmed them, save for Lament whose sword was rather too heavy for anyone to discard. Eventually, however, he took it from his own back and placed it in the cart with the other weapons. Major Deit led them down to the column and forced them in line, marching, surrounded by an eternity of Riit soldiers.

Vaiske pulled on his bonds but even he, with his immortal strength, could not break the rope. He growled and looked to Lament. The shadus walked on, uncomplainingly, though his eye wandered, ever aware. No shadows fell near him and soon midday would come when there would be none at all, except for Vaiske's perpetual second shadow. Lament doubted he could do much with just that.

Major Deit walked alongside them, his hand resting on the shoulder of his son. Arvan had tried to shake him off more than once, only for the hand to return to its place with yet more force and conviction. The boy yielded and let his father hold him. The hand, as if made by some corrosive acid, seemed to burn through Arvan's robe and through his skin. It sat uncomfortably on his shoulder, ever threatening to force its way through. Already the arm beneath no longer seemed to be his own; it belonged to the man who held it in place. Father, abandoner, deserter. Now thief, stealing his son from the freedom he had discovered sanctuary in.

Snow watched with distaste. He had thought Arvan's hatred of the Riit Clan to be simplistic enough; the Riit Clan stole food from Farras so the town went hungry, the Riit Clan killed Darkla's parents, the Riit Clan oppressed the people of the North Lands. But now his father, whom Snow had long thought dead, had appeared as a high ranking soldier in the force Arvan abhorred so. It appeared there were some things Arvan didn't even tell his master.

Darkla watched Arvan shudder at the man's touch. Why hadn't he told her? Were they growing so far apart that he wouldn't tell her anything anymore? She clenched her fists in her bonds until the blood drained from them and they were as pale as Lament's skin.

"Are all adventures like this?" she asked Snow.

He moved his eyes towards her. "Not usually so early on."

It wasn't long before an inelegant carriage, pulled by two great buffalos with horns like the limbs of ancient trees, stopped beside them.

"Finally," Major Deit said and led Arvan inside of it.

The rider drove the buffalos on and the carriage rumbled away.

His father looked across the carriage at him from the velvet seating. So this was the comfort he had been in all these years, while Arvan went hungry and had a thousand sleepless nights. That he shared so many of the man's features was yet another insult. The same grave face, the same dark hair and eyes.

Major Deit folded one leg over the other, his grey trousers creasing slightly.

"It's been a long time, Arvan," he said. "We've much to discuss. Is there nothing you wish to say to your dear old dad?"

Arvan said nothing and looked out of the window. They passed the soldiers quickly, already he knew his friends were far behind.

"I've nothing to say to you," Arvan said.

"I've been gone for fourteen years, Arvan. There must be something you wish to say."

"You abandoned us," Arvan said, his eyes sharpening as he met his fathers. "Do you have any idea what that's like?"

"Abandoned?" Major Deit laughed. "You've no idea why I left. Tell me, Arvan; how many times have we passed on the plains and said nothing?"

Arvan didn't answer.

"I watched you grow up in those moments, when you played with your friends on the plains. I may not have been at home, but I certainly didn't abandon you."

Arvan said nothing. His eyes had grown hollow and vacant.

"I can see I won't change your mind," the Major said. "Let's change the subject; how's your mother?"

Arvan seemed to wake. He stood and struck his father with his bound fists.

"She's dead!" he roared, lifting his hands for another assault. "She died when I was eight of a fever that lasted for years. For her last two years she couldn't even leave her bed, and all she wished, her very last wish, was to see you again! And where were you? Where were you?"

His father's hands shot up and wrapped around his wrists. He forced Arvan back into his seat and didn't let go until the boy had calmed. When he was placated, the Major sat back down.

"She's dead?" his father said wearily.

Arvan nodded.

"I had no idea."

"You weren't around."

"Insolent boy!" his father shouted. "Do you not know why I left? It was no mere abandonment! All my life, all I wanted was a family of my own, especially a son. Did the Riit soldiers ever bother you after I left? Tell me that."

It was true, the Riit soldiers had left Arvan and his mother alone after his father left. They always had more food than the rest of the town and Arvan was spared the tragedies that Darkla was not. Instead, nature stole his last remaining parent from him. What was this world of sorrow he lived in? A world in which he could be forced into solitude both by man and the Planet.

"No, they did not bother you," his father continued. "And they left you alone thanks to my decision to leave you and join Lord Riit. Would you really have been happier if I'd have stayed? Do you think your life would have been better? Splitting the meagre food supplies you had between three instead of two, living in cramped quarters."

"But that's exactly what happened!" Arvan cried. "After Mum died all I could do was live with Mirr and Darkla, who had even less food than we did. Then they split it between three of us, just enough to keep us alive in that perpetual suffering." He paused. "They were the only good to come out of your leaving."

His father looked away.

"That was never my intention," he said quietly.

"Well that's what happened."

"What do you think of me, Arvan?" Major Deit asked. "Do you think fathers are some sort of oracles? We're not. I'm not. I'm just a man who tried to do the best he could for his family. Maybe I made some poor decisions, and they cannot be undone, but at least I made a decision. What would you have had me do? Waited for the hunger to have claimed all three of us, or the soldiers to kill us for hiding food?"

"You broke up the family!" Arvan shouted. "That's unforgivable! You gave us preferential treatment; we never asked for that. Darkla's parents were murdered by the Riit Clan…"

He stopped. The anniversary had come while he was away, and Darkla had said nothing of it. He couldn't speak for a moment, imagining her sorrow. He didn't remember the date of his mother's death, yet Darkla's parents' were imprinted on her mind so fervently so as to tear her soul from her every anniversary, and he had been so selfish as to abandon her when she needed him. He looked at his father. The tragedy that the man's likeness ran in his veins. He felt nauseated by it, but already he was picking up some of his less reputable traits.

"You mean to say you would rather have been slaughtered?" his father asked. "Well, you need not worry about that any longer."

Arvan looked up at the Major. "What do you mean?"

"You are my son, Arvan – the continuation of my line. It is only right that, now, as your only surviving parent, you stay with me. You're a man now, you shall join me in my work."

"I'll never join the Riit Clan!" Arvan shouted. He stood and moved to strike his father again, but the older man caught his fists.

"Now, Arvan" his father said. "You don't want your first action in Lord Riit's army to be one of insubordination."

"I'll never fight for that monster!"

"Monster? Lord Riit is a great man. He fights for peace and asks only that his soldiers join him on his glorious quest. We are honoured to have a lord such as him to rule over us. He will defeat the other warlords, even Great King Eremmerus, and unite the land!"

Arvan weakened and fell back into his seat.

"You all speak the same," he said. "You all fight for peace, but if you all stopped fighting that's exactly what we'd have."

His father seemed not to hear him.

"We evacuated Lord Riit some time before the rest of us," the Major said. "We won't reach him until tomorrow."

On the carriage rolled.

They stopped with the night, setting up tents and dividing the remaining prisoners into two groups. Lament and Vaiske sat outside a tent with around twenty soldiers inside. Their bonds had been re-tied so that their hands were now behind them, and Lament shuffled uncomfortably.

The sky was black and laden with clouds. A light rain fell but gave constant warnings that it wished to rain harder. Still, it seemed not to hinder the large campfire that had been lit. The great flames jumped and flickered as if suggesting caution to the weather.

"Have you any ideas?" Vaiske asked.

Lament shook his head. It felt unnatural sitting so close to the man who stole his shadow, let alone plotting an escape with him.

"Of course," Vaiske continued, "if I didn't have everyone else to worry about I could escape quite easily."

"How kind of you to burden yourself with us," Lament said in his usual emotionless whisper, but his eye let the sarcasm shine through.

"You're a fine one to speak of burdens," Vaiske growled. It was strange to see the shadus without the gargantuan sword strapped to his back, he looked somewhat incomplete.

"Besides," the immortal went on, "I can't break these bonds. I do have a plan though, but I need to be able to trust you."

"That's for you to decide," Lament replied, his amber eye still fixed on Vaiske.

"I know. That's the problem; I don't like the answers I'm coming up with."

Lament shrugged and looked to the fire. "So we wait."

Vaiske sneered behind his mask.

"How much longer do you think you have before the Shadowblight takes you?" he said. "I'm not sure if you've caught your reflection recently but you don't look like a well man."

Lament knew what Vaiske meant. He had struggled to match the pace of the marching soldiers, his footsteps laboured and heavy. His nausea was growing and he was never at a comfortable temperature. But most disconcerting of all was his weariness. A distinct and perpetual tiredness had overcome him, so potent that it made even breathing an effort. He had grown accustom to living with the fatigue that came with his insomnia long ago, but this was something more fervent, as if it attacked him with some virulent rage. And yet, there, within the very drowsiness itself, was an apathy; an acceptance of his fate. He knew this knowledge held no solace.

"At this rate you'll be dead before we even find the Behemoth," Vaiske said.

Lament sighed and then strengthened, forcing himself to sit upright and face Vaiske.

"Very well," he said. "What is this machination of yours?"

Vaiske tilted his head towards the shadus. "How do I know I can trust you?"

"What choice do you have?"

Vaiske laughed, despite the metal it sounded less forced and more human than usual.

"None at all, shadus," he said. "You're the best I've got." He shuffled closer to the shadus. "There's a dagger in my belt that the soldiers missed. Take it and cut your bonds, then mine."

Lament rolled his eye and saw the overly-familiar platinum dagger.

"Yes," Vaiske said. "It's the dagger I stole your shadow with."

Their eyes met.

"Now don't get any unsavoury ideas," Vaiske said.

Slowly, Lament turned his back on the immortal and reached back until he could feel the freezing hilt of the dagger. He gripped it with the slender fingers of both his hands and pulled it from Vaiske's belt.

He lifted himself to his knees as if to give himself more leverage and began to cut through the rope around his wrists. His frown intensified as he tried to imagine how the knot behind his back would look, but soon the bonds began to weaken and the blade cut through the rope entire, meeting his skin with a soft, cold caress.

He turned to Vaiske, still kneeling and flicked the dagger around in his hand so the tip pointed skywards. The immortal looked strangely powerless sat there, his hands tied behind him, in spite of the horrific mask and bullhorns. In those moments the vermillion armour was a mere arrogant statement.

It was then that Lament saw it; Vaiske's second shadow cast by the campfire. It was only a faint outline, as if some non-dimensional apparition lay upon the ground trying to justify its non-existence, only to be gripped listlessly by reality. But, it was there nonetheless.

He passed his eyes between the shadow and the eyes of Vaiske. There was contempt to be seen in them, wide eyed hatred and fear, that could not be diminished by the eye-holes of the mask. That the immortal's pupils were almost completely shrouded by shadows made the occasion seem all the more fitting.

"Now, shadus," Vaiske said, slowly, calmly. "Remember what I said about unsavoury ideas."

Lament slowed his breathing to calm himself as his eye rolled towards the shadow. Unwittingly, he licked his top lip, his tongue sliding from between his rows of teeth like in the command of the mouth of some rampant sexual deviant who wanted only to view pleasure and lust. His breath seemed to curl around inside his lungs, slipping from him unknowingly.

The breeze whispered sensually by and the shadus felt his skin move as if to follow, as if her light touch passed gently across his skin.

His eye narrowed and he leapt for the shadow.

*

His father had been silent for some time. They sat alone in Major Deit's tent, larger than that of the other soldiers, and didn't look at one another. The Major sat on his bunk, staring into some invisible space. Arvan hugged his legs to his chest. How much of him was his mother? Not an awful lot from what he had seen that day. He supposed he didn't have so many more years before he became his father completely, torn from boyhood into an unprepared fissure of a man. Barely even human anymore. Did fighting against the path of time hold any rewards, or only futility?

"Ciadre…" his father lamented wearily. "You could have broken your mother's death to me more gently, Arvan."

"I owe you no consolation" Arvan said.

"She was my wife." His words were barely a whisper spoken within a breath. Arvan was reminded of the shadus.

"You didn't seem to care earlier."

"I have had time to accept a world without her and I do not like the prospect. The fact my son has become less insolent has allowed the news to strike me fully."

"I didn't think it would affect you."

"Then you know *nothing* of love!" his father said more forcefully, twisting his neck to look at the huddled boy. "And I pity you."

Arvan didn't see his father looking at him; he was consumed by his own robe and his own grief. The conversation resurrected emotions he had long thought dead.

"People tend to see those they love more than once every fourteen years," he said.

"It was safer that I stay distant," his father said. "Though I don't expect you, a mere boy, to understand."

Arvan said nothing. He receded further inside his huddle. Soon his father lay down and, consumed by his remorse, fell wordlessly asleep.

As Arvan listened to his father breathe deeply in his sleep, the rain strengthened outside. As his eyes fell upon the short-sword resting by the man's bed, he had an idea that only amused him at first, but, when it did not fade away with its immediacy, he contemplated it.

This was his chance to kill his father.

*

Just as the tip of the dagger was about to plunge into the shadow, Vaiske thrust the horns of his helmet into Lament's chest. The shadus grunted and toppled onto the wet ground by the campfire, though he kept his grip on the dagger.

"Lament, you paltry excuse for a human being!" Vaiske rasped, standing. His hands were still tied behind his back, yet he stood side on, leading with his right leg, ready to fight.

Lament watched lustfully as the shadow grew.

"There are more pressing matters at hand than theft of this shadow from me!" Vaiske growled.

Lament rolled over and pushed himself to his feet.

"No, it is as you said, Vaiske," he replied. "The Shadowblight ravages me with greater and renewed strength with each fleeting moment. If I do not take my shadow back soon this illness will claim me."

Vaiske growled. "Very well. Then make your move, shadus."

Lament dove for the shadow only for Vaiske to gore him with his shoulder. Winded, Lament fell to the ground. His breath soon returned and he was met by the sight of Vaiske falling down atop him. He rolled out of the way and quickly got to his feet.

Vaiske was left inert on the ground. He flicked his legs, trying to push himself up, but Lament kicked him, making the immortal lose his balance. He rolled over on his back, just in time to see Lament go for the shadow again. Using his legs, and the shadus' own momentum, he caught Lament in the chest and vaulted him towards the fire. The shadus landed with a heavy thud.

Slowly, the two combatants got to their feet.

Despite the use of his hands, Lament was at a distinct disadvantage. Aside from his illness and one eye, he only had a hope of stealing the shadow, not hurting Vaiske. As an immortal, the shadus could not break his bones or even cause him pain. He could tackle him to the ground, though the impact would be lessened and Vaiske's recovery swift. Even the dagger could not pierce his skin. It struck Lament that had Vaiske not been an immortal, the result would have been much the same. The armour that covered his body prevented any harm being done to him.

Futility assailing him, Lament fell to his knees.

"You realise your defeat already?" Vaiske asked. "That is your great fault, Lament; you lack resolve. Now, let us end this foolishness and cut my bonds."

His eyes shot to the shadow as an all-too-familiar pain shot through him. The shadow flickered wildly.

"No!" he cried. "Not now!"

He fell on his back and squirmed in pain, the shadow losing shape, only to regain it and fade once more. The immortal's back arched and he writhed.

When his shadow finally calmed he was left there, breathless and paralysed. The shadus stood above with that emotionless expression and the dagger poised.

*

The discomfort of the rain kept Darkla awake. She knew the situation was severe but felt somewhat safer with Master Snow so close. The rope tying her hands together was coarse and too tight, her hands had long been numb. She tried moving them but, limbs anaesthetised through lack of blood, she wasn't sure if she'd succeeded. She groaned in distress.

The darkness was thickest at that time of night, lustre discarded so that the dinge could multiply and swell. They were so far from any of the campfires that she was subject to a miasmic blindness, complete and unending.

Still, in spite of her unbearable discomfort, her thoughts turned to Arvan. Was he in danger? She knew little of his father, but was all too aware that

157

warlord soldiers, especially those in the Riit clan, were not chosen for their good nature or sympathy. But that he had not told her of his father, in fact had lied claiming him to be dead, played on her mind the most. Clearly he was ashamed, but who was she if not someone to share in that shame and lessen it for him?

A shuffling sound distracted her from her thoughts and she found herself being untied. When she turned around she saw Master Snow.

"How did you break free?" she whispered.

Snow smiled. "One of the soldiers realised who I was and untied me. It seemed he feared retribution lest I escaped by my own accord."

Darkla rose to her knees and felt Master Snow take her hand in his. Was that something her parents used to do? She couldn't remember, though Snow had done it so many times during her life that the hand was almost as familiar as her own. Despite his time away and adventures, it felt as it always had; engulfing and vast with comfort.

"I want to find Arvan before we even think of looking for Vaiske and Lament," he said. "Something about the way he looked at his father earlier doesn't sit well with me.

"Stay close, Darkla. You might not be able to see them but there are guards and they are nearer than I would desire. But don't fear; the night is as much in our favour as theirs. Together we will find Arvan, but I need your eyes as much as mine."

"I'm with you," she said.

And with that he led her into the night.

*

Lament knelt over the immortal, dagger held downwards, ready to soak the shadow and take it for himself. Vaiske tried to move, to push the shadus away, but his paralysis was still complete. Lament's hand grasped around the collar of Vaiske's breastplate and the immortal could feel the shadus pin him down in order to ensure his target.

Lament pulled Vaiske to a seated position and cut the rope around his wrists. The immortal turned to him. "Say nothing," Lament whispered.

The rain strengthened and gradually the fire began to wither away. Once it was finally extinguished the shadow disappeared from sight, merging with the rest of the darkness.

It wasn't long before Vaiske regained control of his body, but the two merely sat there, next to one another.

"Why?" Vaiske asked.

Lament shook his head. "Our time would be better spent engineering our escape."

He stood and pulled the immortal to his feet.

Chapter Nineteen

The short-sword was heavier, bulkier, than the katana he was used to. He didn't struggle to lift it, though he knew he could wield it with no great skill; but that was fine. He needed only slit the sleeping man's throat.

Arvan watched as his father's chest rose and fell with each breath, hidden by the thin blanket he lay under. He slept soundly as Arvan had never been able to, fretting over whether or not the Riit soldiers would invade Farras in his slumber. His mother had suffered similarly until her last few years of illness, then she had no trouble sleeping, in fact she had little else to do.

He could no longer remember her face in his mind. When did he lose that last remnant of her? Too many years had passed without reminiscence, so many now that the act of looking back required a daunting amount of effort.

Arvan tightened his grip on the sword and forced the thoughts from his mind. She might still be alive if his father hadn't abandoned them, or at least she would have been more at peace in her final moments instead of that torturous writhing and her screams, "Where is he? Where is he?", until she was so weak she could no longer breathe, much less wail.

"I thought you weren't thinking of that anymore," Arvan hissed to himself.

His hand was worryingly steady as he held the sword over the bed. Could it truly be as easy as he expected? Master Snow was always so mournful of the difficulties he faced when killing a man. The boy exhibited none of these traits.

He smiled and took the time to imagine the scene after the sword stroke. His father's eyes shooting open in surprise and terror, so bloodshot with fear at his impending mortality he would be unrecognisable. His swiftly paling skin as the blood gushed from his throat, rising into a glorious fountain of death with each quickening heartbeat, until it waned into a mere crimson trickle. Of course, his father would try to talk, to tell Arvan he loved him and persuade him to reconsider, but all the boy would hear was a gurgle and, at the very end, a sigh. Besides, once it was done it could not be undone, nor would Arvan wish it to be.

"Enough stalling," he told himself. "This is it: kill him."

He lifted the sword up to his shoulder and aimed at the sleeping man's throat, so like his own.

*

Lament could feel the dark clinging to him and the added encumbrance of

Vaiske holding onto him for some form of direction bade him no comfort. He led the immortal casually through the camp, somewhat suspicious at the lack of security.

"What are you looking for?" Vaiske asked.

"Our weapons," Lament replied. "I shan't imagine we'll be very foreboding opponents for the Behemoth without them."

"And you can see?" Vaiske asked.

Lament stopped and turned to the immortal. All the horned warrior could see in the black nothingness of the night was the amber iris of the shadus.

"Of course," Lament said, before he started searching again.

Vaiske fought the urge to vocalise his amazement at Lament's sight. Instead, he merely said, "Had I known you would be this useful I never would have taken your other eye from you."

"And my shadow?" Lament mused.

Vaiske smiled behind his mask.

"Now, shadus," he said. "You've no better use for that than I."

Lament rolled his eye towards Vaiske and the immortal saw the amber ring seemingly floating in the air.

"Keep that eye pointed away from me, shadus," Vaiske growled. "No good fortune comes my way when you're looking at me."

"Quiet," Lament whispered, stopping abruptly.

Vaiske listened. He could not see them in that near-complete black, but he knew they had been surrounded. He heard the rain collide with the readied swords of the troops around them. From the timbre of the noise he knew they were no more than a few paces away, perhaps closer than that.

Lament passed his eye between the men around them. There were six of them, all armed with broadswords, but he held an advantage over them; he could see.

"Lament, you despicable swine!" Vaiske growled. "I thought you said that you could see!"

"A trap set by the Riit Clan, I assure you," the shadus replied. "If you are so concerned, could I implore you to release me and reach out behind you?"

Rather unenthusiastically Vaiske released Lament's arm. He half-expected to fall into some horrific and unending pit, but, when all appeared to be correct, he turned and grasped a low wooden structure before him. He smiled as he realised it was the cart with the weapons placed on it. His hand fell upon his spear and his smile widened.

"Where are they?" Vaiske growled.

"The even points of the clock," Lament replied.

"Perfect!" Vaiske roared, leaping into battle.

Lament watched. The immortal moved with such skill and speed that, even when he was blinded by the oppressive dark, his opponents could not move in response. It was as if they were paralysed by fear or knowledge of their deaths. But, in truth, Vaiske was just a perfect specimen of war.

Lament gazed upon the scene. In a matter of seconds the six Riit soldiers were dead on the ground, their dark blood pouring from them and merging with the water expelled from the already clogged ground. It soon diluted into just another viscous fluid.

"My eyes are growing accustomed to this dark," Vaiske said. "I even saw that last man die. I would appreciate it if you told no-one of my having to use you as a guide."

Lament turned and took the gargantuan sword from the cart, then strapped it back in place beneath the crimson cape. "As you wish."

*

"Arvan!" the unmistakable voice of Master Snow sounded just as he was about the plunge the sword into the Major's throat.

Arvan didn't move, save for his head that turned to the white clad samurai at the entrance to the tent. Darkla stood silently next to him, staring at Arvan.

"What do you plan, Arvan?" Snow asked.

"I'm going to kill him," Arvan said calmly. "I'm going to slit his throat."

"And that will right the wrongs he has done you?"

Arvan shook his head.

"No," he said. "I hold no illusions. Killing my father will not bring my mother back to life, or Darkla's parents for that matter. Every action he ever committed will still weave through motion and be fixed in its moment. Yet, once his heart has ceased to beat he can commit no more crimes. He cannot hurt me nor any others, save for the memories he has imprinted on us."

He looked to Darkla; her usually gentle, almost passive, eyes seemed to scream to him. 'Do it. Kill him and end this.'

He moved to obey them but was stopped by Master Snow's voice.

"He's just a man, Arvan. And yes, what you say is true; were you to kill him he could not harm you again. He is just a man, as easy to kill as any other. His body has many weaknesses, especially when he is asleep, as he is now. Physically he is easy to kill, yet that does not make it easy to kill him.

"You could slit his throat. You could plunge that sword through his heart. You could even behead him, had you the mind. But once it is done, it cannot be undone, and the image of the corpse you create is unlikely to leave you. Kill him with that knowledge. Kill him with the knowledge what the image of his death will haunt you as the countless I have manufactured haunt me."

Snow turned and left the tent.

"I don't want you to see this," Arvan said to Darkla.

She nodded acceptingly and followed Master Snow.

Arvan sneered at the sleeping man before him. The sword felt lighter now, easier to use, and his father was such a fitting target.

He knelt over him and kissed him on the forehead. He rested the sword next to him and wordlessly left.

"I don't want to know what you did in the end," Snow said, facing away. "I thought I had taught you better than that, to have to have that conversation. I have failed you."

"You meant not to teach me how to kill?" Arvan asked.

Snow said nothing as Lament emerged from the darkness. The shadus handed them their weapons and gave Kyagorusu's staff to Darkla.

"We should all be armed with something for the time being," he said to her. "We've lost the provisions I'm afraid."

"And Vaiske?" Snow asked.

"He's clearing a path for us. I find it distasteful to use his love for the kill in our favour, yet…" He shrugged as if it was a fitting end to the sentence.

Snow nodded. "Yet this whole business is one of distaste." He turned to Darkla, she seemed strangely nonplussed by the episode. "If you wish to go no further I will escort you to Farras."

She shook her head resolutely and said nothing. She held the staff lovingly close to her as Arvan had so many times before.

They walked a macabre path, led by the shadus. The un-drained liquid sloshed around their feet with each running step and they were all nauseated by the knowledge that it was not just rainwater. Even Snow found himself grateful that he could see the scene in no great detail, to the point he held a fervent pity for Lament and his superior eyesight. To Snow the bodies of the dead soldiers were mere outlines in the dark, barely even there. But the shadus could see every cut, every terrified expression as they realised this was their end, even the discoloured rainwater at their feet, at points almost entirely crimson. He never numbed to it.

Darkla could barely see Arvan, yet she could picture his expression almost perfectly. His grave features taking on a sepulchral severity as he thought back to the events inside the tent. She wondered if he had killed his father and what it meant if he had. She understood his feeling towards the man but could not imagine herself in that situation. How she longed for just one living parent. Then again, her parents were not murderous warlord minions.

Supposing Arvan had killed the Major, what did that make him? His father slept at the time, would the noble thing have been to confront him in a duel? However, warlord soldiers were not famed for their nobility.

The morbid path was mercifully brief and the soon found Vaiske on the outskirts of the camp, his spear resting across his shoulders. His breath was quick and deep as if in the throes of some lustful pleasure.

"Are there more to come?" he asked.

"I saw none following us," Lament replied.

Vaiske snorted and looked away as if disappointed.

"They may try and track us," Snow said. "We've done quite some damage here. But we can lose them in the Central Desert; they wouldn't dare follow us in there."

"With good reason," Lament said.

"We've nothing to fear, Lament. I've traversed the desert many times, it's fairly docile at this time of year."

"So we head south," Arvan said.

Snow nodded but said nothing. And with that they disappeared into the night.

Chapter Twenty

They ran in the accursed blindness of the night, their legs working like tireless pistons in some unstoppable machine. None dared look back. An empty horizon was no good sign and one full of Riit soldiers was an even less welcome sight.

The rain was relentless. Thunder called ominous tones to them, warning them not to stop. Sheet lightning flashed, gifting them glimpses of the oppressive landscape laid out before them. On it stretched, an endless vista; verdant at first, growing forever more arid as they neared the desert.

Darkla had kept pace with the more experienced group well, until the night had drawn into its immeasurable time. Only then did she start to slow. She was certain she would be forgotten by the group, each too concerned with their own survival to ensure hers. But Lament fell back with her, grasping her hand in his. The chilling fingers of the shadus took in her own so completely, yet so gently, it made her think of her childhood, when she and Arvan had walked the coastal path together, hand in hand. From that moment she almost forgot that they were running for their lives.

Lament's exhaustion never waned. His nausea flared and feverish sweat soaked through his already rain drenched clothes and hair. But still, he ran on, Darkla's tender hand in his. They were some distance behind the rest of the group, but at least they weren't alone.

They reached the desert just before dawn, the clouds finally dissipating and the sky palling to violent. They waited on the outskirts of the wasteland as Lament and Darkla caught up.

"How many warlord clans must I run from before this adventure is over?" Arvan panted. He looked up, his body held up by his hands resting on his knees, and saw the immortal standing before him with no lack of breath.

"Don't worry, Arvan," he said. "It won't be so long before there are no more warlords to run from."

"Lament!" Snow called between large gulping breaths as the shadus approached with Darkla. "Are they following us?"

Lament released her and Darkla tumbled to the ground, fighting to catch her breath. He knelt beside her, but she smiled and waved him away. He turned, standing, and saw a myriad of tiny silhouettes far away, but getting closer, no doubt.

"They follow," he said.

"Will they track us through the desert?" Arvan asked, gradually straightening himself.

"We go hesitantly ourselves," Vaiske replied.

"Then we should go!"

"Not yet," Darkla groaned. "Please, not yet."

"She's right," Snow said. "They are still some distance away. We would be unwise to venture into the desert in our current condition."

"How can we rest when we know they're coming?" Arvan muttered, falling to his knees.

"Where has this lack of courage come from?" Vaiske said, kneeling to meet the boy's eyes. "You have, at times, been even more headstrong than me. You've an immortal beside you, Arvan; not to mention skills of your own. You've nothing to fear from the Riit Clan, or any warlords for that matter."

Arvan said nothing and glanced to a distracted Master Snow.

Time drew on and true dawn bloomed. The rest did them all good, except Lament whose condition worsened. Once the sky was washed with blue and he knew that his companions could see the approaching soldiers, he stood.

"We must go," he said.

"But you're not ready," Darkla replied.

Lament shook his head and looked to Vaiske. "It is the Shadowblight; I shall never be ready."

Vaiske nodded and they ventured into the desert, Lament stoically doing his best to conceal his sickness.

Time passed slowly in the desert, as did their progress, but eventually they wandered so far into the wasteland they could no longer see the grasslands or the warlord soldiers. The sultry heat seemed to slow everything. It made the air thick in much the same way as the breeze after a battle, yet even the miasmic breeze would have been welcome compared to that uncomfortable heat.

Lament tried not to slow the group, prowling forth as if nothing was wrong. But his legs weakened and he tripped, landing in a cloud of sand. He peered up at the concerned faces of the group and the mask of Vaiske.

They spoke to him in words he couldn't distinguish and he waved them away, forcing himself to his feet. He walked on, for a brief moment leading the group, only to be overtaken by his healthier companions.

The breeze whispered sorrowfully past, seemingly calling to him. He paid no attention until it did it once more.

'Lament,' it appeared to say in those feminine tones. 'Lament.'

He staggered on, trying to keep pace with the group but the breeze wrapped around him as if to hinder his progress.

"You have come for me?" he asked, careful to keep his voice low enough for his companions not to hear.

There was no vocalised reply, but the breeze gripped him tighter.

"Is this real?" he asked. "Is this you or some blissful illusion?"

Still there was no answer. Darkla turned and gave him a concerned look, but the shadus couldn't see her. His half world was melting away, evermore so, until he finally sunk to his knees and released entirely.

Darkness.

"Lament!" Darkla cried. She ran towards him, the sand swallowing her steps, and knelt over him. "Lament!" She shook him but he didn't wake.

When Darkla looked up she saw the others gathered around her and the shadus. Arvan's face was pale and he wore a horrified expression.

"Is he alive?" he asked.

Snow knelt beside Lament and pressed his fingers to his neck. There was a slow, faint pulse.

"Barely," Snow said.

"The Shadowblight," Darkla said. "It's going to take him." She shot her gaze to Vaiske. "Can't you see you're killing him? Give him back his shadow!"

"I've yet to be done with it," Vaiske said calmly. "You underestimate the shadus; he wouldn't let the Shadowblight take him so soon. He needs rest and we must give it to him."

Snow shook his head. "We can't stay here. The desert can be temperamental; there can be sandstorms with no more warning than the slightest change in the breeze."

"Fine," Vaiske said. "I'll carry him."

He gestured for the others to move out of the way and bent to haul Lament off of the ground, but the shadus did not move. Vaiske stood, sighed, and tried again with much the same result.

"Damn wretch can't be that heavy," he grunted.

"It's the sword," Arvan said.

Vaiske turned to him. "Need I remind you that I'm an immortal? No sword is too heavy for me."

"No. All this time only Lament's been able to lift that sword. Maybe it's magic."

"Not magic," Snow said, gazing at the sword on the shadus' back. "Certainly mystic though."

"Cursed, more like," Vaiske growled. "Either way we can't leave him."

Darkla looked up at him from where she knelt next to Lament. "I thought you two didn't get along."

Vaiske sneered behind his mask.

"We don't," he seethed. "But we've an agreement; nothing more than that, little girl. I need his help to kill the Behemoth."

"We're wasting time," Snow said, loosening the leather bonds that strapped the sword to Lament's back. "We'll leave the sword here."

"He won't be happy about that," Darkla said.

"Happy or not, he'll be alive," Vaiske replied. "Besides, he's never happy."

Snow finished unstrapping the sword and it tumbled from Lament's back. Vaiske threw the shadus over his shoulder as if he was some rag doll.

"See?" he said. "Nothing at all."

The sword glistened on the sand as they walked away, the sun almost drawn relentlessly towards it.

Arvan felt as though they were making no progress. For hours they had walked with no change to the landscape. Dunes seemed to rise on the horizon but they reached them, walking an endless path of flat, golden sand. The sky remained as a solid ceiling of blue.

The hopelessness drew on. Lament, draped over Vaiske's shoulder, showed no signs of waking and with each step they made he looked ever less likely to. The sultry heat threatened to deplete their numbers further.

Arvan didn't know how long they'd been walking when the vast carcass of metal first appeared in sight. It lay there, glimmering in the light of the sun like a broken world, long dead. The metal was rusting from its many centuries in the desert, but it shone as if conditioned to do so by some ancient curse. It was a mass of edges and acute angles, precariously placed as if to finish falling from the planet at any second.

They approached it, seeking comfort for Lament.

"What is that place?" Arvan asked.

"A world long gone," Vaiske replied. "The first city destroyed a millennium ago."

"By the Behemoth?"

"No," Snow said. "Man did this."

"Man or Behemoth, the results the same," Vaiske growled. "Let's just get the shadus out of this heat."

Snow saw it first. The gleaming arrowhead shot towards them, trailed by a thin shaft of wood. Arvan only saw it as Snow drew his katana and cut it down just before it struck the boy in the chest, the blade of the sword curling down through the air and cleaving the arrow in two.

Arvan lost all breath and stood panting before looking to his Master. Snow said nothing, sheathed his katana, and looked at the iron carcass.

"Hello there!" called a minute figure from the top of what was once a wall. "Sorry about that! I left my son on guard; he got a little over-zealous! Come on in; we've food and water to spare!"

The figure disappeared from sight and Vaiske looked to Snow.

"What do you think?" he asked.

Snow's expression was one of concerned pensiveness. Arvan had never seen his Master in such a way before, he was usually so calm, especially in situation of danger, or so the stories told. What was different this time?

"I think we don't have a choice," Snow said after a long hesitation.

"It was an accident," Darkla said firmly. "We have to get Lament somewhere he can rest for a while."

Arvan could say nothing. That those so close to him could accept that his near-death was an accident so easily was more-than-a-little disconcerting. But, upon looking at the slumped figure of Lament over the immortal's shoulder, he found himself agreeing. He had never thought of the shadus as a strong man, or even a healthy man, yet this was a terrible condition even for him.

They began once more towards the fortress only to be met by a man whom Arvan assumed had been the one who had spoken to them from the wall. His face was hidden almost entirely by the large, high collar of his garbs, so much so that only his eyes, forehead and messy black hair were visible. His clothes were a mass of waves and obscure lines, made of some soft brown material. What Arvan could see of his skin was heavily tanned and leathery, presumably from his years spent in the desert heat.

"My apologies," he said in a muffled voice. "As I said, my boy got a little excited."

"It's understandable," Snow said. "I shouldn't imagine you get many visitors out here. We've a sick man with us; he needs rest and water. Can you help him?"

The man nodded. "If that's all you need. As you can imagine, we've more room than we know what to do with."

Arvan looked up at the iron city. It was every bit as vast as the Final Resting Place of the Empire, though completely dead. Aside from the man before him and the boy in the wall he couldn't imagine anyone else inside the city. Even in the years when the city could have been said to exist he thought it must have been a lonely place, for some at least.

He turned his gaze to the man. Only then did the desert dweller look upon Lament, draped over Vaiske's shoulder.

"A shadus?" he gasped. Then he looked to Snow. "You expect me to allow a shadus in my home?"

Snow gave the man a perplexed look.

"What exactly are you so concerned about?" he asked.

"I've heard the stories, dark stories one and all. I've no wish to subject my boy to that."

"What exactly do you think he'll do?"

"They manipulate shadows," the man said, drawing a dagger from behind his back. "Leave, now!" He took a step forward.

"Superstitions!" Vaiske roared. "You've more to fear from me than him."

"Please," Darkla said, her sea-green eyes meeting the darker ones of the stranger. "He's very sick."

She looked at Arvan, pleadingly, and he realised he was the only one of the group to have said nothing. Then again, what was there for him to say? The man was right, Lament could manipulate shadows and his fears were well founded. Indeed, Arvan had many of the same fears upon meeting Lament – a pale stranger with a mysterious personality. He supposed he trusted him a little more now, though he couldn't deny the shadus was somewhat dangerous. Yet Darkla's pleading eyes reached him and he faltered.

"He's harmless," Arvan said weakly.

The man fixed his gaze on Arvan and the boy refused to look away. He'd not be beaten by the mere look of those older than him. Not anymore.

Eventually, the desert-man passed his gaze to the unconscious Lament. Then he looked to Snow once more.

"Very well," he sighed, replacing his dagger. "You may stay for a time. But when the shadus has recovered, or you've outstayed your welcome, then you'll leave."

Snow nodded in agreement, though Arvan noticed Vaiske gesture arrogantly with his spear only to stop short of actually speaking.

The man held out a hand to Snow. "My name is Serrin. My son is Banda."

Snow took Serrin's hand and shook it gently. "I am Lawliet Snow. The girl is Darkla and the boy is Arvan. The man in the vermillion armour is a warrior called Vaiske Parlet. The shadus is…"

"No need for that," Serrin said, pulling his hand free and holding it up to silence Snow. "I don't want to know anything about the shadus. You'll do me a great favour if you let me act as though he wasn't here."

Snow's face took on a faint frown, though he consented. Serrin gestured for the group to follow him into the city. They passed a threshold that looked to once have been a great gate but was now a mere fissure in the iron wall, destroyed in an act of war an age ago. There stood Banda, barely half of Arvan's height, dressed much like Serrin, his skin taken on the same sun-tainted look as Serrin. Diagonally across his back was the bow he had used to shoot at Arvan. It was almost as tall as Banda but looked to be made of a light wood. Beside it he wore a quiver of arrows.

Wordlessly, he joined them, walking next to his father.

"We call this 'Avarice'," Serrin said. "The city's divided into four districts, centring on a tower of gold. Well, it used to be a tower, now it's just a toppled monument to a long dead nation."

"What are the other districts?" Darkla asked.

"Don't worry about those. Stay in Avarice and you won't go far wrong."

Arvan looked at the city around him. They passed unused bars and dilapidated homes. Streets were littered with sand and heat shimmered before them. They city continued to decay, on and on into an endless eternity. Immortality through death. Arvan thought it tasteless and morbid, but could think of no better way to describe it. He wondered for a time if Vaiske could understand it.

Eventually Serrin stopped at an abandoned iron building. At the entrance were steps that led down.

"We try to stay underground as much as we can," he said. "The heat can do peculiar things to you."

169

"Only the heat?" Snow asked suspiciously.

Serrin shot him a glance that landed somewhere between fear and malice. He said nothing, turned back to the stairs and led them down into the darkness. Footsteps chimed throughout the stairwell as the soles of their shoes met the iron staircase. Only Snow's steps went unheard. He had long gone barefoot, realising the potential for silence. The first few months had been torturous but, after some two decades, he rarely felt any pain at all.

They soon reached the bottom of the stairs and were engulfed in an almost complete darkness.

"Banda," Serrin said, "light the candles, please."

A quick scuttling noise began and soon the group see. The boy ran from candle to candle, gradually bathing the room in an apathetic lustre. The candle flames flickered inertly, revealing a small, iron clad room with an ancient bed centred against the back wall. Serrin pointed to it.

"You can put the shadus there," he said. "I don't come in here often so I won't have to see it. There are other beds around if you need rest, I'm sure you'll find them easily enough."

He gestured obscurely to a sink on one of the walls.

"The water still runs, just about. I don't expect there's an awful lot left so be sparing. Banda will come to fetch you when it's time to eat."

"Thank you," Snow said, though it elicited no response from Serrin. The man led his son through a jagged hole in the wall.

Vaiske strode over to the bed.

"Miserable fellow, isn't he?" he said, throwing Lament onto the bed carelessly. "Almost as miserable as the shadus."

"I've never met a man who trusted a shadus," Snow said. "Meeting one is a rare occurrence and we don't entirely understand the evolutionary steps they've taken."

"I know," Vaiske said. "I felt the same when I first laid eyes on him and once he lived through having his shadow extracted I came to trust him less. Still, this goes a little further than distrust."

While Snow and Vaiske had been talking Darkla set to work nursing Lament. She was dabbing his forehead with a wet rag she had found in the sink, trying to relieve him of his fever. Arvan watched, pained. Would she do that for him? They had grown so far apart over the past few weeks he wasn't sure. They had hardly spoken to one another since they had reunited and he found himself not caring at this new distance. He was becoming a man and she was a childhood friend.

"Well, either way, we're all at Serrin's mercy," Snow said. "We have to respect his rules. That goes for all of us."

He glanced at Arvan and the boy looked away. He would not rebut. Despite being in the company of four people in that room he was indisputably alone.

"I still don't trust him," Vaiske said, weighing his spear in his hand.

"What was that he said about the other districts?"

"Stay in Avarice and you won't go far wrong," Darkla said absent-mindedly, all her concentration on relieving Lament.

"Abide by that advice," Snow said sternly, his eyes unmoving from Vaiske. "I don't mind you exploring Avarice, in fact I'm going to do so myself, but don't go into the other districts."

Vaiske grunted but nodded in agreement and left up the stairs. Snow freshened himself quickly at the sink then followed. Through all this, Darkla's gaze never left the unconscious shadus.

Arvan sat on the bottom step, fidgeting, trying to think of something to say to Darkla or hoping she would say something to him. But there was only silence. Arvan watched as the covers of the bed rose and fell irregularly as Lament breathed laboriously. After a few minutes of Darkla not even glancing at him he ventured into the next room.

The breeze picked up the littered sand around his feet, only to lose interest and drop the grains back to their earthly prison. The gate stood dauntingly before him, black and ostensibly unmovable. He gazed at it, trying to remove himself from the distinct unease he felt. The desert heat didn't help; it accentuated each nauseating breath he took and drew attention to his spewing bowls. What did he fear? Only that the gate imposed on him myopia.

He scratched at his beard, though it didn't assuage his angst. He thought to turn and leave but couldn't find the will to do so. There was a presence past the gate that led to the centre of the city; vast yet unassuming. The breeze itself seemed to deliver the thoughts to him and that was a messenger he would never escape.

"Intrigued?" a familiar metallic voice said behind him.

Snow turned and saw Vaiske standing arrogantly. His spear was resting on his shoulder, though his posture was as straight as ever. His horrific mask seemed to smile at the prospect of danger.

"It's not quite the word I'd use," Snow replied trying to remove the fear from his voice. "I just can't seem to leave."

He turned back to gaze upon the giant gate as Vaiske stood next to him.

"I know," the immortal said, decidedly more tender than usual. "I'm not entirely sure that I could count myself among the unafraid. Still, as an immortal I feel it is my duty to adventure. I feel as though I must explore inside."

They looked at each other and Snow shook his head reticently.

"We can't," he said. "Serrin is our host, I won't disobey him."

Vaiske gave an incandescent grunt. "How long do you think we'll have to wait before Lament wakes up? A few days at least, maybe a week before he is ready to travel. Do you feel safe with that unknown entity lurking behind that gate? And Serrin so mysterious about it. Doesn't it concern you that he won't even speak of it?"

"I can think of nothing else," Snow said. "Yet I will not disobey Serrin so readily."

Vaiske turned in anger, only to stop short. He nudged Snow and gestured before him with his spear. Snow turned and saw Banda stood a way down the road, his wave-like clothes fluttering in the force of the breeze. He made a gesture with his hands that seemed to say 'Come'. Snow and Vaiske shared a glance and obeyed.

Arvan sat alone in the adjoining room, his head and back resting uncomfortably on the hulking metal structure behind. He listened to the gentle silence, interrupted only by the sound of Darkla intermittently wetting the cloth she used to soothe Lament. Eventually even that stopped and Arvan's old friend appeared in the hole that connected the rooms, holding Kyagorusu's staff.

"I thought you were nursing Lament," Arvan said, looking up at her.

She smiled and sat down next to him. "My sitting by him won't make him heal any faster." She passed the staff over. "You should have this, it means more to you."

"Thank you," Arvan said, taking it.

"I wish I'd known him. From what you say, he was a remarkable man."

"He was," Arvan said. "But already my memory of him has begun to fade."

He hung his head and tried to think of the kindly bald man. Brief images and remnants of feelings ran through him, but they soon wavered and left. Eventually, despite his best efforts, Kyagorusu left his mind completely and his thoughts returned to other matters.

"I didn't do it," he said. "Kill my father, I mean."

"I know," Darkla said gently, her hand resting lovingly on his shoulder.

He met her eyes. "I wanted to. I really wanted to. You've no idea how I've imagined the chance for so long. And there I was. And I faltered, leaving him to sleep soundly."

Darkla said nothing, merely contenting to caress his back softly.

"If I can't kill him, a man who has wronged me so, how can I ever live up to the expectations of being Master Snow's apprentice?"

Darkla grasped his jaw in her hands and placed his face directly before hers. "You did exactly what Master Snow would have done. Have you ever heard of him killing in revenge?"

Arvan shook his head, though his eyes were still full of sorrow.

"But that's not all that's bothering you," Darkla said. "Is it?"

"Everything bothers me," Arvan sighed. "I'm keeping dangerous company and I've gotten you involved. I've disappointed Master Snow after trying so hard to find him. I'm on a journey to kill the Behemoth and I'm of no use." He took her hand in his. "And I feel as though we're drifting apart. I even missed the anniversary."

"Don't," she said quietly. "You have your own troubles, Arvan. You needn't burden yourself with mine as well. And we're not drifting apart, I promise you. These are just strange days for the both of us."

She laced her fingers through his and smiled and infectious smile that Arvan soon shared in.

"My apologies," said the unnoticed Serrin from the other side of the room. "I didn't mean to intrude."

They took their hands from one another and looked to him.

"Dinner's ready," he continued. "It's a few rooms through when you're hungry."

He turned and left.

Darkla looked at Arvan in a way he thought childish. He gave her a mature frown and she kissed him on the forehead.

"I'm starving!" she laughed. Then she ran after Serrin.

They knelt around a small wooden table in a room of iron much like the others. They ate a thin soup, so tasteless it may have been hot water. Vaiske had finished first. After struggling to fit the spoon through the mouth-hole of his mask he had become frustrated and rather rudely decidedly to drink the soup from the bowl.

Necessity dictated that Serrin and Banda remove the cloth covering the bottom halves of their faces, revealing to the group a savage scar snaking its way from Banda's mouth to his throat. He eyed the group self-consciously though they were so hungry they barely noticed. Still, the child watched them warily, every so often glancing at his father for comfort, yet his father didn't seem the sort to give encouragement unsparingly. He made Arvan think of his own father.

Eventually, after her growing discomfort had peaked and she could no longer gestate in the silence of the room, Darkla leaned over to Banda.

"So," she said in her most child-friendly voice, "how old are you, Banda?"

"He doesn't talk," Serrin said shortly. "He can't talk. That scar you've all tried so hard to ignore comes from a sword strike that destroyed his voice-box. And I don't know how old he is. The years have no beginning or end out here."

"That's tragic," she whispered. "Who'd do such a thing?"

"There was a disagreement a few years ago, when there were more of us here than just Banda and I. Some wanted to stay here, others to leave the desert. The talks became heated and, as leader of those who wanted to stay, I was targeted. But they punished Banda, not me. I suppose the guilt is my punishment."

"Where are the others who wanted to stay?" Vaiske asked.

Serrin looked at him menacingly. "There are no others."

Silence washed over the room again and one by one they finished their meals. When all were done, Snow spoke.

"Forgive me, Serrin," he said. "Your hospitality is much appreciated and more than we deserve, but you are in a more talkative mood than when we first arrived and I must take the opportunity. So I ask you; what is it you fear in the other districts?"

For what seemed an eternity, Serrin didn't speak. He stared at the table before him. Eventually he planted his elbows on the wooden surface and placed his hands together.

"Fear doesn't cover it," he said, meeting Snow's eyes, aware that all at the table looked at him. "And I'll ask you not to pry." He stood and motioned for Banda to do the same. "I'll not lie, I don't like you being here. You use my water and eat my food. Yes, I welcomed you in at first; what man would I be to condemn you to the desert? But you are overly inquisitive and you have a shadus with you. I don't want to know what you're planning to do, but once the shadus is well enough to do it, please, leave."

With that he left, Banda following dutifully behind.

"And still we have no answers," Vaiske growled.

"Let's just see how Lament is," Snow said. "We've been here too long as it is."

His condition was no better when they returned to him. He showed no signs of waking and the group was too tired to sit with him until he did. They slept uneasily, but at least they slept.

Chapter Twenty One

Snow rose early the next morning, so early that even the sleepless Vaiske didn't see him rise, much less venture out into Avarice. But, even as morning drew on, no-one mentioned his absence. Arvan and Darkla woke almost in unison and took up their positions caring for Lament.

The shadus was no better. In fact he seemed to have receded further into his slumber, no lustre piercing through the blind-rag and closed eye. He didn't writhe in pain or groan in some comatose dream. He barely breathed, inhaling and exhaling laboriously and irregularly. Had they not known him better or felt his feverish forehead, they might have thought him dead.

They sat there silently for hours, nursing Lament, until Vaiske got to his feet. He wielded his spear in his hands.

"Is this all we're going to do?" he growled. "Sit around and stare at that damnable shadus?"

"What else can we do?" Darkla said.

Vaiske grunted. "Well I'm sick of looking at his miserable face. Everything about him is miserable. His clothes are miserable. His voice is miserable. Even his name's miserable: Lament Strife! Well, enough of it. You can sit around watching him die if you want, but I'll have no more of it."

He turned on his heel and stormed up the stairs, his armour clattering like a marching army, his spear ready in his hand.

For a moment, Darkla stopped swabbing Lament's brow and squeezed the rag in her hands. Her eyes screamed fury until Arvan put his hand on hers. She softened and looked at him.

"He's just restless," Arvan told her. "He's not used to staying in one place for so long."

Darkla said nothing and went on cooling Lament.

"But you don't like him anyway."

"He's killing Lament!" she cried, tossing the rag against a wall with a damp thud. "He might not die right now but how long can he live without a shadow? Even if he's alive by the time we kill the Behemoth and Vaiske gives him his shadow back the damage might already be done. How much longer could he really have left?"

Arvan looked at Lament, so fervently gripped by his sickness that he could hardly be said to be alive. He thought of his mother in her final weeks and the image was little different. He'd never left her side, fearful that she might slip away alone, something he thought nobody should face. And then the moment came. One final sigh that only he heard, his disbelief that it had actually come, something like the relief at the end of her pain, yet set upon that solace was a sorrow so intense that it promised never to leave him fully.

He looked away. Then he got up and fetched the rag for Darkla. Their hands met briefly as he passed it back to her.

"Thank you," she said weakly. She sighed. "I like Lament. He's kind, in his own way; he looks out for the people around him, not that he'd have them know it. Yes, he's cold and taciturn and solemn, but he's a good man."

"That's strange," Arvan said as she began nursing the shadus again.

Darkla gave him a questioning look.

"That's similar to what Lament said of Vaiske."

The immense gate was no different from before, save for its ever growing intrigue. Snow stared at it in the warm morning light. Despite the sultry desert heat he felt a chill and clasped his hand around the lapels of his robe, holding the garment closer to him.

Behind the gate the city seemed to surge, sending a heavy reverberation through the breeze. What was this dead city? What did it hold?

"I hoped I'd find you here," Vaiske growled, taking a place next to him. "I see it's on your mind too."

"I don't feel safe not knowing," Snow said. "No, it's more than that. I don't feel I can protect Arvan and Darkla from that which I don't know. And Serrin's so secretive about it."

"So you *do* think we're in danger."

"I didn't sleep last night," Snow said, finally looking away at the gate and towards Vaiske. The immortal still stared at the gate.

"I don't want to disobey our host," Snow continued. "But I don't want to be surprised later on either."

"He doesn't have to know," Vaiske said, only now meeting Snow's look. "Avarice is large. For all he knows we could be anywhere around here."

Snow looked around. A multitude of streets spawned at the gate, travelling off to different areas of Avarice. He couldn't see Banda down any of them and knew Serrin to be less subtle.

"Very well," he said. "We have to know." He fixed his eyes on Vaiske. "But I need none of your arrogance. If I say to retreat you must do so."

"You do me a great injustice," Vaiske said with a hint of humility. "I may be immortal, but I'm just as scared of the unknown as you are."

Snow nodded, his bearded face typically earnest, and they approached the gate. They opened the daunting iron obstruction with surprising ease and entered the centre of the dead city.

They found themselves in a large courtyard of pure white stone. The slabs were meticulously placed but, after a millennium of disrepair and carelessness, they had become cracked and broken. Snow knelt and touched the stone; it was somewhat like chalk, though less eager to turn to powder.

The sand had invaded even this morbid sanctuary. Snow supposed it had seeped through some miniscule fissure within the city or fallen to the ground in a torturous sandstorm.

Not far from them was a toppled and decaying statue made of the same stone as the ground. Little of it was left, though he could see enough of it to know it was once held in some esteem. He imagined it was a figure of some importance in the history of this oxidised city, perhaps military.

The ground was laced with gold, shattered from a herculean tower, crushing the gate to the west, leading into a new district. The gold shimmered against the sun creating stars upon the ground growing with sharp points as they neared Vaiske and Snow.

The immortal knelt and picked up a shard of gold in his free left hand.

"Were I a less moral man I might take some of this for myself," he said. "But what use is gold while the Behemoth walks?"

He stood, dropping the gold to the ground with a heavy metallic chime. He looked to Snow.

"What do you suggest?"

Snow pointed to the flattened gate to the west. "That seems to be the easiest district to enter," he said. "I feel as though we've little more to find here, unless all Serrin wished to hide from us was the gold."

Vaiske shook his head. "He told us of the tower when we first met him. Besides, we'll be harder to track in the other districts."

Instinctively, Snow's hand wrapped around the hilt of his katana and Vaiske readied his spear as they made for the crushed gate to the west. They clambered over the fallen monument, helping one another as they went. Coming to the end of the golden shaft, Snow lost his balance and slipped into the new district, landing on his feet. Once he saw all was well, Vaiske jumped down beside him.

Before them, endlessly, save for the circling iron wall in the great distance, were hundreds of small rectangular buildings. Snow recognised them to be barracks.

"So this is where the army was once held," Vaiske said. "It can't have been a particularly large one."

"And now all they have is an army of ghosts," Snow replied.

"It's a city of memories; it needs naught more."

"It doesn't make sense," Snow said, relaxing slightly. "What's Serrin so eager to hide? It's not this. It's morbid, but memories hold no danger."

"You don't want to take a look inside these barracks?"

Snow looked at Vaiske. "What do you mean?"

"It's a little peculiar, don't you think?" the immortal said. "All of the other buildings we've found have been destroyed, so much so that Serrin and Banda live in the basements. There are all in near-perfect condition. Look." He pointed to the closest of them. "They've been repaired."

Snow walked over to the building Vaiske had been pointing at and found that the wall had been reinforced. Not only that, a hole appeared to have been covered over. Snow gestured with his head and they walked around to the front. The gap between the door and the frame was non-existent.

"Welded shut," Snow said. "Serrin certainly doesn't want us to get in here."

"Or he's trying to stop something from getting out," Vaiske growled. "Luckily, I've the strength of an age." He looked at Snow's pale, pensive face. "Or are you having second thoughts?"

"I'm not sure," Snow said. He turned and scratched at his beard, noticing the barrack across the way was also welded shut. He looked at Vaiske. "It's certainly suspicious. Frankly I wish there were more of us."

"Distance Valentine and Grimoire Groan," Vaiske growled. "To be honest I'd settle for the shadus."

Snow eyed him suspiciously. Vaiske didn't notice and threw his shoulder against the door. It barely moved, in fact it seemed to push the immortal back. He tried again with the same result. He went for a third attempt but Snow grabbed his shoulder and stopped him.

"You're not getting through that," he said. "Do you think Serrin's welded all of these shut?"

Vaiske let out a heavy sigh and gazed down the immeasurable distance to the final few huts.

"I don't know," he said. "If that wretched shadus was here he'd be able to see the very last one."

Snow looked at him, halted by the mask, and wondered what expression he wore behind that horrific sheet of metal. Did he have an expression at all? Or was he like Lament; emotionless?

"Well, we're not getting into this one," Snow said. "And the ones I can see are the same. It would be too time consuming to inspect them all one by one and I can't say I'm keen on splitting up."

"I say we try for the next district," Vaiske said. "We might find something there that gives us a clue to this macabre scene."

Snow nodded severely and they ventured south.

*

Still Lament didn't awake; he hardly moved. He lay there as a statue of a dying regent, inertly breathing.

"It seems an eternity since he fainted," Arvan said. "Do you think he's in any pain?"

"If he is, I doubt he knows much about it," Darkla replied. "He's so still." She paused and looked to Arvan. "Do you think Vaiske was right? That it's pointless just waiting here for him?"

Arvan shrugged. "He should have someone close when he wakes up. I think it would be better that it's us rather than Vaiske; I can't see that ending well at all."

Darkla smiled in her usual childish way, though she spoke in solemn tones. "No. I don't suppose it would."

*

The gate to the district in the south was every bit as imposing as the first one they had met. Even at noon it cast a colossal shadow over them and all in sight. But, just from looking upon it they knew that they would not pass. Cumbersome chains hung from it, so large they must have been placed by dozen of men. It was not the welding of the barracks before, but it was just as formidable.

"If the shadus was here he could jump through the shadow and tell us what was on the other side," Vaiske said.

Snow planted a hand on the immortal's shoulder. Vaiske turned to him but said nothing. In spite of the horrific mask, Snow didn't remove his hand.

"Come," he said. "Let's rest in the sun for a while."

They walked from the shadow of the gate and sat on the hard stone ground. The heat assailed Snow immediately and already he realised the lull would not be as somnolent as he had hoped. Yet , the thin light held none of the ominousness that lurked within the shadow.

If Vaiske could feel the uncomfortable warmth he showed no sign of it. He sat as stiffly as always, his legs crossed, his hands resting on his knees, and removed none of his armour. His spear lay beside him, though it seemed no further away than when in his grasp.

Snow fanned his face with the collar of his robe but found little relief as the air washed past him. He continued nonetheless and scratched at his beard with his free left hand, considering Vaiske. He wondered whether or not he should converse with the immortal, knowing him to be arrogantly laconic, though he supposed he was still human despite his endless lifespan.

Eventually, his decision was made for him as Vaiske said, "We've had little fortune today."

"At least we know that something is being hidden," Snow replied. "Our paranoia isn't unfounded. That's something."

Vaiske shuffled awkwardly. "That confounded shadus would keep calm in a time like this."

Snow gave Vaiske a sidelong glance. "He seems to be on your mind."

For a time the immortal didn't reply. He merely contented to sit in his serious stance staring into the distance, as if looking for something of reassurance in their desolate surroundings. Snow didn't force him, Vaiske would speak if he wished to. After a few minutes he turned to Snow.

"Look at Lament's shadow," he said. "As still as a calm sea."

Snow looked upon it. The shadow, once forever moving, was disconcertingly motionless and solid, as if it was Vaiske's own.

"Ever since I found out the shadus was alive, the shadow's been

179

squirming," Vaiske continued. "I tried to ignore it, to tell myself it was my imagination, but the shadow knows I'm not its rightful owner. It's aware. All this time it sensed its true master was close and longed for him. But now…"

He picked up his spear as if to distract himself, only to drop it apathetically. He sighed.

"It's like the shadow's forfeiting. It suspects the shadus is dead, as still as it was before his reappearance. If the shadow's given up on him, what chance does he have?"

"And supposing he does die," Snow said. "What then?"

"I'll still kill the Behemoth."

"So your objectives are intact," Snow said. "What's driving this pensiveness? Guilt?"

Vaiske sneered behind his mask and turned away.

"Don't misunderstand," he growled. "I don't like the shadus. He's nothing but a nuisance. That doesn't mean I want him dead. Of course, had he died when I took his shadow, the Behemoth might be dead already. But, since he survived, it's easier to kill the beast with the shadus' help.

"Still, I promised him his shadow back when all this was over. I feel, if he was to die, that I didn't uphold my end of the bargain. Besides, that he went so far to get his shadow back tells me one thing; he fears death. No man should have to face his mortality, especially without a shadow to give him a small measure of solace that he isn't completely alone."

He looked once more to Snow. "That's all."

Snow said nothing. Vaiske didn't want comfort, of that he was certain. Furthermore, he wasn't entirely sure that Vaiske understood Lament's motives for hunting the immortal down. He'd be the first to admit that he hadn't known Lament long (not that one could ever truly know a person as mysterious as Lament) but the shadus wasn't exactly filled with the mirth of life. From what he had heard of him, Lament seemed to throw his life around with a distinctly reckless disregard. Though this wasn't what the immortal wanted to hear. Snow doubted he wanted to hear anything at all, in fact.

"Well," the white clad samurai said, "we won't find Serrin's secret sitting around here all day. Perhaps we should renew our attempts to enter the barracks."

As if waking from a terrible dream, Vaiske's head shot up as the breeze whispered by. It carried a string of sand grains past on it. No, not sand.

Ash.

Black ash.

In spite of the realisation, Snow thought nothing of it. Vaiske, however, knew better and thought to his encounter with the Old Man. Grasping his spear in his right hand, he stood and watched as the ash drifted listlessly away.

"Vaiske?" Snow said. "What's wrong?"

"Nothing, just days gone by," the man-with-two-shadows replied. He looked from the ashen apparition to the sitting Snow. "Immortal business. You do as you must. I'm sure I shall find you soon enough."

With that he darted after the ash, his heavy footsteps silencing with distance until there was no sight or sound of him left.

Snow thought for a time of what he could have meant but came to no conclusions. He sat for a while longer before sighing, rising and venturing back to the barracks.

*

The ash drifted swiftly from him on the breeze that carried it, though never did it seem as if it was trying to escape, more like the immortal was being led. Vaiske chased it relentlessly through the district, between the myriad of barracks, until he found himself alone with the ash, surrounded by the rusting iron of the desert city.

The black ash wavered, creating the harrowing effigy of millions of grains moving, replacing one another as they shook violently in the sultry heat. As if realising it had nowhere to go, the ash made the vague shape of a man, though the grains still vibrated, restlessly. So dark was the human-esque apparition Vaiske had only one thought and he lacked the will to keep silent.

"Lament?" he gasped.

Had the visage been completely human, what would have been the right arm seemed to hold something abstractly sword-like. It rested this on its shoulder and made a strange gesture, as if somewhat amused, with its free left hand.

"Lament?" it said in a frivolous, yet deep, male voice. "Yes, I suppose we should all lament, for the breeze of this city hold many ghosts and I am but one of them."

Vaiske regarded the spectre with a suspicious tilt of his head. The fragmented lunacy of the figure before him made little sense and the very idea that he was conversing with a dead man made of ash was bordering on ludicrous. Yet his eyes didn't lie. Bodies have a habit of obeying their immortal owners.

"You died here?" Vaiske asked.

The being before him had no face to speak of, but he seemed to smile. The ash where his mouth would have been, had he not been featureless, seemed to disperse leaving a gap in the shape of a wry curl, revealing the metal wall behind the ashen apparition.

"'Died' might be the wrong word," he said. "Though this is certainly where I met my earthly end."

"You're a fellow immortal?" Vaiske gasped. "Trapped in the city of your doom…"

The silhouette seemed to shrug. "I ride the endless tides of the breeze wherever I desire, sometimes in a direction opposing where they would will me to go. I feel the term 'immortal' might be rather excessive. Besides," he smiled again, "I've enough titles."

"Then why come here?" Vaiske growled. "Why relive such horrors?"

The man of ash moved his free left hand to the back of his head as if to scratch it in pensive thought. Then it made a similar gesture as before.

"I grew tired and yearned for more familiar surroundings," he said. "Though I can't say I've found them here."

"Grew tired of what?"

"Searching," came the reply, his voice losing the emphatic vibrancy. "All this time I've been looking, even though I told myself I wouldn't. But it's been useless; I haven't found her anywhere. The breeze hasn't welcomed me as I thought it would. I'm spurned. It hides her from me. Wise, I suppose. She's most likely met her love once more in these long years."

He paused and Vaiske felt as though the would-be ghost surveyed him.

"But why am I telling you this?" the entity asked with that almost-smile again.

"Who are you?" Vaiske asked, his voice softer than usual.

"I've many names. Though I don't suppose they mean much to anyone anymore. And who might you be?"

Vaiske smiled behind his mask and gestured arrogantly with his spear.

"I'm the great Vaiske Parlet," he said. "A warrior. No, more than that; an adventurer. I am the man-with-two-shadows. An immortal."

"An immortal, eh?" the man of ash mused, humoured. "Well it's nice to meet a man of similar desires to myself." He moved his head, as if inspecting Vaiske. "Though you seem to delight more in the killing than I ever did." He turned away in a single smooth motion.

"Well, good luck," he continued. "I've adventures of my own to have and I can hear them calling to me." He appeared to turn with his hips and look back at Vaiske. "Beware of your immortality, man-with-two-shadows. That's a burden I shouldn't like bear."

Vaiske snorted.

"Damn Old Man was right," he muttered.

"Old Man?" the figure said, turning to Vaiske hurriedly. "There are many old men, and I doubt we speak of the same one, yet, should you see him again, tell him I still have no use for unworthy ideologies."

With that he disappeared once more into a string of ash particles and was carried away on the lightest of breezes.

Vaiske stood there silently for a time, trying to make sense of what he had just been witness to. He thought of what the man had said, only to realise he had said very little at all, despite the vast amount he had spoken.

"This is truly a haunting place," he said. He left to meet Snow once more.

Vaiske found Snow not long after, sat, waiting for him, at the entrance to Avarice. The white clad samurai looked up at him.

"What did you find?" he asked.

"Nothing pertinent to our situation," Vaiske grunted. "Yourself?"

"The other gates are much the same as the one we came across. I attempted to break my way into the barracks again but I had no luck."

"What now?"

Snow scratched at his beard and sighed. Then he shrugged.

"I suppose we'll have to confront Serrin," he said. "I can't say I like doing so to a host who has treated us with more care than he had any obligation to, but with Lament's condition we could be here for some time longer and I need not the worry of what Serrin's hiding all the while."

Vaiske nodded. "What say we check on the shadus? We may gain some small insight into how many more days our stay will be."

"Well," Snow said, "he is on our way to Serrin."

It was early afternoon when they stepped back into the shade of their quarters and Snow was glad to be out of the glare of the sun. He'd never been fond of the heat and this long stay in the desert was not to his liking.

He wasn't surprised to see Lament was still unconscious, though he had been hoping for a better sight. Darkla still attempted to relieve his fever and Arvan sat dutifully by.

"How is he?" Snow asked as he walked over to the sink. He freshened himself as he had when they first arrived. The satiation surged through him as a relaxing wave and he felt well rested within an instant.

"The same," Darkla replied morosely.

"Not the news we were hoping for," Vaiske muttered.

"No," Snow replied, turning back towards the others. "But at least he's no worse." He looked to Arvan and Darkla. "Vaiske and I need to speak with Serrin, but we'll be back soon enough."

Arvan shuffled uncomfortably, but Darkla nodded and said, "He's somewhere through there," pointing to the fissure in the wall.

Snow looked to Vaiske determinedly and they went after their host. They soon found him in the room they had eaten dinner in the evening before. The leather-faced man gave them a look of suspicion, before sighing and standing.

"I'm glad you're here," he said. "He might not be able to speak, but Banda has his ways of communicating. He tells me you went into the city."

"Indeed we did," Snow said resiliently.

"And what did you find?"

"Only mystery," Vaiske replied.

Serrin passed his glance to the immortal. "Good. See it stays that way."

"I'm afraid we can't do that," Snow said, calmly scratching his beard. "Put yourself in our position; you wouldn't feel safe either."

"I am in your position," Serrin snarled.

"Not quite. You know what's being hidden."

"And you'd be wise not to want to know."

"Then perhaps we are not wise," Vaiske said, his metallic voice echoing once more throughout the room of iron.

Serrin closed his eyes as if to calm himself, but his lids would obey only briefly and he contented to clench his fists.

"I have done for you more than many men would," he said. "In my life I have known men who would have left you in the desert to rot. I have known many more who would have killed you outright. I have allowed you into my home and given you food and water. I have asked for little in return, only that you obey my one rule. You have flouted this and I ask you to leave."

"You would banish us for mere curiosity?" Vaiske growled, kicking a wooden chair at his feet.

"I have done worse!" Serrin cried. "I have done worse to those closer and dearer to me than you!"

He slumped into his chair as if drained of all life. Vaiske likened him to Lament in his mind. Their host's skin had grown pale and his brow was littered with sweat. His gaze was vacant as if he had stared into some unknown oblivion he had insisted on keeping close to himself at all times, but had never acknowledged before.

"What do you mean?" Snow asked in a harrowed whisper.

"You wish to know my secret?" Serrin asked, his gaze becoming more concrete as if waking or pulling himself from some terrible daydream. He rose shakily to his feet, standing weakly and unbalanced.

"Very well," he continued. "Then we must venture into the city. I will take you, though I do so reluctantly. Don't tell the children you have with you, nor will I tell Banda. He needn't witness that horror again."

Chapter Twenty Two

The darkness clung to him as it always had, swirling around his arm as he lifted it into his diminished sight. He waved his other arm before him. Was this true darkness or some strange blindness? Though he could barely see, he knew that there was no ground except the small area he stood upon, as the breeze spiralled around him in a narrow column.

The light met his eye and, for a time, he squinted in fear of looking. But he soon grew accustomed to it and surveyed the haunting scene.

He was stood atop an iron pillar, level with the cloudless azure sky. If he was to take but one step he would plunge to his fathomless death. Yet, despite his peculiar surroundings, he was aware of only the arms draped around his collar bone, obscuring from him the knot of his cape, the body clinging to him as the darkness or breeze usually did.

Her body was pushed lovingly to his back and he felt her head, resting on him, listening to the irregular beating of his perplexed heart. Her wonderful scent assailed him, how long since he had last smelled her, yet the aroma had never left his mind.

"What new perdition is this?" he asked in his usual whisper.

"The best kind," she replied in gentle tones.

He tried to turn and look at her but found himself turning with his eye-less left side. Frustrated, he turned away.

"Is my toil now over?" he asked.

He felt her shrug and fall further into the embrace.

"That remains to be seen," she replied.

Lament moved his arm up to his collar bone and gripped her wrist in his hand. She shuffled further into him.

"Why do you insist I continue?" he asked.

She giggled softly and abruptly. "It is not I who forces you on, my sweet. It appears you are something of a masochist."

Lament said nothing, his hand falling from her wrist.

"I am encumbering you," she said, starting to pull herself from him. His hand shot back to her and held her until he was certain she would stay.

"No," he said. "I enjoy you draping yourself over me."

"I am glad," she said. "I have missed our closeness such as this."

"You have not been so far."

"Perhaps not. But it has felt so much more… abstract of late."

He sighed, knowing exactly what she meant. He had felt her with him, more so every day, but there had been some dream-feeling to the sensation, as if he was the one who was not really there. Her grip on him tightened.

"You haven't asked what I expected you to," she said. From her voice Lament knew she was smiling. "I'm almost disappointed in myself."

He moved to look at her again, this time with his right eye, but she met his cheek with a gentle caress before he had even moved an inch.

"Not yet, Lament," she said, as he returned his gaze to the view before him.

He sighed. "What is it I am expected to ask?"

Her arm fell back into place around his collarbone.

"I can't be expected to tell you that," she said. "I must be allowed some mystery."

"Must I be subjected to your games?" he asked, smiling despite his best efforts not to.

"If you wish to join me," she laughed.

How he had missed her laugh. The sound that encompassed all that was good in life, yet she laughed it at her most joyful when life was melancholic. It was the sound that sprang forth from sorrow when happiness seemed but a hope. How long since he had last heard it; the gentle, short giggle, neither high pitched nor deep? Too long. How exactly he had lived without it he couldn't imagine.

"Why am I here?" he eventually said.

"That's the question," she said, her voice reverberating through his chest. "But who are you asking?"

He paused, for a moment considering the possibility that she knew no more than him. Then it dawned on him; she knew an infinite amount more than him, just not what he expected.

"You," he said. "Though I should be asking myself."

"Well done," she said gently. "So, Lament Strife, why are you here?"

"Because you called me."

"Oh dear," she sighed. "You don't understand at all, do you? Oh well, it seemed you've sought answers prematurely. Back to your shadow-less existence…"

"No!" Lament gasped, his body freezing. "I beg of you!"

He felt her shrug behind him.

"Very well," she said. "Then think."

He looked pensively into the distance. The powdered sky seemed to roll on for eternity but it held no answers. All this time he had thought he could hear her calling him, leading him, and that this, their meeting, was the logical conclusion; the satiation of her will. Could he have been so wrong?

"I think…" he paused, struggling to admit it to himself. "I think I came here to atone."

"Atone for what?"

He closed his eye and sighed. Her touch on him was he truly knew, these words he spoke were almost a mystery.

"You would make me say it?" he said when he opened his eye.

"I would make you acknowledge it."

"Acknowledge? I have thought of nothing else since it happened."

"And yet does it not seem as some long-gone dream?"

"A dream perhaps," Lament said. "No, a nightmare. And a recurring one at that."

"You have relived it?"

"I relive it with each breath; with each breath I take and each you no longer have the ability to."

She froze. "You have thought of it so much?"

"What else is there?" Lament mourned. "One taken by the breeze so young."

She tightened her embrace of him and for a moment Lament thought she did so only to silence him. He obeyed, only to be surprised as she spoke.

"The breeze is not so bad a fate," she said. "Less cruel than life at any rate, and it is infinitely more fitting for my disposition."

He didn't reply. He'd never expected her to be so blasé about her death. That she stayed so close to him on the breeze was, at times, like a haunting and, at other times, like some morbid protection. She seemed not to think of it as either.

Lament gazed once more into the endless distance. Then he peered from the iron pillar into the ceaseless depth below. Could he stay there forever – part of the sky for eternity?

After some time spent in the comfortable silence, he grasped her wrists once more lovingly in his.

"Miata?" he said.

"Yes, my sweet?"

"I'm sorry."

She held him closer. "It is not your fault, Lament."

"I should have seen the signs."

She laughed gently as before.

"You think I was saveable?" she said through the curl of a smile. "And, furthermore, that you were the one who could save me? Lament, this arrogance is unbecoming of you."

She rested her head on his shoulder and he saw her hair, every bit as black as his own. He nuzzled into her in some forgotten kiss and was assailed once more by her perfectly sensual scent; something akin to jasmine, though less potent, easier to ignore, though why one would wish to he couldn't fathom.

"So," he said, "can I stay now?"

She lifted her head and he caught a glimpse of her pale skin.

"If that is your wish then you are not yet ready to."

"What must I do?" he asked with a hint of anger.

"You've yet to atone."

"I thought I had nothing to atone for."

"No, I said you have nothing to atone for, which you do not. However,

187

you still feel some measure of guilt."

"And if you hold me in no blame how am I to atone?"

Miata sighed.

"You have too much of a yearning for death," she said.

"Is that so different to how you were?"

"No, but you are not as weak as I was. Or at least you never used to be."

Lament shuffled uncomfortably in her embrace.

"How am I to redeem myself when you hold me up to such unfair standards?" he asked.

He felt her shrug behind him but she said nothing.

"Do you not wish for our reunion?" Lament asked.

"I wish for nothing more fervently!" Miata cried. "But if I am your enticement towards death then am I not responsible for your demise? You throw your life around as if it was nothing more than something to pass the time with. It is so much more! When you are ended you will no longer breathe or cry. You will be no more than a memory to those you love."

"There is only one I love," he said.

Miata paused.

"That may be," she whispered, more like him than her. "But I could not bear to be responsible for your death."

"Then when can we be together?"

"When you yearn for life!" she said, her embrace tightening and warming him, expelling from him that coldness that had encompassed him for what seemed like an age. "When you have lived and you die naturally, not by your own making. Then we can be together forevermore."

Lament turned, his blind eye-socket not feeling the gentle touch of her hand.

"I will wait here for you," she said.

"Here?"

"Meet me on the breeze, Lament. I will wait here as long as I must."

He felt a brief, soft kiss on the cheek below the rag over his eye.

Her touch became less pronounced until it faded and he knew, in that reflexive dreamscape, that he was alone. He looked to his collarbone, where her arms had been so blissfully wrapped around him and saw only his blood-red cape. His surroundings began to dim to sepia.

"Once more into wakefulness, I assume," he said morosely. "A perdition by any other name."

When all was dark he let it engulf him and lift him from his illusion into that lonely reality.

Chapter Twenty Three

With Serrin at their side, and his knowledge of what the city held, the gate looked even more portentous than before. Even the desert-man stopped with them to gaze at it in awe. He shuddered, more so than them, causing Snow to look gravely at Vaiske. It seemed to him, windless as the day was, that the breeze knew better than to venture into the city with them.

"I don't come here often," Serrin said quietly, as if not to disturb the silence. "I've no reason to. It haunts my memories enough as it is; I've no wish for a ghoulish present too."

"And yet that is what you have," Snow replied. "You live in a city of memories."

Serrin met his look and nodded melancholically. "This is no place for the living. Even Avarice could be called home only to ghosts."

He sighed and ventured towards the looming gate.

Vaiske gripped his spear tighter and followed with Snow. The immortal noted how determinedly Serrin walked considering whatever horror it was that awaited the. Despite his seeming apprehension at the sight of the immense gate he now seemed almost apathetic towards the terrible fate that lurked within the city. So intense was his concentration that he didn't even glance at the toppled tower of gold, which Snow, regardless of his time spent surveying it before, still found striking. The shimmering gold on the white stone floor, contrasting little, save for the matt and the glimmer. But he had no time for wonderment as Serrin strode towards the district with the barracks in.

They clambered over the fallen monument and entered the new district. The barracks stood unassumingly, yet, in the desert heat and the group's reluctance to go any closer than they already were, they acquired the appearance of some demonic effigy, awaiting them. Somewhat like grievous teeth tearing out of the stone ground.

With almost disconcerting abandon and a clear disrespect for the tone of the day, Serrin strode up to the nearest building, forcing Snow and Vaiske to follow. Upon reaching the structure he turned to them, his grave face betraying the confidence of his movements.

"I wish you'd reconsider," he said in a frail voice, so unlike his own he could hardly be said to have spoken at all. "It's not how you think it is."

"We'll decide that," Vaiske growled.

"Fine," Serrin said, hardening. His eyes took on a scowl and he pointed to a metal sheet recently attached to the side of the barrack. "There are your answers. But bear this in mind; once you see what it is that you seek to discover, you cannot un-see it. And this district, along with all those that aren't Avarice, holds a secret so terrible that you will never forget it." He fixed his eyes on Vaiske, before glancing at his second shadow. "And Banda tells me you've a longer time in which not to forget than most."

"You'll not deter me," Vaiske growled. He pushed past the desert-man and thrust the tip of his spear into the top of the metal sheet. He pulled, using the handle as a lever, until his immortal strength began to loosen the welding.

"You'll want to stand back," Serrin said earnestly to Snow.

The white clad samurai took his advice and ventured back a few paces, though his host seemed rather more resigned to his fate; staring listlessly at the barrack as if whatever it was Vaiske was going to free was already before him, assailing his sight and gripping him with such vehement horror he could never know peace again. In those moments his vacant face of terror had more in common with the ghosts of the city he lived in than that of the living. Snow's attention was only drawn away from the broken man once Vaiske succeeded in tearing the fissure in the building.

The stench struck them first; dead flesh, eaten away by bacteria left to feast and breed on those someone had once loved. Snow knew it well, as did Vaiske though it was something they had never grown accustomed to. In that instant, Snow knew exactly what the barracks held and recoiled before he even saw it, vomiting a little as he knelt of the stone ground.

Vaiske didn't have the blessing of being able to retreat and his immortality gave him no immunity to the potent odour. Though so much worse than that was the sight. A pile of dead bodies, rotting, barely human looking at all anymore, fell from the hole in the structure, like some cascading avalanche of flesh and bone. Vaiske was knee deep in the dead by the time they had finished falling. He didn't react, forcing himself not to, amazed at Snow's unashamed weakness and somewhat maliciously pleased by turns. He peered into the building. Corpses piled ten high filled the barrack, so some places so well fitted that he couldn't see the floor, walls or ceiling. He supposed had it not been for the decay of the bodies they would have been so well placed to have not fallen.

His musings on the practicality only assuaged him for a few moments. Death, so definitive an ending, surrounded him. So intense was the demise around him that even the breeze didn't stir and there was no movement. He looked to Snow, crouched and bent; his vomiting ceasing to an ache that froze him. Serrin was little different; staring at the terrifying visage as though the planet had stopped turning. An eternity in but a few short seconds.

What was in the vision that caused them to pause? Was it sympathy for the dead? Vaiske couldn't believe it, with the many dead Snow had on his conscience. If he was truly sorry he would stop and find a new path in life. No, sympathy was a reason the immortal couldn't comprehend. It was fear. Fear that the unknowable sleep that these bodies had entered into would come to them, and the always uncomfortable knowledge that they were heading towards it, ever closer with each passing second. Awaiting them with eternal patience.

And what of the man-with-two-shadows? Once the shadus had helped him rid the world of the Behemoth he would once more simply be Vaiske Parlet. Once Lament's shadow was returned to him, the immortal would be but a man and would have this future lurking in the shadows of time. But was that appropriate: that he should suffer the same fate as all of his species?

He gripped the handle of his spear and charged towards Serrin, nearly tipping over the corpses as he went. For a moment he almost forgot they were human, once like him, and treated them as troublesome cobblestones. When the truth came upon him he felt no guilt.

Reaching Serrin, he grabbed his host by his collar and pulled him towards him, barely inches from the surfaces of that monstrous mask.

"What happened here?" he roared, brandishing his spear.

Serrin showed no fear. He looked into the eyes of the mask as no man ever had; his eyes barely open and meditative. He appeared as if he looked not into the demonic sight before him, but into a love he had long lost and didn't know how to feel about the return.

"After the disagreement," he said weakly, "the one in which Banda was disfigured, I banished the man who did it and all those who sided with him. This meant little to them, they wished to leave anyway, and did so eagerly.

"There were many of us left and, for a time, we lived well. With our numbers slightly depleted we could be less sparing with the food and water, but still we were plentiful enough for the city not to seem desolate. At times it was easy to forget that we were in a desert. Those days were good, the best we had here.

"Then it came... the disease. I don't know what it was; I've never seen anything like it, such a swift deterioration. First a fever, then, within a day, death. No other symptoms. We assumed it was one of the wells, we cordoned it off but, apparently, we weren't fast enough. It spread so quickly. Within a week it had reached every district, except Avarice.

"It took my wife. That's when I decided we would store the dead here. It seemed more humane than leaving them lying in the streets or letting them rot in the desert. Why Banda and I survived I can't imagine. We should have left. We all should have left. Then my wife would still be alive."

Vaiske released him but Serrin didn't react. He looked as if he was unaware of the world around him, somewhat like he was adrift in a spacious nothingness. Vaiske turned away, his shoulders hunched beneath his armour, his head tilted slightly to the side.

Snow gazed painfully at their host. The samurai appeared to have recovered from his earlier bout of nausea, though his curiosity had yet to be fully sated. Serrin seemed not to mind the intrusion, in fact he seemed oblivious to it.

"Is that why you chained the other districts shut?" Snow asked. "To prevent people getting to the infected wells?"

Serrin shook his head. "It was purely selfish. The streets are littered with the dead, in some places so much that one cannot move through them. We couldn't bury all of them, so we decided to just not look at them."

Snow shivered.

"Does that make me a monster?" Serrin asked. "That I would treat the dead with such contempt."

"You had your son to think about," Snow replied. He wasn't sure how much of an answer that was, though Serrin didn't challenge him on it.

"Fool!" Vaiske roared, spinning around and pointing his spear at Serrin. "You were lucky to escape with what you had. Your son still lives and so do you. Yet here you live, in this city of death. There's a world out there, but do you think your son knows it? No. Your own mourning has become a cruelty beyond compare. You keep him and yourself in this prison…"

"Prison is right!" Serrin shouted, suddenly coming alive. "This was my doing. This is my punishment."

"The boy did no wrong!" Vaiske roared. "Yes, you have lost, I won't deny you that. But you've a son still, that is more than many, and there are men out there who yearn for just that. They would think themselves lucky to have lost only what you did."

Serrin's eyes were hard. "Your words hold little solace, warrior."

"Solace? I seek not to give you something so gratifying. No, you deserve nothing of the kind. Your son, yes. You deserve nothing. Since we have arrived I have been asking why the tides of fate led us here; it seemed to have little to do with the Behemoth. But I see now. As an immortal I have a duty to right wrongs and to defend those who cannot defend themselves. I was sent here as your punishment!"

He charged at Serrin, certain of his host's death. But, a few steps before reaching the man, Vaiske was knocked off balance by what, at first, he thought was a mere bundle of cloth. But when his eyes focused he saw the desert-boy atop him. In his daze the immortal saw an effigy from his past.

"Valeron?" he said.

Banda scowled and let Vaiske get up.

"The boy's lost enough, Vaiske," Snow said. "He needn't lose his father as well."

The immortal turned to the samurai but said nothing.

"He might live in hell, or what some would think it, but he is blessed for he knows he needn't walk through it alone. He might not say it, he may not be able, though I believe he knows it. Through all of his trauma he's succeeded in maintaining his humanity. I can think only that the company he's been in is the cause for that."

"What do you know of hell?" Vaiske growled. "You speak of things you couldn't imagine. Things that consume a man."

He stormed off towards Avarice, glancing at Banda as he went.

Serrin knelt before his son.

"You saved me, Banda," he said, embracing the boy. "Thank you."

"You've probably saved him enough times," Snow said. "Through all of your brutality."

Serrin released the boy and gave Snow a questioning look.

"The chains on the gates," Snow continued. "They were there before the majority of the residents were dead, yes?"

Serrin nodded. "Before most were even infected." He looked at Banda lovingly. "What else could I have done? Is it not a father's duty to ensure the safety of his son?"

Snow waited until the vulnerable eyes of Serrin once met his.

"His happiness also," he said. Then he turned and followed after Vaiske.

Lament opened his eye to the candle-lit room. He rolled the orb of sight around, surveying the iron shell. Arvan and Darkla sat either side of him, sleeping. He sighed.

"Will this wakefulness ever end?" he whispered to himself. "Typically cruel of you, Miata. Though I'd expect no lesser mischief."

He felt strong, or at least stronger than he had in some time. Then again, years of sleepless nights have a habit of reinforcing the weakness in a man. He supposed that the enforced sleep he had been subjected to had done him some good, yet he had no doubt it was the work of the Shadowblight. Still, his sickness seemed a greater distance away than it had since he had first discovered it.

Feeling rejuvenated he moved to leave the bed, only to brush against Darkla. She startled and woke. It took her eyes a few seconds to focus, but when they did, they focused on the shadus.

"Lament!" she cried. "You're awake!"

"And from such pleasant dreams," he said mournfully, rising from the bed.

Darkla shook Arvan awake. "Lament's awake!"

It took the boy some time to establish his surroundings, still recovering from a dream he didn't remember. When he was once more lucid, he smiled.

"So we can leave?" he asked.

Lament seemed not to hear. He washed his face at the sink and ran his fingers through his hair. He moved as gracefully as ever, even more so, in fact, without the laborious weight of the sword on his back. Still, the crimson cape clung to him, as if to hold him back from some danger before him.

Darkla shrugged.

"When Vaiske and Master Snow return I suppose we will," she said. She turned to the shadus. "How do you feel?"

"No worse than I was," he said. "Better than I have been in some time in fact. Though I don't know how long it will last."

He paused and turned to them, his frown denoting something Arvan hadn't seen in it before. "Where is my sword?"

Arvan thought the look was something like confusion, but more fraught. Worry, only the shadus had a skill of making even that emotion seem diminished. In fact there was very little different about how he looked from usual, had Arvan not been subjected to him for so long a time he may not have noticed this most subtle of changes.

"We had to leave it in the desert," he said. "We couldn't move you with it still attached to you."

Lament rolled his eye towards the boy. "I should think not."

"So it *is* enchanted!" Arvan said, leaping from the bed.

Lament snorted amused. "I suppose 'enchanted' is as close to what that sword is than other word that is likely to come across it."

"Then what is it? Is it bound to you?"

Lament said nothing as Snow and Vaiske entered. The immortal glanced at him but made no effort to say anything. Instead, he seemed to make a conscious effort to ignore the shadus and strode over to the other side of the room, proceeding to survey his spear.

"Lament," Snow said, nodding in some gentle greeting. "I'm glad to see you are awake."

"Finally," Vaiske grunted. "Perhaps we can leave at last?"

Lament shook his head. "First I must retrieve my sword."

He made for the door only to be stopped by the hand of Snow on his chest.

"Not just yet, Lament," Snow said.

The shadus rolled his eye towards the samurai.

"There's a tension in this room you may not have noticed," Snow continued.

"There has always been tension in this group."

Snow smiled. "Then what say we relieve it?"

It was difficult for the rest of the group to tell whether Snow pushed Lament back or whether the shadus took the few paced voluntarily, but their eyes were perpetually fixed upon one another. Lament crossed his arms as Snow walked further into the room.

"You all know about me," Snow said. "I'm a soldier in the Thean House, my Lord's most trusted retainer. Arvan and Darkla are both residents of Farras; they boy, my student. Even Vaiske has divulged to us the last few years of his life in the hunt of the Behemoth." He turned to Lament. "You have told us nothing."

"That's my business," Lament said.

"Then we will not be leaving just yet."

Snow's eyes were hard and they enforced within Lament a stillness so complete that he could not find the will to shake it. The room was silent for some time until Darkla spoke.

194

"Please, Lament," she said. "Share yourself with us."

He met her look briefly, then sighed and rolled his eye until he could see none of his companions, if companions they were.

"No doubt you've wondered about my name," he said. "It is the Twilight Name; a great honour amongst my people. There were only two others to hold it before me, not even one per generation. One per millennium would even be excessive. No, there have been but two, save for me. The first was a woman called 'Sorrow'. The second was a man by the name of 'Mourn'.

"The Twilight Name is given to children born in the midst of a phenomenon. There is a brief moment in the Shadow Isles that is neither part of the Day Months or the Night Months. A brief few minutes when the sky is at sunset. We call it Twilight, though I suppose it is closer to your Dawn or Dusk and it comes but twice a year. Once before the Day Months, once before the Night Months.

"I was born in the Twilight before the Day Months. This is unheard of. Due to the extreme rarity surrounding the conditions of my birth I was given a second name; the first to be given such an honour. And so I came to be called 'Lament Strife'.

"We are not a warrior nation. We abhor war. One of the reasons we keep to ourselves. Yet, we cannot ignore the fact that the north-men do not feel the same way we do, so we grant ourselves some protection. The holder of the Twilight Name is made the warrior that defends the entire nation. A meaningless sentiment, perhaps. Against an invading force what good is one person? For many generations there may not even be a warrior of the shadus. Yet, such was my place in the world.

"That sword you have left to rust in the desert is my birth-right. Now I must retrieve it."

He looked once more to the group who stared back at him blankly. He shuffled uncomfortably on his feet as he looked at them each in turn.

"Lament," Snow said softly. "I'm afraid all you've done is raise more questions."

Lament's frown intensified. "How so? I told you who I am in much the same way as the rest of your party. You are a Thean Soldier. Vaiske is a warrior. Arvan is your student. Darkla is an orphan. I am the holder of the Twilight Name."

"Yes, but you've explained nothing of how you came to be here."

"Vaiske stole my shadow."

"But why did you come to the Northern Continent?"

"To save Captain Swift."

"And why is it your duty to save him?"

Lament said nothing.

"You see, Lament?" Snow said. "We've too many questions about you. It is unprecedented that a shadus should leave the Shadow Isles; such a thing only happens in tales of horror. Please, don't put our distrust in you down to simple xenophobia. You must admit, there is a certain mystery about you that you have done little to skew."

Lament sighed. "What is it you wish to know?"

"How did you come to leave your homelands?"

Lament looked away. "That is not a happy tale."

"It never is with you," Vaiske growled.

"It doesn't need to be," Darkla said. "We haven't been a group for long, but already we've been through so much together; joy and sorrow."

He rolled his eye towards Darkla. Her look seemed sincere, maybe even earnest. Such frankness had never sat well with him and from one he had known for so short a time was uniquely disarming.

He looked to the shadow-less ground at his feet; the candlelight so dim he wondered if the view would have been any different if he'd had one still.

He frowned in his usual pensive way, staring at the ground.

"She was a macabre beauty," he began. "One the likes of which is rare even in the Shadow Isles. Her skin, so sallow it could have been the thinnest paper lit only by the faintest moonlight. Her hair, so dark as to rival the night itself. Her eyes, amber like all shadus, yet more so, jewels beset on pearls.

"Her name was Miata, the daughter of one of our wisest elders. I'll admit, it was mere lust that attracted me to her at first, though my status as holder of Twilight Name intrigued her and led to her father's approval of our relationship. We courted and, although my appreciations of her physical beauty never waned, she became more to me and me to her. Was it love? I'd like to think it was nothing so childish, yet she insisted that's what it was and I wanted not to argue.

"She was, to me, something more than a romantic interest. I had feelings for her that were neither safe nor wise, to the point where I could concentrate on not even the simplest tasks without being distracted by thoughts of her. Man has, for some time, had the idea of a soul-mate. She was nothing as trivial as my soul-mate. She was my soul itself.

"It is a strange feeling, that of being whole, that of completion. A warmth that emanates from one's chest. Poets speak of the heart as the birthplace of emotion and that feeling proves that they are correct. It was just a tragedy that the day came when that warmth turned to an unflappable cold that has lurked within the marrow of my bones ever since.

"We were forlorn. Our love was not a happiness, but a sorrow so perfect that we could do little than bask in its glory and take joy in the very nature of the melancholy. We wept as we kissed. Our tears soaked each other's bodies as we made love. But even that sadness was mild at what was to come.

"Insomnia is common amongst our people. We have evolved to live in nine months of dark in many ways, yet the ability to sleep in endless darkness followed by three months of ceaseless light has eluded many of us. I never experienced the sleeplessness until I left my homelands. Miata, on the other hand, was an insomniac of the highest order, sleep escaping her for the entirety of our relationship. Fearing my concern she hid this from me until she was driven to near lunacy and I could no longer help. She took her own life while I slept soundly next to her.

"I woke with the taste of blood in my mouth. The tang of iron, unmistakable and horrific. But so much more to my horror was my lack of a reaction. I did not howl with grief at the loss of my tortured soul. I rose, buried her and left the Shadow Isles unnoticed; my heart beating a rhythm it has yet to cease. A rhythm that makes no sense to me.

"As for Swift; I was arrogant in my departure, taking a small fishing boat as I sought a new life among foreign lands. I sailed into a storm, became shipwrecked and almost drowned. Captain Swift came by on the Valhalla and rescued me. He gave me passage to somewhere innocuous enough. Sometime after I heard he awaited execution and thought it was only right to repay my debt to him.

"Yes, I left my homeland, though it was only Miata who ever led me to think of it as 'home'. I feel no duty as the bearer of the Twilight Name. Nor do I feel any affiliation with my kin or race. I sought to make a new life for myself in a new place, perhaps even becoming a varied man. I see that was foolish now."

He looked to the group, his damp eyelashes glimmering in the flickering candlelight.

"Am I trusted now?"

The room was silent and Lament left up the stairs to Avarice, his cape flowing as a tide behind him.

A few moments passed as they sat in silence. Vaiske stood and took it upon himself to break it.

"Damn shadus," he grunted, following after Lament. Once the sound of his armour died away, Darkla looked to Snow and Arvan.

"How could he tell it so emotionlessly?" she asked.

"He's no sadness left to spare," Arvan said.

"Do you think so?"

The boy shrugged.

"One thing's for sure," Snow said. "He left the Shadow Isles so he could die in peace, his title ignored."

"Then why would he feel so strongly about saving Swift?" Darkla asked.

Snow met her look. "Because Swift thought he was doing the right thing."

Vaiske strode from their quarters to find Lament waiting for him in the desolate street.

"How did you know I'd come?" he growled.

"You don't strike me as the indoors type," Lament whispered, observing as the immortal shivered at his voice. "Besides, it's an adventure. I thought we'd be persuading Arvan to wait here."

Vaiske shook his head, his armour rattling slightly as he did so. "He has things to speak of to his Master, and his Master to him."

"So it's just us," the shadus said, turning to the distant gate that led out to the desert.

"Let's just go," Vaiske growled, striding past, forcing Lament to follow. "But know this; I'm only doing this so we can leave this city finally, not to assuage your angst at your missing sword."

Vaiske glanced at Lament and thought he saw his lips take on some eerie smile, like a crescent moon forced on its side. "Whatever you say."

The desert was disturbingly still, as if a quiet it could not understand had come over it. The day was long in now and the afternoon was beginning to wane into night. The sky was bruised into hues of purple as the sun began its decent.

"I'll be honest with you, shadus," Vaiske said. "I'm not entirely sure where your sword is."

"I don't need you to be."

Vaiske tilted his head sceptically and looked at Lament. "You mean to say you know where it is?"

Lament shook his head. "It knows where I am. It's directing me."

Vaiske laughed mechanically. "So you've a sentient sword!"

"Sentient? I'm not sure I'd go as far to say that. It is not alive, it has no will. Yet, it is a curse bestowed upon me that I am ill-fated enough to never shirk, nor shall I. It was forced upon me at my birth and I have come to think of it as my own; as a part of me, though a part I don't much care for. If you lost a part of yourself, Vaiske, would you not know where to look?"

Vaiske snorted. "It sounds to me as if you're talking about your shadow, not your sword."

There was no sound when they did not speak, except the gentle whisper of their footsteps as their boots met the malleable sand.

"I'm not entirely sure that I'm not," Lament said.

Their journey drew on, further into the heat of those desolate wastes; still as history. The sky darkened on but held onto that last remnant of lustre, violet light lacing through the air.

Vaiske looked at the ever-wordless shadus. Lament seemed not to notice him, as if walking through the landscape alone. The diminishing light gave him the look of one risen from death; his dishevelled hair a mere silhouette in the dusk-light, his sallow skin becoming grey. All but his glowing amber eye had faded to sepia and Vaiske had always thought him a resolutely colourless man.

"You know, shadus," he said, the echo from his mask falling more softly than usual against the cooling air. "I wasn't expecting that level of honesty back there in the city."

"It is what was asked of me."

Silence came upon them once more at Lament's laconic answer. After a few more paces, Vaiske spoke again.

"You know, shadus. You're a miserable runt. Everything about you is melancholic. Indeed, a more mirthless man I've never met, nor would I wish to. Aside from the Behemoth you're the closest thing I have to a nemesis and it's only my distinct loathing for the beast that stops you from getting the title in full.

"How is it then that you're the closest thing I have to a friend? Snow shall leave upon reaching the Southern Continent and is a man under the orders of another, leaving my motives a mystery to him. The children are too young to understand me. Yet you; despite your youth, despite the many times you've tried to kill me..."

Vaiske paused, but they kept on walking, Lament seemingly paying no attention.

"Well," Vaiske continued. "I trust you. You trust me too, don't you, shadus?"

Lament rolled his eye towards the immortal. "To an extent."

They stopped walking.

"Of course, it's probably just the shadow," Vaiske said, shrugging. "It's all an illusion, making me feel as though we hold some bond. It's just that I have something that was once yours."

"Once?"

"Don't worry, shadus," Vaiske growled. "I haven't forgotten our agreement." He calmed. "Though, even now that you've woken, the shadow appears to have stopped fighting for the freedom to return to its former master."

"No freedom at all," Lament whispered. He knelt and lifted the gargantuan sword from the sand. Vaiske hadn't even noticed it. Lament strapped in back on himself and moved to return to the dead city, only to glance at Vaiske and stop. He sighed.

"You're a good man, Vaiske," he said. "You've taken a distasteful task upon yourself, though you've done it for honourable reasons. If the Old Man's correct then the Behemoth has to die, both for mankind and the Planet. As I've said, I'll help you fight it, if only to take my shadow back." His look met the immortal's. "I trust you as far as that."

Vaiske shuffled before taking his usual still posture and striding back towards the city.

"Arrogant wretch," he muttered, more than loud enough for Lament to hear. "As if I need his reassurance."

Lament's mouth curled into that mirthless smile again and he followed after the immortal.

Arvan sat on the city wall gazing out into the dusk. He wondered how far the desert stretched on. In his sight it was endless, though he knew that there was a world greater than the one he was trapped in currently. As the years went on would the desert expand or recede? He could imagine the sand sprawling outward until it encompassed the entire Northern Continent, or so seemed the tone of the future. Yet, perhaps if Vaiske got his wish and could kill the Behemoth, the future would be rather more fortuitous. Perhaps, eventually, this desert would be a verdant pasture; a land that was fit to live on.

His thoughts were interrupted as Master Snow appeared beside him. The bearded samurai sat.

"Will Darkla not be joining us?" Arvan asked.

Snow shook his head. "Her sleep during Lament's turmoil was disrupted. Her dreams were so that she woke exhausted. If we are to leave tomorrow she will need to be well rested. Besides, I wished to talk to you alone."

Arvan turned to look at his Master but said nothing.

"I'm sorry for how I spoke to you at the warlord camp. Of course, your teaching has been that of how to kill, regrettable though it is, and I never did teach you when to kill and when to not. That is not teachable, though I would have it that none would kill, ever. Unfortunately, this seems only to be a dream.

"But you are nineteen now, a man, and you have the ability to make your own choices. I must admit, however, as excellent a student as you have proven to be, your temperament has always been of concern to me. You are quick to anger, and those quick to anger are usually the first to draw blood. They are also the first to be killed.

"You may already know this, but it is not the guilt of taking a life that makes it difficult, but the ease with which it is done. We are taught that life is precious, but it is decidedly poorly guarded and easily lost. Perhaps that is where the preciousness comes from.

"I tell you this, not to scare you, nor to comfort you, but to assuage my own feelings of inadequacy. I have been a poor teacher, yet you have learned well. Still, I failed you, instructing you mainly on the physical aspects of the way of the warrior and neglecting the spiritual and emotional side. I was not around enough to teach you these and so you have been plunged, unknowingly, into adult life in a time of war. For that I apologise.

"It is a vulgar path that I have set you on, yet I knew no other to teach. Maybe it would have been better if I had taught you nothing at all. Indeed," he sighed, "sometimes I feel that is exactly what I have done."

"I would have no other path!" Arvan replied, the words surging out from within him as opposed to actually being spoken.

Snow smiled lightly. "We shall see if you feel the same when you reach my age. If you reach my age," he added solemnly.

He stood and looked at his student, so unlike how he was at that age. Snow wondered how many battles he had fought by the age of nineteen, how many campaigns he had been led out on. Far too many, though the number was dwarfed by what it had come to now he was approaching forty.

They smiled at one another and Snow turned to leave.

"Master!" Arvan called, stopping Snow. "I didn't kill my father."

"I know," Snow said, typically benevolent. "I taught you *how* to kill, never *to* kill."

With that he left.

Arvan, peace finding him for the first time in days, gazed out to the desert again. Before the world was left completely in darkness he was granted the sight of two silhouettes nearing the city. One, a horned warrior; the other, a caped shadus.

Chapter Twenty Four

Dawn came swiftly and the group gathered outside in the sand-strewn street as soon as they could, the pale light belying the heat of the morning. Arvan held Kyagorusu's staff as always, eager to continue his journey to lay what was left of the man to rest. Serrin stood close by with Banda, each with a small bag of supplies hung over their shoulders.

"You need give us no farewell gifts, Serrin," Snow said. "You've done more than enough already."

"I'm aware of that," Serrin said. "Actually we're leaving. The life of a child should look to the future, not the past. I realise that now and I can't give Banda that life here."

"How far will you go?"

"There's a town in the South Lands where some of my people went before the disease came. We will go with you as far as that, if it is to your liking."

"You were hospitable to us," Lament said. "The least we can do is ensure you leave the desert safely."

Serrin shuddered at the voice of the shadus but said nothing.

The desert was kind to them, calm as when they had first entered. Serrin knew the land well from his original migration and remembered much of the journey. His excellent sense of direction paired with Lament's sight made short work of navigating their way south. Though, Serrin seemed rather uncomfortable being in the presence of the shadus. Lament realised this quickly and left the remainder of the directing to their former host. Still, they had left the desert by noon.

The grass seemed an alien sight at first, though one Arvan was grateful for beyond belief. The comfort he felt at more familiar surroundings, far closer to home than the desert ever could be, made him feel distinctly unadventurous; though he imagined there were times when even Master Snow yearned for home, wherever he thought that was. For a time the boy concluded that home was where he made it and, for a man as well travelled as his master, that could be any place and all.

It wasn't long before they reached a town, cattle grazing on the pasture, nurturing their young. Sturdy houses weaved the land in a simple circle.

Lament noted a woman sat on the stone step before one of the houses, staring at the group. A girl came up to her; she spoke lovingly to her but sent her away.

"We've friends here," Serrin said. "If one can call those they haven't seen in so long friends."

"I'm sure you can," Snow replied, "and you'd be wise to do so."

Serrin nodded. "Well, I declare us even now. Come on, Banda."

The father moved to venture towards one of the buildings, but Banda stayed where he was. He opened his arms wide and embraced Darkla. She knelt and reciprocated. Eventually they released one another and the boy ran after his father. She smiled.

"Problem, shadus?" Vaiske growled, noting Lament's distraction.

"That woman's looking at us."

"I would have thought you'd be used to curious looks by now."

Lament glanced at Vaiske, then back to the woman. She stood anxiously and approached the group. Arvan supposed she was a few years older than Master Snow.

"You seem to be travellers," she said. "If an unusual bunch."

"We've come from afar," Snow replied. "This way and that."

"As far as the West Lands?"

Snow nodded, looking at Arvan.

Her eyes widened in some uncomfortable excitement and she passed her glance between each of them. "Tell me, did you see a force of men travelling to the Final Resting Place of the Empire?"

Immediately, Arvan thought of the warlord clan that he and Kyagorusu had escaped from and their bloodied corpses as they had left the Wastes. He moved to reply but was silenced by Lament.

"Why do you ask?" the shadus asked.

"My husband led a group," she replied. "He gathered the men from the town to bargain with the Great King as we are desperately low on food. But they have not yet returned and our supplies are almost completely gone. Have you seen them?"

"We've seen no such band," Lament replied. "But your cattle seem to be near-ready for the slaughter. Share them amongst yourselves, but be sparing. You've no idea how long they may have to last you."

Arvan looked around; save for the group and Serrin there were no men, only women and children. That he had demonised men who had wished only to feed their families made his stomach bilious, but a comforting hand was rested on his shoulder by Master Snow.

Wordlessly, Lament passed the woman forcing the group to follow.

"Why didn't you tell her?" Arvan asked as they left the town.

"She will never see her husband again," Lament said. "She thought him an honourable man and it seems he was, though he died in dishonourable circumstances. Do you think it is right that I should sully her memory of the man she loves?"

Arvan said nothing. He was consumed by how much like Farras the town they passed looked.

The group continued on in silence for a time. Their journey from the desert had been simple enough, however the days before still left them too drained to be jovial. Soon, Arvan's restless thoughts became too much for him once more.

"Captain Starling killed that woman's husband," he said.

"Yes," Lament answered. "Though I believe he would have mourned doing so, thinking him only a 'Professional Enemy'."

"I didn't think of them as having families. Not even when I saw their corpses."

"It's a difficult thing to do," Snow said. "In battle I often fail to escape the horrific truth that I am slaying the loved ones of others."

"It's kill or be killed," Vaiske grunted. "They cease being human upon trying to end my life. Eh, shadus?"

Lament gave Vaiske his usual uninterested glance.

"They died for love," he said. "As honourable death as any. Any human who would not die for love is unworthy of the title. Yet, what a melancholic world it is that there is a need for us to die for so important a thing."

Vaiske snorted. "I didn't have you down as being so sentimental."

"I think that was beautiful, Lament," Darkla said, her childish smile beaming through her lips.

Lament gave her look she couldn't quite decipher. "Thank you."

After some time of further silence Arvan said, "Kyagorusu always thought of them as humans." He grasped the dead man's staff. "Though he never had the displeasure of seeing their corpses."

Snow laid a kindly hand on the boy's shoulder. "All this talk of great men I never met. I'm starting to get jealous; your adventures are becoming more exciting than my own."

Arvan smiled a genuine smile but had no energy to reply.

The day drew on and the further they walked the longer the grass seemed and the more laborious their steps became. But, tired and unrested, on they went, walking in the footsteps of the Behemoth. The sky, ever clear, darkened from blue to violet before resting in a hue that was neither the darkest of purples nor true black and there, in the not so far distance, the port town that Snow had spoken of sat, the lucid reflection of the moon glimmering in the sepia sea.

They entered to find the town as one of silence and shadows, as a clandestine friend awaiting them with peaceful, loving arms. The only sound that night was the cooing of the sea.

"We should rest here," Snow said. "There is an inn where the beds are comfortable and the food is filling. After our last few days we could use a night with such pleasures."

They began in the direction Snow led them, only to be stopped by Lament's still eye.

"You won't join us?" Snow asked.

The shadus shook his head. "I have had too much sleep recently and food doesn't please me as it once did."

"The sickness has returned so soon?" Darkla asked, her fragile words coming to nothing in the darkness.

"Even in my slumber I wasn't free from it. It merely affected me in altered ways."

"Very well," Snow said. "Though if you feel the need for shelter we will not be far, otherwise we will meet you at the docks when morning comes."

Lament nodded in his usual stern way. They left him, gradually engulfed in the miasmic black, and he watched them fade. He was only alone for a few seconds before he felt the breeze drape itself over him and the warmth flowed through him.

"Hello, my love."

Vaiske rapped on the door with the tip of his spear. To their left was a window giving them a view of a room, faintly lit by candlelight. The breeze whispered past and Arvan shivered. Darkla smiled and moved closer to him until their shoulders met.

"Who locks the door to an inn?" Vaiske growled.

"A man who is an ally to Lord Thean but lives in a land of feuding warlords," Snow replied in his usual calm manner.

Vaiske snorted in reply. "It seems to me he'd be wiser to side with the warlords."

"Not the immortal?" Darkla asked with a smile.

Vaiske glared at her and she could only assume that the expression he wore behind the mask was even more contemptuous than the mask itself. However, she was spared the full extent of that furious look when the door opened and a small middle-aged man appeared in the frame, holding a candle. The group turned their attention to him and Arvan noted the careworn expression that, judging by the amount of wrinkles that traversed his face, he must have been wearing for some time.

"I'm afraid I've precious few rooms as it is," he said quickly. "I'll not be able to accommodate you all."

"Really, Reed?" Snow asked. "Does that go for old friends, such as me, as well?"

Snow stepped past Vaiske and lit his face with the dim light of Reed's candle. The innkeeper's careworn expression faded and a smile, the likes of which Arvan had never seen appear so suddenly, replaced it.

"Lawliet!" Reed hissed, taking the samurai in his arms. "I'm so glad you're alright!"

Reed released Snow and the Thean man frowned.

"Why would I not be?" he asked.

"Many reasons," Reed replied. "But I can't speak of them outside. Come in, you must be starving! I'll fetch food, and wine. Are there more of you?"

"One more," Snow replied. "Though he won't be joining us. He wants not for food or sleep and is more than content to lay sleepless beneath the stars."

Reed raised a suspicious eyebrow but moved aside and let the group enter. Arvan, the last inside, shut the door behind him and was comforted instantly by the calming fragrance of wood-smoke. Despite now being a week or so into spring, the nights were still bitterly cold and the prospect of spending one somewhere warm, that wasn't the desert, brought him no end of pleasure. He smiled to himself as the group sat around a large table.

Reed rushed back and forth between the table and the kitchen, his bare, clumsy feet padding all the while. After a few minutes the table was cluttered with bread and meat, cheeses the names of which Arvan didn't know and unfamiliar fruit.

Snow laughed. "Reed there's only four of us. I think this should suffice."

The innkeeper stopped halfway back to the kitchen. He turned as if to return to the table, but instead revealed another horrified expression as if some ghoul before him held open the orifices of his face.

"Just one more thing!" he said before scurrying into the kitchen once more.

"What a strange man," Arvan said, eyeing some bread in front of him but not wanting to be the first to start eating.

Snow rolled his eyes and took a slice of meat, causing the rest of the group to load their plates.

"Reed's a good host," Snow said.

"And one we desperately need after Serrin," Vaiske said, struggling to fit his fork in the mouth-hole of his mask.

Reed returned and sat beside Snow, a dark bottle in his hands. "Not the best stuff, I'm afraid. It's made from berries from one of the islands off of the Southern Continent, but, if you haven't had a drink in a while, it should do the trick."

He poured them each a glass of the wine that lay uncomfortably between blue and violet. As the glass was placed before Arvan he was struck by the bitter-but-fruity smell of the wine, that potent alcoholic warmth wrapping itself around the scent. It was closer to loganberries than anything else but, judging by the colour, he imagined it was made from yet another fruit he hadn't encountered before that night.

He'd never acquired a taste for wine, or any alcohol for that matter, as it wasn't easy to come by in Farras and the Riit soldiers were likely to confiscate any that the town did have for themselves. He'd tried some, very carefully hidden, wine at the Fire Light Festival of a few years ago and remembered having a distinct dislike for the stuff. Still, if everyone else was having some he felt rude in declining. He took a cautious sip, the bitter taste making his tongue seem slightly broader than before, and swallowed. It burned as it slid down his gullet, causing him to purse his lips and pray that nobody noticed.

"This is more than generous, Reed," Snow said after a pleasing sip of wine. "But I fear I must know what you meant before."

Reed sighed. "I'd heard some very odious news," he said, staring at the liquid in his glass. "It's been busy recently, yet quiet also. The local problems seem to have dissipated, giving way to the continental ones, maybe even inter-continental. Indeed, the port's been getting a lot of use of late.

"Not even a week ago I had a visit from some very good friends of yours; Distance and Grimoire. I was happy to see them, until I noticed their morbid expressions. They were returning to Lord Thean and thought it prudent to lodge with me before venturing out to see." Reed met Snow's eyes. "They told me you were dead."

Snow smiled. "A popular rumour and one that more than just you have heard. I was tracking the Behemoth and was out of contact for far longer than I had envisioned; it wasn't unreasonable to assume I'd perished. But, Reed, as you can see, I'm fine. More than fine, in fact. I've my student with me and he's shown great progress since my departure. Furthermore, Distance, Grimoire and Lord Thean shall soon discover I'm still alive. Please, Reed, don't trouble yourself with this worry."

"But that's not all, Lawliet!" Reed cried, taking his wine in his hand to calm himself. "There was talk of war."

"Is that so surprising?" Vaiske asked. "The world is in turmoil and all upon it can feel it. Even the breeze struggles to flow with the tension as it is. The warlords strengthen and weaken. Even Eremmerus amasses an army as we speak."

"But you don't think war will come?" Snow asked.

Vaiske shook his head. "I won't allow it to. After killing the Behemoth I shall use the respect I gain to unite those who are currently opposed. War will not come."

Snow sighed. "Judging by the look on Reed's face I fear it may be out of your control."

Reed nodded. "They told me of what happened in the Final Resting Place of the Empire. The loss of so many men will, at best, slow the Great King down, or so Grimoire said. They say Lord Thean is almost prepared and that he will wish to act before the Great King has a full force again."

"That's impossible," Snow said assuredly. "Lord Thean wishes to avoid war. This is good news that Eremmerus has been weakened, Lord Thean can now reason with him. You'll see Reed, I shall return in a few days with news of peace."

Reed nodded but didn't look convinced.

Arvan, now halfway through his glass of wine, struggled to listen. His head felt considerably larger than when they had first entered the inn and he fought to keep it upright. The room did not rotate, though when he moved the room seemed to move in the opposite direction. He had the irresistible urge to retire for the night and his mind was burdened with thoughts of Kyagorusu. The last time he had enjoyed food, something Kyagorusu had demanded, was when they had first started travelling and now here he was, enjoying a meal, when the bald philosopher would never eat again. He couldn't decide if it was guilt he felt or just a profound sadness. Either way, he knew he had to sleep so that tomorrow would arrive and he could come closer yet to laying his dead friend to rest in the town of his birth.

Darkla, quiet throughout, seemed to be suffering similar effects. She gazed wearily back at Arvan, seemingly struggling to stay awake, though her expression was one of serene happiness.

The night washed over the pair and they had no recollection of retiring to bed.

Lament sat on the dock, holding one leg in a strange embrace while the other lay outstretched, his sword placed on the ground beside him. The placid night drew on, the darkness furthering until only the diamond flames of the stars and the hollow light of the moon dared venture out. The breeze weaved throughout the town and caught the waves of the sea, lifting the boats and small ships on the buoyant surface, causing the wood to creak, placated.

"It's not your fault," the breeze seemed to whisper as he felt that familiar presence holding him.

Lament said nothing and contented to stare into the darkness. But even that calming sight could not satiate his nausea. He sighed and pulled his leg further into the embrace.

It wasn't long before he heard heavy footsteps and it only took a glance to see that it was Vaiske, still he decided not to react. It wouldn't hurt to give the immortal the pleasure of thinking he'd gone unnoticed. The shadus only looked up when Vaiske was stood right beside him.

"Not so observant tonight, eh?" Vaiske growled.

Lament looked away. "I thought you wished to sleep."

He moved his sword to his other side and Vaiske sat in its place; his legs resting on flat feet, his spear on his shoulder.

"I'd intended to," he replied. "I need to get used to the things humans must do to stay alive for when I return your shadow to you. I ate tonight and enjoyed it greatly, but it seems my immortality prevents me from sleeping. Besides, the conversation we had over our meal displeased me, encumbering my mind."

Lament rolled his eye towards Vaiske. "Conversation?"

"Damn fool of an innkeeper thinks war's on the way. I'd just dismiss him usually, but the Thean Generals led him to the conclusion. I can't ignore them so easily."

Lament shrugged.

"That's all you can do?" Vaiske said, his voice losing its usual rasp. "War might be coming and you've nothing to say?"

Lament sighed. "Since I first came to this land I have been surrounded by those who feel war is coming, when, as far as I can, it is resolutely here. How many warlord clans have we run into? How much peril did we face at the hands of Eremmerus? Not to mention the Behemoth. We are but men, Vaiske, and have little to say in the turning tides of destiny. Why worry about that which you cannot affect?"

Vaiske looked away.

"Perhaps," he grunted.

For a time they sat in silence, with only the whispers of the breeze and sea to interrupt.

"I don't blame you," they seemed to say to Lament. He shuffled uncomfortably on the wooden dock. His thoughts turned to his coma-induced dream when she had draped herself over him as she had so many times before. But so abstract it was in his mind, how he longed to feel it and know it as he once had.

He paused in his brooding as a faint chuckle came from one of the boats. Lament, permanent scowl intensifying, told himself it was only his imagination. However, it then sounded again and he could not dismiss it so easily. Vaiske turned to him with a suspicious tilt of his head and the shadus nodded. Together, they rose, grasping their weapons, and ventured further up the docks.

Vaiske, immortality at the front of his mind, took the lead and strode tactlessly over to the offending boat. Lament was more relieve than he cared to admit that it was a familiar face inside of the boat. The Old Man sat before them, unchained and smiling.

"I'd hoped I'd run into you two once more," he said. "The boy?"

"Asleep," Vaiske growled, loosening his grip on his spear.

Lament placed his sword upon his back. "What are you doing here?"

"I escaped Sparrus while he was tracking a man with a greater bounty," the Old Man replied, looking pensively out to sea. "I had thought of going to the Southern Continent." He turned towards them, those grey eyes reflecting the light of the moon. "But if you're going there, perhaps it would be best if I went elsewhere."

"Hmph," Vaiske snorted. "Does disaster follow us so obviously?"

"Disaster? Nothing so tangible. Luck. How exactly did you escape the Behemoth at Pale Castle?"

"That was no luck, Old Man. That was determination and skill."

The Old Man smiled. "Either way your path holds far too much excitement for a man of my years. I'd best keep away. You do still plan on killing the Behemoth?"

"You seemed to think it was the right thing to do when last we met."

The Old Man shrugged and looked out to sea again. "I suppose it is. It's in a great deal of pain at any rate; someone should put it out of its misery. The Planet desperately needs to move on and the death of the Behemoth seems to be the only way to achieve that."

"Then what part of the plan do you oppose?" Vaiske growled.

"I'm not entirely sure that I do." He looked at the immortal. "It's just; it's been so long, I'm not certain how the Planet will cope. Of course, it *will* cope. I just wonder how."

"The Behemoth," Vaiske said, his voice dropping. "When it's gone, do you think the tension between men will go with it?"

The Old Man seemed to contemplate this for a few seconds. "I doubt it."

"So war is inevitable?"

The Old Man gave him a curious look. "Inevitable? Not if we *try* to avoid it. We're all after the same things in life, the only problem is that some people want it all for themselves. Besides, war seems to be an environment that a man such as yourself would suit."

Vaiske looked away.

"Perhaps," he grunted.

"And what of you?" the Old Man asked, turning to Lament. "You're as quiet as the last time we met and the breeze seems as fond of you as ever."

Lament met the Old Man's look. "My mind is filled with questions, as it has been since I was a boy. But only one I would ask you."

The Old Man gestured for the shadus to continue.

"What do you know of dreams?"

The Old Man smiled. "Well, I've certainly had a few. Or, rather, one too many times."

"Are they meaningful?"

"To the dreamer. Of course there are those who believe them to be the Planet communicating with us. Needless to say, they tell us our subconscious wants and fears." He noted Lament's unsatisfied expression. "Or are you looking for something more specific?"

Lament looked away and sighed. "I'd imagine an abstract question about an abstract subject deserves an abstract answer."

"Then would you care to ask me something more tangible?"

Lament rolled his eye towards the Old Man.

"Can the..." He paused, glancing self-consciously at Vaiske. Then he turned to the Old Man again. "Can the dead communicate to us through our dreams?"

Slowly, Vaiske turned towards the shadus but said nothing.

The Old Man took on a serious expression, the wrinkles of his face deepening as he frowned in thought.

"It's not something I've heard of as happening before," he said. "But I suppose, for one without a shadow, one the breeze flows through, such as yourself, it might be possible."

Lament said nothing, nor did his expression change. He displayed the same indifference he did to all everyone said.

"What did the dead tell you?" the Old Man asked.

Lament looked away in that habitual moody way of his. "That's my business."

The Old Man sighed. "If the dead have knowledge to impart it should be shared with all the living. Then again, I suppose they chose you for a reason."

"It wasn't wisdom, Old Man," Vaiske said. "It was of a personal nature, just like everything else with him."

Lament glanced at Vaiske and Vaiske met the shadus' look.

"You're sure?" the Old Man asked.

"I know him that well by now," Vaiske said. "Or so I hope." He looked from Lament to the Old Man. "You spoke of one dream."

"A glorious one," the Old Man said with a smile. "One of my death."

Vaiske shuffled uncomfortably. "That sounds more like a nightmare to me."

"And there are many who would agree with you." The Old Man glanced at Lament. "Though there are those who would take an oppositional stance."

Lament rolled an unwavering eye towards the Old Man, the amber iris glowing in the night air. "Is this life such a blessing that we must all wish for immortality? What if we all lived forever; where would the precious nature of life be then?"

The Old Man pursed his lips thoughtfully. "A valid point. One I should muse on if I've the time."

It was then, on the subject of immortality, that Vaiske had a memory, none so concrete as to see something in his mind's eye, nor something so involuntary as a smell or taste. Yet, the conversation, the subject of immortality and the questioning of its significance, evoked in him a feeling that he had never before experienced, save for as a child, when he learned that after his life there would be a vast expanse of time that he, and his consciousness, would not inhabit, and he would cease to be. There was no fury with burning blood and freezing skin. He could not scream or shout in defiance. There was merely a twinge of fear, followed by grim acceptance. It was something akin to the slightest of maladies, one he felt only as something small; there was nothing he could do about it. It was a nausea he had felt only at one other point in his life, when he thought he had come face to face with the morbid effigy of death itself.

"The ash you spoke of at Pale Castle," Vaiske said to the Old Man. "I saw it."

The Old Man nodded. "Just swimming lazily through the breeze, I imagine."

Vaiske shook his head. "No. It formed into a man. He spoke to me, while saying nothing at all."

The Old Man leapt to his feet and cried as he stumbled towards Vaiske. Upon reaching the warrior he grabbed the armour around his shoulders with a strength that even the immortal couldn't match.

"He has reformed?" the Old Man gasped.

"Calm down!" Vaiske roared, pushing the Old Man away, causing the ostensible septuagenarian to stumble back into the boat. "After we spoke he returned to a string of ash. Besides, he was never completely human."

"But he has gained the will to reform!" the Old Man said, standing once more. A smile grew on his face and his wrinkles deepened again. "Then I must go and prepare."

"Prepare for what?" Lament asked.

"I'm not certain, but the Planet shall tell me." He left the boat and gazed at the pair of them. "I suppose, in a way, you have the Planet's blessing to kill the Behemoth. It shall soon have a new defence, or perhaps that should be a defence of old. You need not worry about war, or maybe it's closer than ever. We must still wait, for a while longer perhaps, but the answers shall come. Already I feel it; an age of optimism, of peace; at the hands of one man. I have believed it would come for a long time now, for too long in fact. Each time I spoke to the Planet of it, it said it would not come; he had filled his purpose long ago. Perhaps it told the truth. But, if he has learned to form himself from the breeze alone, then there is hope. Not for eternal life, but for the love of live, for near the end he was so weary..." His eyes widened and he passed his gaze between Lament and Vaiske.

"I suppose it is now the perfect time for me to ask you the question again; my original question, in fact, if not to you. What is your purpose?"

Vaiske snorted. "I gave you my answer. To ensure my place in history."

The Old Man smiled and turned to Lament. "And you? Have you changed your mind? Is your purpose still to do as the breeze wishes?"

For a brief moment, Lament didn't answer. The breeze, the entity that had clung so close to him all night had vanished, as if dissipating into the languid moon.

"My purpose?" he said as if to himself. "I am here for no greater reason than to live until it is my time to die, and we are reunited on the breeze."

The Old Man smiled. "Maybe it is us who give our own lives meaning. He certainly thought so, all those years ago. I hope he thinks this worth the trouble; even if he doesn't, maybe he can teach me something."

With that, something Vaiske thought a rambling statement at best, he left, gradually disappearing into darkness. Vaiske looked to the shadus and Lament looked to the horned warrior, but neither said anything. What can one say to a man who has been waiting his life for an event that he can only tell himself might happen?

Chapter Twenty Five

They were joined at dawn by the trio who had left Reed asleep. Lament noticed Arvan's bloodshot eyes and lacklustre posture from some distance, the mere cooing of the sea beside them seemingly causing him more than a slight pain. Vaiske laughed as the trio neared and realised Lament's observations for himself.

"Someone had quite a night by the look of things!" he roared in a voice lacking his usual mechanical tone.

Arvan flinched and said nothing.

Snow smiled. "As I'm sure you noticed last night, the pair of them didn't react to the wine at dinner quite as well as could have been hoped. However, after going to bed, instead of sleeping as would have been wise, they decided to pilfer more wine from Reed and stay up, reminiscing of glories past."

Darkla smiled in her childish way.

"I'm not quite as bad as Arvan," she said. "Though, I must admit, I've a headache beyond compare."

"Then compare it with mine," Arvan groaned. "And count yourself lucky."

Snow and Vaiske chuckled, though Darkla gave Arvan a sympathetic rub on his arm. Lament appeared not to be paying attention. His eye was drawn to the grey clouds, the burgeoning light trying to protrude through the blanket, but only succeeding in outlining each individual cloud with a white edge. Eventually, Snow's gaze was drawn above as well.

"Not the best day for sea travel," he said.

"Still," Lament said, "we must be on our way."

Snow nodded. "They don't look like storm clouds to me."

"Nor me."

Vaiske turned slowly to Lament.

"Uncharacteristically hopeful," the immortal said.

Lament frowned at him briefly, then began to make his way up the docks.

"Can even I not have moments of optimism?" he asked, his whispering voice camouflaged by his footsteps.

"No, you may not," Vaiske muttered, though nobody showed any sign of having heard him.

The group followed Lament along the boardwalk, the docks gradually coming to life. Fishermen readied their vessels for the day to come, whilst others dismantled their equipment from a night spent at sea. All the while, whether preparing or resting, those around them told tales of heroics rendered on the waves. But, upon the sight of Lament, followed by the demonic

Vaiske and instantly-recognisable Snow, all stories faltered as each weaver of fiction knew they could not rival the extraordinary view of these men, nor could they recount tales that would compare to their encounters. And, slowly, save for the sea and the creaking wood of the vessels, the docks grew silent.

Arvan, consumed in his self-afflicted malady, had not noticed their reception. He murmured, just loud enough to hear, "Perhaps the sea journey will make me feel better."

Snow laughed, despite the looks they were getting.

"You need two things to improve your condition," he said, "water and sleep. There'll be plenty of water, though not for drinking, and I doubt you'll sleep. No, hung-over on a boat; I can't imagine a worse form of torture."

Arvan groaned before his Master continued.

"But don't worry, it will soon pass and then you'll wish for more of the poison you had last night."

Arvan couldn't disagree. In spite of his current sickness and the macabre thoughts the drink had led him to have, he failed to dismiss it as an entirely unpleasant experience. Already he wished to explore the heady feeling of the night before in greater detail, just not at that very moment; perhaps when he had recovered, or as a worthy celebration at the end of the adventure.

Lament had stopped someway ahead of them, his melancholic figure cutting a silhouette, dark beyond compare, even against the grey of the sea and silver of the clouds. He seemed to stare out over the ocean; the breeze, strangely free of the scent of the sea-salt, picked up locks of his hair and danced with them. As they neared he pointed to a boat at his side without looking. It bore the cherry blossom crest of the Thean House.

"That's the one," Snow said, smiling.

"It's not very big," Vaiske growled.

The immortal was right. The wooden boat was only slightly bigger than some of the fishing vessels, yet it was designed like a ship, insofar as it had a hold and a mast with a sail, small though it was.

"She'll suffice," said a voice from the hold. Footsteps followed the utterance and a man Arvan, in his state of diminished lucidity, could only describe as "weasely" scuttled onto what qualified as the deck. He looked at the group with his tiny, rodent-like eyes in a hard, unwavering gaze before fixing the glare on Master Snow. The rattish eyes opened further, for a moment making them look slightly more human and belying the far protruding cheekbones and brow of the man's face. In his look of astonishment he became more than what he had been and Snow gifted him a name with his usual smile.

"Hello, Rafesly."

"General Snow!"

The rattish Rafesly leapt from the vessel and landed awkwardly on the docks. He stumbled towards Snow and held him in an embarrassed embrace, his head only reaching the General's chest.

"*General* Snow?" Arvan asked, too loudly for the preferences of his head.

"Of course," Snow replied with that amiable smile. "You didn't think everyone called me 'Master', did you?"

Arvan said nothing, admitting to himself that he had never thought of his Master as having a rank in the army he served. He was simply 'Master Snow', the greatest swordsman in the world. The idea that he not only knew Generals Valentine and Groan but that he was, in fact, equal to them, astonished the boy, yet, as he thought about it, he realised Snow had talked about them in revered tones, but in the way one would speak of a dear friend. Still, that his Master was so high ranking filled Arvan with a fervent pride and a newfound admiration for his teacher, so much so that he almost forgot his hangover.

Rafesly turned his pointed nose up towards Snow.

"It's good to see you," he said. "General Groan and General Valentine required passage not so long ago; they said…"

"I know," Snow interrupted. "I've had quite enough of what they've said and, as you can see, it's decidedly untrue. Yet, I cannot blame them for believing so."

"And I've had more than enough of standing here, talking," Vaiske said impatiently. "Passage to the Southern Continent is swift enough and the Behemoth waits."

Rafesly gave Vaiske a curious look before returning his gaze to Snow.

"The Southern Continent?" he asked.

Snow nodded. "North Port should suffice."

"Well then, I see no need to wait."

Rafesly gestured towards the boat and they boarded, Lament un-necessarily helping Darkla step onto the deck. After a few minutes' work from Rafesly, the boat started gently south on the buoyant waves, under a blanket of cloud.

"So," Rafesly said, his hands never moving from the wheel, "you've not had quite enough of the Behemoth?"

Snow smiled and looked around the cabin. The wood was in as good a shape as ever and the glass Rafesly used to see what was ahead was cleaned to a gleaming state. He'd always taken good care of the vessel and had nothing aboard that wasn't completely necessary. Briefly, Rafesly glanced at the compass he kept tied to his wrist before looking out to sea once more with a satisfied look.

"I'll have nothing more to do with it," Snow replied. "I'm going to see Lord Thean and inform him that I'm still alive. I crossed paths with those hunters and Arvan was with them. We were headed in a similar direction so I travelled with them."

"And how is the student progressing?"

Snow scratched at his beard.

"He's headstrong," he said. "But show me a man that age that isn't. It's nothing a few years' experience won't remedy. He'll have to learn humility the hard way though, assuming his ability is enough that he can survive to that point."

"You have your doubts about him?" Rafesly asked, still not looking from the sea before them.

Snow shook his head. "I've absolute faith in Arvan. It's my ability as a teacher that I doubt. The boy has a yearning for danger and adventure that no amount of warning or wisdom seems to assuage."

Rafesly smiled, though Snow couldn't see.

"That seems to me to be the way of it," the rattish man said. "He's learned that from you. How many times have you left Mirr now? And for what reason? The call of adventure."

Snow frowned and replied in an annoyed tone, "The call of duty."

"It's your duty to adventure; to create stories for the new generation. To give them hope that there's something more than the fear of the Behemoth or the warlords. To give them the inspiration to grow up to be like you and continue the legacy of heroes for the next generation."

Snow looked to him, but Rafesly still didn't turn to look at the General. Was the rattish man right? Snow had always tried to do the right thing; to protect the innocent and avoid bloodshed whenever possible, that was why he was drawn towards Lord Thean and his quest for peace. Yet, more and more as of late, he saw Arvan finding more in the excitement of battle. Was that his true legacy? Even Rafesly, a man he had known for some many years, if not closely, seemed to misunderstand him.

Snow sat down, wrapping his arms around his knees and resting his head on the wooden wall of the cabin. "I wouldn't wish my way of life upon anyone, and if it is my duty to encourage others to follow in my footsteps then my duty irks me."

"Adventure doesn't hold the allure that it once did?" Rafesly asked.

Snow didn't reply and contented to scratch his beard.

Arvan held Kyagorusu's staff as if for comfort. The buoyant ocean did nothing to soothe his bilious stomach and he didn't like the look of the clouds. He decided to lie on his side and pulled the staff closer.

Strangely, he didn't find himself in the throes of self-pity. Instead, he saw his hangover as just another obstacle to overcome. He had to heal himself before facing the Behemoth.

His eyes fell upon Vaiske, sat calmly across from him, his spear resting across his folded legs. Such a battle awaiting, and so content. How much longer before the boy could learn to be like him?

He removed the thought from his mind and tried to sleep.

Lament rolled his eye from the demonic effigy of Vaiske and looked moodily out to the grey ocean. He found peace in the vista, morbid though it was.

"Depressing isn't it?"

He turned his head sharply and saw Darkla standing beside him, her blonde hair cascading over her left shoulder.

"Did I startle you?" she asked.

Lament pointed to the rag where his eye once was. "My peripheral vision is not what it once was."

"I'm sorry."

Lament looked back out to sea. "No matter."

She smelt sweet with the scented bath-salts of the inn. It cut through the sea breeze as if the salt were nothing more than silk and her fragrance, the essence of which all perfection should be measured against, was a sharp and painless blade. Yet, to the shadus, it meant nothing, for, compared to the scent of his dead beloved, it was a stench so potent he could hardly bear to be subjected to it. Whether it was the fragrance of Miata itself he loved, or whether he just held the wearer of it in such high esteem, he couldn't be sure, though he knew that no other scent could comfort him so vehemently.

"I just wanted to thank you," she said.

"Thank me?"

"You never let me fall behind when the Riit soldiers were chasing us. Thank you."

Lament rolled his eye towards her. "It was nothing. Any of our number would have done the same."

"But it was you who did it," she replied with a light smile.

Lament frowned. "The duty fell to me as I was too weak to keep pace with the rest of the group."

He watched as Darkla folded her arms and followed his former gaze out to sea. Her youthful exuberance seemed to fade and her face was left bereft of the smile, changing to an expression the immortal couldn't quite place. At first he thought that it was almost blank, yet her eyes were too sharp for his suspicion to remain.

"I know that feeling all too well," Darkla whispered.

"I didn't mean to say you were weak."

"I know," she sighed. "Though everyone here has their use in battle, save for me."

"We have eluded battle thus far and that is of far greater use to us than skill within it. You're beginning to sound like Arvan."

Darkla turned to him, meeting that one glowing eye, as a smile broke out across her face. "Yes, I suppose I am."

Lament watched as she turned, leaning on the railing of the boat and lay her eyes on the now sleeping Arvan. The last vestiges of the careworn expression fell from her face and the smile finally took hold in its entirety.

"You spoke of love in your story," she said. "Was it wonderful?"

Her eyes stayed on Arvan, his hair fallen across his face, his body folded into a position of childish comfort.

"It was a sadness so profound to be mistaken for joy," Lament replied as if he were talking only to the breeze. "A euphoria against which all depression would fail. So yes, it was wonderful, if unknowable."

She looked to him, speechless.

Lament glanced at her then looked away again.

"Still," he said, "you chose a strange confidant."

Darkla moved to protest but the shadus waved a dismissive hand and began to walk away, the metronome footsteps singing melancholically as he prowled up the boat. She looked once more to the sleeping Arvan and smiled.

"I'd be careful what I told the shadus, were I you," the metallic voice of Vaiske said.

Darkla turned to him, sat calmly as ever.

"You heard?" she asked, shaken.

"Nothing I didn't already suspect, and there's no shame in it. He'll grow into a good man once he's ready."

"What do you know of love?" Darkla hissed.

"More than you'd think," Vaiske replied in as wistful a voice as his mask would allow. "But I can only warn you; be careful what you tell the shadus."

Darkla frowned and she brushed a lock of hair from her face. "You still don't trust him?"

"Trust has nothing to do with it. I trust him more than I do any other, though I can't explain why. Just remember he's not like you and I."

Her eyes took on that sharpness once more. "You and I are hardly alike, Vaiske."

He shrugged and grabbed his spear, standing.

"Perhaps," he said. "But we're more alike than you are with him. More alike than he is with anyone, even the other shadus people."

"How's that?"

Vaiske glanced out to sea, then back to Darkla, tilting his head in that haunting way. "He doesn't share our will to live."

Darkla took a step back, placing her hands to her chest without noticing. She looked down at them, but didn't comprehend the action.

"Master Snow said something similar," she said. "But you're wrong, both of you."

"Oh?"

She looked up at him, her eyes filled with tears. She tried to force them away, blinking, but they were only replaced by more.

"Maybe he did want to die, but he found a reason to live, or he'll find one. He has people around him now; people who care for him." Her voice was barely a whisper, masked almost entirely by the creeping sea breeze.

"But does he care for the people around him?" Vaiske asked. "His loss was great. Some men aren't strong enough to come back from that."

"But he is," Darkla replied in that same whisper.

Vaiske said nothing. He walked past her, after the shadus.

"What happened to you?" she asked, turning after him. "What made you... *this*?"

He stopped and turned to her.

"Something unspeakable," he growled. And with that he left her alone save for Arvan, sleeping a few metres away.

Snow held his legs to his chest and rested his head on the wood of the cabin wall behind him. Reed's words from the night before were laying heavily on his mind, though he had ignored them at first; lost in the thick haze created by his first tentative sips of wine, when he knew those around him were safe and he could finally relax.

Reed had suggested that Lord Thean planned on attacking Eremmerus while he was at his weakest. But why? Lord Thean craved peace, an act of aggression was against everything he taught, everything he stood for. He had a small army, used only in the most necessary of circumstances; those being defence and protecting those who could not protect themselves.

He tried telling himself that Reed had misunderstood what Distance and Grimoire had said, but the innkeeper had seemed so sure.

How many battles had he fought in now? He couldn't be sure, though he remembered that by the age of twelve he had already lost count. And each time he was promised that it would be the last. Did the killing still irk him? Certainly not as much as it once did and never in the actual moment. But afterwards... The concept of it, being the harbinger of another being's end; that was what troubled him, not the act itself. And what of his own death? Did that trouble him? An eternal darkness. An eternal peace.

"We're almost there," Reed said, ripping Snow from his pensive state.

Snow clenched his eyelids. He let them open, sighed and stood.

"Well," he said. "Once more into..."

He paused.

Rafesly turned and gave him a curious look.

Snow scratched at his beard and shrugged. "Once more in two."

The land grew in their sight in the golden light of dusk. The distant mountains, ever present, rose like devilish fingers from a forgotten wound as they neared, the small continent becoming immeasurably large. Then detail; the white stone buildings of North Port, the terracotta tiled roofs. But, in that blissful scene where the five adventurers stood together at the head of the boat, the languid light dancing lazily on the waves around them, not one of them beheld the beauty. Instead, on their minds was what was to come; their final encounter with the Behemoth.

"Is this silence solemn?" Snow asked, scratching at his beard. "Now you near your destination, do you regret the journey?"

"Ha!" Vaiske growled. "It is a silence of excited anticipation. We near our bounty, eh, shadus?"

Lament rolled his eye towards Vaiske. "Our bounties are not the same" He looked to the immortal's second shadow. "Remember our bargain."

Vaiske grunted.

"I remember," he said. "But I need to get my quarry first."

"And what of you two?" Snow asked, peering past the shadus and armoured warrior at Arvan and Darkla. "Are you still so glad to have joined the journey?"

Darkla smiled. "We've come so far and the world has proved to be infinitely more wonderful than I could have ever thought. Despite its many horrors."

Arvan didn't reply. He merely held the dead man's staff closer to him and watched as the Southern Continent grew nearer still.

Chapter Twenty Six

"Farewell!" Rafesley's thin voice called to them as they walked into the dusk, the silent town of North Port paying them no attention. They walked the deserted streets in an uneasy peace, finding little solace in the near termination of their journey.

Only Snow turned back to grant Rafesly a warm, if firm, wave. Soon they were too far through the town to even see the boat, let alone the man on it, and the night began to fall more swiftly. By the time they were on the outskirts of the town, the faint stars were burgeoning in the darkening sky, becoming ever more lucid with passing time.

Arvan looked at the silent group. They looked weary. He supposed they had never truly had any time to rest, taking into account the heavy thoughts they had shared and the multitude of tensions and perils on their journey. However none, not even the sickly Lament, looked quite as tired as the boy felt. His emotional journey, if not the actual travelling, had drained him to the point of exhaustion from which he was uncertain if he could ever return. Could he ever know the peace he once had? Admittedly, since an early age he had felt a yearning for more, for adventure, to see the world and tell of his conquests. Yet he had always been content to wait for it. Now that he had tasted it he could no longer wish for it. The yearning for an exciting life had not been completely extinguished from his being, he still had an itch in his restless heart, but he could feel it waning with each second, with each loss. And he had lost so much already. Kyagorusu's staff was warm in his hands, the bald philosopher's death not as long ago as it seemed. And what of the boy's confidence? He had yet to prove himself in action, or even mental will.

He looked once more to the tired faces around him. Only the masked warrior seemed to have been unaffected by the journey thus far. Arvan hoped it was only the aid of his second shadow, but something told him it was more than that. He supposed it might have been experience, though even Master Snow had a certain jaded look and few could be said to rival him in experience of adventure. Perhaps some were just born for excitement, and Arvan was becoming increasingly unsure of whether he was.

They stopped at the entrance to the small town, night now almost fully upon the continent. Arvan looked back over the cobbled streets to where the reflection of the moon shivered over the restful, violet waves. A small boat drew away and all was at once at peace. He turned in the opposite direction and saw grassland, only ended by the towering mountains in the distance.

Snow sighed, and it was only then that Arvan noticed just how tired his Master was.

"Well," Snow said. "I suppose this is where we part. My path takes me west, though Lord Thean would loathe me if he knew I'd divulged even that much. Still, it's as nice a night as any to camp, and nicer than most. I could spare one night if you plan to rest?"

Vaiske turned to Lament with a faint clatter of armour. "What do you think, shadus? I'd rather carry on, but if I push you too hard this shadow won't have a master to return to."

Lament looked worse than ever, apparently not soothed by the day at sea. The pullulating moon caught his face with a concerning, languid expression. His amber eye was beginning to glaze over and the sweat on his forehead had returned. He looked at the warrior with his typical proud expression, though his breathing was so laboured that Arvan was amazed he could find the strength to stand.

"I want not for rest," the shadus whispered. "I fear if I was to stop for too long I may never rise again. Besides, you should know by now that I am not one for sleep."

"So we'll carry on," Darkla said optimistically. She turned to Arvan. "Unless you'd like to rest?"

Arvan shook his head.

"I slept on the boat," he said by way of reply. Darkla looked at him with worried eyes but he dismissed them and turned to Master Snow. "So, we are to part here?"

"Yes," Snow said with a contented smile that was just visible through the darkness. "Our paths are different from here. Thank you, all of you. Having some company has made the journey easier. I've much to say to you individually, though we've not the time now and I'm sure we'll meet again." His eyes fell on Arvan. "But, I've some words for my student, if I might have a moment with him?"

"Of course," Vaiske grunted. "Farewell, General. It's been... Well, it has been."

The immortal strode away, followed by Lament who gave Snow an enigmatic hand gesture.

"Goodbye, Master Snow," Darkla said, embracing the samurai. "I'll see you soon."

"Indeed you will," he said, returning the embrace. "Hopefully with Mirr." His voice turned wistful and he released her.

Darkla looked furtively at Arvan before following after Lament and Vaiske.

Snow scratched at his beard and his eyes met those of his student. Arvan blew the fringe from his eyes.

"You wanted to talk to me?" he asked.

Snow smiled. "Of course I do. I always have done." He became more serious. "I suggest you watch your companions carefully. Vaiske and Lament both mean well, but they lack the clarity of wisdom to realise their actions have consequences other than those which they have imagined. Furthermore, they want only to achieve their goals."

"You think killing the Behemoth will end poorly?"

Snow looked away to the waiting group.

"I'm not sure," he sighed. "I'm just very aware that those men have yet to think beyond that which they desire. In Lament's case, I believe that desire to be harmless enough, though it would be pertinent for you not to get too close to him and to ensure Darkla doesn't either. As for Vaiske…"

"You don't trust him," Arvan said sadly, realising his mentors were separate.

Snow looked to his student once more. "He helped me in Avarice and he's been a trustworthy member of the group. Yet, I haven't seen how he reacts when the needs of others interfere with his ambitions. I'd imagine Lament knows slightly better."

"Then why leave me with them?"

Snow smiled. "You've adventures of your own to have and duties to fulfil."

Arvan looked to the staff in his hands.

"Besides," Master Snow continued. "I've taught you all I can. You're a better student than I could ever have asked for. Your ability shall soon surpass my own. You've grown into a better young man than I could have raised; your continued friendship with Darkla is testament to that. Add to that your decision to find me and I see a very conscientious young man before me.

"Yet, you've still much to learn. You're stubborn and you need to control your emotions. But I can't teach you how to do those things. They are taught by time and experience, but learned only by the wise, and wisdom cannot be taught or learned. It is bestowed upon all of us at birth; we must find it within ourselves."

Snow smiled once more. "You'll be a better man than Vaiske or Lament in a few years, with plenty of stories of your own to tell. You'll have an admirable life and bless those around you and, if ever you need advice or guidance, I will be there."

He embraced his student before walking into the night.

Only when he was completely alone, only when the cold of the night burrowed into his bones and the breeze whispered sadly to him, could he ask the question he so longed to ask his Master.

"Then why do I feel so lost?"

They continued as a four, Arvan's new solemnity put down merely to the exit of his mentor and nothing more. Vaiske led the way, the tip of his spear glinting hauntingly in the eerie starlight, surrounded by murk. Far in the distance, the colossal mountains reached up as if to tear the vinyl sky from its heady canvas and bring the tiny sky-candles toppling towards the earth.

Lament's steps were weary and laboured, though he hid this from his companions by maintaining his natural rhythm. He saw that the group hadn't noticed; they had other things on their minds. Gargantuan things. Centuries old things.

He could feel the Shadowblight taking a stronger hold on him. As if there were some viscous fluid in his veins, coursing against his blood and inching its way ever closer to his heart, the beating of which it longed to cease. And what then for the shadus? Death? Abstract and unending. Would he then discover his envisioning of her was nothing more than an illusion or would he at last be granted his wish of falling once more into her loving arms? Uncertainty defined, and it would be prolonged on the re-acquisition of his shadow.

They walked a path cut by desire alone; a strip in the land where the grass was worn down from years of travel. Either side of them the grass grew healthy and thick, rolling on with dotted trees to the west and folding into a cliff in the distant east. They were too far away to see the end of the land and the birth of the sea, but the calming scent of the salient freshness washed over them, seemingly for the benefit of all but the shadus. He shivered with cold sweat, his clothes already damp with lingering moisture.

"Lament?" Darkla said, noticing his slight shudder. "What's wrong?"

He rolled his eye towards her, clearly startling her with his pallid expression as her young face lengthened with worry. Her blue eyes, only maintaining their colour due to Lament's superior sight, grew glacial with concern that can only be born from the suffering of someone that one cares about deeply.

"It's nothing," he said. "Just a twinge of the malady."

Darkla's look didn't change, but Lament turned away, knowing he could assuage her concern no more than he already had and he had done more than he wished to as it was.

Vaiske stopped, causing the rest of the group to halt. He readied his spear. Footsteps.

They were rhythm-less, like many feet walking at once, yet too quiet to be a large force. Still, so silent had been the night, the presence of anyone but the group itself was disturbing.

"Do you see them?" Vaiske whispered, pulling Lament to his side.

Lament shook his head. Even to him the figures were vague, he couldn't even be sure they were human. Silhouetted by darkness, the amorphous shapes continued towards them.

Vaiske grunted in fury.

"Halt!" he growled. "Who goes there?"

Lament shivered with a horrific memory of his first encounter with the warrior.

The effigies stopped.

"I'd know that metallic voice anywhere," said a slightly frivolous voice, as if through the curl of a smile. "And one glowing amber eye. Fitting we should meet you here."

The sound of footsteps began again and the figures drew closer, still washed in darkness.

"I said 'Who goes there?'!" Vaiske growled, gripping his spear.

Lament shuffled wearily, his shadus sight cutting through the black as the figures became closer. No longer were they vague shapes, but two men astride horses, and familiar ones at that.

"It's Captain Starling," Lament said in a tone of voice that was as close as the group could imagine to him sounding glad.

Vaiske grunted but said nothing, calming to a more passive stance.

"You forgot," Starling said, his proximity expelling him from obscurity and revealing his long blonde hair, white cavalry jacket and idiosyncratic wry smile. "My name is Lind. Besides, I'm not alone."

Still slightly masked by the darkness, owing to his black jacket, was Lieutenant Airn Arnamous. Gone from his face was the insecurity he wore in the Final Resting Place of the Empire. His smile was far from the wry one of his Captain; it did not denote contentment or even peace, but the ease of company he was in. It was clear, by his expression alone, that he had ceased to think of Captain Starling as a superior and had started thinking of him as a friend.

"Your group is larger than when last we met," Starling said, spying Darkla and stopping Titus, still that tumultuous grey, just before them. "Or perhaps smaller, though it is doubtful that Generals Valentine and Groan could ever have been considered to be part of your party."

Darkla smiled, taking Captain Starling's noticing of her as a compliment.

"Our group has ebbed and flowed," Vaiske replied. "Not an hour ago we were more still."

"Oh?" Starling mused.

"Master Snow's alive!" Arvan said, rather more excitedly than he meant to. He calmed himself and held Kyagorusu's staff lovingly again.

Starling's smile widened.

"And I just missed him?" he said. "Typical. Still, I'm sure I'll meet him someday."

His smile faded as if exonerated by the moonlight. His attention fell to the east where the sea lay beyond the rolling cliffs in the distance. His thoughts seemed not to hold the amusement he had once conveyed.

"Lind?" Airn prompted, turning to his Captain and brushing a lock of brown hair from his own brow.

Starling came back around to the moment and smiled. "My apologies. These last few days have been trying. Already our time together in the Final Resting Place of the Empire seems an eternity ago. Yet, weariness is no excuse for bad manners." He turned to Vaiske. "You seem characteristically displeased to see me."

225

Vaiske grunted. "You forget what you came to the Southern Continent for."

"Do I?" the Captain asked, smiling.

Vaiske frowned behind his mask.

"To kill the Behemoth!" Vaiske growled. "You're on your way, with a distinctly diminished force. Clearly you've achieved your Great King's goal."

Captain Starling and Lieutenant Arnamous exchanged a look that was hard to place. For each aspect of their faces that appeared grave, there was an equally potent one that made the look appear to be one of almost childlike amusement. Eventually, Starling looked once more to Vaiske.

"I see we've much to discuss," he said. "Airn and I were planning to rest about now anyway. I trust you can afford the time?"

Vaiske looked to Lament, though the shadus refused to look upon the hideous mask.

"It is a necessary expenditure of time," the shadus replied. "Either our continuation is unnecessary or there is a warning of great danger. In any case, my energy has waned almost entirely as it is."

Starling's eyes grew pained with sympathy and he gazed at the moonlit cast second shadow of Vaiske. "Your malady has yet to be assuaged then?"

Lament shook his head. "Worse. It has been given a name. Shadowblight."

Starling smiled.

"My, my," he said, meeting the bulging, anguished eyes of Vaiske's mask. "I hope I don't catch it."

The soldiers dismounted and Starling introduced himself properly to Darkla before introducing his Lieutenant. She struggled to reply, but eased enough to give her name when she started stroking Titus. Starling watched, holding his belt buckle as he stood, the joy leaping across the young woman's face. Lament noticed and wondered just how long it had been since the Captain, only a few years older than Arvan and Darkla, had stroked the horse in so care-free a way. He wondered how long it had been since he himself, again not far their senior, had done something so joyous or calming.

Once everyone was fully acquainted they sat in a circle. A small fire, lit by Vaiske, crackled pleasingly between them. The two horses dutifully grazed a few paces away.

"I'll give you the good news first," Starling began, his face clear of a smile. It looked strangely naked. "My men aren't with us, not because they are dead, but because, after landing on the Southern Continent, I sent them back on the Mjölnir immediately."

"That is good news," Lament replied.

"Hmph," Vaiske snorted. "Your men are of no importance to me. These aren't the details I require."

Starling met Vaiske with a hard look that he seldom employed, though,

226

silencing the immortal immediately, he resolved to use it more often.

"Few men," he said, "even those so callous as you, would assume the deaths of so many and care only that so much demise may have hindered his chance at glory."

Vaiske didn't reply.

Starling calmed. "I'd imagine such insubordination enraged Eremmerus at first. Though, Airn and I may now return, safe in the knowledge that his Blood Lust may have caused him to forget the event."

He shuffled as he sat, moving to a more comfortable position. He unfolded his legs and placed his right foot flat on the ground, resting his matching arm on his knee. He kept his left leg curled and leaned back on his left arm. His grey eyes became distant and the smile that he was forever associated with, became lacklustre. He sighed.

"But you wish to hear of the Behemoth."

Starling fell silent, as if he had no audience at all, or at least none that he wished to have. The flames danced to their own percussive beat, their jumping limbs lighting the Captain's morbid face at intervals. He inhaled, as if to sigh, but let the breath dissipate into no more than any other.

When he spoke again, he spoke slowly.

"You needn't fret, Vaiske," he said, staring listlessly into the star-littered sky. "We haven't stolen your glory. Far from having the means, we had no will. Yet, this was no wish to antagonise Eremmerus, nor was fear of our own deaths. Indeed, the very fact that it has surely angered our Great King so could well lead to our end.

"To say I never had any intention of killing the Behemoth would be untrue – I merely wished not to endanger my men in an endeavour which, for the past millennium, has proved fruitless. It's no secret that I feel no affiliation with my nation, yet seeing the Behemoth so easily destroy parts of the Coliseum did awake something within me. Something I thought long dead."

He paused again, still not moving his gaze from the vinyl sky above. He blinked, deliberately and pensively, but each time his eyes opened they were fixed on the same place.

"Though seemingly it lurks within me still," he mumbled. He sighed and when he spoke again his voice took on its usual theatrical quality. "It wasn't just the Coliseum, but the lives of each man it took." His eyes finally moved from the sky and to the staff in Arvan's hands. "Each death a more personal tragedy than the last.

"Still, despite my wish to avenge the fallen, I couldn't risk the lives of the cavalry. Frankly, I felt a little guilty even having Airn here with me, but he refused to go back with the rest of the men.

"My anger ebbed and flowed, forever waning with the beauty of each dawn and each dusk; the majesty of the distant mountains, far more regal than the ones to which I have grown accustomed. We roamed this land, finding something more akin to peace as we neared the centre of the continent."

He smiled at the memory, all graveness disappearing from his face. "On our third day we found a meadow. Dreamlike in its beauty, too perfectly imperfect with the abundance of colour and life to be real, but far too lucid a sight to be anything other than the most solid of existences. It was there, in the meadow, outlined and crested by the snow-peaked mountains, that we found the Behemoth.

"My first instinct was to reach for my dagger, yet I did this only because I thought it was expected of me. I felt no intent to kill, no wish to see the creature dead and, upon my hand reaching the hilt, I realised this, releasing the weapon and allowing my hand, instead, to run through Titus' mane.

"Sat there, in the meadow, it could have been mistaken for one of the mountains. It was so desperately unmoving that it was only when it finally looked upon us that I was contented to think of it as the Behemoth; the slight movement of its head, aside from those listless white eyes, the only sign of life from the creature.

"We watched, impassive and awestruck, as it gazed upon us, seemingly as surprised by our peace as we were at its. The breeze whispered from the mountains, between the petals of the flowers and engulfed us in the amazing silence of nature. When a sound finally occurred, it came from the Behemoth. It's chest expanded with air and it lifted its head towards the bruising morning light. Despite its calm and our own, I thought it was about to roar, ready to attack us. But, much as anything, as life itself, the air just gathered in its lungs and left with a sigh, and a contented one at that.

"Only then did I realise that the stony face wore an expression. One of reticence, remorse, sorrow. Of course, we had our theory that it wasn't as malevolent as the past millennium had led us to believe, that it attacked and killed only when provoked and this has been proven time and again. Yet, I never thought it capable of... penitence."

He looked into the fire that lit him so melancholically. "It mourns its place in the world. Perhaps we would have been kinder to rid it of the burden of life. Then again," he passed a glance between Lament and Vaiske, "you're here now. And you're better equipped for the task than Airn and I."

His words faded into the night and there was silence, save for the crackling of the fire. Starling shuffled uncomfortably, but didn't change the way he was sitting, as if the words he had spoken hung clammily on the air surrounding him.

Those of the group who could sleep did, though Arvan wasn't among them. He lay there, clutching the dead man's staff to himself, Captain Starling's words swimming around viscously in his mind.

The Behemoth made an enemy only of war, went to war only with war, conflicted only with conflicted and still repented its position in the world.

That, after a millennium, it would still mourn its purpose troubled the boy. He thought of how as a teenager he thought he would have life worked out by the time he was twenty, yet, with that birthday only a few months away, he found himself more confused than ever. It irked him that the Behemoth was just as uncomfortable as him, even if it was of a different species.

Master Snow had told him that he still had much to learn, but if the white-clad samurai could not teach him, who could?

He opened his eyes to the dark night where he saw Vaiske practicing in the dim light. His skill was unsurpassed. He struck with purpose even when he was only training.

Purpose.

Everything the immortal did was full of purpose, and he was never troubled by it. He had created a purpose, a reason to live, for himself and he strode towards his goals, never fearing the consequences of his next step. He didn't let others or circumstance stand in his way like the shadus, nor did he trouble himself with the morals of Master Snow. He did what he thought was right, what would lead him to glory and what would stop his legend from disappearing from the library of time.

As if aware he was being watched, Vaiske paused and turned his immortal head to the boy. Arvan didn't move, barely breathed, and still the horned warrior approached. He sat beside the boy.

"You can't sleep?" he asked.

"I'm eager to continue," Arvan replied, sitting up.

"Eager?" Vaiske said, more pensively than was usual for him. "Nothing troubles you?"

Arvan rested the staff on his shoulder as Kyagorusu used to. "Only what to do and where to go once the Behemoth is dead."

"You won't go back to Farras?"

Arvan shook his head. "It doesn't feel like home anymore, or maybe it never did."

Vaiske grunted amusedly. "That sounds familiar. But fear not Arvan; the quest needs not end upon the death of the Behemoth. Someone has to stop the war from spreading."

Arvan slowly turned his head towards the warrior.

"You mean…" He paused. "You mean you'd take me with you?"

Vaiske laughed mechanically.

"My boy," he said. "I have learned much from life, but nothing so true as this; few, even the most experienced of adventurers, wish for more than the company of others."

Lament wandered far from the group that night, until the feeling he was alone was displaced by the knowledge he was alone. He walked so far that the land ended and the cliff fell steeply before him. On and on in sight ocean met sky, both the deep purple that only the most solemn of nights can create.

He sat at the edge of the cliff, his sword lying beside him. His right leg dangled over the edge while he hugged his left close to him as he gazed at the moon.

It was only a few minutes before the breeze whispered past and that somnolent wave of comfort washed over him.

"Hello, my love."

Chapter Twenty Seven

Arvan woke to a pale, cloudless dawn. During their sleep, he and Darkla had moved closer to one another. They nestled in such a way that her hair was draped across his face. Despite their long journey her blonde locks were still clean and heavily perfumed.

A warmth emanated from within his chest, but he didn't have the words to define the feeling. It was as if his being housed a separate sun, one that would forever soothe him into an indescribable comfort.

He rose, carefully, so as not to wake her. As his head left the grass he noted how quiet the camp was, most often he was the last to wake and he knew that Lament and Vaiske, at least, would not have slept. But the two sleepless men were not there. Instead, he was met by Captain Starling, readying Titus for the day's journey. The man in the white jacket had his back to him, but Arvan knew he was smiling.

"*You* slept well," Starling said.

"When I eventually fell asleep," Arvan grumbled, rubbing his eyes. He blew the hair from his face as if he planned on speaking further, but said nothing.

"Well," Starling said, turning to him and confirming the suspicion of a smile, "at least it was in some comfort."

The Captain glanced at Darkla, then back to Arvan.

Arvan frowned. "We just moved in the night. I wasn't aware of her until I woke."

Starling sighed and turned back to readying Titus.

"Friendship is every bit as sacred as romance, Arvan," he said, tightening a strap on Titus' saddle. "One should feel every bit at home in the arms of a friend as in the arms of a lover. Perhaps more so." He released Titus and turned to Arvan again. "But, as a man of few friends and no lovers, I would say that," his smile widened, "wouldn't I?"

Arvan didn't wish to reply. Instead he asked a question of his own.

"Where are Lament and Vaiske?"

Starling shrugged and ran a loving hand through Titus' bright grey mane.

"Lament was away all night," he said absent-mindedly. "Vaiske left just after you fell asleep."

Arvan frowned. "You were awake all night?"

Starling nodded.

"Why?"

Starling paused. He stopped stroking his horse's mane and glanced at Arvan before focusing his gaze on something outside the camp.

"I rarely sleep well," he said, resuming his care of Titus.

"You're troubled?"

"I don't quite know what I am."

Arvan, every bit as intrigued by the Captain as when they first met (despite Starling's slightly antagonistic nature) was about to pry further when Darkla stirred beside him and he was distracted. She didn't wake.

"You've changed, Arvan," Starling said, moving and crouching before the boy. "You've matured since we last met. You're not the stern faced youth you once were; you're something I can't quite understand, if still a little stern of face. Though, you've still got a lot to learn." Starling smiled. "But less than me."

Arvan looked into the grey eyes. His own were as hard and as stern as ever.

"Well, I have someone to teach those things to me now," he said.

Starling frowned and stood, walking back to Titus. "The less said about that the better."

"You still don't trust Vaiske?"

Starling shrugged, feeding Titus some grain from his hand. "He's not a bad man, in fact he's probably the best of all of us. I just don't hold with hero-worship."

Arvan leapt to his feet, dropping Kyagorusu's staff and placing his hand on the hilt of his katana.

"Hero worship?" he roared. "You dare accuse me of such a weakness?"

Starling gave him a disapproving look but said nothing.

"I learn from others what I must; what else are others for? They are my elders and I respect them, but hero-worship? Master Snow is a great man, but not without his faults."

"And the immortal?" Starling questioned.

"He…" Arvan didn't know how to finish that sentence.

"Exactly," Starling said. "You think him faultless, that each of his weaknesses is warranted, making it a strength. Tell me you don't want to be like him."

Arvan couldn't. He let go of the sword and stood inertly.

Starling shrugged with that wry smile back on his lips. "Then again, what do I know? You'll be a great man when you can see others objectively, but that's a skill I have yet to learn. I see others only as my own arrogance permits."

Arvan sat back down by the long dead campfire and wished that Vaiske was there. He wasn't sure whether to laugh Captain Starling's words off or accept them. They weren't so different to what Master Snow had told him upon his departure. But was he so wrong to look up to others? All he wished for was a little guidance.

He felt a warm hand on his and turned to see Darkla had woken. Her eyes met his and she smiled.

"Good morning," she said.

"Good morning!" Starling called before Arvan could reply. By the time the youth was prepared to reply Darkla had sat beside him.

"How many more mornings do you think we shall have such as this?" she asked, ponderously.

"I don't know," he replied. "Not so many more."

"But enough?" she asked, her soft features turning to his; as if carved from stone.

Arvan didn't answer.

It wasn't long before Lieutenant Arnamous came riding back into camp astride his black horse. It seemed to Arvan that he had gone riding for the mere sake of it.

"Are we going, Lind?" he asked.

"Not just yet," Starling replied. "I've still to say goodbye to Lament and Vaiske and we're in no hurry." He smiled at his subordinate and friend. "Besides, our hosts certainly don't seem to want to be getting on."

Lament watched the sun rise passively from his position on the cliff. The sky was as sallow as his skin and the sun brought no heat as it rose; it had more in common with the moon. The breeze whispered by, picking up his cape and brushing his hair to the side. Yet, it did not bring him the comfort that it usually did as approaching footsteps disturbed him.

"Are you coming back?" Vaiske asked mechanically.

Lament nodded. "I feel rested. The Shadowblight isn't plaguing me as it usually does."

Vaiske remained a few paces behind him. He rested his spear across his shoulders.

"Why did you come here?" he asked.

"I don't know. It felt like it was where I was supposed to be. I just headed off into the night and it felt as though the breeze was leading me here. When I arrived..." He sighed. "I don't know."

Vaiske stared at the shadus. "I feel it too."

Lament turned to him. "I know. It's... disconcerting, is it not?"

Vaiske shuffled in his armour.

"I'm not sure what it is," he growled. "Anyway, staying here brooding won't make it better, will it? I doubt we've the insight to figure it out."

Lament sighed. "Perhaps."

He stood and took his sword, strapping it once more to his back. He turned to the immortal. "How far have we to go?"

"I believe our bounty awaits us in the meadow Captain Starling spoke of. We should be able to get there by noon."

Lament stepped towards the immortal.

"Well," he said. "I suppose I should reclaim my shadow."

Vaiske laughed mechanically. "We've a Behemoth to kill first, shadus."

233

They exchanged a hard look, then started back to the camp.

Vaiske strode towards the waiting group, acknowledging none of them. Lament followed him at his leisurely pace, typically sullen. He noted the men from the Final Resting Place of the Empire on their horses.

"You're to leave us?" he asked.

Starling nodded.

"We've kept Eremmerus waiting long enough." The Captain passed his look between them all. "Well, farewell. The best of luck to you all. If I should happen upon any of you again, I'll wish it once more."

Lament nodded appreciatively but said nothing.

"It was a joy to meet you both," Darkla said, causing a smile to creep across Starling's lips.

Arvan and the Captain's eyes met, but the boy said nothing. He took on that stern face that Starling had thought was gone.

The Captain sighed and turned to his Lieutenant. "Come on, Airn," he said. "Our road ahead is long, and we've travelled further than most as it is."

They went on, pulling the reigns of their horses gently. They set a slow pace, but, as Starling had said earlier, they were in no hurry.

They watched in silence as the men became silhouettes in the morning light, as if waiting for them to turn and give one last sign of their leaving, but neither the Captain nor the Lieutenant turned. They simply rode on into the immeasurable distance.

"Well, come on," Vaiske growled. "The Behemoth can't be so far away. We don't want to be here so long that it starts to expect us."

The immortal strode south and the others followed one by one. Lament went last, gazing east for a time, before walking after the rest of the party at that metronome pace.

The immortal walked with an excited energy towards destiny. Slowly, it osmosed into Arvan, walking beside him. The boy's thoughts had been heavy with self-doubt, incensed by Captain Starling's words. Yet, this dissipated when he realised what a momentous quest he was a part of. Next to him walked a man who would kill the Behemoth and change the world forever. Maybe with the Behemoth gone men really could work out their differences.

Darkla, too, was excited. She had no wish to see the battle to come or Arvan in any danger, but the adventure was to continue, for a while at least. She was unsure of what was to come after. A journey towards Farras, she imagined; a journey towards home. But, what was that pulling on her chest, away from the town in the north?

Shadowblight temporarily assuaged, Lament walked on. He was silent as ever, listening to Darkla's joyful humming, but it brought him no comfort. His steps were lacklustre and he had no wish to hide this, but his companions, lost in thoughts of their own, paid no attention to him.

Still he was irked by the ease-less peace he felt at cliff and just what it meant. That it had taken the arrival of Vaiske to entirely destroy the comfort and let the unease take over was no surprise, but why that of all places? It was far from familiar to him, but he felt he knew those cliffs, that endless vista of sea; as if existed within his being, somewhere his search couldn't reach.

His thoughts were such that, had he been alone, he would have missed it. But he was in company, even if the feeling was unknown to him. Lament stopped, not because he noticed that the rest of the group had, but because the mood to do so fell upon him. Only when he acknowledged the action and the desire did he come around to his surroundings and he shuddered with insignificance.

The group stood, strewn across the path, but their attention did not follow the dirt road south. Instead it led to the centre of the continent. Before them, laid out immeasurably and perfectly imperfect in the presence of the distant mountains, was the meadow that Captain Starling had spoken of. Flowers of as many different species as Lament could name, and a few he had no knowledge of, grew unwieldy long, reaching the hip of even a tall man. The colours were more vibrant than he could ever have conceived possible; shades and hues so vivid to almost be dreamlike, colours he couldn't describe. And the fragrance. Sweetness, sweetness. Yet still, it paled in comparison with his beloved Miata. The milk sallow skin, the obsidian black hair and the indescribable scent.

He stood there, one-eyed and strangely moved, as he compared the art of nature with the most morbid beauty he had ever known and admitted, lustrously radiant as the meadow was, it could never compete with the imperfections of love, nor the wonder that they wrought.

Even Vaiske was silent at the sight. He shuffled in his armour, struggling to take the divine vista in.

Eventually, the godless silence was broken.

"What is this?" Darkla gasped.

"Destiny," Vaiske said in that metallic voice.

"I don't see the Behemoth," Arvan said, curiously confident.

Lament rolled his eye towards the boy but said nothing.

"So we wait," Vaiske answered. "It knows this place. It probably thinks of it as home; as much as it can think."

Lament was about to reply that they knew it could think, it was every bit as sentient as them, perhaps more so. But he realised the futility as his eye turned towards the demonic visage of Vaiske, spear resting across his shoulders, hands hung lazily over the handle.

The warrior, Arvan and Darkla in tow, strode into the meadow. Lament could do little but follow.

Despite almost being noon, the light was cast lazily. A thin powder of clouds was strewn across the sky and the sun was a deep gold. There was a faintly blue hue to the day.

They walked through the meadow, where even the breeze seemed to not wish to venture, in a reverie that belied their intentions. Darkla's hand trailed beside her and she grasped the heads of the flowers lightly as she walked, allowing the myriad of petals to pass between her fingers. She considered plucking one from its place as a souvenir, to remind herself of all the wonderment the world held, but, upon actually moving to do so, she decided the memory was enough. Marring the meadow by taking from it seemed sacrilegious.

Soon, they reached a cherry blossom tree and the scent grew sweeter still. They rested under it, sitting peacefully, the pink-white petals enveloping them.

Lament stood away from the group, but was still engulfed by the majesty of the tree. Its trunk was jagged, as if drawn by two sharp brushstrokes by some restlessly inspired artist. He looked at his surroundings in his typically melancholic way. The mountains drew his attention and he gazed upon them sceptically.

Arvan moved, pleasured, as he lay.

"How long will we stay here?" he asked.

"Until the Behemoth comes," Vaiske said. "I can think of less pleasant places to wait."

The shadus glanced at them, then back to mountains.

"You've not long to wait," he said.

His amber eye narrowed as one of the mountains moved.

Chapter Twenty Eight

The Behemoth rose, tearing itself from the backdrop of the mountains. That its stone-like skin and colossal frame had let it blend in with the formation should not have astonished them as it had. Its listless white eyes fell upon them, glowing as jewels beset in its face, and, only then, was it fully removed from its mountainous surroundings and it cut the figure of itself that was not so different from a man. The shoulders; so broad as to be carved by time itself, holding the strength of a timeless power, that of the Planet itself. The head; held so high to define pride, yet, hung in the eyes it couldn't hide was a remorse the profundity of which only one of the group had the experience to know empathy with it. The sentience of the creature; so old, so ancient, to rival the endless tides of the breeze and the endless tides of life for wisdom. Yet its sagacious existence would ceaselessly be forgotten upon the sight of the eternal figure.

It moved not to attack them, nor to scare them; merely to see them, to look upon them as it gazed upon so much in its millennial life. Even when Vaiske and Arvan leapt to their feet, the immortal brandishing his spear as if faced with no more than a common thug, it showed no murderous intent. Only that all knowing, regretful gaze.

Darkla sat, amazed at the sheer scale of the creature. She had never seen it, only heard the sweeping howls of it in the distant night. She had never expected it to be so... human. She gazed at it, letting the eyes tear into her as her bursting heart beat ever more rapidly, she felt an affinity with it. She thought it not so different from Lament.

Vaiske tilted his head towards Lament. "Ready for glory, shadus?"

Lament rolled his eye towards the immortal. "We should wait for sunset," he replied. "When the shadows are at their longest."

Vaiske threw back his helmeted head and laughed mechanically. Once he was finished he fixed the anguished eyes of his mask on Lament.

"When your bounty lies before you, shadus, you must strike immediately. Make no mistake; your ability to use shadows is impressive, but I do not require your aid to kill the best. You are here only so I can return your shadow to you when I am finished with it."

Lament snorted. "How greatly that speech differs from the one you gave in Eremmerus' Throne Room."

Vaiske grunted and turned to Arvan.

"Ready, Arvan?" he asked.

The youth became stern faced once more and blew his fringe from his eyes. He nodded determinedly.

"Well then," Vaiske growled. "Shall we?"

He broke into a run and bounded through the flowers towards the Behemoth.

Arvan turned towards Darkla, now standing. His carven features were different to usual. She'd never known him to show such malicious excitement.

"Hold this," he said with a grin, thrusting Kyagorusu's staff into her grasp.

"You can't kill it," she said.

His smile widened, like some experienced adventurer, so self-sure of his skills.

"Of course I can," he laughed. "Don't worry, I'll come back."

With that he sprinted after Vaiske.

"No," she whispered. "It's too beautiful to kill."

The forgotten Lament stepped beside her.

"Sometimes," he whispered, "only in death can something become truly beautiful." He rolled his eye towards her and she gazed up at his sorrowful face.

"Stay here," he said. "Stay safe."

Then he followed after Arvan and Vaiske at that laborious pace of his.

Vaiske had long disappeared in Arvan's sight. As his feet pounded on the ground and he tore through the wild flowers, all he saw was the Behemoth. How many times had he seen it now? All the circumstances that led it into his past and him into its, stretched on into possibility and impossibility both. Yet it had happened, and that was all there was to it.

He thought of his encounter with it on the Rock Flats. How long ago it felt, as if he had been journeying to the current moment since the world began. Though still, he remembered the terror he felt at the merest glimpse of it. The sound of its roar, the reaffirmation of fear upon hearing its name spoken. He was still unsure of how far he and Kyagorusu had run from it and felt a fervent emptiness that there was no longer a Kyagorusu to run from it with. So, instead, he ran towards it, prepared to avenge the fallen philosopher.

He thought of the fist of the Behemoth punching through the wall in the Coliseum and how tall the hulking figure had stood above it. He recalled his desire to avenge his presumed-fallen teacher, only to find he lacked to fortitude to continue, being led from the battle by Kyagorusu.

Kyagorusu.

The boulder flying.

The bald philosopher walking beside him one moment, nothing left of him but a trail of blood on the mountain path the next.

Unwittingly, Arvan's legs enfeebled and he fell to a heap in the flowers. He wept, folding into the foetal position as he did so, finding no comfort in anything. He tried to stand, only to fall again, and let the sadness wash over him. He thought of how he had decided to hunt the creature with Vaiske to avenge two men, one of whom turned out not to be dead.

He thought of the Behemoth tearing through the bridge of Pale Castle as if it were nothing more than a remnant of the surface of the water beneath. It moved as if the cannon fire from the castle didn't hit it at all. Then the herculean fist pounded the castle as it had the Coliseum, and everything stopped.

All of the anger.

All of the fear.

All of the fighting.

There was only silence and the breeze as the Behemoth slunk back into the ocean.

Then all there was to be left with was doubt. Master Snow was alive and they travelled south witnessing countless horrors of humanity and the beauty that humanity tried so hard to hide. All the time hearing whispers of the Behemoth, benevolent, malevolent or otherwise.

He remembered the doubt; no, it wasn't so much a memory, for it had long been on his mind; of whether or not the hunt was the right thing. He lay there, sobbing, still unsure.

He opened his eyes and saw Lament standing above him. Arvan rose to his knees and wiped his tears from his eyes with his palms.

"You'd be wise to stay here," Lament whispered, a slight hint of sympathy coating his ghostly tone.

"What do you know of it?" Arvan said weakly.

"Only that you've nothing to prove."

Arvan met the eye of the shadus and scowled.

"I'm a man!" he roared. "I can fight!" He wept again. "I can fight."

"Yes," Lament said. "You can fight. But that doesn't mean that you should."

With that, unknowingly speaking Kyagorusu's words, he left Arvan there amongst the flowers, alone.

It towered above him as it had so many times in his years-long quest. It looked upon him as if it recognised him, remembered him, knew him. Indeed, the immortal thought that by now it should, and when it looked upon him, clad in vermillion armour and horned, it should know that it looked upon an equal. It should know that it looked upon its death.

Vaiske gazed up at the gargantuan visage, the eyes glowing high above him. The foot was a mere few metres away from him and he smiled behind his mask.

"Not much longer now," he growled.

Slow footsteps sounded behind him and Lament appeared. Vaiske looked to the shadus.

"And Arvan?" he asked.

Lament rolled his eye towards the immortal. "He has questions I can't answer."

"And you?"

Lament peered up at the hulking creature. "I have questions I can't ask. Save for one."

"Please proceed," Vaiske said arrogantly.

Lament looked at him once more. "How do you propose we kill it?"

Vaiske smiled behind his mask.

"With ease, shadus," he said. "With ease."

With that he lifted his spear above his head with one hand and pierced the ankle of the Behemoth, as if the skin was mere paper, as if only to provoke the creature.

Darkla watched, stunned, as the Behemoth threw back its head, as if the world around it had ceased to move. It let out a piercing, almighty scream. It tore through her, forcing her to take a step back to stabilise herself.

Daunted, she looked away, holding the dead man's staff closer to her. She closed her eyes, so tight to be ignorant of a world outside of the blackness.

The shriek faded to nothingness.

Silence.

Slowly, she opened her eyes to the dancing flowers around her. The breeze gently entered and whispered through the meadow, sliding past her.

She turned to the Behemoth and shuddered at the conflict the peace around her betrayed.

The creature slowly, but powerfully, lifted a fist above its head.

Vaiske sardonically ripped the tip of the spear from the ankle of the beast. He watched, still impressed at his immortal strength, a thin line of blood trickled down to the creature's hooved foot.

He turned to the shadus, "Ready?"

"I thought you didn't require my help," Lament replied sarcastically .

Vaiske shrugged in his armour. "You may as well join in while you're here."

The fist dove towards them, the air in its path left displaced and rent. Lament gave it a blasé look.

"Should I contend with that?" he asked Vaiske.

"If it's not *too* much bother."

Lament's hand wrapped around the hilt of his sword. "Not at all."

He drew the sword from his back, the gargantuan blade meeting the mammoth fist a mere foot from the shadus' head. It was just enough to stop the momentum of the beast.

Lament, with no hint of effort, took a heavy step forward, throwing the Behemoth's hand from him. He looked to the immortal.

"I assume you've a plan?" he asked.

Vaiske nodded determinedly, ignoring the gigantic palm swinging towards them.

"Care to share?" Lament asked calmly.

Vaiske smiled behind his horrific mask.

"The same as in the Final Resting Place of the Empire," he said. "Get to the head."

Lament rested the gargantuan blade of his shoulder. "And how, with no shadows to travel through, do you suppose we do that?"

The palm drew nearer.

"The old fashioned way," Vaiske replied. The palm sidled a metre or so from him and he thrust the tip of his spear through the cracked skin of the creature. The fingers splayed in pain as Vaiske twisted the spear. "We climb."

Arvan's eyes beheld the battle before him but, bordering on catatonia, he was unaware of what he watched. All around him was a blank. He didn't feel the whispering of the breeze lightly caress his skin as it passed, or the petals of the flowers brushing against his tear-stained cheeks. All that existed for him was sorrow, and all that existed within that sorrow was him.

Sensations slowly left him and he was soon unaware of the feeling of his brain being set afire by his angst. He let nothingness grip him and he lay on the ground, inert and unknowing.

Using the handle of his spear, Vaiske pulled the hand towards him. He moved the weapon as such that he could reach the beast's forearm, the beast too pained to retaliate. He grasped a tuft of the forearm fur and noted the disapproving expression of Lament.

"Hurry, shadus," he growled. "You don't want me to take all of the glory for myself."

He ripped the tip of the spear from the hand, rupturing the skin further. The beast swept its arm upwards and Lament could no longer see the immortal.

The shadus placed his sword upon his back and gazed up at the Behemoth. He noted the fur on its thighs and forearms and remembered similarly coarse hair on the creature's back.

"You're welcome to your glory, Vaiske," he whispered. "I just wish none had to die for so arrogant a pursuit."

He stepped towards the creature's leg and placed a cautious hand on it.

Despite the slowness of the creature, the force that its strength allowed it to move its limbs with created considerable wind resistance. Of course, it was little trouble for the ageless grip of Vaiske Parlet. He gripped the tuft of greying fur in his left hand while he held his spear in his right. It felt to the man-with-two-shadows to be little more effort than standing.

He turned his attention to his objective; the head of the beast. The listless white eyes were forever upon him, but still he held on, undaunted by so lifeless a gaze. The path to the head was, as yet, unclear, but, with his will to rid the Planet of the scourge that was the Behemoth, he knew he would find a way, or the way would find him.

Probing at the possibilities more than anything else, he struck his spear further up the arm of the Behemoth and began to crawl along. The beast, though watching the immortal, seemed not to notice the spear piercing its skin. It did not scream, nor did it flinch. It merely watched Vaiske Parlet continue along its arm with its strange eternal calm.

'That's it, beast,' Vaiske thought. 'Why retaliate? How can you possibly stop the advance of an immortal?'

He smiled to himself behind his mask; how close he was to completing his task.

It was only once he had left the fur covered forearm and reached the stone-like of the forearm that the eternal calm was broken. The listless white eyes seemed to cut themselves apart as the creature frowned.

The Behemoth lifted its other arm and the colossal palm sped towards the immortal.

The fur on the back of the Behemoth's legs was longer than on the front. It dangled, tantalisingly close, just above Lament's head, out of his grasp by a matter of feet. His perpetual frown intensified and he turned his head, eye falling on the hilt of his sword. He drew the gargantuan weapon from his back and sighed.

Lament drove the blade into the ground and clambered onto the oversized guard. Standing on the colossal sword, he reached, stretching as far as his dimensions would allow, until his hand clasped the dregs of the beast's fur. He tested the weight it would hold and gave a satisfied grunt.

He took his sword from the ground and hung from the creature's hair. With difficulty, he placed the sword back in the leather straps beneath his cape and considered how best he could proceed.

He grasped in his free hand a higher tuft of the mangled fur and pulled himself further up the creature. He was glad they had rested during the night as they had, doubting he would have had the strength for such exertion otherwise. Even then he could feel his grip beginning to fail him.

Each pull of himself that slightest of distances up the beast exhausted him, draining him of already low supplies of energy. The Shadowblight lay tauntingly inside of him, threatening to besiege his will with each petty movement he made.

His nausea flared.

He shuddered against the drop in temperature.

Every inch of muscle he possessed whispered to him to let himself drop to the ground beneath. Yet, on he went, though he couldn't quite give himself a reason.

He pulled himself closer to the beast, resting his shoulders momentarily. He gazed up as he hung, panting, halfway up the Behemoth's back. He watched, helpless, as the creature lifted a defiant hand.

Arvan came to to the world around him. The flowers dancing around his crouching body. The soothing touch of the breeze. The Behemoth struggling with invisible adversaries.

Why had he come? Yes, to avenge Kyagorusu, to lay his friend to rest. But before that, before he had even met the bald philosopher. There wasn't just his desire to find Master Snow, but the yearning for adventure he had never been able to satiate. The restlessness that lay within his soul. The peace he didn't know.

All the adventure he could hope for was before him, in some spectacle of wills.

He lifted himself from the ground and wiped the tears from his eyes. Then, hand resting on the hilt of his katana, he ran to join the battle.

The hand rested over the immortal, encasing him between the arm of the Behemoth and the palm. For a moment, all Vaiske knew was darkness. Then, creaking with age, the fingers folded around him, too tightly even for his immortal strength to power against.

The beast held him, helpless in its clutch, only his helmeted head eluding the grasp of the creature. He struggled against it, but his second shadow allowed him to feel no pain. He attempted to scratch at the hand with his spear, yet the weapon was trapped between two of the beast's fingers.

"You look to be having some trouble, Vaiske," that melancholic voice, carried by the breeze, said to him.

He looked up and saw Lament, precariously balanced on the shoulder of the Behemoth.

"Lament, you conniving runt!" he roared. "Don't just stand there: do something!"

Lament rolled a sarcastic eye towards the immortal. "I thought you didn't require my help."

"This is hardly the time for one-upmanship!"

But Lament wasn't listening. His attention had been garnered buy a small, approaching figure. A young effigy, dressed in black rushing towards them.

Unfortunately, the eyes of the Behemoth had been drawn to it too.

Arvan shuddered at the mere sight of it, but kept his hand resolutely on the hilt of his sheathed sword. He charged towards the Behemoth gracelessly.

So there were suspicions that it was benevolent, raised mainly by Master Snow. Could they ever really know? What could mankind understand of such a creature? Their only predator, save for time. And then the tales would speak of the brave adventurers who slew it. Vaiske Parlet and his student, Arvan Deit.

Yet, as he neared, the Behemoth towering skyward, the boy froze; the creature's gaze fixed on him. How could he, so insignificant to barely be called a man, a mere nineteen years of age, hope to pose even a slight threat to this ageless being born from the Planet?

His body turned to fibreless stone as he watched, motionless, the Behemoth raising a free fist, its gaze still lain upon him.

"One sword strike, shadus!" Vaiske roared. "One sword strike and it will release me!"

But Lament didn't hear. He watched as the fist centred clearly on the non-descript Arvan below. He knew what he had to do.

As the Behemoth moved the fist towards the boy, Lament leapt from the shoulder, flying to his destination with the same determined speed as the beast. His clothes flapped deafeningly against the resisting wind; but he knew nothing of it, so resolved was he to save the boy.

He tore the sword from his back and brought the sword down, over his head, as he and the fist both neared the ground.

The gargantuan blade sliced effortlessly through the wrist of the Behemoth and the disjoined hand landed with a quake no more than five metres from Arvan. Lament landed gracefully beside him, sword resting on his shoulder. His amber eye rolled towards the boy.

The beast shrieked. It was far more than anything it had screamed before. Sheer anguish ruptured the breeze.

Despite the noise, Arvan spoke and Lament knew that his lips read, "Thank you."

Instinctively, the Behemoth dropped Vaiske and the immortal landed restlessly in the flowers. He rose from his heap just in time to see his quarry turn and leave through the mountains.

That damnable shadus had once more let the Behemoth elude his grasp. He spied Lament and Arvan not far from him.

"Lament, you contemptible cur!" he roared. The shadus turned to him. "What were you thinking? We almost had it!"

Lament placed his sword on his back.

"I told you we should have waited for sunset," he said, typically calm. "With the shadows at their longest it would have been easier still."

Vaiske strode towards him. "Well, you've made the wait for your shadow longer!"

The mask was a lone inch from Lament's face.

The shadus pointed towards the severed hand with his thumb, his fingers obscuring the bandage on his palms. "Surely that's worth my shadow."

"That's worth a shadow of your hand!" Vaiske snorted. "And until I work out how that's possible you'll have to go without."

It was only then that they noticed Darkla running up to meet them. She still held Kyagorusu's staff and, when she stopped, she rested it across her knees as she fought for breath.

"Is everyone okay?" she asked.

Nobody answered, but Arvan touched her lovingly.

"What now?" she asked.

"We wait for dusk," Lament said, "and we try again."

"And until then?"

"We'll go to Kyagorusu's town," Arvan said. "It can't be far from here."

Vaiske gave a grunt of acceptance.

Lament wiped his fever-ridden brow. "As much as it pains me, I fear I will not make it so far. I shall wait for your return and bid him farewell once I have my shadow back."

Arvan smiled solemnly at the shadus and nodded.

They parted, leaving the shadus in the meadow alone, as the spring sun slid slowly into the afternoon.

Chapter Twenty Nine

The peace he felt in the meadow was ceaseless, yet fragile. The flowers that swayed in their dance of ages spiralled on, far outreaching even his extraordinary shadus sight. The breeze wrapped itself around him, like some playful blanket. It lifted him, far from the experience he knew, the warmth of blissful confusion emanating from his chest and lying next to his perplexed heart. It was far from a religious experience, yet so spiritual he couldn't ignore it. If there was comfort in the world, something he had yet to find and something the existence of which he had long doubted, this was where it was to be found.

His eye turned to the cherry blossom tree, so distant to be a mere speck of pink and white; to be just a petal in the storm of flowers. What was this place? So much more than a meadow. The birthplace of joy? The place where the art of nature and life itself became as one, and the beholder could finally know that they had come to life, if only briefly, and they existed, even if alone, somewhere in the ether. What surprised him most was that he didn't try to shake the feeling off. Lament let it engulf him, until he was no longer sure where he began and the meadow, and the breeze, ended, or if any of them ended at all.

Yet, as it was so often in his life, his contentment was fleeting, and the breeze began to pull itself from him, blowing once more to the east.

"You would lead me there again, my love?" he whispered. "Clearly that place is of some significance. Well, as you wish."

He waded through the groping flowers and headed, once more, for the cliff.

*

As they left the meadow, Arvan found his mind to be strangely unburdened by his failure to fight against the Behemoth. He pictured the trapped Vaiske in the Behemoth's hand, too consumed by the completion of his goal to notice the peril of Arvan. He pictured the melancholic figure of Lament tearing through the air, clothes fluttering apocalyptically in the breeze, and reticently dismembering the creature's hand. But more than that, he couldn't shake the remorse that the Behemoth fought with. The listless eyes suggesting it moved in battle merely for the appearance of fighting back.

His observation confused him. In his hands he still held Kyagorusu's staff. A man so innocent, so good-natured, he gave food and love to one he had just met and one who had met him coldly at that. But, his death was a wrong that could not be righted and it finally occurred to the youth that, perhaps, his sorrow at the philosopher's death was not best directed as murderous vengeance against the Behemoth, but simply as remorse, and acceptance, at the unjust nature of life and its ending.

As they walked further on, tearing through a forest for which Vaiske's voracious pace left no wonder, Arvan's thoughts did not lighten, His reasons for setting out on his adventure had been discarded by fate. He had not found Master Snow, Master Snow had found him. He had lost his desire to see the Behemoth slain and had even more so lost his desire to be a part of its death. Whether or not he could learn anything from Vaiske Parlet was irrelevant; he had no wish to learn the lessons that so heartless a man would teach. Did the yearning for adventure still lurk in his soul? He had no doubt that the answer was yes; he had no wish to return to Farras, the town of his birth and childhood. Yet, he did not yearn for the blood-soaked adventures of the man-with-two-shadows. Then again, every so often, even the immortal seemed penitent at the path his life had taken.

He looked to the horned warrior in the vermillion armour, the lush green of the surrounding forest fading to nothingness against the boy's garnered attention. Vaiske strode though, paying no attention to anything – his thoughts solely on reaching his destination in as short a time as possible. Arvan shivered. Is that how he had been? Running through his childhood to become a man and finally prove himself to the world. And now he was there, at his destination, only, now there, it seemed different than when he had viewed it from a distance; like the future of another man.

Soon, the forest began to thin and Arvan could see through the trees. The ocean, calm and expectant, lay gleaming on the other side of the still obscured land. As the tides whispered, Arvan felt a wave of peace fall over him and he accepted the near-completion of his quest. He could lay Kyagorusu to rest in his homeland, where his family could learn of his death and take solace in the knowledge and in the fact that he died in adventure and his love of it.

The trio stepped from the tree and came to a point slightly above the rest of the town. Arvan gazed down the incline and saw…

Nothing.

Rubble where once there were houses. Scattered stones that once made up a cobbled square. No people. No buildings. No life. Only destruction and disrepair.

Arvan fell to his knees, clutching the dead man's staff, his pulsating heart threatening to leap from his chest and run to the ocean.

"You knew," he seethed at the staff. "You knew and you didn't tell me."

He retched and writhed but he shed no tears. Destroyed though it may have been, he had taken the bald philosopher home.

Darkla wrapped him in her arms.

The immortal gave the pair a furtive glance and took a step forward, eclipsing them from his sight. He took in the once-town with the merest of looks, then gazed to the sea. Two non-descript figures stood on the water's edge; silhouettes in the afternoon lustre.

He tilted his head slightly. "Do you wish to find answers, or only to mourn?"

Arvan lifted his head and Vaiske gestured towards the figures. He felt Darkla release him and turned to her, meeting her gentle look.

"Would answers ease you?" she asked.

Arvan shook his head in reply.

"No," he said. "Far from it. To know that Kyagorusu had suffered such pain and would rather suffer that alone than share it with me hurts me severely. Yet, now he can no longer share that pain with me himself, I owe it to him to learn of it and to understand it, so that I may increase my understanding of him."

Darkla's eyes, giant and unyielding, surged endlessly into his, titillating the smallest of amounts, just enough for Arvan to notice, as her pupils, earthly and unknowing, tried to comprehend his soul.

"Why would you take that pain upon yourself?" she asked.

Arvan's lips shaped into the slightest of smiles. "Because friendship is sacred."

Vaiske ignored their tenderness and strode forwards, forcing them to follow him. Soon, their feet left the hard but unsure ground of the town and they stepped upon the sand of the beach.

The figures were two broad-shouldered men with cyan capes that fluttered in the breeze. One, seemingly the elder, wore heavy silver armour, engraved with regal platinum. His hair was thin and golden, styled into an arrogant quiff.

The other wore the same silver armour but had gold engravings. He wore his blonde locks long, letting them trail down to his shoulders.

Either they didn't notice the group or decided to pay them no attention. They were too engrossed in a conversation of their own.

"It isn't here," the older said.

"The Duke will not be pleased," replied the younger.

"No. Father most definitely will not be pleased."

They spoke in erroneous voices, the younger's a slightly deeper baritone.

"So, what do you suggest?"

The older was about to reply when he paused, his square jaw being compromised in its masculinity as he raised an eyebrow in recognition of the group. "Might I help?"

The younger took a moment to inspect Vaiske, but he didn't even glance at the others. He smirked. "I'll save you the effort," he said. "It's not here."

Vaiske rested his spear across his shoulders and laid his wrists on it.

"What's not here?" he asked in as non-threatening a voice as he could muster.

The two men gave each other side-long glances, then the younger looked back at Vaiske.

"Something," he said. "Something we want, or rather, something the duke wants."

"The Duke?" Vaiske growled.

The older man smiled. "Duke Knightsea of course."

Vaiske took a cautious step back and levelled his spear. "I know of no Duke Knightsea."

"Well," the younger said, waving a theatrical hand. "What would a southerner know of it?"

"Southerner?" Vaiske roared, tightening the grip on his spear. "I'm from the Northern Continent!"

The two men shared a humoured glance.

"And of course, Blight," the younger said, "one can go no further north than that."

"Indeed, Bane," Blight said, smile widening.

Vaiske stood, somewhat stunned that these men would talk so mockingly to him. He thought of felling them, but what answers would Arvan receive then? He looked to the boy, pale and silent; yet it was a feeble silence, one that held only because he could not find the words to speak, not because he had nothing to say.

Vaiske grunted and turned back to the brothers, speaking for Arvan.

"What happened here?" he asked.

Bane ran his fingers through his long hair. "We told you: the Duke wanted something."

"He ravaged the town?"

"No," Blight replied. "He searched it, but he was met by resistance."

"He couldn't find 'it' in the actual search," Bane said. "So he stationed us here. And our results have been less-than-satisfactory. Terrifying, really."

Blight sighed. "This is no job for the sons of a Duke. Two years and nothing to show for it."

Bane raised an eyebrow and turned to his brother.

"There's a possibility we haven't considered," he said.

"Oh?"

"*He* might have it."

Blight frowned. "'He'?"

"Dear brother, this mock non-understanding does not become you. You know very well who I mean."

Blight smiled. "Of course. He seems to have everything else that father lusts after, after all."

The brothers looked once more to Vaiske.

"We'll be going now," they said in unison.

"You've yet to answer my question!" Vaiske roared.

"You've had as much of an answer as you'll get out of us," Bane replied, typically calm. "Besides, the truth would serve only to worry you."

They approached the group, Blight walking purposefully, Bane with a lazy amble. Vaiske stood as a monolith, unwavering and fierce. When the brothers met him, he didn't move.

Bane and Blight gazed into the bulging eyes of the mask, the faint pupils hidden in shadow behind the holes meeting them endlessly. Much like Lament, the brothers showed no fear at the horrific effigy.

Behind the mask, Vaiske sneered. Then he stepped aside.

Bane and Blight passed and ventured wordlessly through a town that was once called Port Fair; a town that was once home to Kyagorusu Kagaron.

Vaiske built a monument to a man he had never met, all the time asking himself 'Why?'. He imagined it was in order to take his mind off of the Behemoth, if only for a short time. Yet, as he placed stone upon stone, he realised his mind rarely wandered from the creature. He eventually surmised that, perhaps, the time of an immortal was not quite as precious as that of a man who would meet an end and that he owed it to those who would die to take some of his endless time to acknowledge death.

He paused as he placed what he planned on being the final stone. The thought crept through his mind, its very stealth drawing his attention.

'Once I give the shadus back his shadow, I will be every bit as vulnerable as Kyagorusu Kagaron.'

"So," Darkla said as they sat on the beach, gazing out at the ocean, "after this will you help kill the Behemoth?"

"That was my plan," Arvan said. "Though now I'm not so sure that is my place."

She turned to him attentively but said nothing.

"For all this time," Arvan continued, "all of this time we've travelled in the footsteps of the Behemoth, I've had my own adventure. I thought… I was *sure*, that I was going to kill the Behemoth. But, as much as we walked the same path, we had different destinations. Vaiske's was to kill the Behemoth. Lament's was to reclaim his shadow."

Darkla met his look.

"Then what's your destination?" she asked.

Arvan sighed. "I don't know," he said thoughtfully. "But my path seems to be winding on into an immeasurable distance, while my companions are leaving the road." He looked at her. "Except one. The one who has walked with me for the longest time."

Darkla smiled.

The breeze whispered by.

They stood at the makeshift monument as a three, though only one of them knew the dead man. Arvan placed his staff against the rocks.

"To a great man," he said. "And a great friend. Sometimes words fail. What else is there to say?"

Vaiske turned from the monument and looked to the horizon. The sun was at a low angle now and he was growing restless.

"If there is nothing left to say, let us return to the shadus," he said. "The shadows are growing."

*

Lament sat on the edge of the cliff, where the breeze had led him once more. He hugged his right leg to his chest while his sword lay beside him. The presence of her familiarity assuaged his Shadowblight while he watched the sunset. The disappearing light coloured the sky a deep orange, and the blue sea glimmered reflections of this on the tips of the waves.

For once he didn't speak to her.

He attempted to ascertain why she continued to lead him there, but, aside from the peace the view gave him, he could understand little reason for it.

His amber eye fell upon a restless part of the tide and narrowed.

Silently at first, the Behemoth rose from beneath the surface of the water, but soon the sound hit the shadus as water cascaded from the almighty frame of the beast. The creature roared, as if to herald the setting of the sun, then made its way towards the cliff.

Lament stood, picking up his sword, as his cape danced in the breeze.

"So you led me here that I might end this, my love?" he said. "So be it."

Chapter Thirty

The Behemoth placed its remaining hand on the edge of the cliff and pulled itself from the ocean. At first it paid no attention to the shadus, but, as it passed Lament, it turned its head towards him, slow as the passing of time itself. It was a look that held no malice, but a diminished love as if mankind had done too much to the creature, and the creature had witnessed too much of man's inhumanity, to ever redeem themselves.

The listless white eyes met Lament's lone amber eye endlessly, all three holding ceaseless sorrow and the fervent hope of finding peace.

"Fear not," Lament said. "I will make this as swift as I can. Though, the man-with-two-shadows would undoubtedly care for some sport in it."

The Behemoth continued to look at him in seeming understanding.

"Lament, you conniving runt!" Vaiske roared charging towards him. "You planned this! You planned to take all the glory for yourself!"

Lament rolled his eye towards the immortal as he stood beside him. "Let's just finish this," he said. "It's been too long a time coming for us all."

"Very well," Vaiske growled. "Just remember, shadus – the kill is mine."

Lament said nothing.

The breeze dissipated and all fell to silence. The Behemoth lifted its herculean fist and drove it towards them, its shadow engulfing the pair. Yet, when the fist met the ground and the Behemoth drew it back, there was nothing there.

He'd never known oblivion like it. The darkness was so impenetrable that Vaiske only knew Lament was there because he could feel him holding him, leading him by the arm. Towards what, he couldn't be sure.

Even Lament, despite his shadus sight, was in complete blindness. He was drawn forwards only by the vehement feeling that he was headed in the right direction; there was little science to it. He could never explain it, even to himself, and had never met a shadus who could. He knew where he desired to exit the shadow and, long as the journey might be, he would always succeed in reaching his destination.

"Is it always like this?" Vaiske growled.

"Always."

"I suppose I should have expected as much. A little more warning might be welcome next time, though."

"I startled you?"

"No," Vaiske growled. "I just wasn't expecting it. Now hurry up, I've had quite enough of drifting through this perpetual dark."

The darkness clung to Lament, like some sentient miasmic fluid, more fervently than usual, as if the shadow realm knew he didn't have a shadow. But soon he reached the outer-blackness; the membrane of dark that led to the outside world.

They were pushed through by the knowledge that they had gone as far as they needed to and emerged to the light of day.

Vaiske squinted behind his mask, shielding his eyes from the bright sun. He looked down, only to find no ground beneath him. Forgetting his immortality, he flailed his arms and legs, discovering one limb wouldn't move. He glanced upwards seeing Lament grasping the Behemoth's back fur in one hand and Vaiske's right arm, spear still in his clutches, in his other.

"A little trust might assuage your concern," Lament whispered.

Vaiske grunted but said nothing. He took a tuft of fur in his free left hand and stole his arm from the grasp of Lament. Wordlessly, they made for the head.

The creature seemed to have forgotten about them, much to the disappointment of the immortal. It took a passive step towards the mountains before settling once more. That slightest of movements was a huge jolt for Lament who immediately lost his grip. He fell a mere few feet before regaining his hold on the back-fur, though he could only save himself with one arm. He grunted at the pain of his shoulder muscle being wrenched.

The Behemoth turned its head.

Unwitting to having alerted the creature, Lament took another tuft of fur in his free hand and began climbing, pushing against the beast with his legs for added balance. He didn't notice the remaining hand enclosing around him until Vaiske stabbed at it with his spear. The creature withdrew the appendage sharply.

"Be sure they put that in the stories, shadus!" Vaiske laughed, continuing up the Behemoth's back.

Vaiske pulled himself up onto the shoulder of the Behemoth and noted how strangely still it was. Frustrated, he leaned over the shoulder once more and pulled Lament up there with him.

"You damn shadus!" he roared, putting Lament down beside him. "You knocked all the fight out of it when you cut off its hand."

Lament shook his head. "You just don't understand, Vaiske. It isn't like you; it doesn't enjoy the kill. I'd wager it wishes for little more than to be left alone."

"Careful what you say, shadus," Vaiske growled, pointing the tip of his spear at the red rag over Lament's eye. "Remember what happened the last time we were up here."

Lament gave him a disapproving look with that one amber eye. His cape fluttered restlessly in the breeze.

"I'd advise against pointing weapons at your only ally when stood upon a millennium old creature, born from the Planet itself," he said.

Vaiske took back his spear. "I just thought you could do with reminding."

"I shan't think I'll be forgetting the man who stole half of the world's beauty from me. Condemning me, whatever path I am on, to walk a path of half blindness."

Vaiske said nothing.

"Now," Lament said, gesturing towards the head of the Behemoth, motionless behind him. "I believe you've a creature to kill."

Vaiske snorted. "But we've had no sport! The stories need a heroic battle to speak of!"

"You and Arvan shall craft the stories," Lament said wearily. "You love yourself enough to elaborate on your exploits and the boy holds you in equally high regard. Besides, there was adventure enough in getting here, let alone killing a creature which endless generations before have failed in killing."

Vaiske tilted his head threateningly.

"You misunderstand, shadus," he said in that haunting metallic voice. "I've been hunting this creature for years. I want it to suffer as it has made me suffer. I want it to feel my spear tear into it and watch the life fade from it, a droplet of blood at a time."

As if in the knowledge of Vaiske's speech, the Behemoth moved its shoulder slightly, unbalancing the immortal at the end of the joint. He fell before the creature's chest, his spear escaping his clutch and plummeting to the ground. His hand found the lone tuft of fur on the beast's abdomen.

Lament peered down at the immortal, then to the spear, so far below. The breeze whispered past and his black matted hair swam before his face.

"Shadus!" Vaiske growled. "Leap through a shadow to my spear, then help me back to the head!"

Lament moved his eye from the immortal and towards the face of the Behemoth.

"Lament, you contemptible cur!" Vaiske continued to shout.

Lament ignored him and continued to look towards the creature. He placed his hand on the hilt of his gargantuan sword.

"Forgive me," he whispered.

He drew the sword from his back and the setting sun shimmered across the blade before he thrust it into the temple of the Behemoth.

Chapter Thirty One

At first it seemed as if the creature took a voluntary step back, then it stumbled. It lifted its anguished stump, momentarily blocking out the light of the sun and, briefly, the entire vista was covered in darkness. When its hand fell back to its side it stumbled back further, before toppling over the cliff and into the ocean. It sent up a colossal fountain of surf and spray and, once even this had died to nothing, there was a profound silence. The world was no longer as it once was.

Aran and Darkla's hands met and clasped around each other.

"They did it," Darkla gasped, her amazement only equalled by her sorrow at the death of so magnificent a being.

"Now we can stop the war," Arvan said.

Their eyes met and they smiled at one another uncertainly. Then they began running towards Lament and Vaiske.

Vaiske rose from the ground, picking his spear up as he went. He turned to the shadus as Arvan and Darkla approached.

"Lament, you conniving runt! You stole my bounty from me!"

The shadus placed the sword once more upon his back.

"I merely upheld my end of the bargain," he said.

Vaiske thrust the point of his spear threateningly at the shadus. "We agreed it would be my strike that felled the beast!"

Lament rolled his eye disapprovingly towards the immortal.

"The Behemoth is dead," Arvan said. "Isn't that achievement enough?"

Vaiske locked eyes with Lament. "It might have been... long ago."

The tattered crimson cape of the shadus moved lifelessly in the breeze. He held out his hand.

"My shadow," he said.

Vaiske turned his head towards Arvan and Darkla, then back to Lament.

"I don't want them to see this," he said, gesturing with the horns of his helmet.

Lament frowned. "Very well."

With one explosion of his immortal strength, Vaiske placed a hand on Arvan's chest and launched the boy and Darkla away, the demonic effigy fading with distance.

They landed, unharmed, some way down the path; so far that Vaiske and Lament were mere wisps of black and red. They looked at one another sceptically.

"I don't understand," Arvan said.

But Darkla knew all too well.

"Now," Lament said, gesturing with his hand again, "my shadow."

Vaiske tilted his head towards him.

"But, Lament," he said. "If I am no longer immortal, who will stop the war?"

Lament shuffled uneasily. "There are forces at work, I'm sure."

He could feel the clammy touch of the Shadowblight upon him, dancing in his palms, holding his brow in a loving embrace. The fever had never been so potent before. His bile spewed, as if in anger or fear.

"You would risk a war to save only your own life?" Vaiske asked. "Since when do you hold life in such high regard?"

Lament frowned. "Perhaps not so high a regard as you."

Vaiske paused.

"You fear death," Lament said. "So much so that you would find any excuse to live forever."

Vaiske said nothing.

"But tell me, Vaiske; what good is immortality? What will you do once the war is over? *How* will you stop the war? By killing every soldier on every side until there is only you left? Is that not war in itself?

"And when that war is ended; to live out eternity. To witness everyone you love die and turn to dust, until there is only you left."

"They're all already dead!" Vaiske roared, brandishing his spear and taking a step forward. He paced wildly. "Do you think I made these my goals with no provocation? Are you so ignorant to suggest that I did these deeds for the mere fame? I know you think me some kind of monster, Lament, and you may not be so far from the truth. But I am a monster with a reason. I am a monster with a cause."

He stopped pacing, setting the gaze of the anguished mask squarely on Lament. "If I removed this mask, Lament," he said with ghostly resonance, "what do you think you would see? A man, not so unlike any other, only perhaps, with a few battle scars too many. Maybe, once upon a time, when the mask was not so necessary. But no more. No, you would see a man every bit as sickly as you. Not with Shadowblight, obviously. In fact, I have chosen a distasteful comparison. I would look more like Eremmerus."

Lament's eye widened but he said nothing.

"Before I became... *this*," Vaiske said, gesturing towards himself with his spear. "I was a soldier. Not in a warlord clan, but in an army most would consider far more benevolent. I was a Thean man. Of course, I knew of Snow and Groan, Valentine had yet to become a general, but they did not know me. I was a lowly private, far too unimportant to garner their attention. We fought bloody battle after bloody battle to protect our lord, never questioning. The pay came and the pay was good. I could feed my family and I knew they were safe. I could ask for little more.

"Eventually, my leave came and I was once more in the loving arms of my family. For a time, it was good. I noticed how my son, Valeron, had grown. He was becoming strong, like his father, to the point that he could almost match me in some of the games we played. My wife was affectionate, more so than she had been in some years.

"Then, my discomfort crept in. It was slight at first, easy enough to ignore. I thought it was some peaceful boredom. But time went on and the feeling grew. I became sick with it – unable to eat or sleep. Unable to look at my wife or Valeron as I once did.

"While they slept, I remembered by efforts in war and the strange pleasure it gave me. It was raining that night, but I didn't know it in the moment. All I knew was the spear in my hand and their sleeping bodies lying before me. I knew only the thrusting of the bladed tip into their unknowing bodies, viscous blood pouring from them onto the wooded floor of the house that we called our "home". I let the spear tear into them, again and again, until I knew they would not rise; until I knew that I was alone.

"Once it was done I felt no remorse. I felt too satiated, my Blood Lust assuaged. I went about making something in memory of them, to thank them for their sacrifice."

Vaiske brought his spear up and tapped the horns of his helmet with the tip. Lament imagined the morbid smile behind the mask, the skin of the immortal's face every bit as languid as his own.

"It isn't easy to carve a tibia, to curve it the amount needed to make it look like a bullhorn. I spent many days on it; until the shavings littered the floor around me, enraptured in the coagulating blood of my family.

"But the satiation of the Blood Lust is every bit as much a sickness as the Blood Lust itself. And as the comfort waned I realised what I had done. For a time I was gripped by reticence, too shocked by actions to attach the horns to my helmet. But my sickness returned and it was soon time to kill again.

"The warlord clans were an easy target. I could tell myself that I was doing some good while I killed them. That was important in the beginning, with my family's corpses still on my conscious. Then, the Blood Lust grew and I was using the good I was doing as a greater excuse, hiding the monstrous part of me even from myself. It wasn't long before killing men did me no good at all and I realised I required something more."

Vaiske turned to Lament sharply.

"Just think," the immortal roared, waving the spear wildly, "of the peace I could have known had I killed the Behemoth! I would not have needed to kill again! For so long I would have known satisfaction that I could call the creature's death a cure." He paused and became calm. "All this time I've said I fought for peace; that is true. But it is not the peace I have suggesting. I fight for my peace; inner peace. So that I might know it and live as an ordinary man once more."

He looked to the sea past the shadus and his spear became loose in his grip. "I suppose that is the most monstrous thing of all."

His voice fell to nothing.

In the pink twilight the men stood opposite one another. Vaiske looked away, to the ground, as the blades of grass danced miserably in the breeze.

Lament looked to the distant mountains. "You're wrong," he said. "To kill so many and live forever, you would never know peace."

"What would you have me do?" Vaiske asked. "Walk gladly towards the abyss as you do? To know all fear and horror in each instant."

Lament rolled his eye towards the immortal.

"No," he said. "It is release. To be held in the arms of love itself, though perhaps not to know it."

Vaiske shook his head.

"No," he sighed. "I would rather drift through eternity until all else is dead." He met Lament's eye. "Though, truth be told, to me; it already is."

The breeze dissipated and Lament's cape fell back around him. He shivered, telling himself it was the cold, or the Shadowblight, though he held a fervent terror that it was something else.

"You would make me take my shadow back by force?" Lament asked weakly.

Vaiske shrugged. "I have had a strange thought of late. For how long would your death assuage me?"

He lifted his spear above his deathly horns.

Lament drew his sword.

"Will this killing never end?" he asked.

"Soon enough, shadus. Soon enough."

The amber eye observed the half black world unrelentingly. The demonic effigy stood, framed by the distant mountains, the tip of his spear glinting in the twilight sun.

Vaiske moved first, stabbing for Lament's remaining eye. The shadus spun away, striking Vaiske hard in the chest with the gargantuan sword, but it did nothing.

The immortal moved his elbow sharply and struck Lament on the chin. The blackness grew briefly as the shadus stumbled away. Vaiske went to stab him, only for Lament to sink into the relative safety of Vaiske's shadow.

"Damn shadus," the immortal growled.

He prowled, as his opponent so often had, seeking where Lament may rise from. He walked in a wary circle, eyes fixed upon his two shadows and the many around him.

He felt different; strangely uncertain, as if something about his person had changed. He brushed the thought away as paranoia brought on by the completion of his years-long quest.

His second shadow flickered.

The gargantuan sword came first, leaping from the shadow so fast that he could do nothing to stop it. The tip pierced his chest as the shadus followed it, kneeling.

Vaiske looked down at the blade, the blood gently seeping from the wound and sliding down to the hilt. Just as he asked himself 'how?' he noticed, in the sword-less hand of the shadus, the platinum dagger; its blade thrust into the second shadow, draining his immortality from him.

Lament gazed up at the mask and, in those moments, it finally made sense to him. The bulging eyes, beholding an eternal darkness. The skin, so pale to be drained of all blood. The mouth, slung open in some terrible scream of fear. The face, agonised as the wearer gazed at his death.

As the last of the shadow entered the dagger and it turned obsidian black, Lament tore the sword from Vaiske and stood.

Vaiske Parlet, no longer supported by the man whose shadow he had stolen, fell backwards, his eyes meeting the cloudless sky and his body meeting the ground strangely silently, all for the last time.

Darkness.

Chapter Thirty Two

Lament looked down at the lifeless body of Vaiske Parlet. Blood seeped from the wound in his chest, discolouring the grass he lay on. As the shadus placed that gargantuan sword, once more, upon his back, he thought it strange that he had just killed the closest person he had to a friend.

Only then, gazing at the fallen demonic effigy did he remember the now obsidian black dagger in his hand. He brought it up to the level of his eye and inspected the tip, every bit as sharp as the horns on the dead man's helmet. Inside was his shadow, that most elusive of prizes that he had chased for so long and only now did he have it back in his possession, albeit in a state that was unfamiliar to him. Peculiarly, merely holding the dagger in his hand seemed to abate his symptoms. Yet, as the breeze began to blow lightly by, he couldn't help but think it was just his imagination.

"Goodbye, Vaiske," he whispered, as the breeze took upon its new recruit.

Lament turned to where Arvan and Darkla stood, watching. Despite his shadus eyesight he could barely tell them apart. He wiped his brow in frustration, finding it littered with the sweat he thought had gone. He shivered, the cold of the breeze too much for him. Then that presence, distant yet close, so familiar as to almost be a part of him, came over him.

He looked down and saw her arm, skin as white as the listless eyes of the dead Behemoth, wrapped around his collarbone. Uncharacteristic though it was, he smiled.

"What illusion is this?" he asked.

He felt her nestle further into him, her sweet scent swathing down upon him.

"As much illusion as love," she replied. "No illusion at all if you accept it"

Lament sighed, pleased. "I'd wager I have no choice but to."

He felt her chest convulse lightly against his back and he knew she was stifling that laugh he loved so vehemently.

"Now, Lament," she said in her light tone. "That's a dangerous wager. In this love, you won't ever get too far from me."

"Then I accept it wholeheartedly."

Although gazing at his surroundings, Lament was unaware of all but Miata and the dagger in his hand. In those moments, there was no cliff from which the Behemoth had toppled into the ocean. There was no breeze blown grass at his feet in which Vaiske Parlet lay, lifeless forevermore. There were no companions, silhouetted by distance, edging their way closer, determined to see the outcome of the duel. There was only Miata, Lament and the dagger.

Lament brought the dagger up for inspection once more, only for one arm of Miata to leave his chest and her hand wrapped around his wrist.

"No, my love," she said. "I believe you've had toil enough."

Lament frowned, moving his eye from the dagger and turning to Miata, only to find her head resting on his shoulder. His gaze fell over the cliff into the calm seas below, then the dagger. He rolled his eye towards his approaching companions.

*

Their feet pounded beneath them, shuddering and reverberating through their beings with each step that met the ground. Darkla drew further ahead before stopping abruptly.

"That's Lament!" she called as Arvan stopped beside her. "Lament killed an immortal."

"Mournfully, I'd imagine," Arvan said.

"But he survived!" Darkla laughed. "He's alive."

Arvan didn't reply. Instead he looked to the pool of vermillion at the feet of the shadus. What had Vaiske Parlet been to him? Hero? Villain? Or some strange mixture of the two, like all men? All the boy knew was that the warrior was now dead. He would learn no more from him.

Although the urge to reach the shadus still held them, they moved no further as they noticed his gaze return to the obsidian black dagger in his hand.

"What's he waiting for?" Arvan asked, for a moment forgetting the death of his mentor.

Darkla stared forwards, her blonde hair shadowing half of her face as Lament's did.

"Do it," she said as if to herself. Then louder. "Do it!" Her voice fell on the air, almost as the breeze itself, but such a cry knew no peace.

They watched as Lament lifted his head and lay his amber eye once more on the pair.

*

"Do it!"

The cry shuddered through him, ravaging his whole being, corroding his just-beating heart. But it caused him no pain. The arms draped around him so lovingly allowed only for acceptance. He smiled at the affection of Darkla and her wish for him to live.

He moved further into Miata's embrace and let out a somnolent sigh.

"Is this comfort?" he asked. "Peace? Home?"

"It is what it is," she whispered to him. "My arms around you, now and forevermore."

The sad smile he employed intensified.

"Toil enough indeed," he said, his gaze falling once more upon the ocean over the cliff.

*

That first glance, that mere passing look, was all the sign he gave of having heard Darkla's plea. Arvan stood watching, attentive and inert, as Darkla's eyes, fixed upon Lament, welled with tears. She could not look away despite all before her becoming a mere blur and Arvan could not look away from her.

*

"You made your decision long ago," she whispered, her head still lain upon his shoulder, her hair trailing down his chest. "Long before I gave you ultimatums, before I gave you my blessing, and yet I doubt either of these would have changed your mind. You were never one so lustful of life, were you?"

With her question she lifted her head. Lament turned, wishing to look upon her as he was constantly denied, only to find her dissipated on the breeze.

"I don't much know what I am," he whispered in reply. "Especially without you."

He turned away from the distant visages of Arvan and Darkla and towards the edge of the cliff. The setting sun cast light, the colour of which was not dissimilar to that of a fading autumn leaf, and set it shimmering across the ocean in shards. A thin dappling of clouds didn't blight the scene, but revelled in it.

He smiled, knowing it was the last sight his remaining eye would ever behold, and arched his arm behind his head. In a movement as laborious as one would expect from a man on the cusp of death, he rolled his arm into the air, releasing the shadow-filled dagger and casting it into the ocean.

He fell forward, hitting the grass laden ground with a guttural thud, his gargantuan sword encumbering any will he might have to rise. His cape followed listlessly, dragging through the air, until it lay upon him once more, crimson and torn.

Darkness.

*

Darkla fell to the ground, her pained wails leaping far into the dusk. She clutched at her heart, as if to tear it from herself. How much more death would she have to face?

262

Arvan fell with her, only as a source of comfort. As she wept he wrapped his arms around her and she moved further into his embrace. He held her until the tears ended. Until night had fallen. Until she felt like a part of him and their souls entwined.

She turned to him in the hollow light of the spring moon and their lips met, though she kept her eyes closed. When they opened she didn't look at him, but through him.

She brushed the hair from his face. He brushed the hair from hers.

"What now?" she asked wearily.

"Back to Farras?"

She shook her head as best as their position would allow. "How could it feel like home after all of this?"

Finally, their eyes met. His brown orbs gazed into her green ones and at once they knew peace and truth and they held one another tighter.

Their eyes never left one another and they lay there, silent but together. Their silent agreement; to roam the earth together in the quest of the orphan. That search without end. That seemingly eternal quest to find home.

Lightning Source UK Ltd.
Milton Keynes UK
UKOW04f0039100216

268022UK00002B/72/P